A Place of Refuge

A COLLECTION OF 7 NOVELLAS

A Place of Refuge

JALANA FRANKLIN — EILEEN KEY
K. MARIE LIBEL — CONSTANCE SHILLING STEVENS
MARJORIE VAWTER — RALPH VOGEL
DARLENE WELLS

Under His Wings © 2015 Marjorie Vawter
The Calling © 2015 Ralph Vogel
A Shadow in the Daytime © 2015 Constance Shilling Stevens
Chosen © 2015 Darlene Wells
Promise for Tomorrow © 2015 Jalana Franklin
My Best Shot © 2015 Eileen Key
My Dwelling Place © 2015 K. Marie Libel

Published by Wings of Hope Publishing Group
Established 2013
www.wingsofhopepublishing.com
Find us on Facebook: Search "Wings of Hope"

Printed in the United States of America

All rights reserved. No part of this publication may be reproduced, stored in a retrieval system, or transmitted in any form or by any means—for example, electronic, photocopy, recording—without the prior written permission of the publisher. The only exception is brief quotations in printed reviews.

Franklin, Jalana; Key, Eileen; Libel, K. Marie; Stevens, Constance Shilling; Vawter, Marjorie; Vogel, Ralph; Wells, Darlene
    A Place of Refuge
    Wings of Hope Publishing Group
    ISBN-13: 978-0692400579
    ISBN-10: 0692400575

This is a work of fiction. Names, characters, incidents, and dialogues are products of the author's imagination and are not to be construed as real. Any resemblance to actual events or people, living or dead, is entirely coincidental.

Cover design and interior layout by Vogel Design in Hillsboro, Kansas.

Table of Contents

Under His Wings
Marjorie Vawter
PAGE 7

The Calling
Ralph Vogel
PAGE 35

A Shadow in the Daytime
Constance Shilling Stevens
PAGE 79

Chosen
Darlene Wells
PAGE 141

Promise for Tomorrow
Jalana Franklin
PAGE 193

My Best Shot
Eileen Key
PAGE 229

My Dwelling Place
K. Marie Libel
PAGE 283

Under His Wings

Marjorie Vawter

Be merciful unto me, O God, be merciful unto me: for my soul trusteth in thee: yea, in the shadow of thy wings will I make my refuge, until these calamities be overpast.
Psalm 57:1

To my wonderful husband, Roger, for being my hero.
Thank you, honey, for your support and encouragement
in pursuing my dreams.

Chapter 1

Sawyer's Gap, Wyoming
July 1878

"Mr. MacKenzie?"

"Yes'm." Duncan rose from the chair beside the stone fireplace, tamping down the worry burning a hole in his stomach. "How's m' wife?"

"She's fine. For now." The midwife—Mrs. Fisher?—seated herself in the chair opposite his. "Sit down, Mr. MacKenzie, please. We must talk."

"Duncan, uh, Mrs. Fisher." He took a chance at the name he vaguely remembered. But when she didn't correct him, he took his seat again.

"Duncan, then." Mrs. Fisher smiled. "Bonny is okay. Nothing that a little bed rest won't fix up, given time."

Duncan frowned. Hadn't Bonny told her? "She's been resting when she can—"

Mrs. Fisher snorted. "In a bed that jerks and twists with every rut and stone along the way? That's not what she needs, Duncan."

So Bonny *had* mentioned they were on the wagon train heading to Oregon Territory. "But we must go . . ." Why did the blasted woman keep shaking her head?

"No." Mrs. Fisher leaned forward and placed a firm hand on his forearm. "Not if you wish her to live and bear the child she's carrying."

Duncan shook off her hand and stood to pace between the door to the hallway and Mrs. Fisher's chair. They had to go on. Uncle Robert had promised work. If they didn't get there before winter, he'd hire someone else. Probably out of their wagon train.

Nae, the midwife must be wrong. The God who had led them to leave Scotland in search of a better place, a better life, in America wouldn't abandon them now.

Mrs. Fisher stood, and the compassion in her eyes brought his pacing to an abrupt halt. "Mr. MacKenzie, Duncan, if you do go on, you will kill your wife *and* the unborn child."

Duncan set his lips in a grim line, in an effort to keep in the words he shouldn't say.

She sighed. "At least talk it over with your wife."

He gave her a short nod, not trusting himself to speak even a simple "aye," and followed her into the hall.

Mrs. Fisher tapped on the last door to her right before opening it, revealing a nicely furnished bedroom. Bonny lay on the bed, huddled in a semicircle. Her pale hand caressed her rounded belly, and her face bore the signs of recent tears.

"Bonny, m' lass." Duncan strode to the side of the bed and slipped to his knees so he could look into her beautiful sky blue eyes. Molasses colored curls had slipped their pins and ringed her pale face.

He reached to rub away the fresh tears running down her cheek. "What's wrong, m' love?"

Confusion clouded her eyes. "Didnae Mrs. Fisher tell you?"

"Aboot your needin' bed rest? Aye. But we cannae stop now, lass."

Behind him Mrs. Fisher clicked her tongue—a sound that clearly spoke her displeasure. He looked at her over his shoulder, but she turned away.

"I'll leave you to talk some sense into this husband of yours, Bonny." And she swept out of the room, muttering something about "thick-headed men," and closed the door firmly behind her.

He shrugged and turned back to Bonny with an attempt at a smile. "Wonderful upbeat woman, isn't she?"

"So ye daen't believe her?" Bonny struggled to sit up, but Duncan put a hand on her shoulder to stop her.

"That both you and the baby will dee if we go on?" Why should he? He had only the wagon master's word that Mrs. Fisher was the best midwife and herbalist in Wyoming territory.

Bonny's soft sigh soaked through his thoughts.

"What?"

She closed her eyes.

"You believe her?"

"How can I not?" Her hand pressed her stomach, and he saw her dress bulge in a series of kicks from the bairn inside her belly. "I know the signs."

His pretty, gentle wife had quite a reputation for her midwifery skills before they left Scotland. "What are you saying, m' lass? You know how important it is that we geit to Oregon."

"I know how important it is to *you*, yes." She still wouldn't look him.

"But?"

Bonny sighed. "But you will have to dae it without me or the bairn."

Even Bonny? He could handle an unknown woman's scorn when he ignored her advice, but Bonny's? He jerked his hand from her shoulder, but she grabbed it in both her tiny ones.

"She speaks truth, m' lad." She peered intently into his eyes, as if trying to read his mind. Though, truth be told, he'd never been able to close his mind to that probing gaze of hers. "I have nae told ye what I suspected, because Oregon and your Uncle Robert are so important to you, I didnae want to stand between you and your dream." Fresh tears stained her face, but her grip on his hand kept him from attempting to staunch the flow.

"Ye must gae on wi'oot me." Bonny squeezed her eyes shut, but the tears slipped through. "For if I dae go with ye, I will dee. And the babe with me."

Bonny clenched her eyes shut, but the tears still came. She couldn't look into Duncan's eyes knowing that what she feared—that his dream of Oregon and working with his uncle Robert was more than his love for her—would be there. And she didnae want to be the cause of his not realizing that dream.

Still, she had hoped that if the midwife agreed with her self-diagnosis, he would listen. But nae. If he wouldn't listen to her, his wife, why would he listen to some stranger's advice? Bonny knew she should have told him the full extent of the bleeding that she'd been unable to stop, even with making herself lie down instead of walking alongside the wagons as the other women did. But the herbs she'd taken in hope of staunching the flow had done little to help.

She saw no other way. She would have to stay behind if she wanted to save the life of the bairn growing within her. Surely if she went on, both she and the bairn would dee. Duncan would come back for her once his carpentry business was established, wouldn't he?

How long would that take? One year? Two? She didnae know how she would bear the separation. It already felt as though her heart were tearing in two.

Duncan's whispered words broke through her thoughts. "Oh, Father God, gie wisdom. You know I cannae bear to be separated from m' Bonny lass. But the bairn, too?"

His shoulders shook with restrained sobs. "What would you have me dae, Father? Show us. We will dae as Ye ask."

His prayer was balm to her troubled mind, and Bonny's heart swelled with love for the man God had given her. Yes, he could be stubborn, set in his idea of how things should go, but He loved God with a passion she'd not often seen, even in those who preached His Word. She stroked his shaggy head. His hair was longer than he usually wore it, but there hadn't been time to give him a proper haircut, even if she had felt well enough to dae so.

Duncan lifted his head, his gray eyes were calm, not the stormy sea she'd seen earlier. "Dae you think Mrs. Fisher would let ye stay here a little longer?"

Bonny's heart tumbled from her chest to the lowest part of her swollen belly. So he was going to leave her behind. God hadn't heard her pleas for a different solution.

"Only long enough for me to find some place to build us a small cabin where we can live until it's safe for ye and the bairn to travel."

She stopped stroking his hair. Had she heard right?

"You will be able to finish the journey next summer, right, m' lass?"

Such a peace flooded her midsection, her heart rose to its accustomed place, and she laughed out loud. "Aye, of course, m' love. I'm sure I can rest here while you look."

Chapter 2

In the morning, Duncan returned to the wagon train. If they were to stay, he'd need to gather their meager belongings in their covered wagon and their livestock. He located the wagon master and told the man they would have to leave the wagon train.

He reared back, his bushy eyebrows rising. "What about your job with your uncle? What am I supposed to say when you don't show up?"

"You daen't have to say anything. Tell him all he wants to know is in here." Duncan handed the wagon master the letter he and Bonny had written the evening before. "Would you please make sure m' uncle Robert geits this?"

"Aye." The man slid the envelope into his shirt pocket. "What you be doing with your oxen?"

"Is there someone who can use them?"

"Not at present." The man looked over his shoulder at the rugged road that lay up the side of the mountain to the west. "But we always need extra to get everyone over the passes." He paused to spit out tobacco juice.

Duncan repressed a shudder.

"What do you want for them, lad?"

They quickly came to an agreement. As the older man counted out the money into Duncan's palm, he said, "There are better places to settle. This is nothing but a supply depot with a few ne'er-do-wells who couldn't face the passes. The only good people here are the owner of the general store and his wife, the midwife I sent you to." He led the oxen away, flinging one last parting word over his shoulder. "Get out as soon as ye can, lad."

Duncan hitched his horses to the wagon and pulled it to the livery where he stabled the horses and stored the wagon for a minor fortune. The money for the oxen helped, but their funds were dwindling. He needed to find a place of their own soon.

He stepped out of the dim livery into the morning sunlight and looked closer at the buildings that lined Main Street. Most were thrown together and looked as though they wouldn't stand against a blizzard. Yet the Fisher's house was well built, and so was the general store. Once again he wondered who had built them. Maybe he could find work with him once he'd built a cabin for Bonny.

Bonny. He loved her so. He didnae want to lose her. While he grieved over his lost dream—at least for now—he would rather lose his own life than to risk Bonny's.

Duncan stopped and looked around for a church building, but found none. At least nothing that had a steeple on it. He would ask about that too. It had been many months since he and Bonny sat under the preaching of a minister of God.

He pushed open the door to the general store and stepped inside. He blinked a couple times to let his eyes adjust to the indoor gloom after the bright sunshine.

"Ah, there you are, MacKenzie." The man behind the store's counter greeted him with a smile. "I thought you might stop by." He motioned to his left. "I'll meet you at the Land Office window."

Duncan returned Mr. Fisher's smile with a short laugh as the man disappeared through a doorway and removed the board hiding the interior of a tiny room. There was barely enough room for the minuscule desk and chair, let alone Mr. Fisher.

Looking around, Duncan noted a post office. "Are ye also the postmaster?" Duncan raised his eyebrows.

"Well, you don't see anyone else in here, do you?"

"No, but I thought maybe you had some help."

Mr. Fisher shook his head, tightening his lips. "No one in this town I can trust. That is until you and your lovely wife showed up yesterday." He spread a map on the counter. "Where are you thinking to settle? In town?"

Bonny's instructions rang clearly in his mind. *"Find a place outside of town. I daen't want to feel cooped up. A piece of land that speaks refuge to you."*

Duncan had laughed at her fancy. *"How does a piece of land speak to you?"*

Bonny didnae laugh. *"Ask the Lord. He will show ye the right spot. A level place for the house, room for a shelter for the horses and a campsite while you build."*

"Why, lass? Ye will stay here with the Fishers while I build. Nae need for you to be there, too."

Even lying on the bed, she could look formidable when she put her hands on her hips and looked up at him with her most serious countenance. *"I am going with you. I can dae bed rest there as easily as here. Dae nae leave me here. I couldn't bear to be parted from you."*

Duncan raised his hands in surrender. *"Okay, lass. I'll come for you as soon as I find the right place."*

"One more thing, Duncan love." Her face was once more serene. *"I want a place close to a spring or stream. We need a good water supply, especially after the bairn is born."*

Duncan now relayed the information to Mr. Fisher who wrinkled his forehead as he stared intently at the map. "Hmmm. I don't know."

Duncan's heart sank to his toes. "Is there any place like that?"

Mr. Fisher shook his head. "There is one place, but Old Man Prescott owns it."

"Would he sell?" Duncan tried to keep the desperation out of his voice.

"I don't know. He's pretty miserly." Mr. Fisher put his finger on the map a short distance from town. "Here's the spot. You might want to look at it before approaching Prescott."

Duncan leaned over the map. The plat Mr. Fisher's finger rested on was a couple miles to the north and west of town. "Is there a road that goes by there?"

"No. At least not all the way. But you can continue the same direction on horseback and find the place."

Duncan shrugged. He would look, but he wouldn't get his hopes too high. He'd already dug into their savings for a place in Oregon, and if he wanted to go on next summer, then he needed to be as frugal as possible. "Is it all right if I wander a bit? To geit a lay of the land."

Sam smiled. "Sure." He pointed to another spot on the map. "All this land to the south and west belongs to the government, waiting to be settled. But . . ."

Duncan waited. When Sam didn't speak, he asked, "But what?"

"It's untamed land. No one in their right mind would find a place to settle there."

Duncan smiled. "Well then, maybe I'm nae in m' right mind." He took another quick look at the map, nodded a good-bye to Sam, and returned to the livery.

He saddled his sorrel horse, Gabriel, and they walked out of town on a narrow road that looked more like a footpath. Duncan whistled a tune. Gradually the words came to him: *Oh safe to the Rock that is higher than I.* "Hiding in Thee" was Bonny's favorite hymn, ever since Mr. Sankey had sung it in a revival meeting she'd attended back in Scotland.

An hour later Duncan came to the end of the path. Frowning, he knew that even if Mr. Prescott would sell him land here, it was too far from town for their needs. He urged Gabriel forward, searching for the land Sam Fisher had pointed out. But after another half hour, he gave up. Nothing matched Bonny's description.

In a way it was a relief. He didn't look forward to negotiating a fair price with a miserly man. "Whoa, Gabriel. We might as well geit a bite to eat before heading back."

He jumped down from the horse's back, hobbled Gabriel in an open, grassy spot, and sat down on a rock overlooking a small meadow to unwrap a sandwich Mrs. Fisher had put together for him.

"Fathir, Ye heard Bonny. But I'm nae finding what she wants. I can't go back to her and ask her to settle for less." The potential disappointment reflected in her eyes was too much for him to even think about. "Nae, Father, if there is such a place, take me there this afternoon."

Bonny had never felt so useless in her entire life. So far, bed rest went against her grain, but Mrs. Fisher, Sadie, had turned down every offer of help. Even mending.

She let out a deep sigh. She longed to sit up, but fear of displeasing Sadie kept her flat on her back. She supposed that was why Sadie had refused her offer to mend their clothes. It would be difficult to sew lying down.

Gabriel had been gone for hours. He said he wouldn't return until he'd found a place for them. But she didnae expect it to take more than a day. Much as she liked the midwife and her daughter Rose, she longed for Duncan's company and a place of her own. A place of refuge.

Rose tapped on the open door before she stepped into the room. "Do you need anything, Miss Bonny?"

Bonny looked at the fifteen-year-old and smiled. The girl was cheerful, even when tending to Bonny's private needs. "Can you read, Rose?"

The girl smiled. "Yes'm. What would you like me to read?"

Bonny reached for the heavy family Bible her father had given them as a wedding present, but Rose beat her to it. "That's too heavy for you to lift, Miss Bonny." She took a seat in the chair next to the open window. A slight breeze ruffled the girl's collar.

"Psalm 91, please, to start with."

Rose ruffled the pages then began speaking. " 'He that dwelleth in the secret place of the most High shall abide under the shadow of the Almighty.' "

Her voice was clear, and she read at a speed that allowed Bonny to picture the secret place of the psalm. Only it looked a lot like the description she'd given to Duncan that morning. Was there such a place around here? *Please, Fathir, if there is, show it to Duncan.*

Rose patiently read Bonny's requests until the light began to fade. Bonny knew most of the portions by heart, but she loved hearing them read out loud. She closed her eyes.

"Miss Bonny, do you want me to read more?"

Bonny looked around the dusky room. She must have fallen asleep and yet the girl still read.

"Miss Bonny?"

"Yes, lass?"

"If you want me to go on reading, I'll need to light the lamp." Rose motioned to the kerosene lamp on the table under the windowsill.

"Have you been reading all this time, Rose?"

The girl grinned wryly. "Well, I did stop for a little bit when you began to snore."

Sudden heat flared on Bonny's cheeks. "I hope it wasn't too loud."

Rose laughed. "Oh no, Miss Bonny. Your snores are nothing like my dad's. Very gentle and ladylike."

Still, how awful that she'd drifted off in the middle of the day. And to have snored too! Goodness. What must the child think of her? "Have you heard Mr. Duncan come in?" Bonny's voice trembled a bit.

Rose shook her head as she stood and placed the Bible back on the bedside stand.

Bonny swallowed a sob. Where was he? It had to be close to suppertime.

Rose put her hand on Bonny's restless ones. "I'm sure he's fine, Miss Bonny. Don't worry. I'm sure he'll be back soon."

Bonny nodded, wanting to believe her. What would she dae if he didnae come back? Who would know if he were hurt . . . Or worse?

Chapter 3

Duncan looked at the mountains rising above Sawyer's Gap in the twilight and quickened his steps. Bonny would be worried. He hadn't meant to be so late, but he also hadn't wanted to come back without a place that would suit.

He quickened his steps to the land office to talk to Mr. Fisher before he closed the store for the day. But once he pointed out the spot on the map, Mr. Fisher shook his head and stared at Duncan's finger over the spot on the map.

Mr. Fisher took a deep breath. "Sorry, son, but that's in the middle of Stanley Prescott's holdings."

Duncan's shoulders sagged. In his excitement over finding the perfect spot, he never considered that someone else might own it. "You mentioned him this morning. Who is Mr. Prescott and where can I find him?"

Mr. Fisher's lips turned down, and he wrinkled his nose. "He owns the saloon and . . . um, brothel."

Duncan raised his eyebrows. "Dae ye mean to tell me this town has a saloon and br-brothel"—heat flowed up his neck and into his face—"but no church?"

"Ah, you noticed that, did you?" Mr. Fisher shook his head. "A few of us meet at our house on Sundays to worship the Lord together, but we don't have a pastor or even a church building if we did manage to find a man willing to stay longer than a few days. We'd love to have you and the missus join us."

"Aye, that we will dae with pleasure." He knew Bonny would be pleased. "But what aboot this plot of land? Dae you think Mr. Prescott would be willing to sell?"

"Don't know." Mr. Fisher's face looked like he'd bitten into one of his lemons. "He's a hard man. Bitter and vengeful. No one knows why." His fingers worried the edge of the map. "But I guess you could ask. Maybe he would sell to a stranger. Then again, it's smack-dab in the middle of his holdings."

Duncan had no choice. He had to get this piece of land. For Bonny.

"Where does he live?"

Now it was Mr. Fisher's turn to raise his eyebrows, higher than Duncan had ever accomplished. Duncan hid a smile. "Right now?"

"Why nae?"

"He lives in rooms tacked onto the back of the saloon. But business will be picking up soon, and Prescott is a drunkard, a mean one." He shook his head and put a hand on Duncan's arm. "Wait until morning. Or give up owning this piece of land."

After a lifetime of living with his mean drunk of a father, Duncan's heart lifted. "I know how to deal with mean drunks." Duncan grasped Fisher's hand and gave it a hearty shake.

Bonny stirred restlessly on the soft bed. The babe gave a mighty kick, and she placed a soothing hand on her swollen belly.

"Hush, child. Daddy will be back soon." *I hope.* What was keeping him? She had put her Bible down twenty minutes ago when the room got too dark to read. A lamp stood on the small table next to the bed, but no one had been in to light it. She looked for matches in the gloom and saw a familiar box on the edge of the dresser across the room.

Bonny sat up. She'd light the lamp herself. Surely that would be allowed. Her bleeding had stopped, and she felt strong after a whole day of sleeping and reading. She threw the quilt off her and swung around until her bare feet touched the cool floorboards.

"Bonny!" Duncan's voice stopped her from standing as the door flew open and banged against the wall.

She startled and the baby kicked, harder this time. "Ugh." Her breath exploded out in a grunt. She patted her stomach. "Goodness, Duncan. Dae you have to tear the door doon?"

He came to a stop just inside the door, a huge grin stretched his lips. "Bonny, m' lass, you won't believe it."

"Whatever it is, it kept you out much longer than I expected." She glanced at her feet then pulled them up onto the bed, settling the quilt around her. "And you scared us with the doors banging and all."

He turned to look at the door that had bounced half closed. Turning to shut it, he asked, "What were you up for? You know what Mrs. Fisher said."

"Sadie."

"What?"

Bonny rubbed the spot on her ribs the child chose to kick. "Mrs. Fisher's name is Sadie."

"Oh." Duncan looked around the nearly dark room. "Where are the matches? I would have thought the lamp should have been lit already."

Bonny sighed. "Sadie was called out to help with a birthing, and Rose is preparing our dinner. Nae one else is here to dae it." She gestured to the box on the dresser. "I was just getting up to dae that when you burst into the room." How she hoped the bleeding wouldn't come back after her foolish attempt to get out of bed.

Duncan grabbed the box, struck a match, and lit the lamp.

Bonny blinked in the light as her eyes adjusted. "Now what has you so excited?"

Duncan sat on the edge of the bed beside her and clasped her hands in one of his. "I found the perfect place."

Bonny couldn't quite squelch the hope rising in her heart. "Perfect?"

"Everything you wanted. A flat area for the cabin. Grazing space for Gabriel and Patsy. A spring close to the cabin. A bigger stream a short distance away. And trees of all kinds—aspen, pine, dogwoods—ringed around the building site." He held his hand up ticking off the points as he spoke. "And best of all—" He pulled in a breath and grinned.

Bonny tugged her hands, trying to free at least one from his grasp. But his fingers tightened. She gave up. "If I could I would kick you."

The grin broadened. "Daen't you want to know what the best of all is?"

Bonny pooched her lip out. "Nae." She tried her best to sound nonchalant. "I'll see it soon enough."

He sobered. "You won't be there until I geit a house built."

"What are you saying? You mean to go without me? But ye said—"

Duncan shifted to face her better. "I'm going to set up a camp site with the cover off the wagon."

Tears stung the back of Bonny's throat. "But—"

"Nay, lassie." He ran his fingers through her hair, pulling it away from her face. "Ye canna come. It's too far in case something happened."

She couldn't bear to be parted from him. The tears squeezed past her squinted eyelashes and slowly descended her cheeks, as she cast about for something that would change his mind.

A knock on the door startled them both, and Duncan let go of her hands. "Who is it?"

Mr. Fisher's deep voice—almost like the rumble of thunder, Bonny thought—answered. "I thought I heard your voice back here. May I come in?"

Duncan looked at Bonny. She nodded, and he said, "Aye."

The door opened slowly, and Mr. Fisher stuck his head into the room. "How did you fare with Prescott?"

Duncan grinned and pulled a folded sheet of paper from his shirt pocket. He handed it to the older man.

Mr. Fisher's eyebrows rose, and he stepped all the way into the room to take the paper. "Really? He let you have the land?" He unfolded the sheet and read the contents.

"Aye."

Bonny's heart clenched. Why was Mr. Fisher—she cast around for a word as she searched his face. Incredulous, she decided.

Bonny tugged Duncan's hand. "Duncan?"

He gave her a quick wink before turning back to Mr. Fisher. "Is it legal?"

"What?" Mr. Fisher looked up. "Oh. Yes, it's legal." He shook his head. "How on earth . . . ?"

"I told you I knew how to deal with mean drunks." Duncan shrugged. "M' father could have kept pace with Prescott. All I did was tell him how Bonny had her heart set on that land since we had to stop our Oregon journey on account of the bairn."

"And that did it?" Mr. Fisher's voice held a note of skepticism.

"That . . . and the right price." Duncan made a face. "Took almost all our funds for setting up in Oregon."

Bonny tightened her hold on Duncan's hand. He'd given all that money for her sake? Her heart swelled with the tears she choked back. After she had cost him his dream. "Oh, Duncan."

He turned to face her, and Bonny saw Mr. Fisher slip out into the hallway and shut the door with a small click.

Bonny swallowed hard. "I have cost you so much! And I can't even repay you with keeping house and cooking for you."

Duncan leaned forward and kissed her gently on the lips. "Anywhere you are, m' Bonny lass, is hoom. Besides, I didnae marry you to have a housekeeper and cook." He kissed her again. "I married you to keep you by m' side till daith dae us part."

Bonny sat back against the pillows. "Does that mean I can go with you while you build our little house?"

Duncan sighed. "I thought that subject was closed. Nay, lass. You need to stay here to geit the proper rest until our little bairn makes his appearance."

Bonny smiled. "She will come when she's ready."

He grinned. Ever since she'd known she was carrying their first child, they'd carried on this banter. Bonny didnae really care whether the bairn was boy or girl. She only prayed that the child was healthy. She winced as once again the babe kicked within her.

Duncan laughed and placed his large hand over hers on her stomach. "See? He agrees with me. You will stay here while I build."

Bonny smiled sweetly and kept back the retort. Duncan would not be going alone to the place he'd found for her.

CHAPTER 4

Two weeks later

Duncan dragged a large pine into the clearing where he planned to build. He'd hoped to be farther along with a house, but Bonny's insistence that she come with him forced him to build an outhouse first.

He glanced at the makeshift shelter he'd erected from the canvas-covered top of their wagon. It perched next to the wagon where it would be easy to shelter from bad weather.

Rose tended to the cooking fire, preparing their dinner. Duncan had at first been reluctant to accept the help the midwife offered, but one look at Bonny's grateful face squashed the words he'd planned to say. Now he, too, was grateful, for the girl waited on Bonny with such devotion and care that was beyond his ability, especially if he were to build a sturdier shelter than the tent before the bairn was born.

"Thank Ye, Father!" the words broke forth out of his full heart. "Ye have been more than faithful in providing our needs." He was especially thankful that Bonny's bleeding had quit once they were off the rough trail leading over the mountain passes between Sawyer's Gap, Wyoming Territory and Oregon Territory.

He thought of the letter he'd written in haste to Uncle Robert and entrusted to the wagon master's care. He could only pray that Uncle Robert would wait for him until next summer. The weather would close the passes to all travelers before the bairn was born. They had no choice but to wait.

"Dinner's ready, Duncan," Bonny called from the bed just inside the tent.

He raised his sap-stained hands up for her inspection. "I'll be there as soon as I wash up." He smiled, his heart swelling with the anticipation of spending the mealtime with his beloved.

Rose brought him some warm water from the kettle she kept at the side of her cooking fire and filled the basin on their makeshift washstand. He dug at the lye soap and lathered up his arms as well as his hands. The sap from the lodgepole pines that grew in abundance around the cabin site was difficult to remove, but he couldn't ask for straighter poles to use in framing up the small house. Especially as there was no sawmill in Sawyer's Gap.

The sound of fabric rustling through the grass and wildflowers behind him made him turn from his ablutions to see what the stifled giggling meant. Next to the cooking fire, Rose spread one of Bonny's tablecloths. On the opposite side, Bonny reclined on the straw mattress that doubled as their bed.

Her grin spoke volumes as she waited for him to join her.

He strode to kneel behind the mattress and dropped a kiss on her cheek. "Are you playing the part of the Queen of Sheba?"

Her hazel eyes twinkled. "In Solomon's court?" Her laugh rang out. "Hardly. But I am glad Rose let me out of the tent. I dae want to watch you as I embroider this afternoon."

"Daen't trust me?" He dropped another kiss and then lowered himself to the stump he'd used as a chair since they'd moved away from town. "Aye, I'm a rascal, for sure." He winked at her, winning a giggle from her.

Rose set a bowl of steaming stew in the middle of the tablecloth, then laid the plates and silverware in front of each of them.

"Aren't you eating with us?" Duncan asked Rose when a third plate didn't appear.

"No, sir." Her head dipped, refusing to meet his gaze. "I'm to town as soon as you say the blessing." She nodded to Bonny. "I put her out here so you can keep an eye on each other."

Duncan's eyebrows rose. "On each other?" He put special emphasis on rolling the r, since it seemed to fluster Rose, and he watched the heat rise in her cheeks as expected. "Why dae I need watching'?"

Bonny placed a hand on Duncan's. "Daen't tease." Her voice was mock serious, and one look into her eyes proved she was holding back a laugh. "Go ahead, sweet Rose. I'll explain."

"Yes'm." Rose pulled her apron off, laid it over the edge of the wagon, and disappeared down the path to the wagon road that led into Sawyer's Gap.

Duncan watched her go before turning a questioning eye on his wife. What was going on?

Bonny turned his hand over and reclasped it with their palms together. She nodded for him to say the blessing. He obliged with a short prayer, but when she started to pull her hand away, he clasped it tighter. "Nay, lass, nae until you tell me what's going on."

Bonny's dimples flicked into sight and were gone. "Oh! Nathing to upset yourself." Her free hand waved in the direction the midwife's daughter had taken. "She promised her father, that she'd come tell him when you found the ridgepole." She glanced over her shoulder at the log he'd dropped on the ground in front of the cabin. "That's it?"

Duncan nodded. "Nae sure how to geit it in place, but I'll rig up something after dinner." He released his hold on Bonny's hand in an attempt to spoon some of the stew onto his plate. He didnae want to waste any time.

But Bonny's fingers tightened. "That's what Sam Fisher was afraid you would dae."

His eyebrows climbed his forehead. Why should Sam care about his ridgepole?

Bonny's smile, full of understanding, worked its magic and his eyebrows lowered. He sighed. "Tell me, lass. I'm hungry, and I need to geit back to work if the house is to be done before the bairn is born."

She shrugged. "'Tis nothing much. Sam made Rose promise to let him know so he could come with help." She glanced doubtfully over her shoulder at the massive log. "That's more than one man can handle, I'm thinking."

She released her hold on his hand as she leaned back against the pillows propping her into a semi-sitting position they'd devised so she could eat. He grabbed the serving spoon and ladled stew first onto her plate, then his. He swallowed his first bite before answering the question he knew she didnae like to ask.

"'Tis fine, m' lass. I welcome any help I can geit on raising that log into place."

Bonny picked up her fork, but hesitated before putting a bite in her mouth. "You won't try it by yourself?"

He grinned. "Nae. I still need to clean it up a little before it's ready. By that time Sam Fisher will be here . . . wi' help."

She opened her mouth as if to say something, but then she picked up her fork and started eating. Not for the first time did he thank the Lord for sending him Bonny. She seemed to know the best way to "handle" him, the best way to get him to see sense. And when she couldn't get through to him, she stepped back and let the Lord have him. Two weeks ago he had no intention of stopping their journey west to Uncle Robert. Today, the little community of Sawyer's Gap was wrapping another tentacle around them, making the thought of moving on next summer an unpleasant one. How could that happen so quickly, if it weren't for the prayers of his wife? She definitely knew how to capture the desires of the Almighty.

From her makeshift day bed, Bonny watched Duncan stride toward the log he'd dragged into the clearing earlier. She knew he'd been looking for the "perfect" tree to use for the ridgepole, so when he dragged that one into camp this morning, only a look passed between her and Rose before the girl hurriedly moved the mattress out of the tent.

Now, with the dishes piled up near the washbasin waiting Rose's return, Bonny repositioned herself to face the little house quickly taking shape under the shadow of the mountain. The bairn kicked her under her ribs, making her catch her breath. She pressed a hand on his foot, attempting to shift him away. At least the bairn was in position if her bruised ribs indicated anything.

The foot shifted, and Bonny smiled and picked up her embroidery. With the cabin walls up—and soon the ridgepole so Duncan could finish the roof—they would be able to move into the cabin in a few days. She wanted this piece ready to hang over the mantel.

Pulling a section of the rich green thread through her needle, she again studied her surroundings. Her piece was little more than a mountain, a verse, and the name of the cabin, but she'd tried to make her colors to those surrounding her.

A sharp cry followed by a thud came from inside the cabin.

"Duncan!" Bonny was on her feet and running toward the cabin before the echoing cries diminished.

Chapter 5

The next morning Bonny raised her eyes to the mountain rising into the sky behind their new home. But the lighting wasn't right. The sun hadn't risen over the mountains behind her. Still the verse taking shape beneath her needle brought the comfort she sought.

Drawing the needle through the fabric, Bonny recited the words to Psalm 57:1. " 'Be merciful unto me, O God, be merciful unto me: for my soul trusteth in thee: yea, in the shadow of thy wings will I make my refuge, until these calamities be overpast.' "

Silently she thanked God that Duncan's injury was only a sprained knee. It would slow him down, but it wouldn't totally incapacitate him. Her impromptu race hadn't started her bleeding again. The bairn was active this morning.

Once more she dropped the embroidery into her lap and studied the rock face rising up behind the house. Duncan's voice right next to her ear, made her start.

Clasping her hands to her chest, she willed her heart to slow down. "Oh! Duncan, m' laddie. Ye frightened me!" Dropping a hand to her swollen belly, she added, "And the bairn." She took a deep breath and swallowed hard. "What did ye say?"

Duncan's arm stole around her shoulders, but his grin did more to settle her heart rate. "What dae ye keep looking for in the mountain?"

She shrugged. "Probably just m' imagination."

"What dae ye mean?" He settled down on the ground next to her and gazed up at the mountain.

"'Tis nothing, I'm sure." She didn't want to tell him, afraid he would laugh at her fancies. But she couldn't help glancing once again at the huge rock face.

And there it was! "Ahh!" Delight swelled her heart and her eyes widened. The sun shone off the rock face, causing a display of light and shadow in the form of a dove with outstretched wings rising above the cabin's new roof.

She gripped Duncan's hand, pointing his gaze toward the sight.

"*Fo sgiath*. Underneath the wings." He let out his breath in a soft whistle. "So that's why you wanted to call our cabin *Tearmann*. Our place of refuge."

"Aye." The word came out on a breath, as she drank in the sight. "Under His wings. God truly led you to the right place for our cabin, Duncan, lad."

Duncan didn't answer, but he didn't need to. Not for her. Too soon the sun rose higher and the shadows shifted, and the outline of the magnificent bird disappeared.

Duncan reached for the abandoned embroidery in Bonny's lap. He ran a finger across the Gaelic words next to the outline of a mountain.

He cleared his throat. "I came to tell you, we can move into the cabin tomorrow."

Bonny thought her heart would burst with the delight surging through her blood vessels. "Tomorrow? We must send word to Sadie."

Duncan laughed. "I told her yesterday." He wrapped his arms around her, cocooning her in his love. "She'll be here to help."

Bonny sighed. "Are you still upset about having to stay behind?"

"Nae." He pulled back to study her face. "The Lord truly had this spot waiting for us here."

She pulled his face down to hers for a sweet kiss. "Aye. He did."

Gideon dug his knees into Gabriel's sides, urging him to fly along the road to town. The sun slipped behind the mountains behind him, plunging the narrow valley into deep dusk. In a few minutes he'd have to slow down, but every moment lost spoke death for Bonny and the bairn.

"Father God, please!" Duncan shouted above the horse's frantic hoofbeats. But even that much took too much energy. Energy he needed to reach Sadie as fast as he could.

Why, oh why, had Bonny thought she could do some "light" work around the house while he was away today? Whatever she'd done, she was bleeding and in labor when he got back. Her tears fed his fears as he sped through the deepening dusk.

The light through the thinning trees ahead caused Duncan to urge the horse even harder. He was nearing Sawyer's Gap. "Please, God." Sadie had to be there. He couldn't bear the thought of what might happen if she weren't.

Gabriel came to a sliding stop outside the Fisher's front door, and Duncan leaped out of the saddle almost before he stopped. He pounded on the door, shouting Sadie's name. She opened the door just as her husband came running around the side of the house.

"What . . ." Both started to ask in unison. But one look at Duncan sent them scurrying for her midwifery bag and another horse. Duncan jumped back onto Gabriel and turned him back along the road to the cabin.

Back under the trees, Duncan was forced to slow his mount, and soon the Fishers caught up to him in their light buggy. Sam handed him a lantern to give some light to the road, allowing horse to speed up a little.

Gideon fought the urge to tighten his knees, but he couldn't risk losing his faithful mount, too.

"What happened?" Sadie asked, once they settled into a safe pace for all of them.

Duncan's heart clenched at the question. "I daen't know exactly." He took a deep breath. "I went hunting." He forced his fingers to loosen on the reins. "When I got back, Bonny was on the floor, covered in blood and water."

Sadie's hand covered her mouth.

"She said the birth pangs were strong, too strong." He drew in another deep breath. "I didnae stay any longer. Gabriel was still saddled." He patted Gabriel's neck absently.

Sam shook the reins of his horse into a slightly faster pace. Duncan had never been more thankful for understanding friends. And a God who had found them the perfect place only two miles from town. Still the ride through the dark seemed interminable.

They drew to a stop in the flat area below the cabin, and Sadie was out of their buggy and halfway up the mountain to the cabin before Gideon could dismount. He ran after her, vaguely hearing Sam say he would tether the horses before coming up.

When Gideon burst through the door, Rose met him with her hands outstretched. Hot water steamed from the basin on the washstand beside the bed. And Sadie washed her hands while clucking quietly in response to Bonny's soft whispers.

"Mama said for you and Daddy to stay on the porch." Rose pushed on Duncan's arm to get him to move.

He shook her hand off and moved toward the bed. "But . . ."

Rose jumped in front of him and grabbed his other arm. "Please, Mr.

MacKenzie!"

Sam grabbed his other arm, and turned him toward the door. "Come on, Duncan. We're better out of the way."

"But . . ."

"I'm all right, Duncan lad." Bonny's soft voice shook him to the core, reinforcing his need to go to her. "Go with Sam. The bairn will be here before ye know it."

Chapter 6

Sadie, with sweat dewing her forehead, placed the slippery, squirming bairn in Bonny's eager arms and grinned.

Bonny, still panting from her exertions of birthing the child, stared at the baby boy—her baby boy—with wonder. Joy bubbled into her chest, filling her heart with a love she didnae know was possible.

"Geit Duncan," she said softly.

But she needn't have spoken. Rose already was guiding him inside. Bonny caught his gaze and smiled as he cautiously approached the bed,

She held out a hand and when he grasped it, she pulled him close to the bed. "Meet your son, Mr. MacKenzie."

He went down on his knees and reached a finger cautiously to touch his face. "Is he . . ." He swallowed hard. "Well?"

The tiny bairn opened his eyes, took one look at his father, and let out another lusty cry. Duncan looked so startled, Bonny let out a laugh. "Of course he is. Meet your da, wee Colin."

"Colin." Sadie leaned over the other side of the bed. "A perfect name for the wee one."

"Aye." Duncan said and the babe's flailing hand wrapped around his finger. "His name speaks of God's faithfulness and protection."

"Yes, God definitely has His hand of protection on this little one." Sadie stood up, making shooing motions with her hands. "Now, Duncan, we need to clean him and his mother and then let him nurse and rest so he can regain some strength after his hard work. I'm sure there's some chores needing done outdoors for a bit." And then when Duncan didnae move, she repeated. "Go along with you now."

Bonny laid her hand over Duncan's as he continued to stroke their tiny son. "Duncan, laddie, dae as Sadie says. Soon you can join us again."

❖

Late Spring 1879

"Bonny! Bonny, lass, where are you?"

Bonny rubbed her lower back as she straightened from the packing box lying open on the table. Glancing at the cradle where Colin slept, she moved to the door to hush Duncan's shouts. Too many times in the last few months, she'd had her hands full settling a startled baby awakened by his father's inability to speak quietly.

Stepping out onto the porch and drawing the door closed behind her, she smiled at her husband running up the hill with a letter in his hand. "Hush! Colin is sleeping." She stepped down from the porch to stop Duncan before his large boots pounded on the wood flooring.

"What has ye so excited?" She reached for the envelope and looked for a return address. Only there wasn't one. "Where did you geit this?"

"Johnson, the wagon master, found me at Fisher's store." Duncan grasped her about the waist and swung her around. "It's a letter from Uncle Robert."

"Put me doon, Duncan." Her fist beat on his shoulder as she grasped the shoulder of his shirt and the letter with her other hand. "How can I see it with you swinging me . . ."

He set her on her feet and held one elbow to steady her. Her head still whirled as she tried to focus on the writing on the envelope. She wrinkled her nose. "Are you sure this is from Uncle Robert? It disnae look like his handwriting."

She had seen the other letters Uncle Robert had written to Duncan. This handwriting could be his, of course, but something wasn't quite right.

"That's what Johnson said." Duncan peered closer at the envelope, his brow furrowed in concentration.

"Then it must be." Bonny slipped a hairpin from her coil at the base of her neck and slit the envelope open. Secretly she'd been hoping that something would happen to keep them in Sawyer's Gap.

Once Duncan finished their cabin, the residents of Sawyer's Gap had kept him busy. Even Mr. Prescott, who wanted a new house. Duncan had earned back most of the money he'd spent out of their meager savings for Oregon Territory. But there were plenty more people who wanted Duncan's carpentry skills here, and Bonny dreaded the journey ahead of them to get to Oregon.

Eager as a small boy, Duncan reached for the letter as she drew it from the envelope. "What does it say?"

She unfolded it, turning away to keep Duncan from pulling it from her. She slapped at his hand and laughed out loud. "Let me open it, Duncan."

She'd been right. It wasn't Uncle Robert's handwriting. She stared down at the short letter. Duncan peered over her shoulder, read the short paragraph, then groaned and pulled away.

"Uncle Robert is dead?" Bonny stared at the words swimming before her eyes. She dropped the letter and reached for Duncan, wrapping him in her arms. "Oh, laddie." She swallowed back the tears but couldn't speak through her tight throat.

Duncan groaned again. "Aye." He pulled away from Bonny and reached to pick up the letter from the ground. Then he shook it at the sky. "Why, Father, why?" His voice shook.

When he lowered his arms, Bonny reached for the letter again. "Look, Duncan, laddie." She pointed to the date at the top of the page.

He stared. "Why, it's dated last summer." He took the letter and read it slower. Bonny watched as his face registered shock, anger, frustration, and then amazement and wonder.

"He dee'd before we had to leave the wagon train." He grabbed Bonny around the waist and swung her around again. "Dae ye know what that means, lassie?"

When he set her down, she leaned against him until her head stopped swirling.

"Dae ye know?" Duncan repeated.

She nodded and pulled back to look into the gray depths of his eyes. She put her hands on each side of his face. "God knew there would be nothing for us in Oregon Territory."

"Aye, lassie." He shook his head. "He sheltered us from losing everything . . ." He laughed. "And all this time I've been upset with Him for ruining m' dreams."

Bonny grinned. She had dreaded having to pack up and move farther west. Dreaded leaving this place of refuge.

Duncan pulled her into his side as he pointed at the face of the mountain rising up behind the cabin. "He protected us under His wings . . . We didnae even realize how much. Just this morning Fisher asked if I'd build a church in Sawyer's Gap. Guess the townspeople are ready for God to bring a preacher to town."

God was so good. She had her husband, her son, and her place of refuge.

And now they would be staying in Sawyer's Gap. Colin's cries announcing the end of his nap brought Bonny out of her silent praise. She could unpack until Duncan built them a home in town, but even then she still planned to leave the Bible on the mantel under the embroidered piece. Someone might need the encouragement one day.

THE END

The Calling

RALPH VOGEL

*For I can do all things through Christ
which strengtheneth me.*
PHILIPPIANS 4:13

Dedicated to those who think they can't.
I have good news for you: you can.

CHAPTER 1

Northeast Kansas
September 25, 1892

The sun exploded above the eastern horizon, bathing all creation in a brightening glow of breathtaking pastels. Long fingers of shadows spread out across the landscape, shortening ever so slightly as the orange ball climbed higher. Illuminated in the fresh morning dawn, a single rider seated on a long legged mule slowly ambled across the dew laden prairie grass. A flock of crows, aroused by the sun's eruption, flew across the shadows of man and beast and headed for their early morning feeding fields, their hoarse calls echoing in the early morning hour.

John Roane watched the crows' departure and gave his mule's sturdy neck a pat. "Well, Cautious, I reckon we did get us an early start. Should make good time today if'n we don' dawdle too much. Sure do want t' get beyond that pass t' Willamette Valley afore winter sets in. Don' want t' get caught in no deep snow or something."

He took off his old gray hat and wiped a sleeve across his forehead. "Reckon we both could use a mite of a clean up, you and me. 'Course you don' care none, but Grandma Roane would be a tad upset if'n she could see how unkempt I've become since leaving Anderson Flat. It jes' ain't respectable for a person t' become too unpresentable.

"Now take my grandpappy for instance. Not a finer lookin' gentleman did the South create than Grandpappy Roane. If'n he could see me now he would take a switch t' my britches. He would for a fact. Him dressed up in his fine Brigadier General uniform and all of a Southern gentleman. I was tol' he was a handsome cut of a man, he was all that an' more according t' Grandma Roane, an' she should know. Sure too bad he had t' up and get hisself killed in that dreadful war. Never could see the way and wherefore of it then and still don' now. The good Lord didn't put man on earth t' kill each other. No sir!"

Emitting a short snort, the mule nodded up and down as if to signal agreement with the discourse aimed at no one in particular. Beneath a small stand of cottonwood trees, several deer appeared as statues in the dark shadows of the trees, peering out at the intruding strangers. Only an occasional twitch of a nervous tail gave way to their silent presence.

"Yes sir, Grandma Roane would agree with me. After all, she's the one who figured out that I had the calling. Told me herself that the good Lord done gave me the blessings o' talk and the sweet desire to gentle folks. On'y thing that bothers me though is the pure fact I'm not too sure I really have the stuff t' be a preacher." Pulling up on the reins, he drew the plodding beast to a stop. "Fact is, Cautious, I don' rightly figure I have any right at all t' even think that I could be a preacher. A preacher has t' know things like all the happenings in the Bible, an be able t' convince folks that they need t' change their ways from evil living t' peacefulness."

He hung his head low, defeat weighing on him. "No, Cautious, I reckon I should forget the calling and concentrate on finding some good farming ground in that Willamette valley place somewhere in Oregon Territory."

The sun mounted higher, and the day took on a bright, warm glow. Giving a gentle nudge to Cautious' ribs, John prodded the mule into continuing his calm walk toward the west. "Something else, Cautious, I need to think about Lilly Mae. She's done expecting me t' send for her once I get settled. Sure hated to leave her, but I needed t' find myself a proper way t' support a wife and make a livin' for a family. One thing I know is I can't go back, nor can I send for her 'less I find a way t' be successful, and that ain't goin' to be easy. I hear tell that Oregon territory area has some mighty good farm ground. You reckon we could maybe find some for ourselves and settle down there?"

A warming breeze rattled the leaves in the cottonwood trees, sending chattering squirrels scurrying. Rising up in his stirrups, John shaded his eyes from the bright glow of the sun and peered intently at the receding western horizon where he detected a slight movement. "Reckon there's something out there. Wonder if'n maybe it could be Injuns or other travelers?"

He guided Cautious to the shade of the trees then halted and continued to stare at the slow movement on the horizon. The mule raised his head and also stared ahead. John gave his ears an absent scratch. "Don' look like anything movin' too fast, do it, Cautious? I reckon we'll just sit here a spell and see what comes." Gradually the objects began to take form. "Well, I'll be! Lookit there, Cautious. Them's buffalo! Curious looking beasts, ain't they? No offense t' you, Cautious. Let's us jus' rest here and let 'em pass. No sense hurrying and maybe scare them into stampeding."

After what seemed like an eternity, the herd ambled its way past the grove of trees and out of sight, emitting short grunts to one another as they made their way southward. John shook his head in wonder, staring after the hairy animals. "What a sight they was. Do you think maybe someday there won't be room enough for such animals? Not likely, I'm to think. This here prairie is too big to ever become anything less than a large piece of grass and sky. Well, we best be taking t' hoof afore the sun burns itself out for t'day." With a few bounces of his heels, he set Cautious in motion.

In the early evening, John made camp near a burbling stream. He hobbled Cautious, consumed a meager meal of beans and hard tack, then rested beside the fire while night fell gently on the eastern horizon, spreading its soothing blanket over the rest of the sky. Little flecks of stars began to wink to one another as the sky totally darkened. Softly the birds of night began their bed time calls to each other, accompanied by the mournful call of a coyote seeking its mate. An owl, somewhere in the nearby trees, began questioning the presence of man and mule, only to fall silent as the dying embers of a cooking fire began to cool and then glow a soft red, speckled with flecks of black. A slight breeze awakened the embers for one brief curtain call and then they retreated backstage to mark the end of their performance.

Using his saddle as a pillow, John lay back on his blanket and gazed at the stars. "Cautious, you reckon Lilly Mae is restin' easy tonight? Sure do miss her company, I do. That soft, corn silk hair and those deep searching blue eyes of hers that just seems t' stick in your soul. And that slender body with her loose, feed sack dress that Grandma Roane made for her, the one with little yeller flowers all over it. Yes sir, she's a mite sightful, she is. Can't wait 'til I gets myself settled in that Oregon country."

Loneliness pressed, so he kept talking to his only companion. "Cautious, you reckon we're on the right track? Seems t' me that we ought t' be running into covered wagons or such. Ain't seen hide nor hair o' any other living thing but you, me, and that bunch o'spikes earlier t'day. Don' seem normal no how. Oughten t' be some other folks head'n t' this Oregon territory, too. Do you think maybe we're not on the trail? I know we haven't crossed any big stream, so I feel pretty sure we haven't run into the Platte yet, and I ain't seen any sign o' what they call Chimney Rock. That ought t' be somewhere close t' where we're fixin' t' go."

Cautious gave a soft snort and stuck his nose to the grass.

John chuckled. "Oh, well, the good Lord looks out for fools and beasts, so I reckon we'll be all right. Come morning I'll do some figurin' and decide where t' head."

Taking a small, well-worn Bible from his woolen shirt pocket, he fingered the faded pages. When Grandma Roane gave him the Bible, she said it was the one his grandpa had carried all through the war. She said it was special, and that a person who was called should have a Bible that was specially meant for him. What would Grandma Roane say about him running from the special call? With a sigh, he slipped the little Book back into his shirt pocket, laid his head against the saddle, and closed his eyes.

He bade the quietness of night lull him to sleep, but guilty thoughts made their way into the recesses of his mind. *What are you running from, John? Did God call you away from your calling? What are you afraid of, John? Is Grandma Roane wrong about your destiny? Are you a Jonah, John? Remember, you can't run from God.*

Chapter 2

Even before the sun came up, John rose. He fried up four strips of bacon, cut with his waist knife, and washed them down with tepid canteen water. He saddled Cautious then tied his supplies in a pack behind the saddle. Using his poncho as a blanket, he lovingly wrapped his Kentucky long rifle and secured it through several leather straps. After kicking dirt over the remaining coals of his fire, John mounted the mule and made his way northwest.

A cool breeze stirred the leaves overhead, sending down a fine cascade of dew droplets which dripped off his hat brim and onto his hunched shoulders. He squinted through the early morning shadows, hoping for a glimpse of the North Platte. Once he found it he could follow it all the way to where Fort Kearney once stood. He muttered to himself, "I do believe the old Oregon Trail went the same way as the river. I know I'll surely feel better when we strike 'er."

Keeping Cautious in a northwesterly direction, John rode across the empty landscape. To pass the time, he kept up a one-sided conversation. "Cautious, I think maybe I know why we haven't run into any wagons. Most o' the folks have probably already been by. After all, it is gettin' late in the year for slow wagons t' be making the South Pass. Makes me t' wonder if'n maybe we too might be a tad late for the pass. Guess we'll be t' findin' out when we gets there."

As the sun rose, the prairie grasses absorbed its warmth and radiated it back with gentle caresses. By noon both rider and mule were sweating, and John was ready for a long rest and a cool drink of water. "Cautious, I'm thinking maybe I should take a little time and place my heels on the ground. Let's stop."

He gently pulled the reins, expecting the mule to stop, but he didn't. So he pulled harder. And Cautious stuck out his neck and trotted ahead.

"Whoa, mule! What're you doing? Let's stop and rest. Here, now, slow down like I done said!"

The mule broke into a run, and all John could do was hold on. Cautious crested a short rise, and finally John saw what Cautious smelled: water. There spread out before them was a wide ribbon of glistening, shimmering water.

John let out a whoop of delight. "Well, I'll be, you done foun' the Platte, Cautious! Keep going, and we'll see how quick we can get wet, you an' me."

Loping headlong into the water, mule and man created a grand splash. Cascades of the precious liquid flew in all directions. Mule, man, and all belongings tied on the back of the saddle received a soaking, but John only laughed. "Pay no never mind, Cautious, all will dry. We foun' the Platte!"

When John was convinced all he wore was as clean as the sparkling water could get it, he spread his clothes and blankets out in the grass and let the sun bake them dry while he lazed on the bank. With everything loaded once again, he climbed onto Cautious's broad back and the pair set out in a westerly direction, following what John was certain was the route most wagons took to the Willamette Valley of Oregon.

Excitement kept him alert in the saddle, and he couldn't help sharing his thoughts with the spotted mule. "We must've missed the point o' rocks, but lookit here, Cautious, see all o' them worn out ruts? Them's wagon tracks. Look how far t' the sides they go? Must be fifty t' a hundred fifty feet or more across. Sure can tell that a lot o' wheels came over this trail, and I'll bet you Aunt Maple's knitting basket that most all of 'em headed west. Can't be too long 'til we run into the place where Fort Kearney used t' be. Heard they done moved 'er back in 1871. Tore down the whole thing, they did, and carried 'er off. Somethin' about a railroad coming. Sure do wish it was still there. We could use some supplies. If'n the Pony Express was still running, we could post a letter t' Lilly Mae and Grandma Roane, but I do doubt that we'll find anything there anymore."

They passed several mounds of rocks—burial spots for poor souls who didn't complete the trek. "'Pears to me, Cautious, that folks would have t' put a whole lot of stock in t' the notion of finding a better place than they done left. Rolling from St. Louie clear to this here Oregon place has t' take a whole lot o' gumption and hope. Hear tell the whole thing stretches for 'bout two-thousand miles! Wonder what possesses folks like that t' risk property and family t' take such a long trail? By the number o' stone-piled graves we're a-seeing, a person tends t' think that maybe the idea was not all it was thunk up t' be."

Tossing the pioneers' intents and efforts back and forth in his mind as Cautious carried him westward, he was struck by the difference in his own reason for heading West. He wasn't a brave pathfinder looking to better his lot in life but a coward, trying to escape the call God put on him. A chill wriggled its way up his back. He yelled to the blue sky, "So I'm like Jonah after all!" As if emphasizing the announcement, Cautious raised his head and brayed.

His excitement dwindled, bringing a rush of mingled shame and fear. He hung his head. His heart felt heavy, as if all matter in his torso had suddenly vanished and only a boulder remained. Curiously, the little Bible in his pocket seemed weighted enough to drag him from the saddle. Salty tears made their way down his cheeks, creating warm paths past his nose and under his chin. He could almost hear God's voice saying, *"I know where you are headed. Are you going where I want you to go? Will you be doing what I want you to do? Think, John Roane, think."*

Tears blinded him. He drew Cautious to a stop and wiped the tears with the back of his fist. Gently sobbing, he formed a defense. "But, God, I don't got enough learnin' to teach others. I'd shame You 'cause I'm not set for such a job. Don' know if the calling is right." He cried out, "How do I know I have the calling? Where's the fleece, God? I need a fleece!"

Chapter 3

Guilt wore at John the long, lonely day of travel. Try as he might, he could not shake the dark shadow that seemed to hover over him like a black cloud. A light rain fell, making every tree, rock and grass blade appear to be covered with a fine sheet of silver-white threads. Lovely to the eye, but the dampness chilled him. He removed a coat from his pack and pulled it on. Several buttons were missing. He should've asked Grandma Roane to mend his things before he left home.

He criss-crossed the coat front and huddled into it. "This ol' coat's kind of like m' life here lately, full of holes and needing mending. I reckon I'll never 'mount t' much. I probably done did Lilly Mae a favor by leaving. Now she can find herself a real man, one who has the skills to 'mount t' something, someone she can look up t' and be proud of. That surely can't be me."

Riding onward, hunched over, with water dripping from the brim of his hat, misery gripped him. The goal of reaching the Willamette Valley seemed too far off to even dream about. "What do I do now, Cautious? I don' seem to have what it takes t' keep going, and if and when I gets there, what is there for me?"

With light fading rapidly, John decided to stop and camp early. Finding a dry spot seemed impossible, but he hoped he'd at least be able to find a few pieces of dead wood he could coax into burning. He climbed down from Cautious's back and searched the thick grass. To his surprise, he found a board.

He showed it to the mule. "Strange that a board should be here. Must've fallen off a wagon some time ago." Carrying it, he continued to rummage, and he found several more pieces of lumber scattered about. Could this be where Fort Kearney had been? They'd closed the adobe fort and soldiers had carted off whatever they could way back in 1871, but maybe these boards were from a small building that had been left behind.

John made a pile of the boards, his gaze drifting over the open prairie in all directions. "Small wonder they done left, Cautious. Sure is a lonely place.

I'm guessin' that the Injun troubles were about over an' they didn't need it no more. Maybe there warn't any more wagons t' protect." He paused. "An' maybe we are on a fool's chase, you and me, Cautious."

He wished the fort was still in operation. Be nice to have some company besides his old spotted mule. He'd also like to visit the sutler store where soldiers and travelers could stock up on provisions. His supplies were getting low, and he wouldn't mind refilling his packs.

With a good stock of wood ready for a fire, he turned his attention to finding a partial adobe wall—something tall enough to shelter him from the drizzly weather. He settled for the south side of the highest wall remaining. After fastening his poncho to the broken top, he draped it outward and held it down with several stones. Hands on his hips, he observed his half tent. It would do. He turned to Cautious, and pity rose. The mule stood with his head down, large drops of water running from his sides. "I truly wish I could invite you in, Cautious, but you'd never fit."

After several failed tries, he managed to start a small fire within a ring of stones under the rubber poncho. He retrieved his few rations from the saddlebags and returned to the tent. "More salt pork tonight, Cautious. Maybe with all this wet I'll settle on a corn dodger or two. That is if'n I can still break off the pieces. One thing Grandma Roane made plenty of were these here corn dodgers, and they don't spoil none. Got some coffee left, too, so I'll have something hot to drink before I sleeps."

The meal wasn't fancy, but his belly was comfortably full when he wrapped himself in his blanket. He lay listening to the *tap-tap* of falling water droplets. The quiet loneliness of the prairie wore on him. He tried to conjure up the excitement previous travelers must have felt on their way toward a dream. But he failed.

When he reached Oregon Territory, would things be better there than they were here in his soggy tent? Maybe he should turn around and go back. But how could he go back home to face shame and embarrassment in front of those he loved and who loved him? A vice clamped on his heart, squeezing the life blood out of him.

Lamenting about his lot in life, listening to the soft rain pelting the poncho above his head, he searched through memorized scripture to soothe himself. A story jarred his mind. A son left his father with grand ideas but had to return home in shame and humiliation. Would he be forgiven if he returned home? Grandma Roane surely would forgive, but would God forgive him for disobeying?

"I might not be sittin' in a pig sty but these accommodations aren't much better. A leaking poncho, a dying fire, next t' a smelly mule in the middle o' nowhere with nothin' good looking me in the face for tomorrow." He didn't want to think anymore. Pulling his blanket tightly under his chin, he fought his way to sleep.

A cold nose woke him from troubled slumber. Pushing Cautious's head away, he struggled out from under his blanket and stood, inhaling the freshness of early morning air. The rain had stopped and low, heavy looking clouds slowly dragged their way south. Patches of clear sky appeared between the dark masses. Every blade of grass sparkled with the shine of untold numbers of diamonds as the sun peeked through.

He rummaged in his saddlebag for a few pieces of jerky and then munched, his thoughts rolling much like the clouds. Go on. . . or go back? Going back meant listening to Grandma Roane urge him toward the calling. He shook his head and tossed aside the last bit of jerky. That calling was surely meant for someone else. He'd go on. Find a different road than preaching.

He cupped Cautious's muzzle in his hands and looked into the mule's wide, unblinking eyes. "Grandma Roane always did say that we Roanes were a powerful determined bunch. It's that determination that keeps me from up and quittin' this whole shebang. But what's I gonna do when I gets t' where I think I want t' be? I s'pose my best bet is t' be a farmer, like I first thunk t' be. Reckon if you pull the plow, I'll guide it, all right?"

While he loaded his belongings on Cautious's back, he kept jabbering to the mule. Talking meant he didn't have to think. "Sure will be glad when we gets t' civilization an can find some real vittles. I calculates that we must be somewheres on the way t' Fort Laramie. Maybe you an me can become more respectable then."

A biting breeze nipped his cheeks—sharper than the breeze he recalled from back home in Anderson Flat. Would he make the South Pass before snow fell? "I just got t' get to the Rockies soon. On'y problem is, I don' know how far I needs t' go. I'm t' think that Fort Laramie can't be too far. One thing I knows is when I gets t' Laramie, I'll be in Wyoming Territory and that will make me close t' the Pass."

He kept up a steady stream of words all day, but the talking didn't erase the sting of guilt. Would reaching Fort Laramie make it better? Maybe being around other folks would divert the pang of his conscience. Leastwise, he could hope.

Chapter 4

The days melted together as John and his mule plodded weary mile after weary mile. No matter how many times he prodded the mule with his boot heels, Cautious refused to trot. The mule was wearing down, but so was his food supply. He had to get to Fort Laramie. One cool morning a full week after finding the Platte, John spotted several riders in the distance. Excitement roared through him when he recognized they wore uniforms.

"Hallelujah, Cautious! We done reached the fort!" He spurred the mule toward the body of horsemen, shouting, "Howdy! Hold up there!" The soldiers reined up and waited for him to approach. He drew Cautious alongside them and smiled so wide his face felt sure to split. "I am just plumb joyful t' see you fellers. Ain't seen folks for some time now. You sure all look good t' me! Be ye from the fort, be ye? Sure am glad t' be able t' see ya. Yes sir, sure am glad."

The soldiers chuckled and invited him to accompany them to Fort Laramie. John followed along, joy flooding him. Civilization! Well, sort of. The fort was nothing more than a rambling group of sod buildings set in an open field. A wooden flag pole rose high in the center of a dusty parade ground, and soldiers lounged around hitching rails and under porch verandas. The door to the largest sod house was open, and an officer stood in the doorway. John surmised by the marking on his sleeve he must be the one in charge.

When the group reached the hitching rail in front of the building, John launched himself off Cautious's back and pounded straight to the officer. He grabbed the man's hand and shook it with vigor. "Sure am glad t'see you. Yes, sir, I am! Been on the prairie for some time now. Don' rightly know how long but I knows it's been a long time. My name's John Roane. Hail from Anderson Flat, Arkansas. Hoping to go through the South Pass and on t' the Willamette Valley place. Didn't think I'd ever find m' way, but I found myself to here."

The soldiers lingered near, seeming to listen in. John sensed their amused grins aimed at him but he didn't mind. Entertainment was probably rare in a lonely fort.

"Welcome, Mr. Roane. My name is Captain Wainscot." The officer pulled his hand free of John's grip and looked John up and down. "It appears you could use a good meal and a hot bath. After that, we'll talk. I imagine that you'll want information as to where you are and what you should expect this time of the year. You probably have noticed that there aren't many travelers on the trail at this time."

Everything the officer said met with John's approval. He nodded emphatically.

Captain Wainscot gestured one of the soldiers forward. "This is Corporal O'Rourke. Whatever you need, he'll provide it. It's getting late. After you and your mount's needs have been met, come and see me." He stepped into the building and closed the door behind him.

O'Rourke shook John's hand. "Mr. Roane is it? Come with me and we'll get your mule tended and you cleaned up."

John settled Cautious in a stall with oats and then enjoyed a bath in a small room at the back of the stable. When he came out smelling like soap, O'Rourke pointed to his bundle of gear.

"Grab your things there and come with me."

John gathered up his belongings and followed the soldier across the small compound to a building where a painted wood sign announced "Sutler's Store." He entered and couldn't squelch a pleased grin. Such a marvelous place! John scanned the shelves of food, clothing, guns, cloth, and countless items. The soldiers certainly weren't left wanting.

O'Rourke took John to the counter where a tall man wearing a bibbed apron eyed him in curiosity. "Mr. Roane, meet Warren Damen, he runs the store. He'll fix you up with supplies. We have a saying around here: 'If Warren doesn't have it, you don't need it.'" With a grin, O'Rourke tipped his hat and left John with the storekeeper.

Warren rounded the counter, rubbing his hands on his apron front. "By the looks of it, you will want some new clothing. And by the way, I'd throw away that old white rebel hat if I was you. It might not set well with the troopers in this fort."

John set his gear down beside the counter and removed the hat. He fingered it, fondness rolling through him. More gray than white after all these years, he still couldn't imagine not wearing it. "It's true I needs some things, but I am most partial t' this here hat. You see, it belonged t' my late grandpappy. It and a little Bible is all I have t' remember him by."

The storekeeper grimaced. "I'm not one to interfere with anybody's decision making, but don't say I didn't warn you. Troopers aren't the only ones in these parts who don't look favorably on anything Southern. I thought to save you some problems that will probably come sooner or later. But you do as you like."

The man's serious tone prodded John to follow his advice. John rolled the hat and stuck it his back pocket. "If'n you have another of another color, I'd be obliged t' wear it."

Warren nodded. "Come with me."

John trailed him to a set of shelves. The sutler took a black felt hat from the top shelf, then chose a red linsey-woolsey shirt, a pair of heavy trousers, and a pair of cotton longjohns from other shelves.

He placed the items in John's arms. "These should do nicely."

John wouldn't argue. "Thank you, sir."

Warren headed for the counter. "Let's get you tallied up and you can pay."

"Pay?" John hadn't considered being charged for the supplies after Captain Wainscot's greeting. He had a little money but probably not enough to pay for these items and necessary food supplies. He laid the new clothes and hat on the counter, reached into his pocket, and withdrew several coins and a bill. He put the money next to the clothes. "Do I have 'nough t' pay for all o' these here things?"

The sutler frowned at the coins. "Mr. Roane. . ." He shook his head, and all at once his frown disappeared. He picked up John's rifle and gave it a caress. "Say, isn't this a Kentucky long rifle? Haven't seen one of these in a long time. I collect old guns, you know, but I don't have one of these. Would you consider parting with it?"

John didn't like the proprietary way Warren's eyes gleamed when he looked at John's gun. "It belonged t' my grandpappy's pappy. Been in the family for some spell now. Don't know how I could rightly part with it." He leaned on the counter to get closer to his rifle. "Y'see, my grandma told me how a whole crew of Kentuckians used these rifles during the War of 1812 to raise havoc on British troops. Them troops, they had muskets with short barrels, and they couldn't begin to compete with the Kentucky sharpshooters and their long rifles."

The man nodded impatiently. "Yes, yes, I know. They're very accurate at long range, more than any other rifle. That's why I'd like to have it."

John reached for it. "Well, I—"

"Tell you what, Mr. Roane, I'll trade you the rifle for those clothes, plus all the food supplies you can carry. I'll even throw in another gun that would do you. How about it?" The sutler's eyes gleamed.

John stared at the rifle, torn. Which did he need more—the rifle or the supplies? He spoke slowly. "Might do it if'n you were t' sweeten the pot a bit. Maybe put some new shoes on my mule and gimme another set of clothes so I don't have to sit around shiverin' in my underdrawers, waitin' for that set to dry the next time I jump in a river."

The sutler let out a whoop. "Yes, sir, you got a trade! Just help yourself to the supplies. Flour, sugar, dried apples. . . Whatever you want." He cradled the rifle in his arms as gentle as a mother cradled her newborn babe. "I've got a used Snider breech loading rifle. You don't have to use powder or lead balls. It uses a self-contained cartridge. It's fast to load and fire. I'll also throw in a handful of shells for it. Yes, sir!"

John slid a pouch across the counter. "You might as well take this here powder horn and lead shot, then." He swallowed against a lump in his throat. He needed supplies, and the Snider breech loading rifle sounded fine, but it sure hurt to part with his great-grandpappy's gun.

True to his word, Warren arranged for the blacksmith to shoe Cautious. The smithy chuckled when John led the animal into the barn. "What kind of mule is this any way? I ain't never seen a mule with appaloosa spots before."

John smiled. "Well, sir, Cautious is special in that his daddy was a donkey and his momma was an appaloosa mare. That makes him an appaloosa mule. Ain't many of his kind 'round. He's special in more than one way, too. He's smart and never will he go where he knows it ain't safe for him or me. That's why I named him Cautious, 'cause he's all o' that."

"That's right interesting." The man pulled an iron shoe from the flames, placed it on the anvil, and gave it a few whacks with his hammer. Then he dipped it in a water bucket. He spoke over the hiss of steam. "How'd you get Warren Damen to pay for these new shoes?"

Still smarting over the loss of his family heirloom, John shrugged. "Oh, I reckon you can say we worked a trade."

"That does surprise me some, mister, seeing as he never does anything that isn't in his favor. Maybe he's mellowing some." The smithy continued working as he talked. "Scuttlebutt has it this fort won't be here much longer.

Guess the old trail is becoming rather peaceful of late. The old sutler probably knows his days of making money off of us soldier boys is about over."

As the blacksmith attached the last shoe to Cautious's hoof, Corporal O'Rourke entered the barn and crossed directly to John. "There you are. Are your needs being met?"

John patted the button placket of his shirt. "Got new duds, and Cautious here got new shoes. Got a pack full of supplies." He was also short one rifle, but he wouldn't complain.

"If you're finished, the Captain asked to speak with you."

The blacksmith gave Cautious's hindquarters a slap. "He's done. I'll put him back in the stall. He'll be here for you when you're done with your talk."

John returned to the captain's quarters, and Captain Wainscot invited him to sit in one of the matching upholstered leather chairs facing a small rock fireplace. John eased into the chair. It sat nicer than his leather saddle.

The captain shoved his saber scabbard aside and sat next to John. "Well, Mr. Roane, I understand you are anxious to proceed to the South Pass."

Anxious for a new beginning, for sure. "Yes, sir."

"I must caution you that I sincerely doubt you will be able to go through the pass until next spring when the snow melt is nearly complete. However, there are several small towns in the vicinity. Perhaps you can winter in one of those."

John would do his best to make it. He needed to get as far from Anderson Flat as possible. Even so, he'd pick the captain's brain for suggestions. "If'n I can't plow m' way through, where'd be a good winterin' spot?"

"There is a fairly new settlement by the name of Sawyer's Gap, near the Sweetwater River. The settlement is growing and shows promise of being a fine town. South Pass is about forty miles further south. Were it me, I would spend the winter in Sawyer's Gap. However you do as you please. Every man has to make his own decisions as to his welfare." He rose and extended his hand. "I bid you good luck and God's speed, Mr. Roane."

Taking his cue, John left the captain's room and returned to the sutler's store. He begged paper and a pencil from Mr. Damen. The man happily obliged. John bent over the paper and wrote:

Dear Gramma Roane and my beloved Lilly Mae,

I am well and at Fort Laramie at this time. Might spend the winter months in a town called Sawyers gap. Hope to be in Orygon come spring. Shore do miss you all. Hope all is well for you. I will send for you, Lilly Mae, as soon as can be.

Lov, John

He spent the night in the stable with Cautious and rose with the sun. As he left the fort, Captain Wainscot's words rang in his ears. *"Every man has to make his own decisions. . ."* Was he making the right decision by pressing on? The knot in his stomach told him probably not, but he urged Cautious forward anyway.

Chapter 5

For the next two months, John followed the rivers. First the Platte and then the Sweetwater. The calendar moved steadily toward winter as Cautious moved steadily toward Sawyer's Gap. John began to appreciate the wisdom of finding a warm place to wait out the snowy months. Some days he feared his ears would freeze right off his head. But it didn't keep him from traveling onward.

On a clear day in mid-November, he watched a rabbit wearing a coat of half brown and half white disappear beneath a scraggly bush. Rabbits made good eating, and he considered taking aim, but decided he didn't much care to skin and cook it right then. He sighed, his breath a cloud in the cold air.

"Sure do miss Grandpappy's Kentucky long rifle, even if the new one loads fast and easy." He reined Cautious to a stop and held the black hat over his chest. He squinted skyward. "Grandpappy, if'n you be paying attention t' what I been up to, I truly hope you are in a forgivin' nature for me partin' with your favorite gun. But you see, I had needs and it seemed the on'y way t' go."

A gust of wind swept through the dry grass, bending the blades to resemble the riled waves of ocean water on a high sea.

John shivered. "Sure hope that wasn't Grandpappy sendin' down his anger on me." He patted Cautious's neck. "More'n likely it's Mother Nature stirrin' things up. Let's get movin'."

Nightfall came earlier with the colder days. John didn't mind riding on while stars freckled the graying sky—beauty marks on the face of night, Grandma Roane always said. The dots of light gave him company beyond the old spotted mule. But on this night he noticed a different kind of light promising a different kind of company.

"Lookee there, Cautious. Does that 'pear like a campfire to you?" Eagerness for human companionship bade him push Cautious on. "Let's go see."

Nearly an hour later, John stopped the mule well outside the circle of light thrown off by the flames. "Hello, there at the fire. Can I come in?"

A gruff voice responded. "Come ahead, but come slowly. I ain't hankering to be surprised."

John approached the circle of flames. A man stood close to the fire, his shadow stretching long over the flattened grass. John couldn't see much of his face for all the hair growing thick along his jaw and chin.

The man looked John over. "You don't seem to be armed. You daft or just a trusting soul?"

"I ain't one t' carry guns lessen I hafta. Figure the on'y people who tote'em are those look'n for trouble or are terrible scairt of things. I ain't neither."

The man chuckled. "In that case climb on down and sit. Got hot coffee on the fire, and I could use a little company. Been out here nigh on to two months now. Most people have been staying close to home so I haven't seen many of them. Guess they figure there is to be an early snow. What's your name, stranger?"

John crouched by the fire and took the cup the man offered. "John Roane. I come from Arkansas way. What's yorn?"

"David Pretty."

"What's kept you on the prairie for so long, Mr. Pretty?"

David stretched out his legs and tugged his collar closed. "Been trapping the Sweetwater, hoping to make a little to tide me and my missus over for winter. I'm fixin' to head back to home soon though, seeing how the cold is here and my mule has enough to tote already. Where you be heading, John?"

"A place called Sawyer's Gap. Hear it's the place where the South Pass lies."

David slapped his knee. "Well, I smile! Sawyer's Gap is home to me. If you don't mind, you can tag along, give me someone to talk with."

John marveled at his good fortune. "I'd be right proud to ride alongside you." Now he knew for sure he'd find the town without trouble. For the first time in many days, John slept with no worries plaguing him. It was good to have company and to know his route was secure.

John enjoyed David's presence over the next ten days even though each day the cold grew more bitter. John had never been happier to see a town than the evening they rode into Sawyer's Gap.

David led John up the snow-dusted main street. Lamps glowed behind store windows and a tinny piano played a joyful if off-pitch tune in some distant building. David pulled up in front of a small wood frame house off of a side street. Its chimney sent up a welcoming ribbon of smoke, and John's body shuddered in eagerness to hunker before the fire. David climbed down, but John stayed in his saddle.

"David, is there an inn here in Sawyer's Gap?"

"An inn?" David gawked at John. "This ain't a big city, John. No hotels at all. But you're welcome to spend a night or two with us. Don't know where else you'll go."

John scratched his chin. David had been gone a good long while. His wife might not take to having an extra person underfoot. "What about your missus?"

David looped the reins in his hand and headed for the side of the house. "Aw, I don't think the missus will mind. Much."

John slid down and followed behind his friend. "I do 'preciate the offer, David, but mebbe I oughtta just bed down with old Cautious. Been him and me now for so long I'm not sure I can sleep without him."

"Well, I know my missus won't let him in the house," David said. "Cautious can stay in the stable with my mule and horse. You're gonna sleep in our loft. An' that's that."

David's missus welcomed John and made up a pallet for him on the floor in front of the fireplace instead of the loft. Lying there warm, snug, and secure, thankfulness walked through John's mind. He'd made it to the South Pass. All he had to do was go over the pass and into the promised land of the Willamette Valley. Everything had worked out after all. So why, instead of sleeping, did he lay there with a nagging feeling that something was not as it should be?

He rolled over, and the small, worn Bible in his shirt pocket pressed against his chest, heavy as the guilt weighing down his soul.

Chapter 6

Winter moved in with lightning speed during the night, spreading a generous coat of snow over the entire landscape. Mrs. Pretty declared the scenery beautiful, but John didn't see beauty. He stared out the kitchen window at the fluffy mounds of white, trying his best to arrive at a solution that would take him to his goal. He was at the threshold of the pass that would take him to his promised land, only he couldn't get there.

David pressed a cup of coffee into John's hands. "Watching the snow fall will not make it go away. You best come to a resolution that says you ain't going anywhere for a spell."

John gripped the warm mug and shook his head. "But I gotta go on. I'm wantin' to reach Oregon."

"I know what you want, but old Mother Nature ain't going to let you do that, at least not for a spell." David slurped his coffee. "It's early in the season yet for winter to be coming, and it might let up and melt some, but that doesn't mean the pass will be open. If you wait for a warm spell to melt the snow here, chances are the snow will not be melted in the pass. Funny what a little elevation will do. You could get a ways but you also could get caught, and then what?"

John sighed. "I'm a tad bothered. Can't stay here with you good folks all winter, but I also don' have a place t' go t'. I'm not sure what t' do. Seems like nothing no how is workin' out for me. Maybe I could find some work so's I can winter without being a bother t' folks." Hope flickered through him. He turned to his friend. "You reckon there be work about town? I would do mos' anything."

"Hm..." David crossed to the table and sat. "Before I went trappin', I heard tell that the MacKenzies were wanting to find a fellow to build a lean-to for a horse or two out at their cabin."

John hurried to the table. "A lean-to?"

"Uh-huh. 'Course, I been gone a while. Could be they've already found somebody, but I reckon we could ask."

The flicker of hope became a tiny flame. "Do you think I can find this here MacKenzie person? I sure do want t' ask him if he thinks I can have the job."

David chuckled. "Findin' him's no trouble. The MacKenzies started a construction business, and there's always one of 'em around their office." He set his empty cup aside and stood. "C'mon. I'll introduce you to them."

Mrs. Pretty cautioned them not to be late for lunch, and John couldn't resist giving her a smile. She was a nice lady—as nice as Lilly Mae. He and David tromped through the soft snow covering the streets. As they passed stores, he peeked in windows, taking note of neatly arranged shelves lit by glowing lanterns. The sight of those well stocked shops pleased him as much as Mrs. Pretty's kindness. Sawyer's Gap seemed a fine place to spend a few months.

His toes were fair to freezing by the time they reached a tall false front building at the far edge of town. The hand painted sign above the door read, "MacKenzie Construction Co." David gestured for John to go on in, and for a moment John considered kneeling to pray. But why would God listen to him when he'd spent so much time running away from Him? He took one wide step over the threshold and John came in behind him.

A woman seated behind a fine carved desk looked up. "Good morning, gentlemen."

John crossed to the desk. "'Morning, Miz MacKenzie."

"Welcome tae you, Mr. Pretty." Mrs. MacKenzie sent a curious glance at John. "Are ye needin' some building done, or are ye just visiting?"

David waved his hand at John. John stomped his feet clean of snow and then hurried forward. David said, "Neither, ma'am. My friend here, by the name of John Roane, is new to town and needs a little work to get him through the winter time. Your mister was talking about building a horse shelter at the cabin, and I thought if hadn't got done yet, maybe he'd hire John to do it."

Mrs. MacKenzie looked John up and down. "Duncan is wantin' tae put a barn behind the cabin. Are ye capable of workin' with building materials, Mr. Roane?"

John snatched off his hat and nodded. "Yes, ma'am. Done a bit o' it back home in Arkansas. Lot o' trees there so I'm used t' chopping and sawing. Helped t' build a cabin back home for some folks. I think I could build a horse barn without too much trouble." He grimaced. "On'y problem being, I was planning on going through the South Pass and on t' Oregon, so I didn't bring

The Calling

no tools or nothin' with me. Guess you might say this early winter caught me a tad unprepared."

His last comment tore at his heart. How often had he lamented that he was unprepared to represent God because he wasn't ready or equipped? He was even unprepared to do something as simple as wood working.

Mrs. MacKenzie wrote notes a piece of paper. "Mr. Roane, come back at hauf past four. I'll have an answer for ye from Duncan."

By the time John left the construction office, the bright hope of morning had faded away. Why would an important man like Duncan MacKenzie give some unknown traveler a job? The snow stuck to his boots, making his steps plodding. He had no money, no tools, and probably no chance.

Mrs. Pretty kept up a flow of chatter during lunch, and David added his comments about the joys and travails of trapping, but John stayed quiet. Feelings of failure made it hard for him to swallow the good meal. Talking took too much effort.

David lightly smacked his arm. "Tell you what, John, I could help you out at the cabin, if you want. Ain't got much else to do this time of year. I could hold boards and help you dig holes for the framing."

John sighed. "I doubt if'n they will hire me t' do the work. Ain't much has gone right for me for a long spell. Don't know why it should change now." He left the table and moved to the fireplace. He sat in one of the homemade chairs and spent the afternoon staring at the dancing flames. When the clock on the mantel showed a quarter after four, he put on his coat and headed out the door.

The walk to MacKenzies seemed longer by himself, and he was chilled clear through by the time he reached the construction office. He crossed directly to the desk and began the speech he'd formed while watching the logs in the grate burn. "I appreciate you talkin' to me, ma'am, but I understan' if'n you can't use me for the work. Me bein' unknown about town, not having tools and all, and you not knowing iffen I can handle them. I just come by to say thank-you for speakin' kindly to me." His duty complete, he turned to leave.

Mrs. MacKenzie stood and held her hand to him. "Wait, Mr. Roane, you hae not heard what Duncan said."

He offered a sad smile over his shoulder. "Don' need to, ma'am. I understan' your concerns and all."

The woman laughed softly. "Mr. Roane, I fear ye daen't understand me a bit." She moved around the desk and stood before him. "Sawyer's Gap is growing. Our carpenters stay busy. Duncan is happy ye are willin' tae take on the project at the cabin."

John stared at her in wonder. "He is?"

"Ay. When I told him you have nae place to stay, he suggested offerin' ye a trade."

His last trade left him without his great grandpappy's rifle. For a moment he hesitated. "What kind of trade?"

Mrs. MacKenzie laced her fingers together and rested her hands on the waist of her skirt. "If ye are willing tae spend the winter buildin' the horse shelter, ye may stay at the cabin. He'll gie ye food supplies an' lend ye the use of a wagon to tote tools an' lumber from town tae the cabin."

John could hardly believe his good fortune. "You'd let me live in the cabin?"

"'Tis only two miles away, so ye won't be far from town. There's no indoor pump, but there is a running stream close tae the cabin wi' fresh water. Ye should be quite comfortable." She sighed. "'Tis a grand little cabin, Mr. Roane."

John fairly twitched with excitement, envisioning settling in for the cold months. "I thank you, ma'am. I thank you very much."

She smiled. "Thank ye, Mr. Roane, for bein' willin' to build the shelter. Duncan will hae a wagon loaded an' ready for ye first thing tomorrow morning. So please be here by eight tae meet him an' ask any questions ye might have."

"I'll be here, ma'am! I surely will."

John headed for the Pretty's house with a bounce in his step. A place to stay, money for food, and a means to keep his hands occupied. What more could he want? He couldn't go on now that the snow had come, but for the time being life was looking up. That knot in his stomach shrunk some, but the little Bible in his shirt pocket, over his heart, still weighed heavily.

Chapter 7

With a full wagon pulled by two company horses, the trip to the cabin took only thirty minutes. Unloading took a good bit longer. John stacked the lumber on the covered porch so it would remain out of the snow, then he carried the tools, nails, and food stores into the cabin and arranged it all in the tiny pantry off the kitchen. The cabin itself was a simple log structure of two rooms. A small kitchen at the front led to a bigger room holding two beds and a smattering of random, mismatched furniture. A stone fireplace stood centered on the north wall of the big room. With a front door facing east, the morning sun warmed the entrance. John glanced about the space and gave a satisfied nod and spoke to the quiet room.

"I am t' think that this here cabin will do nicely. Even have covers and plenty o' blankets for the bed. Wood for the fire place and stove shouldn't be a problem, there's plenty o' that outside. Yes, I think I'll be comfortable here. Sure beats sleeping outside on the ground. Might get a tad lonely with Cautious staying in town but he'll get good care at the livery stable. Sure was nice o' the MacKenzie's t' have him put up."

He stepped close to a small table between two chairs and ran his finger over its top. Not a speck of dust. How could an empty cabin be so clean? It didn't seem natural. But then he shrugged. "Must be really sealed proper with good chinking and tight fittin' logs. So much the better for keeping warm." He inwardly vowed to build the shelter with the same attention to care whoever had built this cabin had used.

After fetching his personal effects, he crossed to the wardrobe in the corner. As he passed the fireplace, he noticed the framed square of embroidered cloth hanging above the mantel. A strange writing was stitched in delicate handwork, which he could not make out, but below the writing were words he could understand: *Place of Refuge*. He leaned close and recognized two scripture references stitched in small letters: *Isa. 4:6*.

His gaze dropped to a Bible placed neatly on the mantel beneath the sampler. The Book seemed to beg to be opened. Respectfully, he picked up the Book and gingerly turned pages until he found the first verse inscribed on the sampler. "'And there shall be a tabernacle for a shadow in the daytime from the heat, and for a place of refuge, and for a covert from storm and from rain.'"

His chest fluttered, and he smiled. "Makes sense t' me. This here cabin is all that." He leafed forward a few pages, scanning scriptures, and he came across a verse that made his smile fade. He whispered, "'Because thou hast forgotten the God of thy salvation, and hast not been mindful of the rock of thy strength, therefore shalt thou plant pleasant plants, and shalt set it with strange slips.'"

He stared at the scripture, his heart thumping. How could this frame of cloth an' sewing lead him to read such a message? He carefully returned the Bible to its place on the mantel and stepped backward, shaking his head. "Can't be what I am thinking it t' be. I know that God speaks in strange and wonderful ways, but here? In this place?"

There was time enough to return the wagon and horses to the livery, and he felt the need to escape the fierce tug the words from Isaiah had on him. So he hurried outside, climbed up on the wagon seat, and gave the horses' backs a flick with the reins.

The trip back to town took only twenty minutes with an empty wagon, hardly enough time to muddle through the meaning of the verses so aptly given. He was still working through the revelations when the horses stopped in front of the livery stable. He dismounted, strolled into the large barn, and went straight to Cautious's stall. "Cautious, you an' me got some figurin' t' do. I know you probably don' care none, but I done got me a problem an' I don' rightly know how t' handle it."

"You always talk to mules?"

Someone spoke behind him. The voice held a level of amusement. John whirled around and found a short, older man smiling through a face full of gray whiskers. The man said, "I guess if I was to be out on the prairie for a long time, I'd probably be talking to anything that was warm and breathing."

John wouldn't argue. "You work here?"

The man nodded. "I own this livery. I'm taking care of your mule."

"Well then, glad t' meet you." John stuck out his hand. "My name's John Roane. What's your handle?"

"Most people call me Les."

"That your whole name? Just Les?"

Les ducked his head for a moment. "Well, sir, I generally don't use my whole name. Truth is, most people in town don't know my whole name."

"Why's that?"

The bit of skin showing around the whiskers turned red. He looked around and then whispered, "My whole name is Lester Beenblossom. Never did like the name Lester."

John hid a smile. "I won't tell a soul. Truth is, I got me my own problem that on'y I can handle. Problem is, I don' rightly know how t' do that."

"Sometimes helps a heap to talk to someone besides a mule, John. Now I'm not to say that I'm the one to talk to, but I figure I know who is."

Something tickled John's stomach. He recognized the tickle as need. "Who might that be?"

"Reverend Bishop. He's been here even afore Sawyer's Gap became a suitable place. Used to drive a buggy around the country visiting folks. Now he has a fine church painted white with a large cross above the front door. Folks have been trying to get a bell to hang there, too, but no luck so far. It will happen though because folks here admire the preacher a whole lot."

"If you fancy him that much, he must be good."

"Why don't you go see for yourself?" Les waved his hand toward the livery doors. "He ain't hard to find. Generally in the church of a day. He's getting up there in age and doesn't go around much anymore."

John thanked Les, gave Cautious a loving stroke on the neck, and then headed through the snow to the large white building waiting at the end of the street. He stepped inside and walked through a stream of fading sunlight flowing through high pointed windows on both sides of the room. A white haired man in a black parson's suit sat on the front pew, his head down, apparently in prayer. John stood silently and waited for the man to lift his head.

After several quiet minutes, the man rose, turned, and faced John. A well used smile creased his kindly face. All at once John felt at ease. The preacher extended his hand. "I'm Reverend Bishop. May I be of some help to you, friend?"

John briefly explained why he'd come and then said, "But if I be a bother t' you, I can come another day."

The preacher gestured to the pew. "Nonsense, sit down here. We'll talk and become friends."

Slowly, with some hesitation, John told the kindly minister how he'd left

Anderson Flat and set out for Oregon to get away from the calling Grandma Roane claimed was on him. Not once did Reverend Bishop interrupt or frown or say anything to make John feel bad. He just listened, and John found himself relaxing more and more as he talked. When he finished, the minister invited him to return and talk again whenever he needed to. John wondered why the preacher didn't tell him he'd done something wrong or cast blame on him, but he also appreciated the man's kindness. He decided he'd come see the reverend every time he came to town.

He left the church. Evening was fast approaching. He'd intended to post a letter to Grandma Roane and Lilly Mae to let them know he was safe and at the Pass, but his visit with the reverend took up his extra time. He'd have to do it another day. Oddly, he didn't mind putting off writing the letter.

The thick snow slowed his progress, and the two miles between town and the cabin took much longer on foot. Shadows of early evening began stretching out over the trees, causing the animals of night to awaken to their new day. An owl took quiet flight above his head, scarcely disturbing his thoughts that occupied his bothered conscience. Finally, as night closed its fist to end the day, he stepped onto the cabin's creaky porch and entered the structure.

Dimly glowing coals in the fireplace cast enough light to outline the room's furnishings. John shrugged out of his hat and coat and hung them on the back of a chair. He set his boots beside the chair and then laid his trousers and flannel shirt across the seat. Tiredly he scuffed across the floor to the bed, drew the covers down, and slid in.

Immediately a high pitched scream knifed through the stillness of the room.

Chapter 8

John leaped from the bed, ran to the table and fumbled for the kerosene lamp and tin box of matches he'd spotted earlier. Hands shaking, he managed to strike a match and touch it to the lamp's wick. He swung the glowing lamp in the direction of the bed and froze in place. There, in the center of the bed, sat a wide-eyed woman clutching the blankets tightly under her chin.

The woman squeaked, "What are you doing here?"

John stared back at her, more confused than he'd ever been. "I was goin' t' sleep. What are you doin' in my bed?"

"Your bed? *Your* bed!" The fear in her voice changed to anger. "What makes you think this is your bed? Are you one of those evil men of the West that girls are warned about? Well, are you?" Her voice elevated with every word uttered.

John shook his head hard. "No, ma'am, I'm not evil. At least I don' think I am."

"Then why are you in my room in your underwear?"

He looked down at himself. Gracious, he was practically naked. Grabbing his hat, he held it in front of himself, trying to shield as much as he could. "Forgive me, ma'am, I didn' know you was there." He blew out the lamp so she wouldn't be able to see him so clearly. He stood there holding his hat and the dead lamp like a small boy who got caught with his hand in the cookie jar.

Silence fell in the room, heavy and stifling. Then a soft chuckle came from the bed. "Do you know how silly you look with only a hat for cover?"

John shrugged. "Well, no, ma'am. I reckon not. Never had this happen afore."

"What do we do now, Mr. Silly?" Her voice lost its mad sound and became almost pleasant.

John didn't know how to answer, so he stayed quiet.

She knew what to say, though. "You can't stand there all night, and I can't stay here with you present, so one of us has to leave. I think it would be best if it was you. Good-bye." She flopped onto the mattress, rolled to her side, and pulled the covers over her.

Now that she wasn't staring at him, he recovered his senses. He spoke to the lump in the bed. "Why should I leave? The MacKenzies gave me the right t' be here. Besides, I was here first."

She didn't even twitch. "Correction, I was here first. Besides, their son, Colin, said I could be here for as long as I wanted. So there!"

"Colin? He's not even full-grown. What business does he have t' tell you that you could be here?" The words fell flat and sounded like a school boy arguing on the playground, but he went on anyway. "I have a deal with Mr. MacKenzie. I aim t' build a horse shelter here."

She yawned. "Then go sleep in it and leave me alone."

"Can't."

"Can't what?"

"Can't sleep in it."

"Why?"

"It ain't built yet."

A heavy sigh carried from the bed. "Oh, for goodness sake, then grab a blanket and sleep in front of the fireplace. Just don't bother me anymore, and when morning comes I expect you to be gone."

John squirmed. "Can't."

"Can't what?"

"Can't be gone. Still have the horse shelter t' build."

The woman yawned again. She snuggled further into the mattress. Heavy breathing let John know she'd fallen asleep.

Staring at the bed to make sure she wasn't peeking, he put his hat back on the chair. Then he scurried to the wardrobe and found a spare blanket. He wrapped the blanket around himself and curled up on the rag rug in front of the fireplace. He doubted he'd sleep, but he closed his eyes.

The smell of bacon and coffee teased him awake. He popped his eyes open and looked at a tumble of cold coals. Then a lilting voice came around the corner from the kitchen.

"Good morning. Were you planning on sleeping all day? It must be at least 5:00. I thought you had a barn to build?"

John forced his stiff limbs to unfold. He struggled to his feet, still holding the blanket around himself. He inched to the doorway between the two rooms and peeked at a slender woman standing in front of the stove with her back to him. "Ain't no barn. It's on'y a small horse shed."

"You should probably get dressed." She flipped slices of bacon in the pan. "I'll keep my back turned if you promise not to surprise me again."

She'd surprised him, too, but he decided to just do what she said. He ducked to the corner and quickly donned his shirt, pants, and boots, keeping one eye aimed at the doorway. Fully dressed, he stepped into the kitchen. "Done."

The woman turned around, and for the first time he had a good look at the person who ordered him around the night before. He found her plumb pretty with a cute little nose that turned up a bit on the end. Her hair was as black as a crow's wing, and she had greenish eyes. Maybe she was part Irish. She carried herself proud. John decided he better watch this one. So he eyed her carefully as she dished bacon and fried potatoes into the plates set out on the table. She poured coffee into two tin cups and then motioned to the table.

"Sit."

Lured by the smell of breakfast, he did, and made use of the waiting fork.

Mary slid into the chair across from her intruder and sipped her coffee, holding the tin cup with both hands and resting her elbows on the table. He ate like a man half starved, stabbing up the food and shoveling it into his mouth without a hint of shyness. His shadow last night had shown his broad shoulders and narrow hips, but without his ridiculous hat, she realized he was more than half handsome. She liked his thick brown hair and sapphire eyes. Gentle eyes. She sensed she could trust him.

His fork stopped midway between his plate and his open mouth. He shot her an uneasy glance. "What're you starin' at? Ain't'cha never seen a man eat afore?"

She answered honestly. "I was thinking you aren't frightening at all. You embarrass easily, but that is a good thing for a man in most cases."

Red stole up his cheeks. He set the plate aside. "What you fixin' t' do about our problem here? We both can't stay livin' here. You got a place t' be? By the way, what're you doing here anyways? This ain't the time o' year or the place for a woman t' be. This is winter and this cabin sure ain't a fancy hotel or boarding house. I don' even know your name."

His voice wasn't harsh, but his speech made her cringe. She'd never heard a more atrocious run of words. "I guess it's only fair to tell you what I'm doing here since I already know why you are here. As for my name, it's Mary Badger. My father is William Badger. Maybe you've heard of him. He's a rather famous painter." She waited, but no recognition flickered in his eyes. She sighed and continued. "We live in Boston, and I work for the *Boston Globe* newspaper as a sketch artist and reporter."

His jaw dropped open. "You work for a newspaper?"

She wasn't certain why the idea astounded him, but she felt the need to explain. "Yes. I attended Boston University to study art and writing, which is why the paper hired me. People in the cities want to know more about the West and the people who travel this way. The paper's owners thought that articles showing what the country looks like and sharing stories about the people who cross the South Pass would be well received."

The man scratched his cheek. His fingernails rasped on his short whiskers. "You say your pa's a painter? He ought t' come to Sawyer's Gap then. There's a lot o' unpainted buildings in town jus' hollering for a coat or two."

Mary released a short laugh. "No, silly. He's a portrait painter, and a good one."

The man's face blushed bright red, and he looked away. She'd shamed him. She swallowed her humor and spoke kindly. "My father has painted the faces of some of the most famous people in Europe and the United States. I suspect he will go down in history some day."

Slowly the man turned to face her again. "Why don't you paint por. . . portraits like your pa does?"

"Because the newspaper needs a different kind of artist. And I'd rather sketch landscapes or flora and fauna." She took a sip of her coffee and smiled at his puzzled expression. "There's a box of my pen drawings over in the corner, but I'll ask you to not bother them. I need to take them with me when I return to Boston."

"When'll that be, do ya reckon?"

"Oh, surely not until spring. I'll spend the winter finishing my drawings, and then in the spring I will interview travelers. I anticipate returning to Boston in late spring."

He sat gazing at her, his lips pinched tight, for several seconds. Then he blurted, "I don't much like bein' called 'silly.'"

She appreciated his honesty. "Then you'd better tell me your name."

"John. John Roane."

The Calling

His name was solid and unpretentious. Like the man. "And what brings you to Sawyer's Gap, Mr. Roane?"

"Never intended to settle myself here. I was hopin' t' get through the pass afore winter and find me some land in the Willamette Valley, but I got here too late, so I took up this job t' tide me over 'til spring and the snow melts."

Mary clanked her cup onto the table. "Perhaps I could interview you. You're one of the travelers the people in Boston find intriguing."

He chuckled. "Oh, them Boston folk won't wanta hear about the likes o' me. I ain't nothing special." He sobered. "But y'see, I gotta stay in this cabin 'cause I agreed t' build a horse shelter for the MacKenzies. It's too cold for me t' sleep outside, and it's hardly decent for me t' sleep inside with you here. Can't put you out, an' I can't put me in. I don' rightly know what I should do."

Mary gazed into his face. Not a hint of duplicity showed in his square jaw or clear eyes. She made a snap decision. "Mr. Roane, I believe we can work this out. Let's divide the cabin. I'll take the half where the bed is, and you can have the kitchen. I'll keep warm with the fireplace, and you can keep the iron stove going. Of course, I'll have to trust you to stay on your half, but I think you are a man of honor."

Once more his face flooded with pink, but she suspected the flush was from pleasure rather than embarrassment. A slow grin formed on his handsome face, and a self-conscious chuckle left his throat. "I gotta say, Miss Badger, I can't recall ever bein' called such a thing, but I am t' be thankin' y' for it."

She grimaced. "You're welcome. But if we are going to exist together like this, one thing must change. We need to work on your butchering of the English language." He gaped at her in horror, but she gave him a firm look. "That's right. Every day we're going to work on your speech patterns."

CHAPTER 9

While Mary worked in the cabin, dipping her pen and applying it to paper, John worked outside. Although she tried to stay focused on her own work, she couldn't resist peeking out the window frequently and watching him. He labored with such diligence. Despite the chill temperatures and frozen ground, he carved out holes to hold posts and filled in around the wood with dirt and small rocks gathered from the stream bed just south of the cabin. He always moved quickly and with purpose, claiming the quick movement kept him warm, but she was certain he was also reluctant to waste a moment of sunlight. She admired his hardworking attitude.

Late afternoon, like clockwork, he bundled up and trekked into town for a visit with the old reverend. She wondered what the men talked about, but she never asked. She did, however, study John's face when he returned from the visits. Some days he looked worried, others peaceful, and still others determined. Whatever they discussed, the conversations apparently impacted him deeply.

She liked evenings best. When the sun slunk behind the mountains, they enjoyed a pleasant supper together and then they sat together at the table for "speech lessons." At first he resisted her teaching, but she never teased him and always gently corrected, and eventually he relaxed. She found she enjoyed their evening talks.

And not once did he enter the sleeping room once she'd turned in for the night.

Three weeks into January, she watched him attempt to raise one of the roof rafters. Time and again he heaved it upward only to have it fall back into the snow. Finally he plopped down beside the rafter. White puffs of steam emitted by short breaths cast a vapor cloud around his head. Sympathy filled her. She donned her thick coat and went out to him.

"Would you like my help?"

"What can you do?" He slapped the sturdy length of wood. "This here beam is too heavy for me, so how could you do any better?"

She plunked her fists on her hips. "Just like a man, always thinking women can't do as well as them." She crouched down and touched his snow-covered boot toe. "I do not intend to lift it myself. But maybe the two of us together could lift it. That is, if you are capable of working with a woman." She deliberately challenged him, and it worked.

He pushed to his feet. "All right, let's just see if'n you can do your share."

Hiding a smile, she rose and scampered to the opposite end of the beam. He lifted his end above his head and secured it on the top of one wall. He aimed a grin at her. "Well, let's see you do that!"

She rubbed her palms together and then gripped the end of the beam. Grunting, she lifted. When the beam reached her shoulder height, she took an awkward side step and her foot slipped. She tumbled backward, the beam falling with her. John leaped forward and caught it, but he lost his balance and fell beside her with the beam on his other side.

She clutched her heaving chest, grateful to be safe. She shifted to look at John and found him gazing at her, a soft expression in his eyes. The tenderness sent a strange spiral of feeling through her. "J-John?"

For a long time he lay there without speaking. Long enough that she wondered if he'd knocked the wind out of himself. Finally, he said, "Yes, Mary?"

She loved how her name sounded on his lips. She sat up. "I think we should approach this a different way. Perhaps we both could lift the same end. Together."

He slowly sat up, too. "I thinks so. Don't want to t' hurt ya none."

She shook her head. "John Roane, haven't I been working with you on your grammar?"

"Well, yes, but you see, I ain't had much learning, and. . ."

"You *haven't had* much learning."

"That's jus' what I done said. You're not hard of hearing, are you?" An impish grin curved his mouth. He was toying with her.

She suddenly broke out in laughter. "John Roane! We have a long way to go, you and me, and I intend to see my goal to make you speak properly be one that is achieved." She also hoped he'd recognize how well they worked together. On speech, with roof rafters, and in life.

❖

By working from morning until dusk, John finished the roof on the pole barn the last week of February. Large enough for two horses and a good supply of hay, it wasn't all that pretty to look at, but it was sturdy and should serve the MacKenzies well. He was as proud of the accomplishment as he was of his improved grammar. He hoped Mary would be proud of it too.

Eager for her to see the completed structure, he stomped his feet clean and entered the neat kitchen. Mary was at the table in front of the window with her pen and paper laid out. She worked so intently, he didn't have the heart to disturb her. Instead he turned around and headed for Sawyer's Gap. Now that the barn was finished, he could bring Cautious out to stay. What with working so hard to finish up the barn, he hadn't seen the good reverend for several days. He'd go visit the preacher before he fetched the mule. The thought pleased him, and he sped his steps.

He went straight to the church, as always, but to his surprise the reverend wasn't there. As he left the building, Lester Beenblossom trotted up the street toward him.

"John! I been watching for you."

John met the man in the church yard. "What for?"

"Reverend Bishop said if I saw you, I should send you to the parsonage." The liveryman sounded sad. "He took powerful sick and ain't been out of bed in days. He said he wants to see you as soon as possible."

John wasted no time making his way to the small parsonage located behind the church. His hands shook from something other than cold as he knocked on the door. An elderly woman greeted him and ushered him through the shaded parlor and to the reverend's bedroom. John stopped right inside the door, shocked by how old and fragile the strong minister appeared lying there on a feather pillow.

The older man's eyes were closed, but when the woman touched his shoulder, he opened them with a snap. His gaze found John, and his eyes took on a brighter glow. Weakly waving his hand, he beckoned him to enter. "Come in, my friend. Pull up a chair. It's good to see you."

John did as the reverend requested, gripping his hands in his lap and leaning close to the edge of the bed. "It's good to see you too."

Reverend Bishop reached out and put his hand over John's. "Been wanting to speak to you about something, and I think the time is right. As you can see, my journey on this earth is nearly finished."

John gave a start. "Why, surely not. You have a lot time yet."

The preacher gently shook his head. "No, John, the Lord is calling me home. I can tell."

John wanted to argue, but looking at the man's ashen face and hearing the rasp in his voice let him know the preacher was right.

Squeezing John's hand, the reverend said, "John Roane, there's something I want you to do for me."

"You just name it, and it will be done."

"I want you to take my place when I'm not here."

John felt as though a horse kicked him in the stomach. "Me? Take your place? Reverend, you can't mean that."

"Oh, but I do."

All of the old reasons for running from the calling came flooding back. Shaking his head, he tried to find the words to express why he was unworthy. Why this request was impossible. John sputtered, "I'm not ready. I haven't had experience with a bunch of people depending on me. I don't know all of the Bible like you do."

"John, Mary has done a wonderful work with you and your speech, and over our hours together I've come to know your heart. It's soft for people, and you have a way of making others feel comfortable.

"But, Reverend, I—"

"No buts, John. God has called you. I know it, you know it, and God certainly knows it. Now all you have to do is trust and obey. You know, that is all the Lord requires of us, to trust Him and obey Him."

"But—"

"Don't interrupt an old, dying man of the cloth, John. Your biggest problem is that you feel you don't know enough to lead. I felt the same way many years ago. I found out a secret, John, and I'm going to share it with you now. God rarely calls the prepared. Instead, He prepares the called. Take your Bible and read Philippians 4:13, and when you have done that, come back and see me—but don't wait too long."

"Yes, sir." John rose and slowly walked to the door.

The Reverend's voice called out to him. "And John, marry that woman. She's the one for you."

John froze. "What woman?"

"Mary, of course."

John stared at the preacher. "How do you know about Mary?"

"Oh, John, how could I not know about Mary? You talk about her every time we meet. And by the things you say, I'm sure she loves you. You'll want to get married quickly. I'm the only one who can perform the ceremony."

John didn't know what to say, so he hurried out of the parsonage and to the livery stable. While riding back to the cabin, a million thoughts tormented him. Could he really step behind the pulpit in Reverend Bishop's place? Did Mary love him? Did he love her? She did bring a rush to his heart, different from anything he ever felt for Lilly Mae. Matter of fact, he couldn't recall the last time Lilly Mae traipsed through his mind. But Mary was always there, lingering. His pulse set up its familiar thrum as he pictured her sweet face, and he wanted more than anything to look into her green eyes right that moment. Nothing else would do. Was love this exuberant feeling that could not be satisfied any other way?

Reverend Bishop had told him not to take too much time, and he understood why. Geese flying north warned that winter's grip on the high country was slowly losing its hold. The pass would open up soon, and Mary would return to Boston shortly thereafter. He groaned. Why did everything have to happen so fast? The truth that Reverend Bishop was dying made him sad, and his request for John to take his place scared him. It was all too much.

"Whoa, Cautious." He slid to the ground and knelt in the snow. "Lord, you know I've been avoiding Your hold on my life. You know I've made excuses why I can't be what You want me to be, and You know that I shouted for a fleece. I guess You gave me one in the words from Reverend Bishop. So I want You to know that right here and now I'm opening myself up for Your leading. I don't know what else to do. What I'm saying is. . . Lord, have Your way!"

The tension drained out of his body. He stood and looked up at the sky where the first flicker of stars winked. The very God who hung those stars in the sky had called him to speak His truth. For the first time the challenge excited him rather than frightened him. Past doubts crumbled into powder. He smiled and gave a nod at the sky. "I know what I'm to do, God." Yes, he knew. And Mary must know too.

Remounting, he encouraged Cautious to hurry. Time was fleeting and there was much that needed to be done.

CHAPTER 10

Upon reaching the cabin, John dismounted and led Cautious into the horse shed. He latched the door behind him and hurried to the cabin, shouting for Mary even before he reached. the porch. He clattered into the kitchen, continuing to call. "Mary, I have many things to tell you!"

Silence followed.

He explored every corner of the cabin, but Mary was nowhere to be found. Could she be out drawing? She often traipsed into the woods to add to her collection of sketches. He started for the door and then stopped. Dark was falling. She couldn't possibly be drawing. Then where was she? He turned a slow circle, still seeking her, and his gaze found its way to the corner where she kept her drawings in a flat box. The box was gone!

A sinking feeling of loss swept over his entire body. Surely she was gone. She would never have left her drawings. He'd waited too long to find himself, and now he'd lost her. Stumbling back to one of the chairs, he sank down heavily and placed his head in his hands. The horrible sensation of loss overwhelmed him. *Dear Lord, why when I finally give myself to Your service did I have to lose the one I wanted by my side?*

"Good evening, John. Did you enjoy your trip into town? I suppose you and Reverend Bishop a good visit."

To John, it was a voice from Heaven. He jumped up so fast the chair tumbled over behind him. He rushed to Mary and took her in his arms.

"John, what are you doing?" She gently pulled free of his embrace and looked up at him in surprise. Then she touched his cheek, where tears crept downward. "Why you're crying. What happened?"

He wiped his tears away. "I thought I had lost you, but now everything is all right. It will never be wrong again. You'll see."

She frowned at him. "Whatever are you talking about?"

"Mary, you and I are going to get married."

She gasped, "What?"

"Married. Just as soon as we can get into town. This very evening, even."

Mary scooted a few feet away, holding up her hands. "This is very sudden. Shouldn't I be asked first? After all, that is usually the way it happens."

He came after her. "We don't have time. Reverend Bishop is dying, and he is the only one who can make it legal, and he wants me to take his place, and I had a talk with God, and I feel at peace with his calling, and—"

She took a couple of more steps in reverse. "Let's slow down and take things one thought at a time." She folded her arms over her chest. "As for my marrying you, what makes you think I want to? After all, you haven't made a proper proposal, and you haven't said you love me. Shouldn't that come first?"

Since Reverend Bishop knew he loved Mary, how could she not know? He'd better tell her. He moved slowly toward her. "I love you, Mary. I guess I always have. I just didn't know it or how to show it, or how say it for that matter. But I'm saying it now. I love you." He paused, searching her face. "Do you love me?"

With no delay, she leaped into his arms. "Yes, I do. I think I have since the moment you held your ridiculous hat in front of you, with a look of total innocence on your face. Of course I love you."

John pressed his cheek to Mary's hair and held her close. He whispered, "What about becoming a pastor's wife? How do you feel about that?"

She remained nestled in his embrace. "Doesn't the Bible say that where you are I shall be also? And didn't God make man and woman to be a partnership, cleaving to each other out of love? John, when we're married we will be one. I will be your partner. For the rest of our lives."

John drew her to the table and they sat down, still holding hands. "Thank you, Mary. You've made me so happy. When I came into the cabin to tell you of the wonderful change and understanding that was given to me by both the Reverend Bishop and God, and you weren't here, I thought you had left. I don't want to ever be apart from you again."

She squeezed his hands. "What made you think I had left?"

"You weren't here, and your box of drawings was gone, too."

"While you were gone, I walked to town and sent them to Boston. The *Globe* wanted them by the middle of March, so I needed to send them." She gave him a firm look. "And I'm not going back to Sawyer's Gap tonight even to marry you. It's too cold. We'll go first thing in the morning."

John decided first thing in the morning would be just fine. There was something he needed to do before he committed himself to Mary. He took out paper and pencil and wrote a letter that would bring joy to Grandma Roane and bring closure to his past.

> *Dearest Grandma Roane,*
> *Just a short note to let you know that I'm getting married tomorrow. Mary is a wonderful girl. You'll also be glad to know that I've stopped running from the calling and will be taking over church responsibilities very soon. Please tell Lilly Mae that I will not forget her friendship and that I wish her well.*
> *Love, John*

As he sealed the letter in an envelope, Mary approached him and laid the Bible from the mantel on the table. She pointed to a verse. "Look, John. I found a scripture that fits you so well." She read, "Ezekiel 22:30, *'And I sought for a man among them, that should make up the hedge, and stand in the gap before me for the land, that I should not destroy it: but I found none.'* Reverend Bishop must have been looking for someone to take his place, and God brought you."

John took the Bible and stared at the words, "I sought for a man among them. . ." He smiled, nodding. Yes, he was that man. This Bible must have been left for him to use when he took over for Reverend Bishop.

Removing the small, well-worn Bible from his shirt pocket, he took Mary by the hand and led her to the mantel. "I'll leave my great-granddaddy's Bible here in the hope that someday someone else will be able to use its wisdom for their life."

The morning dawned clear with a warm sun shining down. God had granted a beautiful day for their wedding. A small assembly of people gathered in the pastor's bedroom to witness the event. The Prettys, Les, and the MacKenzies were all present, including Colin MacKenzie. John couldn't resist giving the younger MacKenzie a hug. "Colin, if it hadn't been for you, this union would never have happened, and I thank you for it."

From his bed, Reverend Bishop presented a short wedding challenge and simple vows. "Mary, do you take this man to be your wedded husband?"

Holding John's arm she responded, "I do."

Reverend Bishop asked, "John, do you take Mary to be your wife?"

With a grin as wide as Cautious's ears were long, he stated, "Well, I shore do reckon I'll do jus' that!"

Mary jabbed her elbow into his ribs, then she burst into laughter. He pulled her close for their first kiss. He couldn't say for sure, but the story was that the moment their lips met, a mule joyfully brayed in the distance.

THE END

A Shadow in the Daytime

Constance Shilling Stevens

"And there shall be a tabernacle for a shadow in the daytime from the heat, and for a place of refuge, and for a covert from storm and from rain."
ISAIAH 4:6

To all those who have served our country with pride and honor.
Know that your sacrifice is held in the utmost respect.
Thank you!

Chapter 1

Casper, Wyoming 1919

Beads of sweat popped out on Aaron Forester's upper lip as he stared at the ambulance, his feet rooted to the ground.

It's just a truck. The war's over. There are no guns, no wounded soldiers.

It wasn't the first converted ambulance he'd seen since returning from the war in Europe, but the memories didn't disappear when he was discharged from the army. He sucked in a deep breath and ordered his feet into motion. His boss, Duncan MacKenzie, and Duncan's son, Colin, loaded the last of the tools into the back of the work truck and slammed the doors.

"C'mon, Aaron, let's go." Colin's grin punctuated his statement." There's a little diner on the other side of Casper where they serve the best hotcakes you ever tasted."

The three of them crowded into the cab and Duncan double-clutched and ground the gears. The truck lurched forward.

Once chugging down the road, Duncan started whistling "Standing On The Promises," and Colin added his baritone. Aaron knew all four verses by heart, but he didn't join in. He mentally closed his ears, not wanting to think about the promises he'd made—and broken.

Colin squirmed sideways. "So, Aaron, Dad tells me he's hired you to build the addition on our cabin."

Aaron nodded. "The place sounds nice." And quiet. And isolated. "I appreciate you offering me the job. I wasn't sure where I'd go next after the work on the Casper courthouse was finished."

Colin nudged him with his elbow. "After seeing the kind of work you did on the courthouse, I suspect we're the ones getting the better end of the deal. Some of that trim work was as good as I've ever seen."

"Thanks." Aaron squinted as the sun streamed through the truck windshield.

Duncan pointed to the distant mountains. "I've niver found a place better suited to communing wi' God. We can talk to God anywhere, o' course—while we're working, in church, even in the middle of a crowd. But sometimes we just have to geit alone wi' Him in order tae hear Him."

Duncan was a godly man and a fair boss, but Aaron didn't feel much like talking about God. Drifting from one construction job to another since returning home from the war, he'd felt at a loss for purpose. He'd had a purpose...once. Now he floundered. One thing was certain—he was no longer of any use to God. So hearing God speak to him was as unlikely as hearing an aria sung by hound dog.

Aaron hadn't shared everything with Duncan or Colin about his time in the army. Some of the horrific memories of the war haunted his dreams—the combined smell of the gun powder, blood, and sweat, and even the charred dirt. Colin would likely understand, since the boss's son had spent some time in France. But his role had been much different than Aaron's.

They stopped for breakfast at the diner Colin had mentioned. Duncan and his son chatted about the next job while Aaron pushed pieces of hotcake around on his plate. After paying for breakfast, Duncan eyed him as they returned to the truck. The older man patted his shoulder. "If ye need tae talk about whatever is troubling ye, I'll listen. Meanwhile, there is a Bible at the cabin. I hope ye'll read it."

Aaron nodded, unsure why he agreed. Perhaps only to satisfy the old man. The roar of the truck as it climbed necessitated shouting to communicate, so the remainder of the drive passed with little conversation. The higher they ascended, the road resembled more of a rutted and rocky trail than a navigable highway. The converted ambulance jarred his insides with every pothole, but the view took Aaron's breath away. Craggy peaks reached into the lapis sky as if trying to grasp the clouds and soar on eagle's wings. Below the tree line, the deep green of pines and firs mingled with the fading foliage of the hardwoods. Already showing a few hints of yellow, several trees appeared in a hurry to bid farewell to summer.

Duncan slowed as they passed a fork in the road. He pointed toward the left and hollered over the engine noise. "Just doon that road is the town of Sawyer's Gap. Once we drop off your gear at the cabin, I'll take ye intae town and show ye where Trapnell's Sawmill is." He clutched and downshifted. The truck coughed and growled its way up the dusty road. "I'll let Roth Trapnell know ye'll be stopping in tae order lumber. Past the sawmill, down the street, ye'll see Owen's General Store and Rawling's Hardware. Anything ye need in the way of supplies or building materials for the cabin, charge tae my account. I'll let them know ye're working for me."

The truck crawled around a hairpin turn. Duncan shifted gears and let out the clutch, propelling the truck further up the mountain road, away from Sawyer's Gap. "The cabin isnae much farther."

Aaron craned his neck, taking in the scenery and memorizing the way into town.

True to his word, less than ten minutes later, Duncan steered the truck around a bend and wove between a maze of white pines and cottonwoods, coming to a halt in front of a small, rustic cabin nestled among overhanging branches, much like a mother hen protecting her chicks.

The trio climbed out of the truck. Aaron planted his hands on his hips and surveyed the place that would be his home for the next couple of months. Wind whispered through the pines, divulging secrets of the seasons. Other than the rustling of the tree boughs, the only sounds were the cry of a red tail hawk, and an argument between a squirrel and a magpie. The place was a sanctuary, a refuge from the demons of his past.

Duncan led the way around to the right side of the cabin where the stone fireplace took up a large portion of the exterior wall. Stakes had already been driven into the ground, indicating where the walls of the addition would be, and slabs of granite anchored the corners. "This is going tae be an extra bedroom and the door will be cut here." He gestured to a place a few feet from the stone fireplace. "Let's go inside. I want tae show you something else."

Once inside the rustic, but well-built cabin, Duncan described an overhead loft he envisioned perched above the main room. "What dae ye think aboot a stairway here?" Duncan motioned along the wall beside the fireplace.

Aaron studied the corner and the slope of the ceiling. "I'd put in five or six risers, and then a landing here. Then turn and go up the rest of the way. That way, whoever is climbing the stairs won't bang their head on the rafters." He moved his hands as if running them along the imaginary stairway. "I could put storage cabinets under the stairs so the space won't be wasted."

A satisfied smile stretched across Duncan's face. "Good thinking."

Colin came in the door with an armload of firewood and dropped it into the wood box next to the stove. "There's coffee and some canned goods in the pantry. You can pick up anything else you need at Owen's General Store in town."

Duncan picked up a small, worn Bible from the mantel and held it lovingly between his palms like a cherished thing. Guilt smote Aaron so hard he nearly staggered. He used to cherish God's word at one time. But it seemed like an eternity ago. He didn't even own a Bible anymore.

Duncan placed the Bible on the arm of a chair beside the fireplace, no doubt so Aaron wouldn't forget his promise. "C'mon. Let's go intae town. We have an old mule at our place that ye can use to get back and forth. He's not very fast, and he's kind of fat and lazy, but it beats walking."

Riding a mule? Aaron shrugged. Why not?

Lainey Garrett dragged the sleeve of her chambray shirt across her forehead and replaced her sweat-stained Stetson. Ever since Uncle Phillip's accident, she'd tried her best to fill in for him, sending Mama to the office to deal with the ordering and invoicing. Daddy sorely needed the help and Lainey couldn't bear to see her fragile mother pushing logs through the saw blade or loading lumber. She dusted off the seat of her dungarees and pulled her leather gloves back on.

"Excuse me, sir." The unfamiliar voice behind her drew her attention. She turned and came face to face with the bluest eyes she'd ever seen on a man. Even bluer than Lance's eyes. She bit her lip.

A deep-throated chuckle rumbled from the opening of the mill bay. Her father stepped out onto the loading dock wearing a grin. "Lainey girl, I keep telling you wearing men's britches and that hat are going to get you in trouble."

He stepped past her and extended his hand to the stranger. "Afternoon. I'm Roth Trapnell and this my daughter, Lainey. You must the young fella Duncan MacKenzie told me about."

Lainey snapped her mouth shut on the retort that clamored for escape while heat scorched her face.

The stranger raised his eyebrows at Lainey's attire and shook her father's hand. "Good afternoon, sir. Miss. I'm Aaron Forester. Mr. MacKenzie told me I could order lumber here."

Lainey eyed him while he conversed with her father. She shouldn't care that he mistook her for a man. Why did it fluster her? She peered over her father's shoulder and watched Mr. Forester make a crude sketch. They discussed board feet and square footage, and decided on a plan to deliver the lumber in three separate loads.

"Talk to Lainey here, and she'll write up the order." Daddy gave her shoulders a squeeze. "I see Duncan gave you old Moses to ride." He grinned. "That mule's near as old as me."

Mr. Forester turned a rueful smile toward the gray mule. "We're getting acquainted."

Lainey bit back a grin. Everyone in Sawyer's Gap knew the animal's reputation for orneriness. She wondered if Duncan MacKenzie had mentioned it to Mr. Forester.

Daddy pulled his leather gloves back on. "We can probably begin cutting by the day after tomorrow, and deliver the first load by Friday. Will that suit you?"

"Yes, sir, that'll be just fine. I need to do some clearing first and make sure the footers are secure." Mr. Forester turned his mesmerizing blue eyes back to Lainey and her breath caught in her throat for a moment. She reached for her clipboard, but dropped it along with her pencil.

For heaven's sake, when did I become so fumble-fingered?

She tore her gaze away from him and dove for the clipboard before it slid halfway down the log flume. But Mr. Forester snatched it first.

"Th-thank you. I'm not usually so clumsy." Heat returned to her face. She tugged her Stetson a bit lower.

"No problem." A small dimple put an exclamation point on his smile. He handed her the clipboard and pencil, and she got the distinct impression he was amused by her.

She pulled her composure back into place and assumed an all-business posture. "All right, Mr. Forester. What will you need for the first order?" She tapped her pencil on the board.

"Aaron."

"Excuse me?"

"Call me Aaron. Mr. Forester is too stuffy."

Fiddlesticks, if he didn't unsettle her again! She cleared her throat and took a deep breath, the tapping pencil picking up cadence. He rattled off his list of needed lumber while she scribbled it all down, reminding herself to breathe normally.

"If that will be all, I'll ask you to sign it right here." She turned the clipboard around and pushed it at him. He scratched his signature across the bottom of the page. "Thank you, Miss Lainey. Could you please point me in the direction of the general store?"

Lainey took the opportunity to put a bit more space between them. She stepped toward the road and pointed. "Turn left at the first street you come to."

"Thanks." He scrambled aboard Moses, pulled on the reins to turn the beast around, and nudged with his heels.

Moses didn't budge.

"C'mon, mule, let's go."

Lainey turned her head to hide her smirk. After a full minute of the poor man trying in vain to get the animal to move, Lainey stepped over, pulled one of Moses's ears down and whispered to him. The mule took off like he'd been stung by a bee, galloping down the street with poor Mr. Forester hanging on for dear life.

A swell of laughter from deep in her belly couldn't be suppressed. My, but it felt good to laugh. She wiped her eyes, shook her head, and went back to work.

Chapter 2

Lainey dropped to her hands and knees and groped under the bed for her boots. In her weariness last night, she'd kicked them aside instead of setting them neatly in her closet. Her knuckles thudded against a corrugated paperboard carton. Without thinking, she sat on the oval braided rug and pulled the box from under the bed.

Her hand stilled. The glow of the electric lamp on her bedside table fell across the return label: *US War Department, American Expeditionary Force*. But the cold and impersonal address sent a chill through her. *The next of kin of Corporal Lance Garrett, General Delivery, Sawyer's Gap, Wyoming.*

The box had sat, unopened, under her bed since the day it arrived. She couldn't bring herself to break the seal and open the flaps. She knew what was in it—or at least had a good idea. Lance's things. His wallet, his uniform, his dog tags, perhaps a letter he'd received from her or one he was in the process of writing.

She slowly drew her hand across the top of the dusty box and fingered the seal. All she had was a small photograph she and Lance had taken on their wedding day. She pulled the memory from the recesses of her mind—those remote shadows to which she'd relegated the images of her brief marriage. She'd not allowed herself to dwell on the past, what might have been if Lance had come home.

But this morning, in the stillness before dawn, the memory's power to intimidate remained in the shadows. She'd met Lance at the University of Wyoming, and they'd been immediately drawn to each other—love at first sight, some said. Their wedding day had been a whirlwind. They'd both been so nervous, standing out in front of the courthouse in Laramie. Had they been foolish to marry so quickly? They'd courted for less than two months and were so certain of their love. Despite both of them still being in school, with the war in Europe escalating, Lance convinced her they should marry before he joined the army.

Lainey had tucked their wedding photograph away in the bureau drawer, and there it had remained, much like the box. She stared at the neatly typed address label on the container, as if everything Lance was could be packed in a sixteen by sixteen inch carton. The box didn't know how charming he was, or how smart, or how funny.

Or how scared.

After a two-day honeymoon, he'd shipped out for basic training, and she'd left school to come home to Sawyer's Gap. "Daddy and Mama never even got to meet you," she whispered.

Oh, she'd written them about him. She told them Lance was in two of her classes at the university, and they studied together in the library, and he took her out to the malt shop where they shared a cherry phosphate with two straws. She'd gone on and on about how Lance had made the dean's list and his ambitions to go into business. But the war changed all that.

And now all she had to remember him by was a single photograph and this unopened box. And a receding grief that had lost much of its sting.

Should she feel guilty over her dried tears?

Lainey squeezed her eyes shut and pushed the box back under the bed. *Boots.* She needed her boots. She continued groping under the bed until she hit leather. Her shabby old boots, scuffed by rough encounters with everyday life—much the way her heart felt. But sliding her feet into them was like greeting an old friend. The stitched leather hugged her feet without complaint. No introductions or explanations necessary.

She tucked the legs of her dungarees into the boot tops and scrambled to her feet. Purple, pink, and gold streaks stole across the horizon to the east, evidenced the stretching and yawning of the sun. Stirrings from the next room indicated Mama was shuffling about. Lainey headed for the kitchen to stoke the fire in the stove and start the coffee. She had too much to accomplish today to worry about the past.

Aaron worked at a pesky thorn in his thumb and berated himself for not wearing his leather work gloves while clearing the underbrush away from the side of the cabin where the new addition was to be built. Scripture rose in his mind unbidden: the apostle Paul's thorn in the flesh that rendered him weak so he had to depend on the Lord's strength. Those verses in Second Corinthians had sustained him through many difficult times during his eight years of pastoring a church. But even more so on the battlefield when he'd held a young soldier in his arms who sobbed out his grief after seeing his buddy killed, or prayed with the men in his battalion to have courage in the heat of battle.

What had he told them? *God's strength is perfect in my weakness.*

He'd lost that assurance. When he'd made the choice to step across the line as a chaplain, he'd misplaced his ability to trust. If he could go back and change his decision, would he? Could he bear the consequences?

He shook his head and picked at the thorn again, grimacing as it bit into his flesh. It was too deeply embedded. There was nothing he could do but let it fester.

Aaron crossed the rocky yard to the small barn where Moses hung his head over his stall. He patted the mule's nose. "Hungry, old fella?"

Moses snorted in response. Aaron scooped some oats into the feed trough and tossed an armload of hay into the stall. "Enjoy your supper."

He tramped inside and poked a few pieces of kindling into the glowing coals in the wood stove. After working construction jobs over the past several months, a little brush clearing shouldn't tire him. He suspected it wasn't the activity but rather the musings he fought to dismiss that sapped his energy. He rummaged through the canned goods on the pantry shelves and decided he wasn't terribly hungry. He opened a can of beans.

While his supper heated on the stove, he grabbed the bucket by the door and headed outside to the spring. The short hike took him up a gentle rise where he came upon a doe rooting through the leaves and brambles for acorns. She lifted her head and observed him for several moments, stamping one front hoof in agitation. He stood still and admired the beautiful creature, wanting to apologize for having disturbed her. When she bounded off through the woods, he approached the spring. First, he filled his bucket with cold, sweet water. Then, stripping off his chambray shirt, he knelt and dunked his head in the pool, scrubbing at the grit on his face and neck with his calloused hands. The bracing chill sent a shock through him and he shook his head like a shaggy dog, sending water droplets flying in every direction.

He grabbed his shirt and the handle of the bucket and trudged back down to the cabin, trying not to slosh water on his pant legs. The towering trees to the west cast long shadows across his path, creating a mottled pattern of light as the sun sank behind the mountains.

He paused beside the cabin, surveying his day's work. Besides clearing the brush, he'd dug trenches in which he'd stack the rocks he planned to haul from the surrounding mountainside to form a strong foundation.

He is like a man which built an house, and digged deep, and laid the foundation on a rock; and when the flood arose, the stream beat vehemently upon that house, and could not shake it, for it was founded upon a rock.

The trouble with memorizing so much scripture over the years is that it came back to preach to him. He huffed and plodded the rest of the way to the front porch. After depositing the water bucket beside the dry sink, he stirred the pot of simmering beans. A tin of crackers and a wedge of cheese provided extra sustenance.

He sat at the table and bowed his head. What did one say to the God of heaven in the light of failing so badly at one's calling?

"Thank You, Lord, for this food..." Aaron swallowed hard. "And I'm sorry," he finished in a raspy whisper.

The meal went down like sawdust. He tossed the remainder of the beans and a half-eaten cracker out the door, rinsed the pot, and settled into the chair beside the fireplace. Cool air wafted in the open windows, carrying with it a hint of coming autumn, but still not chilly enough to warrant building a fire.

He struck a match and lit the oil lamp. The glow fell on the small Bible Duncan had left on the arm of the chair. The book called to him, as if it had been waiting for him all day. Remembering the promise he made to Duncan, he picked up the Bible and flipped it open. Keeping a promise he'd made to a man was much easier than keeping the promise he'd made to God.

Enough scripture had already manifested in his mind over the past few days to last him a while. Nonetheless, he turned to the "safe" part of the Bible, the Psalms. His grandmother had always called the Psalms her sugar-sweet blessings from God. How disappointed she'd be in her grandson if she knew he'd let God down.

He turned to the first Psalm, but couldn't get past the third verse. The man described there wasn't him. No, he was the man the Psalm compared to the chaff driven by the wind. He closed the book and laid it aside. Restlessness stirred him into motion and he wandered out to the porch.

In the fading minutes of light, he barely made out the doe threading her way through the brush and trees down the hillside. She stopped and sniffed the air. If she picked up his scent, she didn't show it. She edged a little closer and began nibbling on the cracker he'd discarded earlier. Crumbs fell from her muzzle and she quickly retrieved them, but apparently leftover beans didn't appeal to her. She lifted her head and appeared to stare straight at him, as if to ask, "Is that all?"

Aaron chuckled, and the sound spooked the doe. She bounded away, leaping gracefully into the thickening darkness. The creature moved like she knew exactly where she was going, sure-footed and confident. He couldn't see more than a few feet, but the deer plunged into the darkness like she knew the gloaming cloak was a refuge.

A refuge. If only he knew for what his wounded soul searched.

If he closed his eyes and allowed the nightmare to gain a foothold, he could still hear the artillery, the gunfire, the screams. A tremble shuddered through him at the sickening choice he'd been forced to make.

Chapter 3

Lainey poked her head in the office where her mother was working on invoices.

"Daddy's gone to deliver a load to the MacKenzie cabin. I'm going to go visit with Uncle Phillip." Lainey checked the clock on the top of the file cabinet. "If I hurry, I'll have time to stop at the General Store before he gets back."

Mama tapped her finger on her chin. "Pick up a tin of cinnamon from the store for me."

Lainey brightened. "What are you planning?"

Mama's hands continued stuffing the invoices into envelopes. "The apple trees are nearly breaking their branches. Perhaps this evening we can make apple butter, if you aren't too tired."

Lainey pasted on a cheerful smile. "That sounds like fun."

Truth be told, she trudged home exhausted every day from the backbreaking work at the sawmill. The horrific accident that mangled Uncle Phillip's legs meant Lainey had to try to fill her uncle's position. While Lainey couldn't wrangle the huge logs into place on the conveyor that carried them into the saw blade, she did as much as she could. She feared it wasn't enough, however.

Her mother beamed at the prospect of the two of them working in the kitchen together tonight. Lainey just prayed she could stay awake and not fall over into the pot of apple butter.

"I won't be long." She kissed her mother's cheek and hurried out the door. She trotted two blocks down and turned onto the narrow lane that led to her uncle's cottage. Knowing how difficult it was for him to come to the door, she opened the door and poked her head in.

"Hello, Uncle Phillip. May I come in?"

The sound of rustling paper met her ears. "Come in, Lainey girl."

She followed her uncle's voice and found him in the kitchen in his wheelchair reading the newspaper. "How's my favorite uncle today?" She leaned down and gave him a peck on his whiskery cheek, noting he'd not shaved in several days. His disheveled salt and pepper hair drooped over one eye, and his rumpled bathrobe needed washing. She made a mental note to come back tomorrow and do some laundry for him.

"Lonely. Useless. Tired of sitting here doing nothing." He set his newspaper aside. "Help yourself to some coffee. At least I can still make a decent pot of coffee, even if I can't do much else."

Lainey retrieved a cup from the shelf and filled it, topping off her uncle's cup as well. She chatted with him for a while, filling him in on what was happening around town and what Pastor Roane preached about last Sunday. Her description of Myrtle Hargrove's new hat prompted a chuckle from him.

"There's a man staying at Duncan MacKenzie's cabin. He's building a room onto the cabin for Mr. MacKenzie." A warm flush filled her face when she spoke of the visitor.

"That right?" Uncle Phillip cocked his head. "Is he ordering lumber from us?" A hint of regret flickered over his features at the reference, and Lainey guessed he no longer felt a part of the sawmill operation.

"Yes." She took a sip of coffee. "He came by two days ago. His name is Aaron Forester. I think I heard Mr. MacKenzie tell Daddy that Mr. Forester was in the war."

Uncle Phillip nodded like he already knew the man. A lot of young men were returning to civilian life since the armistice, but just as many didn't come home. Her young man didn't. Time to change the subject.

She leaned closer to Uncle Phillip, propping her elbows on the table and waggling her eyebrows. "Mr. MacKenzie gave his old mule to Mr. Forester to use while he's here."

Uncle Phillip cackled. "Old Moses?"

It was good to hear her uncle laugh, his face wreathed in a huge grin.

"Did Duncan remember to tell the young fella how to get Moses to move?"

Lainey giggled. "I don't think so."

Uncle Phillip's countenance fell when Lainey stood to leave. "You'll come back and visit an old man, won't you?"

She leaned down and hugged him. "I don't see an old man, but yes, I'm coming back tomorrow to do some laundry and give you a haircut."

Uncle Phillip's mantel clock struck ten as she scurried out the door. If she wanted to finish her errands before her father returned from delivering Mr. Forester's lumber, she'd best hurry.

Henry Owen glanced up from his sweeping when she stepped into the general store. Balding on top and skinny as a lodgepole pine, his apron nearly wrapped around him twice. "Mornin' Miss Lainey. How's your Uncle Phillip doin' these days?"

"The doctor says he has healed as much as he's going to." Lainey smoothed her wind-blown hair. "He could use some company. If you have time, why don't you drop by for a game of checkers. I know he'd enjoy it."

"I'll do that." Henry's gap-toothed grin punctuated his promise. "Now what can I get for you today?"

Lainey dug a folded piece of paper from her pocket. "Here's Mama's list." She glanced around. "Is Miz Dorothy here today?"

Henry's smile drooped. "No, she's home."

"Not feeling poorly, I hope."

"Got a letter from our daughter." A frown deepened the lines in his brow. "We was hopin' she and her family would come for a visit this summer, but they couldn't. So we invited 'em for Thanksgiving, but it don't look they're comin' in November, either. It's been pretty hard on them since her husband come back from the war missin' an arm."

At least he came back.

She dug money from her pocket and paid for the few grocery items. "Tell Dorothy I said hello. Mama and I are making apple butter this evening. I'll bring you a jar."

She scooted out the door with her purchases, the tired screen door slapping the frame in her wake. She paused briefly in her hike back to the mill to shift her packages in her arms.

Up ahead, a man jogged across the road and strode up the hill to the sawmill office. Lainey's heart stilled. Even with his back to her, she recognized Pete Cooper by his customary sleeve garters and navy blue visor. Loathing rippled through her—not for the man. It wasn't his fault people dreaded seeing him come toward their door. The trepidation generated from what he did, what he carried.

What he delivered.

The last time Pete Cooper came to the mill, he bore a telegram from the War Department, informing her of Lance's death.

❖

Aaron measured and cut another two-by-six, precisely ninety six inches. He blew away the sawdust, but before he could nail the piece into position, gunfire echoed through the woods. Aaron dropped to the ground, his breath abandoning his lungs.

He crawled on his belly, his face scraping across the dirt, to the trench filled with stacked rock. Sweat beaded on his forehead and upper lip as he frantically looked to the right and left for the men of his battalion. Was anyone hit? A huge knot encompassed his throat and he tried to call out for Sergeant Tucker, his squad leader. There was no answer. Without knowing the enemy's position, Aaron couldn't risk giving away their own.

The roar of an approaching engine—a tank?—cut through his swirling thoughts. But was it Allied or enemy?

The rumbling thunder grew closer and then the engine cut off. A door slammed.

"Hey, Aaron. Where are you? I brought you something to eat."

The battlefield faded but Aaron's heart continued to pound. He sat up and brushed dirt and leaves from his shirt.

"Aaron? Are you here?"

Moses brayed from the small barn in response. Aaron hauled himself to his feet, bent at the waist with his hands on his knees and sucked in a deep breath.

"Hey, there you are. Didn't you hear me?" Colin approached from the side of the cabin. He stopped short. "You all right?"

"Yeah." Aaron stood upright and dragged his sleeve across his brow. He heaved a sigh. "There was... gunfire." He tilted his head toward the wooded hillside above them. "Up there."

Understanding slowly spread across Colin's face, followed by commiseration. He clapped Aaron on the back of his shoulder. "C'mon. My mom sent you some stew and a fresh loaf of bread. Let's go eat."

They followed the trampled path from the work site to the door of the cabin. Colin picked up a basket containing a covered pot and a cloth-wrapped bundle. They stepped inside and Colin set the stewpot on the stove and shoved a few pieces of stove wood into the fire box. Aaron rummaged through a wooden tray for a knife to slice the bread and tried to hide his trembling hands.

"Aaron, there are a lot of hunters around here, especially at this time of year. What you heard was most likely a couple of guys hunting deer or turkey."

Aaron realized the truth of Colin's explanation and took a measure of comfort in it, but still felt foolish for allowing his imagination to run so out of control.

Colin pulled out a chair and straddled it. "Where did you serve?"

Aaron riveted his eyes on the knife and continued his sawing motion across the loaf of bread. "Second Division, Ninth Infantry, Twelfth Artillery Unit." The knife no longer carved the bread, but rather sliced across his very soul. "Bouresches. Belleau Wood. Chateau-Thierry. Saint Mihiel." He stopped short of mentioning the Argonne.

He placed the uneven slices on a plate and set it on the table. Colin nodded slowly, a pained expression in his eyes. He didn't speak for a long minute, but the silence cried with mute empathy. Finally, Colin looked up, his eyes blinking back moisture.

"Aaron, if you need to talk, I'm always here to listen. Or you can talk to Pastor Roane."

Aaron swallowed back a lump threatening to choke him. "Didn't your dad tell you?"

"Tell me what?"

Aaron turned back to the stove and stirred the stew with a wooden spoon. "That I used to be a preacher."

A few seconds ticked by. "Used to be?"

An ache the size of the entire state of Wyoming squeezed Aaron's chest. He scooped the stew into two bowls and carried them to the table. "This smells very good."

Colin's gaze locked on his. "My mom's a great cook."

A fleeting smile twitched Aaron's lips. Colin wasn't going to press. He sat across the table and offered a single-sentence prayer of thanks for the food. When he said amen, however, neither of them reached for their spoons.

Aaron placed both palms on the table. "I pastored a church in Nebraska for eight years. When the war escalated, and it became obvious the United States couldn't remain neutral, a lot of young men in the community signed up." He drew in a slow, even breath. "And God called me to be a chaplain."

Colin leaned forward with his elbows on the table, his hands clasped together. He simply waited.

Aaron took his time. "As an army chaplain, I was attached to the Ninth Infantry and then to the Twelfth Artillery. Some of those boys were so young."

He shook his head at the memory.

Colin reached for a ragged piece of bread and tore it in half. He extended one half across the table to Aaron. Aaron reached for the bread and their eyes connected—a silent invitation to let go of the burden that had held Aaron prisoner for so many months.

"I killed seven men. It was at the Battle of the Argonne. The Germans had our battalion pinned down. Our boys were being picked off...dying right in front of me. I couldn't—"

His voice broke. He blew out a breath and swallowed. "I couldn't let any more of those young men die. I had to do something. So I took the rifle off a dead soldier, took his grenades too. And I ran up the hill. I was hit in my upper leg and my shoulder. I threw one grenade. I saw—" Bile rose in his throat. "I saw two Germans hit by the shrapnel. I threw the other grenade, and then I just kept firing the rifle until there wasn't any more return fire."

Tears ran down his face and his stomach turned over. His trembling voice was a whisper. "They awarded me the silver star. Gallantry under fire, they said." He covered his face with his hands. "I was a *chaplain*. A non-combatant. I took an oath to minister to the hearts and souls of men. But I killed seven men and they called that gallantry."

Chapter 4

Aaron shifted on the hard church pew. Despite the guilt that ate at him for not being able to remember the last time he was inside a church, he still wished he was anywhere but here. Colin sat beside him singing along with the rest of the congregation.

" 'I need Thee every hour, most gracious Lord; no tender voice like Thine can peace afford...' "

Peace. The cease fire had been declared, the armistice signed, and the newspaper headlines proclaimed peace reigned throughout the world. But within Aaron's heart, war still raged. Pouring his heart out to Colin had loosened some of the bonds that still held him captive, but whether he labored on a mountainside cabin, sat on a church pew, or crawled through a battlefield trench, he'd never forget the gut-wrenching feeling of having taken seven lives.

The hymn singing ended, and Pastor Roane opened his Bible and cleared his throat, looking out across the congregation with a smile. "How many times have we said, 'In that day...', meaning some day when we are in the presence of Jehovah God. God's word teaches that we will have tribulations in this world. Our nation has just come through a horrible time of war, and strife, and heartache.

"In the book of Isaiah, the prophet spoke of the future house of God in all its wonder and glory and sweetness. He proclaims the day of the Lord as a time of peace over all the earth." The preacher lifted his Bible and read, " 'They shall beat their swords into plowshares, and their spears into pruning hooks; nation shall not lift up sword against nation, neither shall they learn war anymore.' "

Aaron bit his lip. God could have stopped that awful war before it started—the bloodshed, the carnage. Stopped man from hating one another.

The pastor droned on, but Aaron set his jaw and tried not to listen. Unless Pastor Roane had walked in his shoes, listening was pointless. The shame of which the preacher spoke was the shame Aaron lived with every day.

"But in that day... Isaiah says it shall come to pass that the Lord's house shall be established in the top of the mountains, and many people shall say, 'Come ye, and let us go up the mountain of the Lord.' "

Pastor Roane's voice rose with conviction. But Aaron's heart sorrowed and he found no solace in the preacher's words, even when he spoke of God's mercy and grace: " 'And there shall be a tabernacle for a shadow in the daytime from the heat, and for a place of refuge.' Oh, brothers and sisters, that place of refuge is the Lord Jesus. He is our shelter, He is our shadow in the daytime."

Aaron wanted to clap his hands over his ears. He didn't want to embarrass Colin and his family, or draw attention to himself, but he couldn't sit here a minute longer. He rose and moved quickly toward the door.

Once outside, he sucked in deep draughts of crisp autumn air, hoping to clear away the dishonor and unworthiness. But it clung like a burr.

A man sat on top step off to the right of the door. He glanced up at Aaron, and hesitantly stuck his hand out. "Pete Cooper."

Aaron shook the man's hand, wondering why he was sitting outside. "Aaron Forester. It's... a little stuffy in there. I needed some air."

A cynical half-smile tipped Pete's lips. "Know what you mean."

Bitterness in the man's tone arrested Aaron's attention. Having been in the ministry for more than eight years, he'd seen his share of disillusioned people, but this man's demeanor went past discouragement.

Aaron sat down beside him. "Care to tell me why you don't want to go inside?"

Pete released a soft snort. "I used to go to church. Before the war. Now it makes folks uncomfortable when I'm around."

The defeat in his voice pierced Aaron's heart. "Why?"

The muscles along Pete's jaw line twitched. "It ain't my fault, y'know. I just deliver telegrams for the Western Union. Durin' the war, folks hated to see me comin', 'cause it was usually bad news. It got so I felt like one of them people in the Bible who had that disease."

"Leprosy?"

Pete nodded. "Yeah. Nobody wants me around. 'Specially since I couldn't go in the army, on account of I have a bum knee."

Poor fellow. Empathy tugged at Aaron. How many letters had he written to the next of kin of fallen soldiers? He'd hated signing his name, thinking the families would somehow blame him.

"Pete, you have to understand, those people who got the telegrams lived in fear day after day during the war. I'm not saying it's right to shun you for doing your job. But maybe if you go out of your way to show those folks some kindness, they'd see you in a different light."

"You mean do somethin' nice for them same people I had to give the telegrams to?"

"That's right."

"Like what?"

Aaron pursed his lips and shrugged. "I bet you'll think of something. You know the folks around here better than I do."

Pete rubbed his chin and appeared to ponder Aaron's suggestion a moment. "I can try. Can't be no worse'n havin' folks hate me."

"I don't think they hate you, Pete. They're just hurting."

A look of contemplation came over the fellow. No doubt he understood how it felt to hurt. He gave a slow nod. "Yessir, I'll try." He rose and ambled off down a wooded trail.

Aaron watched until he disappeared into the woods, and then he remembered why he'd exited the church. The service would be over soon, and he wasn't in the mood to explain to Colin why he'd left. He pushed away from the step and headed toward the road.

Before he took a dozen steps, a young woman headed his way in an ivy green dress with some sort of lacy shawl around her shoulders. When she came closer, Aaron realized it was the woman he'd met at the sawmill, the one he'd mistaken for a man.

"Miss Lainey."

She stopped and looked past him to the church. "Is the service over already?"

He cast a quick glance over his shoulder, half expecting to see the door flung open and people shaking Pastor Roane's hand at the door. "Uh, no. Not yet."

Lainey arched her eyebrows, a question in her expression.

He schooled his features into an indifferent stare. "You're a bit late for church yourself."

A tiny smile played at the corners of her mouth, and she dipped her head briefly. "Yes, I suppose I am. I went to look after my Uncle Phillip this morning. He seemed lonely, so I sat and read to him until he dozed off."

"Colin MacKenzie told me your uncle had been injured. It's good of you to care for him."

Her expression softened. "Uncle Phillip tries not to complain. He says a lot of our soldiers came back from the war with physical injuries, and many didn't come back at all."

A wince flickered across her face, matching the one that skewered his heart. He muttered, "And some came back with scars on their heart."

Lainey cocked her head. Had she heard him correctly? His remark sounded more like he was talking to himself. She couldn't help wondering what kind of wound he meant. What about the invisible wounds in the hearts of the ones who received those awful telegrams?

She ducked her head and caught hold of the dainty watch pendant hanging around her neck, clicking it open with her fingernail. Nearly a quarter of twelve. She snapped the cover closed again. "I've already missed most of the service, and walking in this late would only be a distraction. I think I'll just go for a walk. Good day, Mr. Forester."

"Aaron."

She paused mid-turn and looked back at him. Was he trying to annoy her? He held out his open palms at his sides for a moment, in a gesture that only communicated a need for friendship. She conceded his request.

"Aaron." The sound of his name on her lips had a pleasing effect that caught her off guard. She swallowed hard. "W-would you like to accompany me? There's a pretty spot by the creek."

Now why did she say that? The little hidden thicket beside the rushing water was her secret place. She'd played there as a child. She'd gone there to write letters to Lance when he was fighting in Europe, and it was her private sanctuary the day that cold, impersonal telegram came, where only God witnessed her tears. But it was too late to rescind the invitation.

A slow smile relaxed the tension in his face. "I'd like that."

He fell into step beside her and they spoke of the pleasant weather, the chilly autumn nights, and the beautiful mountainous panorama. Less than fifteen minutes later, the sound of the creek tumbling over rocks called to her through the trees. The path became a barely discernible trail—she liked to think nobody but her and local deer knew about it. But now Aaron Forester would know about it as well.

She pushed aside thick, low-hanging hemlock boughs that swept the ground to reveal the secluded retreat. She turned to gauge Aaron's reaction. His gaze traversed the tall, overhanging trees and the sunlight sparkling off the water as it danced over the rocks. He swept his gaze to his right and left, his eyes widening and his lips silently forming an O as he took in the beauty.

"This place looks like a picture postcard."

Gratified over his appreciation, Lainey perched on a rock and let the image of the creek carrying gold aspen leaves downstream soothe her spirit. "I've been coming here since I was little."

He took a seat on a rock adjacent to hers, drew in a slow, deep breath, and let it out easily, as though releasing his troubles along with the lungful of air. "I can see why you love this place." He turned and connected his gaze with hers. "Thank you for bringing me here."

A tiny smile curved her lips. The timbre of his voice blended with the song of the creek and the whisper of the wind through the pines, as if he were as at home in this place as she. She hated to interrupt the sounds of nature, but sharing them with Aaron felt too intimate. They needed a topic of conversation.

"How long have you been working for Duncan MacKenzie?"

Aaron picked up a gold leaf and twirled it between his thumb and forefinger. "Not too long. I signed on with his crew when they were working on the courthouse in Casper. When that job was finished, he told me about his cabin and the addition he'd been wanting to build. He and Colin are the experts at building, but Duncan said he liked my work." He shrugged. "Since I didn't have another job to go to, this seemed like a good option. It's nice, staying in the cabin. Quiet. Beautiful view."

He turned to face her. "Have you ever been up there? The view of the mountains from the front porch looks like eagle's wings."

Amusement tickled her. He obviously didn't know she'd grown up in Sawyer's Gap. With the exception of the semesters she'd spent in the dormitory at the university, she'd never lived anywhere else. When she and Lance married, she couldn't bear to stay at the university after their two-day honeymoon. The day he shipped out with the army, she packed her things and moved back home. "Yes, I've seen the MacKenzie cabin. It's a lovely place." She cocked her head. "So, you just go from one construction job to the next?"

A faraway look fell across his expression. He gave a brief nod. "Yeah, pretty much." He tossed a pebble into the creek. "Colin told me your uncle had been injured, but he didn't say how it happened. Was it a logging accident?"

"Not exactly." Lainey's stomach clenched at the memory of the gruesome event that nearly claimed her uncle's life, and robbed him of the use of his legs. "He and Daddy were working at the sawmill, and a log had gotten hung up coming down the conveyor. Uncle Phillip jumped up onto the track to kick it loose, and the log rolled into him, caught his pant leg, and dragged him. Both his legs were broken. Daddy got the belt and saw blade shut down in time, but the doctor says the tendon and nerve damage will never heal correctly." An involuntary shudder shook her as she remembered her uncle's screams. "Uncle Phillip's injuries will keep him from ever working at the sawmill again. My heart aches for him. He feels useless. I wish there was a way to convince him his life isn't over."

She glanced at Aaron. Moisture gleamed in his eyes and he looked away. She'd obviously stirred something painful in his mind. She'd heard Duncan MacKenzie mention Aaron had been in the war, but he'd come home in one piece—at least physically. A whisper in her spirit hinted at the unseen emotional injuries Aaron might have endured.

She stiffened her spine and pushed the notion away. What could be worse than being buried on the battlefield?

Chapter 5

Aaron drove the nail into the rafter with a sure stroke of his hammer. He poked his hand into the pocket of his carpenter's apron and came up empty. He gave a huff of annoyance and cast a glance to the makeshift corral where Moses cropped grass. The ornery mule likely wouldn't be terribly cooperative, but he needed the supplies if he was to accomplish any more work today. As long as he had to make a trip into town for more nails, he might as well pick up a roll of tarred paper and order the shingles.

Moses eyed him with suspicion when he approached the corral carrying the animal's bridle and saddle. Aaron looped the bridle over his arm. "I don't like this any more than you do, but could we just this once put our differences aside and try to work together?"

Moses snorted and swished his tail, smacking Aaron on the back of the head.

"Hey! Keep your tail to yourself, you wretched beast."

Aaron set his jaw and tightened the cinch. *Stupid mule.* He climbed aboard and nudged his heels into the mule's ribs. Predictably, Moses planted his feet and refused to move.

"C'mon, I have work to do and I can't do it until I get those supplies." He raked his hand through his hair. He'd give a month's wages to know what Lainey had whispered in Moses's ear two weeks ago.

After ten minutes of threats and cajoling, Moses finally ambled out of the corral and plodded toward town. When Aaron passed the sawmill, he looked to see if Lainey was about, but didn't see any sign of her.

Just as well, after their conversation last Sunday. Perhaps talking about her uncle's accident made her sad. Her description of his depression certainly touched a chord in Aaron's heart, and for some reason, she became aloof and distant.

He pulled Moses to a halt in front of Rawling's Hardware Store and dismounted, tying the reins securely to a post.

A cowbell clanked against the door as Aaron entered. When he'd been here his first day in Sawyer's Gap, he hadn't noticed the picture of a young soldier on the wall behind the counter.

Nor had he noticed the black drape around it.

The proprietor entered from a doorway that likely led to a storeroom. A black arm band hugged Mr. Rawling's sleeve, and lines mapped the man's face. His eyes were hollow pools, empty of life. Aaron shuddered. He'd seen that look...too many times.

"Good morning, Mr. Rawling."

"Mornin'." The word ground out more like a growl than a greeting. Mr. Rawling gave a nod and moved woodenly to stand behind the counter. Aaron was loathe to break the silence, as if doing so would be an intrusion on the man's obvious grief.

Aaron tipped his head toward the row of bins lining the wall behind the counter. "I need three pounds of roofing nails and five pounds of flooring nails, a couple dozen carriage bolts with washers and nuts. And a roll of tarred paper if you have it."

Another mute nod accompanied Mr. Rawling's acknowledgement as he went about the task of scooping the nails into the pan on the scale. Aaron watched the man move instinctively, his mind elsewhere. But Aaron couldn't tear his gaze from the black arm band. He'd seen enough of those black bands to fill several lifetimes. The chaplain in him—the part of his heart he kept trying to bury—ached for the merchant. Dread clamped his lips closed and all he wanted to do was flee. But his feet were anchored in place.

Mr. Rawling turned with the sacks of nails. Pain filled every inch of his face. Aaron stepped to the end of the counter where nothing came between him and Mr. Rawling.

Quietly, Aaron let his focus fall on the arm band. "Tell me about him."

Initially startled at Aaron's gentle request, Mr. Rawling's face melted into wonder. He cleared his throat once.

Twice.

And he swallowed hard.

"My boy, Joseph. Today is his birthday. He would've been twenty-one." Moisture collected in his eyes, and he had to blink several times before he could continue. "H-he was...k-killed...one week before the armistice."

Aaron kept his voice quiet, soothing. "I can see you loved him very much. He was blessed to have you as a father."

Mr. Rawling shook his head. "I was the blessed one. Joseph was a good boy, smart, strong. He loved God. When his mother died a few years back and it was just the two of us, Joseph was more than my son, he was my friend. Sometimes we'd close up early and go fishin'. My, that boy loved to fish. And he always caught a bigger one than me." Mr. Rawling chuckled. "Joseph had a sense of humor, and he loved to joke. Guess it brought him pleasure, seein' other folks laugh." He patted his chest, over his heart. "Him and me—we was real close."

He turned when his voice broke, but not before Aaron caught a flicker of a sad smile on the grieving father's face. Mr. Rawling pulled a handkerchief from his pocket and blew his nose before turning back to face Aaron.

"Thanks for askin' about my boy. Lots of folks are sorrowin' these days. Nobody wants to hear about someone else's pain. Reckon they expect talkin' about him'll just make it harder. But even if it's hurtful, I don't never want to stop talkin' about my son."

A deeper understanding than Aaron wanted to claim twisted his gut. He reached out and gripped Mr. Rawling's shoulder. "Anytime you need to talk about your son, I'll listen. I never got to meet him, but if he was anything like his dad, he must have been pretty special."

A tremulous smile tipped the corners of Mr. Rawling's mouth. "Thank you, young man. Duncan MacKenzie hired himself a fine one." He slid the invoice across the counter for Aaron's signature.

Aaron scrawled his name across the bottom of the sheet and shook Mr. Rawling's hand. He grabbed the sacks of nails and hoisted the roll of tarred paper onto his shoulder. He turned toward the door and found Lainey Trapnell a few feet behind him.

The expression on her face staggered his footsteps. She looked at him, wide-eyed, as if seeing him for the first time. He walked to the door where she stood framed in sunlight.

"Hello."

A long moment passed before she replied. "H-hello. I saw Moses tied up outside and figured you were in here."

Aaron nodded, and turned back and lifted his chin to Mr. Rawling. "I'll come by again."

Mr. Rawling smiled. "I hope so."

Lainey stepped aside to allow Aaron to carry his purchases out and tie them onto the saddle. As he lashed down the heavy roll of paper, he glanced sideways at her. She scuffed her boot against the sidewalk.

She finally hooked her thumbs in her pockets and spoke. "I wanted to apologize for last Sunday. I'm afraid I wasn't very good company."

He turned from his task to face her. "You were lovely company. But I did notice talking about your uncle's injuries was hard for you. For that, I apologize. I shouldn't have brought it up."

She shook her head and waved her hand, as if brushing the subject aside. She stepped over and stroked Moses's muzzle while he finished tying down the roll of paper.

"What made you ask Mr. Rawling about his son?"

He tugged on the final knot and patted Moses's neck. "His black arm band. The pain in his eyes. Like he said, most folks assume people who have lost a loved one don't want to talk about them, so they act like the loved one never existed. But usually the grieving person *wants* to talk about them—*needs* to talk about them. It's an invitation to let the person whose heart is broken know it's all right to enjoy the good memories, even while you're grieving."

She wrapped her arms around herself. "How did you know that?"

Aaron rubbed his hand across his face. This conversation was getting too close to dangerous. "I've been around a few people who have lost loved ones."

She peered at him through a lock of hair that had fallen across her eyes. "In the war?" She pushed the hair away, her tiny smile wavering and her brows pulling in.

He yanked his focus back to the mule and pretended to double-check the ties. Strange how his insight kicked in, knowing why Mr. Rawling needed to talk about his son. But the opposite was true for him personally. The last thing he wanted to talk about was what happened in the war.

"I'm sorry. I shouldn't have asked that." Her soft apology was almost lost on the whisper of the wind. "So many people experienced heartache during the war, the ones overseas and the ones who stayed home. But sometimes it's hard to know what to say. That's why I asked about Mr. Rawling. You seemed to know he needed to talk about Joseph, like God sent you to ease his grief today."

Aaron curled his fingers into fists and he laid his forearms across the saddle. "No. God didn't send me. I guess it was just dumb luck."

She touched his elbow and he turned. "I don't believe that. Whether or not you want to admit it, God used you to give Mr. Rawling a special gift."

Her words rattled through him like dry leaves in a winter wind. Aaron turned slowly. Lainey's wide eyes, so full of unfeigned sincerity, implored him to accept what she said as truth. Aaron nodded slowly. "Mr. Rawling gave the dearest thing he had in all the world for the cause of liberty. Maybe asking him about his son was a gift—I don't know. But who deserves such a gift more than a grieving father?"

Lainey sat on the back porch, the book she'd been reading neglected in her lap. The lantern light flickered beside her, creating a spooky dance on the floorboards. Aaron's response to her observation haunted her mind. From what Mr. MacKenzie had said, she knew Aaron had been in the war, but that was all she knew. There was something else, something deeper. His affinity with Mr. Rawling's grief touched a place in her heart she usually kept closed and shuttered. The dusty box beneath her bed bore testimony of her reluctance to expose her inner feelings to prying eyes.

The back door opened and her mother stepped out on the porch with two cups of steaming cocoa. "I thought I'd join you." She handed Lainey a cup.

"Mm, thank you." Lainey took a tentative sip.

"Would you like to talk about it?" Mama settled herself into the sturdy rocker.

"Talk about what?"

"Whatever is weighing so heavily on your mind. You've been mighty quiet this evening." Mama set the rocker in motion.

After a minute, Lainey told her mother about her encounter with Aaron at the hardware store. "There is something about him, Mama. He knew just what to say to Mr. Rawling. It seems to me that a person has to experience grief to know how to talk to someone else about it."

Mama's rocking chair squeaked in harmony with the wind in the pines. "You're probably right."

They sipped their cocoa in silence while a coyote howled in the distance.

Finally, Mama rose. "I'm going inside. Don't stay out here too long and catch cold."

Lainey smiled up at her mother. "I won't."

Mama paused at the door. "Sweetheart, it might be time to open the box."

Startled, Lainey jerked her head to look at her mother.

"Yes, I know it's still under your bed. Honey, I'm not sure you'll ever be able to reconcile your own feelings until you face the contents of that box."

A sigh borne of confusion escaped Lainey's lips. "Mama, I'm not even sure what I feel anymore. I thought Lance and I were so in love. We only knew each other a couple of months, and we were only married three days when he shipped out. It felt so right at the time." She stared out across the porch railing to the woods, now cloaked in darkness. "How does a person grieve for someone they were supposed to love, but barely knew?"

Chapter 6

Aaron sucked in a lungful of crisp air and headed down the narrow dirt road toward town. He didn't feel like fighting with Moses today, so he left the ornery mule in the barn. Aaron's list was short, so his purchases wouldn't be difficult to carry back to the cabin.

He hoped to look in on Joe Rawling, to let the grieving father know he wasn't forgotten, and then pick up a few groceries at Owen's General Store. Since he also planned to stop by Trapnell's Sawmill to order some trim, he stood a good chance of seeing Lainey. He brushed his hand over his fresh chambray shirt and ran his fingers around his belt, ensuring his shirttail was neatly tucked in.

Leaves in various shades of yellow fluttered in a spiral autumn dance, cascading from the treetops to keep him company as he walked. He hummed as he tramped down the hill. Autumn in Wyoming was breath-taking.

Forty minutes later, he rounded the bend in the road leading to Sawyer's Gap and strode up the hill to the sawmill. He paused between the loading dock and the office but saw no sign of Lainey. Disappointment trickled through him, and he chided himself. Just because they'd shared a few conversations didn't mean she desired his company. He shoved the thought away as the noise from the sawmill captured his attention.

Roth Trapnell grappled with a huge log, trying to maneuver it onto the conveyor. Aaron hopped up onto the decking that ran the length of the conveyor. He gave Mr. Trapnell a wave—the racket making a verbal greeting impossible—and he grabbed a pole to assist the older man in the task of steering the log into the giant blade.

Sawdust spewed and planks of bark fell away as the two men pushed the log through the blade, squaring it up and readying it for cutting into boards. A half hour later, Mr. Trapnell shut down the saw and pulled off his leather gloves.

"Thank you, young man." He stuck his hand out and Aaron gripped it. "Sure appreciate you coming along when you did. This order has to go out today. It's not easy wrangling those big ones down the belt."

"Especially for one man working alone." Aaron brushed wood chips from his clothing and swiped his sleeve across his forehead. "Lainey told me your brother isn't able to work anymore."

Mr. Trapnell nodded and slapped his gloves against his pant leg. "Phillip was hurt pretty bad. The doc says he'll likely never walk again. Even if he does, he won't be able to do this kind of work. Lainey tries to help as much as she can, but she can't do this heavy labor, and I don't want her to."

Aaron rubbed his hand over his jaw. He had to agree—even as capable as Lainey was, the work was too strenuous for a lady.

Aaron followed Mr. Trapnell to the water barrel where they both scooped up a cooling drink with the tin ladle. The older man wiped his mustache and eyed Aaron. "You handled that log like you knew what you were doing."

Aaron shrugged. "I worked at a sawmill for two summers while I was studying for—" He cleared his throat. "While I was going to school. I need to order some milled trim. Window frame, baseboard, door framing. I won't need it until next week."

They determined the amount and Mr. Trapnell wrote up the invoice. "I'm grateful for your help today, but I don't suppose you came by to help out an old geezer like me, or to order trim you won't need for another week." A grin split his face and a twinkle gleamed in his eye. "My guess is you stopped by to see Lainey."

Aaron's face heated and he chewed on his lip. Was he so transparent? "Yes sir, I suppose I was hoping to see her."

Lainey's father clapped him on the shoulder. "She's over at her Uncle Phillip's house today. She does some housework and laundry for him, makes a couple of his favorite dishes, and just keeps him company. I get over there when I can, but Phillip is mighty discouraged. I don't know what to say to pick up his spirits." Mr. Trapnell's brow drew inward.

Aaron hung the ladle on a peg by the water barrel. "Seems to me if your brother knows the sawmill business, he still has something to contribute, even if he can't do the physical work."

The two men walked to the edge of the loading dock. "Lainey told her mother and me about the way you talked to Joe Rawling, and Duncan MacKenzie is real pleased with the work you've done thus far on the cabin. You and I working together sure made short work of that log." Mr. Trapnell's grin broadened. "You're a good man to have around—could be a real fine addition to our community."

Odd, how the man's comment didn't seem as undesirable as it would have a few months ago. Instead of slamming the door on the idea, Aaron simply shrugged.

Mr. Trapnell crammed his gloves into his back pocket. "What are your plans after you finish working for Duncan?"

"I don't know. Haven't really thought much about it. The work on the cabin will probably take me at least another five or six weeks, and the old barn out back needs some repairs." Aaron hooked his thumbs into his belt. "After that, I suppose I'll move on, look for another construction job."

Mr. Trapnell planted his hands on his hips and squinted at Aaron. "What would you think about staying in Sawyer's Gap, working with me here at the sawmill?"

The unexpected offer took him by surprise. Staying in Sawyer's Gap? He looked past the man standing in front him to the little town just down the road where he'd already made a few friends. The surrounding mountains made the invitation more appealing, not to mention the idea of seeing Lainey regularly. "I'd have to think about that."

Mr. Trapnell shook his hand. "You do that. Take all the time you need, pray about it, and let me know."

Aaron thanked Lainey's father and departed down the road toward the hardware store. For the first time since the war, Aaron entertained the thought of putting down roots. Was he just tired of moving from place to place, from one job to the next? Or was he tired of running?

His steps slowed and the whisper of God fell over his heart. He could have died that day on the battlefield. Countless times since then he'd wished God hadn't allowed him to live—the memories of that awful day too grievous to carry. Why God chose to deliver him he didn't know. Last night as he sat by the fire, his gaze fixed on the framed piece on the mantel, and he'd stared at it for a long time. Embroidered in colorful threads, someone had taken great care to draw attention to a scripture that obviously had ministered to them.

Tearmann - A Place of Refuge - Isaiah 4:6

Was it true? Duncan had suggested the cabin was a sanctuary in which to get alone with God. Had God brought him to this place so he could hear His voice? If so, why was God calling him?

112

Lainey stamped her foot when she realized her mistake—the third one this morning. First, she'd added up Henry Owen's order incorrectly, and then she'd loaded Fred Wilcox's lumber into Sam Greenfield's wagon. Now she stood, her face aflame. The order in her hand clearly stated six dozen eight-foot posts, and she'd told her father to cut eight dozen six-foot posts.

"Don't fret so, Lainey girl. We'll sell the six-footers—they won't go to waste." Her father gave her shoulders an awkward squeeze. "It just means you'll have to help me cut more posts so we can deliver the order on time."

"I'm sorry, Daddy. I just can't seem to keep my mind on what I'm doing today."

Her father smirked. "I noticed."

The heat in her face intensified and she bit back the words that tried to escape. She was thankful her father hadn't teased her further after her reaction to the news that she'd missed Aaron's visit to the sawmill. She must not have done a very good job of hiding her disappointment, because her parents exchanged a look and her father winked at her when he'd told her he'd offered Aaron a job.

His presence in church yesterday had added to her chagrin, especially when he smiled and greeted her after the service. It was a good thing nobody had asked her what Pastor Roane's sermon was about, because she'd spent the entire time studying Aaron's profile across the aisle and two rows ahead of her.

Once again, confusion nipped at her. How could she nurture feelings for Aaron after having known him such a short time? Her whirlwind courtship with Lance should have taught her something, at the very least that she should keep her guard up and not foster feelings she had no business entertaining. The trouble was her traitorous heart refused to heed the advice.

"I'll start unloading the six-footers. Where do you want them stacked?" She tugged her gloves back on.

"Just stack them over at the far end of the loading dock for now." Daddy patted her shoulder. "Come and help me as soon as you can."

Sweating out her frustration on moving the fence posts, she disciplined her thoughts to keep her mind on her work. From time to time she glanced back at her father working a new batch of logs down the conveyor. He needed help, someone better suited for the work than she. But who else in town knew the sawmill business? Other than Daddy's teasing over offering Aaron the job, she couldn't think of a single person who could work alongside her father the way Uncle Phillip had.

If it hadn't been for her bone-headed mistake, this fence post order would be finished by now. Instead of helping her father, she'd only added to his work. Not that this side of the business had ever been her goal.

Uninvited memories flooded her mind while she worked. The days she'd spent at the university studying toward a degree in business management seemed misspent now. She'd always planned to come back to Sawyer's Gap and help her parents take Trapnell's Sawmill into the next decade, expanding the business, subcontracting with other mills to supply the larger operations, growing their company so her parents could one day retire comfortably.

Meeting Lance was a fork in the road. Leaving school without finishing, she'd come home, but not the way she'd planned.

"I wish I knew what You wanted me to do, God. I've tried to reconcile Lance's death and being a widow, but the guilt won't leave me alone. Why do I feel guilty? Is it because of the flutters in my stomach every time I look at Aaron?

"And I wish I knew how to help my father." She grabbed two more fence posts and stacked them with the others. "Show me what to do. I know I should be more patient and wait on You to answer, but Daddy really needs help soon."

"Hello, there. Need a hand?"

Lainey startled at the sound of the deep baritone voice and dropped a fence post on her toe. She yelped and grabbed her foot, hopping up and down and gritting her teeth.

"Here, sit down. I'll finish this."

She looked up to find Aaron's deep blue eyes, hooded with concern, boring into hers.

Chapter 7

Aaron straddled the ridge of the roof, nailing shingles into place. The picture he had in his mind of Lainey hopping around on one foot brought a smile to his face—not because stubbing her toe was funny, but because she'd looked so cute. Tendrils of dark hair had escaped her hat and clung to her dirt-smudged cheeks, and her brows were drawn in to a little scowl, but she was still the most appealing thing he'd ever seen. He positioned another roofing nail and brought the hammer down, narrowly missing his thumb.

The familiar rumble of a truck engine coming up the rutted road pulled his attention away from the roof. Must be Duncan coming to check on his progress. Aaron hoped he'd be pleased that the roof was nearly complete and the interior studs were nailed in.

He swung down from the roof and rounded the corner of the cabin, but it wasn't Duncan's converted ambulance chugging around the bend and into view. It was the Trapnell Sawmill's flatbed truck. He shaded his eyes. Was that Lainey behind the wheel? And who was that in the passenger seat?

The truck halted a few feet from the front porch. Aaron ran his hand through his hair and dusted off his dungarees as Lainey hopped out of the truck. In place of her usual work attire, she wore a pink blouse and a denim skirt with a patchwork jacket that had some kind of frilly stuff around the neck. She jerked her thumb toward the flat bed.

"I brought the trim pieces you ordered, and some additional lumber for the loft."

"Thanks. Sooner than I expected." His gaze took in Lainey's passenger. The man bore a striking resemblance to her father.

Lainey tugged on Aaron's sleeve. "Before we unload the lumber, there's someone I'd like you to meet."

He followed her to the passenger side of the truck.

"Aaron Forester, I'd like you to meet my uncle, Phillip Trapnell. Uncle Phillip, this is Mr. Aaron Forester."

Aaron stuck his hand through the truck window. "Glad to make your acquaintance, sir. Lainey has told me quite a bit about you." He leaned closer and lowered his voice, as if divulging a secret. "I think you're her favorite uncle."

Phillip Trapnell chuckled. "Don't put too much stock in what Lainey tells you. She's a bit prejudiced."

Aaron quirked a smile in Lainey's direction. "I'm not sure that's a bad thing." He clapped his hand on Phillip's shoulder. "You stay put while I get this lumber unloaded. It shouldn't take but a few minutes. If you have time, I'd like to chat and get to know you better."

Brightness illuminated Lainey's uncle's eyes. "I'll be right here."

With Lainey's assistance, Aaron made short work of unloading and stacking the pieces of lumber on the front porch. He glanced her way as she carried the thin strips of trim. "I was surprised to see you at the wheel."

She arched her eyebrows. "Hmph. You don't think I can drive a truck?"

Aaron grinned and shook his head. "Quite the contrary. Nothing you can do would surprise me."

A most charming blush stole into her cheeks and warmed Aaron right down to his toes. "I meant I wasn't expecting this delivery until tomorrow, and your father is usually the one who comes." He dropped the last few boards onto the porch and shoved them into a neat stack. "The surprise was a pleasant one."

She turned her head, but not before Aaron noticed the rosiness in her cheeks deepening. She dusted off her hands and took a couple of steps closer, her voice lowered. "This is Uncle Phillip's first outing since he was injured." Her eyes communicated an unspoken plea.

Aaron nodded in understanding and returned to the truck window. "View sure is breathtaking from up here, isn't it?"

"That it is, young fella. Lived here all my life, and I never get tired of lookin' out across those mountains." A wistfulness eased into Phillip's expression. Aaron discerned the man's love for the mountains and the trees.

Phillip craned his neck and looked out the truck window toward the cabin addition. "Duncan MacKenzie tells me you're a fine carpenter. I have to say I was surprised Duncan allowed anyone but himself or his boy to do the work, but it appears like he made a good choice." He looked sideways at Aaron. "My brother says you're pretty handy around the sawmill, too."

Aaron shrugged. "He had an ornery log that didn't want to cooperate. I just helped out a little."

Phillip's snort indicated he didn't fully agree with Aaron's assessment. "It was an ornery log that did this to me." He tilted his head down to indicate his lame legs. "Glad you were there to give my brother a hand."

"Me, too." Lainey's soft voice reminded Aaron of her presence.

Aaron just smiled, but Lainey cocked her head. "Daddy said you worked at a sawmill before."

"I worked a couple of summers between school." Aaron returned his attention to Phillip. "In fact, I learned most of what I know from a man like you—someone who had lived and breathed the lumber business all his life."

A scowl creased the space between Phillip's brows. "Not anymore. Can't do much of anything now. Even my niece here has to help me in and out of my chair. You shoulda seen her tryin' to get me into this truck." He shook his head. "No, I'm of no use to anyone now."

"I disagree." Aaron dragged his sleeve across his forehead. "You have a wealth of knowledge—not just of trees and cutting wood into boards, but of the lumber business itself—about hiring loggers and filling lumber contracts. You're a man with valuable experience. You know, it takes someone like you—someone who's had the actual experience—to conduct the day to day business operations of a growing lumber mill."

Phillip's eyebrows rose momentarily, and then dipped into a frown of contemplation. Aaron sneaked a peek at Lainey from the corner of his eye and found her nodding and blinking back tears.

"Oh, Uncle Phillip, he's right." A thread of excitement colored her tone. "Remember a few months ago when you started to form a co-op of the area sawmills so we could contract with the bigger operations? Nobody else had the business sense to do that."

"Well, yes, but that was before... I can't do that now." Phillip slid his gaze between Aaron and his niece.

"Why not?" Aaron sent Phillip a pointed look. "Phillip, if God was finished with you, you wouldn't have survived that accident. Managing a co-op takes brains and experience and business savvy. Seems to me all you need is someone to build a ramp for your chair so you can get up to the loading dock and the office, and you can go back to work."

The silence that hung between them was broken by the wind through the trees. Aaron glanced at Lainey. She appeared to be holding her breath waiting for her uncle's response.

Finally, Phillip met Aaron's gaze. Life sparked within the depth of his dark eyes. "You know, young fella, you've given me something to think about."

Aaron shoved his hands in his pockets. "You supply the lumber, I'll build the ramp."

Phillip rubbed his hand over his chin. "Maybe it's time I have a talk with my brother."

A grin stretched Aaron's face and he gave Phillip a nod. He turned to Lainey. "Just let me go secure the tailgate before you pull out."

He strode to the rear of the truck, and when he seized the tailgate he discovered Lainey had followed him.

"Thank you."

Aaron shoved the tailgate in place and bolted it. "For what?"

"For talking to Uncle Phillip like that—man to man. I'm afraid we've all been coddling him for the past few months. Perhaps it's partly our fault that he feels useless. We haven't encouraged him to do anything. You were the best medicine he could have had."

Warmth crept up Aaron's neck. He secured the safety chains and turned to Lainey. Her face glowed. As much as Aaron wished her delight was from being in his presence, he conceded the anticipation that danced in her eyes was because of her uncle's renewed purpose. Nevertheless, he took advantage of her good spirits.

"May I have the privilege of escorting you to church this Sunday?"

She gave him a shy smile. "Yes, but I have a better idea. Why don't you plan on staying after church and we can take a picnic basket to the creek."

Sleep eluded Lainey. Muted moonlight filtered through her bedroom curtains and fell in patches across her quilt. For the past two days, anticipation tickled her stomach at the thought of enjoying Aaron's company this coming Sunday.

The veil of her memory drew aside and she recalled her first date with Lance had also been a picnic. Conflicted emotions smote her, and her mother's gentle suggestion crept back into her mind. Lainey stared into the dark, resisting the call of the box under the bed. If she never opened it and allowed herself to come to terms with the way her brief marriage to Lance ended, it didn't mean Lance didn't exist. Nor did it mean she was never married.

She tried to close her eyes and divert her thoughts, but it was no use. There was nothing she could do to change the past, and part of her past still remained in a dusty, sealed box, the contents of which she needed to release and say goodbye.

She slipped from beneath the covers and turned on the bedside lamp. Kneeling on the rag rug, she dragged the box out from under the bed. Nothing had changed—the return address still declared the US War Department, American Expeditionary Force as the sender, and the cold, impersonal label directed the box to Lance's "Next of kin."

"I guess that's me." She breathed out a soft sigh and gave herself permission to break the seal. As expected, Lance's folded uniform lay within the pasteboard confines, along with his ID tags. Her fingertips lingered over his name for a few minutes. "God, there is so much about Lance I didn't know. Daddy and Mama are so bonded together, they are almost like one person. They know each other's heartbeat. I don't even know what size shoe Lance wore."

Lance's wallet fell from the folds of his uniform. Lainey opened it and found four dollars and a copy of his orders with blurred ink. A pocket knife, a canteen, and a broken watch came next. In the bottom of the box, Lainey found a Bible. She lifted it out, startled to realize that she didn't know Lance owned a Bible. Maybe that's what had been holding her hostage for the past year and a half. Shame filled her with the realization that she and Lance had never talked about faith together. Did he know the Lord? Was he a believer? She couldn't answer that question.

"Oh, God, I'm so sorry. How could I have let myself fall for a man without knowing whether or not we shared the same faith? What if he died without You? Please forgive me for not putting You first."

She bowed her head and wept, broken-hearted over blithely running ahead of God during their whirlwind courtship. When the box had arrived, it was the not knowing that she didn't want to face. She wiped the tears from her face and stared at the Bible in her hands. The cover appeared worn and the page edges well-used. The tattered condition of the Book gave her a glimmer of hope that her husband had read it.

She opened the cover. There was something written on the first page in a flowing script: *This Bible presented to 1st Lt. Aaron Forester, Chaplain, 2nd Div, 9th Inf.*

Lainey's mouth fell open. Aaron Forester? Aaron knew Lance? Had they served together?

Below the inked inscription Lainey found pencil scrawling in Lance's handwriting: *Chaplain Aaron Forester gave me this Bible, 29 May 1918, on the day of my salvation.*

Chaplain. She re-read both writings again and tears dampened her face once more. Lance was killed on June 6th—just a week after he'd come to know Jesus as his Savior.

A tangle of gratitude and confusion spiraled through her. Why hadn't Aaron told her he knew Lance, that he'd led him to Christ? Why would he keep something like that from her?

CHAPTER 8

Aron stood beside the woodstove, savoring its warmth as he buttoned his shirt. He shoved his shirttail into his trousers and hummed "What A Friend We Have In Jesus," one of his favorite hymns. He couldn't remember the last time he'd sung it. Funny how he'd purposely pushed such memories away a couple of months ago. He'd attended church services for the past six weeks—albeit reluctantly, more out of respect for Duncan and Colin MacKenzie than anything else. But today the precious words of the song encouraged him, and he looked forward to church. Not just because he'd spend the afternoon with Lainey Trapnell and a picnic basket, but because God had whispered to his heart over the past few weeks. True, some questions still roiled through his heart. Despite the long hours he'd put in yesterday on the cabin, he'd sat up until past midnight reading the old Bible from the mantel. With the first light of the morning, those questions remained, the most prominent of which was, *God, can you still use me?*

Yes, he wanted to hear from God. Wanted confirmation that despite going against everything a chaplain stood for, God still loved him and still desired for him to be His servant.

The sun had risen above the treetops and sparkled off the melting frost. He snatched his jacket from the peg and slipped Duncan MacKenzie's Bible into his pocket. A bounce in his step carried him out the door. He paused for a moment to look over the finished roof and the sturdy walls of the addition. Tomorrow he'd begin laying the floorboards. The way the cabin addition was taking shape gave him a sense of accomplishment, but seeing a smile of comfort on Mr. Rawling's face and hope in Phillip Trapnell's eyes gave him a satisfaction that far exceeded the pleasure of work turned by his hands. Perhaps God was still using him.

Moses eyed him dolefully when he approached. He patted the mule's neck and whistled while he fitted the bridle in place and fastened the saddle's cinch. "It's Sunday, old fella. Time to go to church."

Moses brayed his opinion of having to work on the Lord's Day.

"Moses, you and I haven't exactly been the best of friends for the past several weeks. I sure wish I knew what Lainey whispered in your ear to get you to move. At any rate, your cooperation would be greatly appreciated this morning." Aaron led Moses to the gate and climbed aboard. Gathering the reins, he nudged the mule with his heels. As expected, Moses planted his feet.

"C'mon, you ornery beast. I don't want to be late." He bumped his heels against the animal's sides again, with the same result. Aaron blew out an exasperated breath. Of all the times for Moses to act like ... well, like a stubborn mule. "You know if you were the real Moses, you'd go and part the Red Sea."

Moses took off like a cannonball down the road toward town, with Aaron hanging onto the saddle horn. Had he just discovered the magic words?

Lainey propped her elbows on the table and sipped her second cup of coffee, avoiding her mother's scrutinizing gaze. She could count the number of hours of sleep she got last night on one hand with fingers left over. Discussing the contents of the box wasn't something she was prepared to do just yet, at least not until she'd had a chance to talk to Aaron.

"You've been working too hard, sweetheart." A tiny scowl creased Mama's brow. "I hate seeing those dark circles under your eyes."

Lainey mumbled through a yawn, "I didn't sleep very well last night."

How could she? Discovering that Aaron knew her husband, served together with him on the battlefield, and yet never even broached the subject with her. She felt foolish. How many times had she and Aaron talked? Did he wonder why she'd never thanked him for praying with Lance?

Praying with Lance. Something she'd never done. She could have shared her faith with Lance, but she didn't. She'd spent time in prayer last night asking God's forgiveness for neglecting the one thing her Savior asked of her—to share the Gospel. God, in His graciousness, poured out His comfort over her aching soul. But that didn't change the fact that Aaron had not been forthcoming.

The clock on the mantel had struck three o'clock around the time the realization had hit her. It was her own fault. If she'd opened the box a long time ago, she would have known Aaron Forester was the army chaplain who had led Lance to Christ. But frustration still seethed through her. Why hadn't Aaron told her? He hadn't even mentioned being a chaplain. She couldn't blame him for knowing Lance, for giving him a Bible. What she couldn't comprehend was Aaron coming here to their tiny community tucked into the Wyoming mountains, and then never uttering a word about her husband.

Mama scurried back into her bedroom and emerged a minute later with her Bible and coat. "Hurry now, dear. Your father has already left. He said he'd meet us at church."

"Yes, ma'am." She shoved her arms into her coat, but instead of grabbing her own Bible, she picked up the one she'd discovered last night in the box, and tucked it under her arm.

The church was only four blocks from the house, so unless it was raining or brutally cold, Lainey and her parents usually walked. When she and Mama made their way past the collection of vehicles and wagons in the churchyard, Aaron was already there, standing with a small cluster of folks, talking with Daddy. When the church bell rang, the group parted, and Lainey caught her breath. Uncle Phillip sat in his wheelchair, smiling up at Aaron.

Without asking, she knew Aaron was largely responsible for Uncle Phillip's decision to re-emerge back into the community. From the smile on his face to the crisply ironed shirt and trousers he wore, her uncle's appearance reflected the joy within.

She watched Aaron and her father guide Uncle Phillip's chair up two planks that had been shoved together to form a makeshift ramp. Tears stung her eyes and emotion welled in her chest. But her elation was short-lived.

Aaron turned his head and broke out in a smile when he caught sight of her. Everything in her wanted to stomp over to him and demand that he explain himself, but she refrained. That challenge must wait until they were alone.

She sent him a brief nod, noting the puzzled expression that dipped his brows. If he was confused, that was just fine with her. She looped her arm through her mother's and followed Daddy and Uncle Phillip into church.

Between her perplexed thoughts about Aaron, and lack of sleep, she had a hard time concentrating on the hymn singing. Her traitorous gaze kept slipping across the aisle to where Aaron sat. More than once she caught him looking her direction as well.

Pastor Roane opened his Bible, and she directed her attention to the preacher as he began to read the day's text:

" 'Fear not: for I have redeemed thee, I have called thee by thy name; thou art Mine. When thou passest through the waters, I will be with thee; and through the rivers, they shall not overflow thee; when thou walkest through the fire, thou shalt not be burned; neither shall the flame kindle upon thee. For I am the Lord thy God, the Holy One of Israel, thy Saviour.' "

While the pastor began his message, Lainey kept reading from Lance's Bible—Aaron's Bible. The next verse said she was precious in God's sight, that she was honorable, and He loved her.

Oh God, I wasn't honorable. I didn't even share my faith with Lance, yet You still love me and claim me as Your own. You've not withheld Your forgiveness.

Tears formed and she blinked them back. She stared straight ahead, her gaze unfocused. The compassion in the scripture was clear. Lainey couldn't hoard it for herself. If God was so gracious and faithful, and showed such mercy to her, how could she harbor resentment toward Aaron? That same compassion God extended to her was meant to be passed on, shared. If Aaron had an explanation, at the very least, she needed to hear him out.

Her muscles cramped sitting still on the hard bench, but she forced herself to remain motionless until the final hymn. She smiled at a few parishioners, shook Pastor Roane's hand, and turned. Aaron stood behind her, a tentative expression in his eyes.

"Good morning, Lainey. I've been looking forward to our picnic."

Picnic? She'd nearly forgotten. She studied him for a moment, looking for evidence of guile, but instead read concern.

He gently cupped her elbow as they turned toward the door. "Are you feeling all right?"

She paused before stepping over the threshold onto the stone step. Was she all right? She hardly knew, but she nodded. "I'm fine. Shall we stop by the house to pick up the picnic basket?"

He held out his arm to Lainey. "Shall we?"

A shiver rippled through her. She laid her hand lightly on the crook of his arm and they walked the short distance home. Daddy and Mama had said they were having dinner with Uncle Phillip. Aaron waited on the front porch while she retrieved the basket from the kitchen. She returned with an old quilt and the basket, both of which Aaron took from her. She slipped her hands into her coat pockets, and her fingers found Lance's Bible.

As soon as they were away from the house, Aaron cleared his throat. "Lainey, you're awfully quiet. I sense something is wrong."

She drew in a deep breath. "There is something I need to talk to you about, but I'd rather wait until we're at the creek."

He nodded. "All right."

The rest of the walk passed in awkward silence. She held thick evergreen branches aside for him as they made their way to the secluded spot. Lainey took the quilt, but instead of spreading it for them to sit upon, she laid it on a rock.

Aaron faced her, waiting.

How did she begin this conversation? She ran her fingers over the quilt stitching. "Aaron, you were in the war, but you never told me where you served."

He stiffened visibly. "It's not something I like to talk about."

She tipped her head slightly. "You were a chaplain."

His eyes widened. "Y-yes. How did you know?"

Cold invaded her bones, but it had nothing to do with the crisp autumn temperatures. She pulled the Bible from her pocket and his face lit with recognition.

"That's my Bible. I mean, it— I gave it—" He swallowed. "How did you...?"

"You gave it to my husband."

Aaron blanched and his breath seemed to desert him. "Your—your h-husband?" He barely croaked the words out.

She opened the cover and pointed to Lance's handwriting. "My husband."

Confusion screwed Aaron's expression into a collection of deep creases. "There was a young soldier in my battalion. His name was Lance Garrett. I gave that Bible to him."

Lainey's throat tightened and a shudder trembled through her. "That's right."

"But—" Aaron shook his head as if trying to find reason and sanity in the conversation. His eyes filled with disbelief. "But your name is Trapnell."

She swallowed hard, but her voice still broke. "Elaine Trapnell Garrett."

His mouth fell open and his brows quivered. Clearly learning that she was Lance's widow was as much of a surprise to him as finding the Bible had been to her.

Weakness attacked her knees. "Can we sit down?"

Slack-jawed, he couldn't seem to find his voice, but he reached for the quilt and opened it, laying it where she could sit. He lowered himself across from her and rubbed both hands over his face, and mumbled through his fingers. "Lainey, I had no idea." Then he suddenly jerked his hands down. "But you had the Bible. My name is in it."

She clasped her hands in her lap in an attempt to stop their shaking. "When the box with Lance's belongings arrived from the War Department, I couldn't bring myself to open it. It's been stored away, still sealed. Until last night."

His eyes narrowed as he still obviously struggled to understand. "Last night?"

She lowered her gaze, finding it easier to explain without looking at him. "My mother has been encouraging me to open the box so I could come to terms with Lance's death and move on. I finally opened it last night and found the Bible. That's when I realized I had never—not once—" Her throat ached. "I'd never spoken of my faith to Lance." Tears burned her eyes. "I was so ashamed, but at the same time I was grateful that someone—you—had told him about Jesus."

Aaron's faraway look reflected the calendar turning backward in his mind. "He was afraid to die, he said, because he didn't know if he was good enough to go to heaven." He reached across the quilt and took the Bible, and leafed through it. "I showed him that none of us are good enough, but Jesus paid the price for us anyway."

"Amen." Her whisper got lost in the wind.

Her hand met Aaron's halfway between them, their fingers joining in a connection of empathy.

Chapter 9

Aaron always knew when company was coming by the sound of the truck engine laboring up the hill. Aaron tossed the last of his wet laundry over the branches of the scrubby underbrush behind the cabin and tramped around to the front. Duncan's converted ambulance coughed to a halt and Colin and Duncan climbed out.

"Morning, Aaron." Colin sniffed. "Do I smell coffee brewing?"

Aaron grinned and tipped his head toward the cabin. "Go help yourself."

Duncan shook his hand and walked around the side of the cabin, looking over the nearly finished addition. "Ye're doing a fine job, Aaron. Looks like I hired the right man for this job." He studied Aaron for a moment. "How are ye?"

Aaron gestured to the completed portion of the addition. "It's all weather tight now. As you can see, the window is in. Tongue and groove paneling is finished inside and the baseboards are done. I just have to finish the doorframe and hang the door, and then I plan to start on the loft. I'm glad you're here, because I wanted to ask you if—"

Duncan held up his hand. "I'm not talking aboot the work. I'm talking about *ye*. Ye were a mighty troubled young man when ye first arrived here. I've been praying that ye could use this time alone at the cabin to hear from God an' find restoration from those hivy burdens ye've been carrying."

A stiff breeze rattled the leaves and created a shower of gold around them. Aaron nodded. "Yes, sir, I have." He sent his focus out across the mountains where the rock formation resembled eagle's wings. "I was so sure I'd let God down, that He'd never again fill me or walk with me. That's why I drifted from job to job."

Duncan's eyes crinkled at the corners. "I dinae suppose God agreed wi' your assessment."

A soft chuckle eased from Aaron's throat and he pulled his gaze back to stare at the toes of his boots. "No, He didn't. And I didn't really know what my purpose was here—other than building the addition onto the cabin."

"God always hae a purpose. Sometimes He leads us where we donae expect, and we have to trust that He's got something in mind." Duncan put his hand on Aaron's shoulder. "But, son, aerguing with God is niver a good idea. Ne'er is running from Him."

A sheepish smile pulled at Aaron's lips. "You're a very discerning man. And you're right. I may not have admitted it, but I was running. I was afraid to get too comfortable here because God might confront me with the past. Before I knew what was happening, God brought people into my life, and—" He jerked his thumb toward the cabin. "I wasn't looking for God to use me. I didn't even want to crack open that Bible in there. But I'd made you a promise. I might not have lived up to the promises I'd made to God, but I was determined not to let *you* down." He heaved a sigh. "So I read, and tried to pray. And then—"

Duncan quirked one eyebrow, but waited in silence.

"Then I met Lainey."

A gentle, knowing smile broke across Duncan's face and crinkled his eyes.

Aaron bit his lip. "I've never met a young lady with such courage or fortitude, generosity of spirit, and tenderness of heart." A warm flush crawled up Aaron's neck to his face. How did he justify the feelings for Lainey that had emerged within him?

Duncan's smile deepened. "She told me. Ye were the chaplain who led her husband to Christ days before he died."

Aaron dipped his head. "I didn't even know she'd been married. Discovering she was a war widow definitely caught me by surprise, but finding out her late husband had been the young soldier to whom I'd given my Bible rocked me back on my heels."

If his dad were still alive, he'd seek out his father's advice and counsel. But in place of his dad, God had seen fit to put Duncan MacKenzie. The man's quiet wisdom and steadfast faith calmed Aaron's spirit.

He looked up into Duncan's gray eyes. "All these months, I believed God was so disappointed in me. I missed His fellowship, and I felt so alone. So when I met a few folks here, I suppose I was hungry for companionship. It wasn't hard to be a friend to Phillip Trapnell or Joe Rawling or Pete Cooper. But Lainey is different. When I'm around her, when I think about her, I experience feelings I've never felt before. I thought maybe she had feelings for me, too, and then last Sunday we discovered I had known her late husband..." He shook his head.

"Hmm." The contemplative sound rumbled from Duncan's throat. "Ye think ye've hurt Lainey because ye led her husband to Christ?" A muted chuckle rolled from Duncan's lips. "Nae, Aaron. Lainey has been burdened since the day she got that telegram because she didnae know if Lance was a believer. She told me this morning she blamed herself for that. When she found that Bible, she found freedom an' forgiveness an' mercy. Your coming to Sawyer's Gap was the moving of God's grace in Lainey's life."

Aaron blinked back burning moisture from his eyes. "I thought I'd destroyed any chance that God could ever use me again."

Duncan rubbed his chin. "Nae laddie. Don't ye go thinking God cannae use you anymair. I've seen new determination an' purpose in Phillip Trapnell's eyes. I saw Joe Rawling smile the other day—first time since his boy was reported killed. And Lainey? She was radiant this morning."

Duncan's observation was gratifying, but did the man have the insight and discernment to advise him on a deeper level? "You know I was a pastor for eight years before I was an army chaplain. A question keeps running through my head—since God has forgiven me and restored me to fellowship, does that mean I should return to the ministry?"

The older man's eyes softened into a wise smile. "I cannae answer that for ye, Aaron. Keep praying, read His word, listen for His voice, be sensitive to His leading, an' He will make all things clear. I will tell you this, though: there are many ways to minister. A man daen't have to stand in the pulpit to win souls, nor does he have to be a pastor to serve God. Just something for ye to consider."

Aaron nodded slowly, thankful for Duncan's sage counsel. *All things clear.* He hoped that included Lainey, because at the moment, his heart was in turmoil.

Duncan pulled his watch from his pocket and clicked it open. "Almost eleven o'clock." He beckoned to Aaron. "Your presence is requested at a meeting. Come on. If we daen't hurry, we'll be late."

Aaron started picking up his tools, but Duncan waved his hand. "Ye nae need those. G' find Colin and tell him to quit guzzling coffee. I'll g' crank the truck."

The distinctive growl of Duncan MacKenzie's truck chugging up the incline to the sawmill drew Lainey to the window. Squinting in the glare of sunlight off the windshield, she tried to determine if there were two or three people in the cab. The truck ground to a halt and the doors opened.

Duncan. Colin. And Aaron.

Her heart fluttered. She checked her reflection in the window glass and ran her hand over her unruly hair to smooth it into submission. "They're here."

Her father grinned. "Come on. You're part of this meeting." Anticipation and apprehension collided in her chest. The plan Mr. MacKenzie, Uncle Phillip, and her father had laid out sounded wonderful, but she had to admit to mixed feelings.

She followed her father out to the loading dock where Uncle Phillip sat in his chair next to a makeshift table—two boards laid across a barrel—and a couple of benches. Mr. MacKenzie led the way up the steps to the platform and greeted her father. When Aaron's gaze connected with hers, butterflies tap-danced in her stomach.

Daddy shook Aaron's hand. "Glad you could make it. Let's all sit down over here."

Aaron greeted Uncle Phillip and took a seat on one end of the bench nearest Phillip's chair. Daddy cleared his throat.

"There are a couple of things we'd like to discuss. Aaron, a while back you offered to build a ramp for Phillip's chair." He pointed to the two planks off to the side angled from the ground to the loading dock. "I assume you would agree those aren't acceptable for the long term."

Aaron craned his neck to see the boards and pursed his lips. "I don't know. Might be exciting to roll up and down those every day. What do you think, Phillip?"

Uncle Phillip laughed along with the others, but quipped, "I think I'd rather avoid the adventure."

Hearing Uncle Phillip sound like his old self again tickled Lainey, and part of the reason for her uncle's new outlook on life was sitting across from her. Lainey's heart swelled as she fixed her focus on Aaron.

He sent her a subtle smile, causing a hiccup to catch in her throat. She pressed her lips together and pulled her gaze away, lest she embarrass herself.

"Colin and I were just up at the cabin, and the new addition is aw but finished." Duncan cast a look of approval at Aaron. "An' Aaron has daen a fine job. I suggest, however, that he postpone working on the loft, and start building the ramp, since it's o' greater importance."

Lainey's father nodded. "The second thing that needs doing is widening the door to the office. The reason we're sitting out here on the loading dock is because Phillip's chair won't fit through the doorway."

Aaron and Colin turned in unison and looked toward the office, but a slight frown drew Aaron's brow downward. Lainey could only guess that he was wondering why a committee was necessary for such decisions. She suppressed a smile.

Lainey's father rubbed his hands together. "Now for the real reason we dragged Aaron away from the cabin for this meeting."

Lainey shifted her gaze across the space that separated her from Aaron. His expression reflected a plethora of questions. He looked from one man to the next, presumably for answers.

"I was wondering why the building of a ramp and replacement of a door required a conclave." He nailed Lainey with a quizzical look. "What's going on?"

"We've been talking." Daddy reached behind the bench on which he was sitting and extracted a rolled-up paper. "This is a very rough sketch." He stood and unrolled the paper across the wobbly table, and anchored it with a couple of pieces of scrap lumber.

Aaron rose and bent over the table, studying the sketch. "What am I looking at?" Aaron looked up at Daddy, and then Duncan.

Her father nodded to Duncan who leaned forward with his elbows on the edge of the table. "Roth and I have decided to partner together to purchase some timberland aboot eighty miles north of here. Trapnell Lumber Company and MacKenzie Construction are forming a joint operation up in Green Valley, not faer from Pinedale. What ye're looking at is a rough layout o' the yaerd." He ran his finger across the sketch. "This will be an area for the decking an' sorting process, a large pole barn for stacking an' drying lumber, a boiler to provide steam power, and the mill itself." Duncan pointed to the opposite corner of the layout. "Over here is a construction office to handle the building end of the business."

Aaron shot a look to Duncan. "Eighty miles away—you're relocating your business?"

"Nae relocating. Expanding."

Her father joined in. "I will remain in Sawyer's Gap to manage this mill, just as Duncan will continue to manage his construction business here. What we're proposing will enable us to build a co-op to compete with the big operations."

Lainey kept her eyes on Aaron, watching his expressions as he rolled the information over. How would he decide once Daddy and Mr. MacKenzie revealed their entire plan?

Duncan tapped a pencil on the corner of the table. "'Twill tak some time to finalize everything, but we'd like to begin hiring men an' felling trees by February, using the snow to slide the timber from the mountainside to the site. That way we can begin construction by April."

Lainey's father straightened and crossed his arms. "Colin will become the manager of the construction of the Green Valley location, and Phillip will take the reins as business manager for the entire operation of MacKenzie-Trapnell Enterprises."

"Thanks to you, Aaron." Uncle Phillip grinned. "After listening to you, I decided you were right. My legs might not work anymore, but my brain does."

Moisture pricked Lainey's eyes to hear her uncle's declaration, and she silently nodded to add her affirmation. But her father wasn't finished yet.

"That leaves us with one other position to fill. Aaron, we'd like you to consider taking the job as manager of the new sawmill. I know I offered you a job here, and that offer still stands if you'd rather do that." He glanced at Lainey before continuing. "We also know you may not be interested in either job. After you finish up at Duncan's cabin, you might decide to move on like you planned." He thumbed his suspender. "We just want you to know we'd like you to consider becoming a part of our company and our family."

Lainey held her breath, unwilling to think about Aaron moving on once he was finished doing the work for Mr. MacKenzie.

Aaron turned toward her with widened eyes. "I—I wasn't expecting this. I hadn't planned on. . ." He bounced his focus between her father, Uncle Phillip, and Duncan. "I'll have to think about this."

Duncan reached out and laid his hand on Aaron's shoulder. "An' pray, son. Pray."

"Yes, sir."

Lainey barely heard his reply. What had he started to say? That he hadn't planned on... staying?

Chapter 10

Aaron measured and calculated the angle at which the ramp for Phillip's chair would rise from the ground to the loading dock, figuring the height of each of the support posts. Freshly sawn lengths of lumber sat, ready for him to choose which piece to use. If only choosing a direction for his future were as simple.

Since Roth and Duncan had laid out their proposal, Aaron's thoughts had spun an intricate web of possibilities. He'd just about made up his mind to accept Roth Trapnell's job offer at the sawmill where he'd earn a decent wage and be able to put down roots. After months of drifting from job to job, settling down in one place was no longer disagreeable—if the place was Sawyer's Gap. He'd made some good friends here, and through the help of those friends, he'd found peace with God again.

He hauled a twelve-foot long four-by-four from the stack and measured off and marked the locations of the notches to accept the support pieces. With careful precision, he began his cut.

Precision.

A fraction of an inch off and the ramp would be unstable. No guesswork. It had to be right.

The trouble with making decisions was they weren't made with painstaking exactness resulting in a predetermined end. Only God knew the end from the beginning, and for the past week, Aaron had yet to receive clear leading one way or the other.

Being asked to take the managerial position at the new location was an honor, to be sure. From what he could tell, the expansion plans were well-defined, and Phillip and Lainey had prepared a sound strategy for forming a cooperative with other area lumber companies. But this decision was not just about working for Roth in Sawyer's Gap or working for him in Green Valley. If God called Aaron back into the ministry, he must go.

He glanced up at the office window, and Lainey smiled back and waved as if she'd been watching for him. Yesterday they ate their lunch together, and the day before that they went for a walk down by the creek. He'd taken her hand to help her across some rocks, but didn't relinquish his hold even after they were on solid ground again. The memory of her hand in his warmed him all over again—which pulled his heart in still another direction. What about Lainey?

Sawyer's Gap meant more than new friends and a nice, little town. Truth be told, his main reason for finding Sawyer's Gap so appealing was Lainey. Seeing her smile every day, hearing her laugh, and watching her move around the sawmill weren't joys he wanted to forfeit by moving eighty miles away. And if the feelings that warmed his thoughts by day and graced his dreams by night were real, he'd already fallen in love with the girl and his heart desired to make her his wife. But he couldn't court her until he knew with all certainty what direction his future would take him. If God did direct him back to the ministry, he couldn't make a commitment to Lainey without the assurance that she supported that call. If she did, it meant moving away from her home, her parents, and their family business. Sawyer's Gap already had a fine pastor in John Roane.

A few minutes later, a decrescendo of the saw blade's whine indicated Roth had shut down the machinery. Aaron looked up from the plank he was cutting to size. Lainey's father headed in his direction. The older man hopped down from the loading dock.

"Aaron, got a minute?"

"Sure." He straightened and laid aside his folding carpenter's rule.

Roth tucked his thumbs under his belt. "I don't mean to pressure you, but I was wondering if you'd made a decision yet about either the job here or the job at Green Valley."

Aaron rubbed his index finger across his chin. "It's never far from my thoughts. I've been rolling everything over in my mind and asking God for His leading. Sometimes I wonder if maybe I'm not listening hard enough."

Judging by the thoughtful dip to the man's brow, he had something on his mind. "Pete Cooper stopped by here a while ago." Roth removed his hat and dragged his hand over his salt and pepper hair. "You know Pete works for the Western Union part time. His brother-in-law was killed in the war and Pete is trying to help support his sister and her two little boys." He replaced his hat and crossed his arms. "He needs a second job. I offered you the job working here first, and I don't want to withdraw that offer if you're still interested, but—"

Aaron held up his hand. "There's nothing more to discuss. Pete needs that job."

"Are you sure? I know my daughter would be disappointed." Roth's eyes twinkled. "I think she's getting used to having you around."

After repeatedly asking God to direct him, and remove those things that hindered his decision, it appeared God just narrowed down his choices. "I'm sure. Pete has a family to support."

"Lainey girl, are you listening?"

Lainey jerked her attention away from the window. Uncle Phillip's gaze nailed her and she bit her lip. "Sorry. Guess I was day dreaming."

Her uncle leaned his elbows on the arms of his chair. "The contract with Wilson Lumber Company? Adding them to the co-op?"

Her face warmed. Uncle Phillip's tone wasn't scolding, but the poor man must certainly be exasperated with her. He'd had to direct her concentration back to the business at hand three times already this morning. She'd never been very good at waiting. Keeping her foot from tapping out her impatience was almost more than she could manage. She knew her father and uncle hoped Aaron would take their offer—the plans spread across the desk between her and her uncle still had an empty hole to fill—but eighty miles seemed like half a world away. Her feelings for Aaron pulled her into a tug-of-war.

Uncle Phillip tipped his head toward the window and smirked. "Seems your young man out there is more interesting than your old uncle."

A flock of hummingbirds took flight in her stomach at hearing Aaron referred to in such a way. "Uncle Phillip!"

He cackled and reached to squeeze her hand. "It's all right, Lainey girl. Why don't we pick this up after lunch?"

The office door opened and Aaron stepped inside. Lainey's hummingbirds fluttered upward to her heart. Aaron sent her a smile and her breath hitched.

"Can you break away for a while?"

She rose from her chair, anticipation tickling her. "Sure." Perhaps he was ready to tell her his decision.

"I need to run an errand. Want to go along?"

A pang of disappointment nipped her, but she'd take any stolen moments with Aaron she could get, even if it was simply walking to town. "I'll get my coat."

Aaron helped her with her coat, leaving his hands on her shoulders for an extra moment. "I need to stop by Rawling's Hardware for some carriage bolts." He grinned at Uncle Phillip. "I want to make sure this ramp doesn't come apart."

The older man smiled. "I appreciate that."

Lainey looped a scarf around her neck against the crisp autumn wind. "If you don't mind, I need to pick up a few things at the mercantile."

Aaron discreetly took her hand as they exited the office and descended the stairs. "Don't mind at all." Instead of releasing her hand once they reached the bottom step, he solicitously tucked it into the crook of his arm as they made their way down the street.

Aaron slowed their steps. "I need you to pray about something."

Her heart accelerated and her breath caught. "Yes?"

"You know that I was in the ministry before becoming a chaplain."

Lainey's stomach tightened and she nodded mutely, her thoughts spinning.

"I'd like to ask you to pray for God to make clear to me whether He wants me to return to the ministry." His quiet entreaty pulled her feet to a halt.

Aaron turned to look at her, and their gazes locked, unspoken communication filling the space between them. They stood there for an eternity before she whispered, "Of course, I'll pray, Aaron."

In that moment, God confirmed her love for this man. Regardless of his decision for the future—even if it took him away from her—she knew she'd always love him. They resumed walking, the raw wind tugging at her scarf. But deep within in her, a fire burned.

They arrived outside the mercantile and Aaron opened the door for her. "You take your time with your shopping. I'm going to go across the street to the hardware store. But I'll be back in time to carry your parcels for you."

"All right. I'll only be about fifteen minutes." She stepped inside and let the door swing shut behind her, but she watched from the window as Aaron crossed the street. She could no longer base her prayers on her selfish desires, but rather on what God willed for both of them.

The cowbell over the door clanked when Aaron entered the hardware store. Joe Rawling's face lit up when he greeted him. But before Aaron could tell Joe what he needed, Joe jerked his thumb toward the window and the street outside.

"Have you seen it?"

Pausing mid-step, Aaron glanced over his shoulder. "Seen what?"

Joe caught Aaron's sleeve and pulled him to the window, pointing down the street. "Looky there."

A half-block away, in front of the small brick building that served as the courthouse, justice of the peace, and sheriff's office, a flag waved in the stiff breeze. On one side of the flagpole sat a wooden bench. On the opposite side, a sign of some kind leaned against a log frame, but they were too far away for Aaron to make out the details.

"You hafta go see it." The insistence in Joe's voice couldn't be denied as the man nudged Aaron toward the door.

Joe accompanied him out the door toward the site where a handful of people now stood, pointing. Aaron glanced back at the mercantile. He'd promised Lainey he'd return to carry her purchases in just a few minutes, and he didn't want her to think he'd forgotten. But Joe's urging was resolute.

"You gotta see it."

As they drew closer, Aaron noticed a neat row of rocks bordering the flagpole and stepping stones leading to the bench. What he'd thought to be a sign was actually a plaque, meticulously carved and polished. Across the top, skillfully engraved letters sculpted the words: *Served with honor—Gave all they had.* Beneath the heading there appeared six names, presumably young men from the area who had died in the war. At the top of the list was Corporal Joseph Rawling.

"Ain't that somethin'? That fella from the telegraph office, Pete Cooper, done this." His voice breaking, Joe pointed to the plaque, and then to the bench. "He done all this—to honor my boy and all them that died. Ain't that somethin'?"

Across the back of the bench, another carved inscription bore testimony of Pete's offering. *We will always remember.*

"Oh, my. . ."

Aaron turned to find Lainey at his elbow. He followed her line of vision back to the plaque. The last name that appeared on the list was Corporal Lance Garrett.

Aaron squeezed her hand, and turned back to Joe who was wiping tears away. "Yes, Joe. That's really something."

The pressure of Aaron's hand surrounding hers made Lainey catch her lip between her teeth. Neither of them spoke for a long minute, but Aaron brushed his thumb back and forth across the back of her fingers, the sensation of his touch sending a tingling all the way up her arm.

Finally he turned, as if he'd suddenly awakened. "Where are your parcels?"

She had to swallow before she could form words. "Mr. Owen said I could pick them up later. I saw you and Mr. Rawling hurry down the street. I was afraid something was wrong."

He drew a deep breath, and fixed his gaze on their connected hands. "No. Nothing is wrong. In fact, I didn't realize until now how right everything was."

He shifted his glance from side to side. "Can we go for a walk?"

Her voice deserted her, but she nodded.

A wobbly smile pulled a dimple into his cheek, and he tightened his grip on her hand. They headed toward her favorite place by the creek. Thick evergreen boughs closed behind them as they made their way to the rocks, and the tumbling creek sang a welcome.

Aaron faced her and took both her hands. "I asked if you would pray that God would reveal His will, but I should have asked if you would pray *with me*." He looked all around them. "This place is a sanctuary, a refuge, where we can hear from God. So, will you? Will you pray with me?"

Moisture in her eyes made her blink and her breath became rapid. She nodded, and with their hands still joined, they both bowed their heads. Aaron began in a quiet, reverent voice.

"Oh, Lord God, more than anything, we want to be in Your will. And so we come before You together, praying in one accord, that You might give us both a peace for what I am about to ask.

"Father, I love this woman whose hands I hold, and I cannot imagine a future without her by my side. I've spent the past week trying to make a decision—one direction, one path—thinking I couldn't follow my heart and still be in Your will. A wise man told me not long ago there are a lot of ways to serve You. Taking the Green Valley job means a whole new mission field, hiring men to whom I can minister, maybe even preaching in the lumber camps. So I am asking You now, Father, to grant me the desire of my heart.

Lord, I pray that Lainey will say yes, and become my wife."

Lainey's eyes burst open and tears overflowed. Her voice no longer held captive, she lifted her face to take in every angle and plane of Aaron's countenance. "Oh, Lord, I pray You will pour out Your blessing on us." Happiness and contentment seeped through her. "Yes."

Aaron opened his eyes. Awe filled his expression and he bent to place a gentle kiss on her forehead. He pulled her close and whispered against her hair. "You answered my prayer, Lord. She said yes. She said yes."

THE END

Chosen

DARLENE WELLS

*"Before I formed you in the womb I knew you,
before you were born I set you apart..."*
JEREMIAH 1:5

In memory of Marion and Frieda Dodds
in appreciation for the spiritual foundation they laid
for the Dodds family. Thank you!

Chapter 1

Near Sawyer's Gap, Wyoming
Fall 1935

Rogan Meuller aimed his face toward the open window of his Model A Ford truck and breathed in, filling his lungs to capacity with the fresh Wyoming air, then released the cleansing breath. Sunlight streamed through the evergreens lining the road, painting yellow ribbons across the truck's hood. A boy trudged along the road, carrying a fishing pole and small tackle box. The fishing pole sent Rogan's thoughts backward in time.

Preacher Dodds used to take him fishing whenever he needed a good talking to. The man always seemed to know the best way to approach him. Rogan drummed his thumb on the worn Bible lying on the passenger seat. A gift from preacher Marion Dodds. A smile tugged at his lips as he recalled the man's regret at not being able to give him a brand new Bible. But, given the choice between a stiff new Bible, or the preacher's personal Bible, Rogan would choose this one. Marion had written his own notes in the book, underlined his favorite verses. Rogan felt as though he took a little bit of the preacher with him as he set out to start his new life.

The biggest question he faced was where that new life would be. Marion suggested Sawyer's Gap. A small town about forty miles north of Rogan's hometown, Lander, Wyoming.

His stomach grumbled. Rogan looked up at the sky through the Ford's windshield. The sun hung high right overhead. He pulled the car to the side of the road and parked. He snatched the paper sack next to him and got out of the car.

Rogan stretched his back and arms and scanned his surroundings. The sound of gurgling water summoned him down an embankment several feet away from the road. Clear mountain water swirled around large rocks and cascaded over smaller obstructions in its path. Rogan sat on the bank and watched the water, so clear he could see the sandy bottom, and German

Brown trout meandering their way through the river's path. Rogan's fingers twitched at the sight of the fish. He'd love to grab his pole out of the truck bed right now. But the fish would go bad by the time he reached his destination.

Rogan rummaged through the paper sack Mrs. Dodds gave him. He found an apple, four sugar cookies, a jelly sandwich, and a mason jar of iced tea. As he bit into the sandwich he thought about the man and woman that had saved him from state prison. They'd spoken up for him and agreed to take him into their custody for one year on probation.

He'd felt a little foolish standing before the judge at the time, listening to the deal being made between the court and the Dodds'. In the end though, he didn't mind, seeing as how it saved him from a long stay in the big house.

What he hadn't counted on was how much his life would change as he lived in the couple's home. They already had six children of their own, four boys and two girls, plus the church they pastored. But they spent time investing in him, sharing the gospel. Frieda was just a slip of a woman with bright blue eyes, and the easiest person on earth to tease. Marion, a tall, quiet man—except when he was preaching—possessed more wisdom than anyone Rogan had ever known.

Rogan snatched the apple out of the sack and lay on his back, staring up the blue sky through the canopy of tree limbs. He didn't want to think about what kind of person he'd be today if it hadn't been for those two people and their family.

Startled by a scurrying sound next to his ear, Rogan's eyes flew open. He spotted a lizard wriggling its way under a rock. How long had he slept? The sun had moved a bit to toward the west. Much as he'd love to close his eyes again, Rogan wanted to make it to Sawyer's Gap before nightfall. He gathered the paper sack and its contents—what little was left—and made his way back up to the road.

Catherine Whitmore turned the mother of pearl hairbrush and mirror set this way and that, admiring the shimmering pearl and silver.

Dorothy Owen's voice held a trace of defensiveness. "It's a fine set. I ordered it straight from that little store you told me about."

Catherine lifted her gaze. "Bergdorf's is not a 'little store,' Mrs. Owen. It is the finest department store in New York City. In the entire country, as a matter of fact."

Dorothy set her hand on her hip. "Well, I'm sorry to be so uninformed. I don't get out to New York very often."

Returning her attention to the brush, Catherine ran her fingers across the bristles. Flexible, but strong enough to brush out her long hair. She set the brush down in front of Mrs. Owen. "I'll take them. Please wrap them."

Catherine ignored the woman's raised brow. She knew what most people in Sawyer's Gap thought of her. A spoiled, rich girl. Even two years later, Catherine still resented her father's insistence they open a Whitmore's grocery store in this hovel of a town.

A bell above the store's door jangled. Catherine turned to see a tall, blond-haired man enter the store. She quickly turned back to Dorothy.

The store owner set down the brush set to address him. "May I help you?"

The man walked to the counter. "Yes, thanks. I'm looking for Pastor Cecil."

"Oh! You must be Rogan." Dorothy held her hand out. "I'm Dorothy Owen."

Catherine took two steps to the right, putting distance between herself and the unseemly man. From the corner of her eye, she saw him take Dorothy's hand.

"Good to meet you, Mrs. Owen."

Dorothy looked to Catherine. "Excuse me, Catherine, I need to get Mr. Owen."

Catherine opened her mouth to protest, but the woman scurried to the back room before she could. With no one else in the store besides the strange man, she tried to maintain an air of disinterest. Although his voice had a strangely calming affect on her. Wanting to take a second look, but afraid of drawing his attention, she surreptitiously glanced to her left, at his shoes.

Dirty. Worn. And the hem of his pants didn't look much better. He didn't seem to pay her any mind, so she decided to be a little more bold. Pretending to look past him to the door, she quickly scanned his face. He was staring at her.

Heart racing, Catherine turned her back to him and fingered a silk scarf on display by the counter. Was he still staring? Why didn't he speak? And what on earth was taking Dorothy so long to return? She could feel those blue eyes boring a hole into the back of her head.

Finally Dorothy returned with Mr. Owen, who introduced himself and led the man out the door. Catherine released a breath she hadn't realized she'd been holding. Her last glimpse of the stranger was of him walking away.

She caught Dorothy watching her with an amused grin. Catherine smoothed her skirt and lifted her chin. "What is the total of the brush set, please?"

With smirk, Dorothy rang up the purchase. "Nine dollars and twenty-six cents."

"Fine. Put it on my father's charge account."

"Of course."

Catherine gathered her pocketbook. Her fingers trembled. "Thank you." She hurried out of the store. She would avoid the good-looking but oddly behaving stranger in the future.

Chapter 2

Rogan set his Bible on the pew beside him and stood for the closing hymn. Pastor Cecil's sermon had held him in rapt attention. Learning about Queen Esther and her role in saving the Jewish people replayed in his mind like a reel at the picture show.

After the hymn, congregants milled about greeting each other and the pastor.

Sheriff Kernshaw approached and patted Rogan on the shoulder. "Hello, Rogan. Good to see you made it this morning." The man's silver mustache lifted with his smile.

"Wouldn't have missed it." Rogan's stomach clenched briefly. Even though he'd encountered the sheriff several times in the past few days, he still had work to do when it came to trusting lawmen. He turned his attention to the stout pastor who interacted with his church members. "He sure knows how to make a story come alive."

"That he does." The sheriff slipped his hands into his trouser pockets. "I especially liked the way he made it relevant for today. What with Hitler on the move in Europe, seems they could use an Esther over there right now."

Pastor Cecil stepped beside the sheriff and shook Kernshaw's hand. "Now, don't you get the sheriff started on politics, Rogan. We'll all be here until next week!"

Kernshaw chuckled and lifted his hands. "All right, all right. I'll stop there. I'll see you around, Rogan." He turned to the preacher. "Stop by for a cup of coffee one day this week, Cecil."

"That I will. See you then, Russell." Cecil looked to Rogan and opened his mouth to speak.

Dorothy Owen bustled over with a basket of fabric squares cradled in her arms. "Oh, I'm glad I caught you, Pastor. Your dear wife offered to take these off my hands. I don't have the time to quilt like I used to."

Cecil took the basket. "I'm sure she will, Dorothy. Thank you."

Dorothy offered her broad smile to Rogan. "It's lovely to see you again, young man. You really should come over for dinner one night."

"I'd like that. Thank you."

"How about Tuesday?" The woman's eyes glowed with a warmth Rogan still wasn't used to receiving from others.

"Tuesday will be fine."

"Wonderful. We'll see you at six o'clock." She hurried off.

The pastor clapped Rogan on the shoulder. "We best get going. Elizabeth is probably tapping her foot and checking the clock already."

Rogan's mouth watered at the thought of Elizabeth's baked chicken and vegetables. As a pastor's wife, she embodied everything that was kind, generous and loving. How had he been blessed to be a part of not one, but two pastor's families?

He walked with the pastor to the church entrance. Halfway down the aisle he spotted the woman he saw in the store four days ago. She wore another expensive looking dress, her brown hair combed into a perfect chin-length flip, and her posture as rigid as he remembered. Everything about her screamed money. And snobbishness. An older version of the young woman stood beside her, along with a distinguished looking man with graying temples.

The man approached Rogan and Cecil. "Pastor, that was an inspired sermon."

"Thank you Michael. Have you met Rogan Mueller?"

"I have not." He offered his hand to Rogan. "I'm Michael Whitmore." Mr. Whitmore's smile seemed genuine and his eyes friendly. "This is my wife, Deborah, and my daughter, Catherine."

Rogan accepted his hand and nodded to his wife before settling his gaze on Catherine.

Her eyes ignited with surprise before she quickly regained her composure. She offered a slight incline of her head and a pinched smile before turning away.

While Cecil visited with Mr. Whitmore, Rogan wandered to the church doors. He'd known women like Catherine Whitmore before. And he had no use for any of them. Prancing around like the world owed them its undying service, looking down on anyone they deemed unworthy of their attention. *No thanks, buster.* Rogan dreamed of a woman like Esther. Godly. Beautiful. Courageous. Kind hearted.

Catherine Whitmore was clearly none of those things.

Except beautiful.

He pushed all thoughts of Catherine aside when Cecil joined him and they walked to the pastor's home. He tugged his jacket tighter around his neck. "Sure is getting colder. I keep thinking about the day I came here. That creek I stopped at, and how warm it was."

Cecil nodded his agreement. "Well, you've lived in Wyoming long enough to know that when the seasons decide to change, they change right quick. Just two weeks until Thanksgiving." He looked up at the sky. "I wouldn't be surprised if we got a heavy snow."

Rogan looked up at the gray clouds forming. Cecil was right. When the weather decided to change, it never asked permission. They passed by Whitmore's Grocery, and a question found its way from his mouth. "Michael Whitmore . . . does he own the grocery store?"

"Yes, he does. And that is just one of many. He came here a year ago to open that store. Michael grew up here in Sawyer's Gap, so the town has always held a special place in his heart. When he heard how bad things were after the market crashed, he started making plans to bring the business to Sawyer's Gap. He has helped a lot of people by providing jobs, and even gives away boxes of food when folks can't afford to buy it."

Rogan cast one more glance at the store as they walked. Mr. Whitmore sounded like a good man. He seemed quite the contrast to his wife and daughter.

A light sprinkle began to fall, moistening the dirt road. Something about the smell of wet earth took Rogan back to his childhood. He couldn't say he'd had an altogether happy childhood, but there were some happy memories. Like one very sweet lady who worked at the orphanage and would let the boys stomp around in mud puddles. She didn't mind cleaning their shoes and clothes afterward. She said it did her heart good to hear their laughter.

His reflections ended when Sheriff Kernshaw stalked out of the Five and Dime.

"Uh-oh." Cecil stopped. "I know that look. Something's wrong." He caught Rogan's elbow and propelled him along the boardwalk to the sheriff. "Russell, what is it? Are the Owens all right?"

The sheriff released a snort. "Jack and Dorothy are fine, but someone robbed the Five and Dime while they were at church."

"A robbery? Here in Sawyer's Gap?" Cecil scanned the quiet Sunday afternoon street. "I can't imagine who it could have been."

"Me neither." The sheriff cast a quick glance at Rogan.

Rogan crossed his arms. His stomach tightened. "I was with the pastor all morning."

Cecil nodded. "He certainly was."

Sheriff Kernshaw's gaze lowered to his boots. "I appreciate you letting me know that, Preacher."

Cecil's brows lifted. "Russell, you couldn't possibly suspect Rogan. He's brand new to our town, true, but he's been a huge help to us at the house and at the church."

"That's why he suspected me. Because I'm new." Rogan swallowed his anger, but it bubbled just beneath the surface.

Holding out a hand, Kernshaw met Rogan's gaze again. "It's nothing personal. You understand, don't you? I have to cover every possible angle. If I don't, then folks will be breathing down my neck, thinking I'm afraid to really chase down criminals."

Instead of accusation, Rogan read pleading in the sheriff's eyes. The anger clawing its way to the surface dissipated and empathy replaced it. He held his hand out to the sheriff. "I do understand. And I hope you find the guy responsible."

Kernshaw accepted Rogan's gesture. It felt good. To shake a lawman's hand, to be on the same side for once. But what really made Rogan's heart swell was the approving smile on Cecil's face.

Rogan and Cecil hurried on to the preacher's home. Rogan stepped in to the aroma of roasted chicken, carrots, and potatoes, and—if he weren't mistaken—a pecan pie. The table was set for three, and his mouth watered when the preacher's wife, Elizabeth, carried the food from the kitchen into the dining room.

"Looks too pretty to eat." Rogan winked.

Laughing, Elizabeth wagged a finger at him. "I haven't seen that stop you! Now, go wash up before it gets cold."

"Yes, ma'am." Rogan went into the washroom connected to his bedroom and lathered up his hands beneath a flow of warm water. Such a luxury, to have his own washroom. Cecil and Elizabeth had told him how blessed they felt to have a home like this, the biggest they'd ever had in their ministry. Apparently when a local business man moved back to Sawyer's Gap, he wanted them to have a comfortable place, and he paid to add on to the house.

Rogan rinsed and dried his hands. A local businessman... Could it have been Michael Whitmore? As far as he could tell, Mr. Whitmore was the most recent transplant in Sawyer's Gap.

He slid into his chair at the table and bowed his head for Cecil's prayer. Dinner was every bit as delicious as Rogan had anticipated. The chicken melted in his mouth. The buttery carrots and potatoes filled his stomach with a warmth he had only experienced one other place—the Dodds' home.

Elizabeth spooned more chicken and vegetables on his plate. "So, I hear you met the Whitmores this morning, including Catherine."

"Elizabeth . . ." A warning tone came from across the table before Cecil took a drink of milk.

"Oh, you hush." Elizabeth swatted him with her napkin and turned her attention back to Rogan. "She's a beautiful young lady, don't you think?"

Rogan bought some time chewing a bite of chicken and swallowing. Then a swig of milk. "Uh, yeah. She's pretty."

"Hmmm."

Her tone drew Rogan's attention.

Her steely blue eyed gaze semi-paralyzed him. "I understand. I really do." She patted his hand. "But I believe there is a sweet young woman hiding under all that ice."

Rogan nearly choked on his bite of carrots.

Cecil coughed, "Elizabeth!" He patted his mouth with a napkin, eyes closed.

"Oh, Cecil." She reached for his hand. "I am not gossiping. I'm just telling Rogan what a sweet woman I think Catherine is."

"Under all that ice?" Cecil challenged, picking up his fork.

"Well, you have to admit the girl is a bit cold." Her blue eyes found Rogan again. "I just think there's more of her father in her than she shows. She tries to emulate her mother, and her mother is very—"

"Elizabeth!" Cecil slapped his fork down.

Sighing, the pastor's wife closed her eyes for a moment. Then she smiled politely at Rogan. "I apologize."

Rogan nodded once and glanced at Cecil.

Elizabeth continued. "As I was saying, Catherine tends to try to emulate her mother. But I do think there is more of her father's influence there, deep down." Her voice softened. No one could dismiss the compassion in her tone. "She just needs to meet Jesus. She needs a one on one encounter with the One who loves her more than life itself."

"That's right." Cecil picked up his fork again and stabbed a piece of chicken. "She needs to meet Jesus. Not Rogan."

"Well, Rogan is a wonderful godly man." Elizabeth arched one eyebrow. "What better way for her to meet Jesus, than through a handsome young man who knows Him?"

"She already has a handsome young man, Elizabeth. She is engaged to be married. You know that."

"But he doesn't know Jesus." Elizabeth's eyes flashed. "And you know that wedding is all her mother's doing. It's not what Catherine wants."

The minister jabbed a chunk of chicken into his mouth and spoke around it. "And how do you know what Catherine wants, dear? She hardly speaks two words to anyone."

"I can sense it. And you know my senses are always right."

Cecil looked at Rogan, a smile tugging at his lips. "You see what I have to deal with?"

"And you love it." Elizabeth picked up Cecil's hand and kissed it. "You wouldn't have me any other way."

Rogan wondered at the magical way her kiss could reduce Cecil to a lovesick boy. And who was Catherine marrying? He hadn't seen a ring the day he first saw her at the Five and Dime. A woman like that, she would have a ring. So why didn't she wear it?

CHAPTER 3

Catherine set her embroidery aside. She toyed with the diamond ring on her left hand. The closer the day of Benjamin's arrival approached, the tighter the ring felt.

She rose from the fine jacquard print sofa, walked to the large bay window, and pulled the gold silk drapes aside. A squirrel ran across the expansive lawn and up an oak tree. A bored sigh escaped Catherine's lips.

Every day was so much the same. She rose around nine each morning, ate a light breakfast, bathed, dressed, styled her hair and applied the appropriate amount of subtle makeup. Then the day stretched out before her. Embroidery. Reading. Playing the piano. Browsing catalogs. Gardening. But planting and blooming season for the lovely colors of the Indian paintbrush flower was long over.

Of course, lately, her mother smothered her with wedding plans. She closed her eyes and balled her hands into fists to stop the tremble. This was all about her mother. Every bit of it. How was she to endure marriage to a man she didn't love?

Catherine looked up at the sky. The clouds had moved in last Sunday after church, and hadn't left. She turned and faced the room again. Mother was upstairs with a headache. Again. Though she understood her mother's dislike of Sawyer's Gap, Catherine thought Mother's constant punishment of Father was childish and unfair. But she would never have the courage to say that out loud. At least for today, Catherine was spared from talk of florists and linens and bridesmaids.

Sighing again, Catherine crossed her arms. Maybe she could go to the Five and Dime. No. She'd seen everything they had to offer. The Depression had hit Sawyer's Gap terribly, and people didn't have money to buy things that weren't absolutely necessary. Therefore, the Five and Dime carried few luxuries.

Father had left early for the grocery store. She could walk over there and say hello. It was the best she could do, seeing as how she had no friends here.

The other women in town ignored her, sometimes making plans with each other within ear shot but never asking her to join them.

Forcing down the growing angst in her stomach, Catherine went to her room, checked her reflection, pulled on a coat, snatched up her pocketbook, and left.

The crisp air filled Catherine's lungs, sweeping away her brooding thoughts. A light sprinkling of snow floated down from the swollen clouds. She walked in the direction of the grocery store, her heart lifting with each step.

A woman approached, holding the hand of a young boy. His shoes had holes in them, as did his trousers. The woman didn't wear a coat and her dress had definitely seen better days. Her shoes weren't in any better shape. She looked at Catherine, but quickly averted her weary gaze. Catherine wanted to say something. But there were no words. A sting of shame pierced her middle. Not for the first time, she felt ostentatious in her fine clothes.

Catherine quickened her pace and continued on. How she missed New York! She fit in there. She had friends. People who didn't look at her with contempt.

She reached Whitmore's Grocery and frowned at a commotion in front of the store. Her father was talking to Sheriff Kernshaw, and several employees gathered around, chattering amongst themselves.

Catherine approached the small crowd, ignoring the glances and whispers. "Father?"

He turned. A smile spread across his handsome features.

"Catherine, what a nice surprise." He pulled her into a hug.

Did he know how safe, how loved his hugs made her feel? "What's happening here?"

"Oh. This." Father's smile disappeared and his eyes saddened. "We've been robbed."

"The second robbery this week." Sheriff Kernshaw shook his head as he wrote on a notepad.

"The second one?" Catherine's pulse increased. "Who else was robbed?"

"The Five and Dime." Russell motioned down the street. "Last Sunday morning. And now your father's store."

She looked at her father. "What did they take?"

"Just some food, darling. It's fine." Her father brushed a strand of hair behind her ear. "Nothing to worry about."

Catherine gawked at him. "Nothing to worry about? What if you had been here? What if you had been hurt?"

"They were just looking for food." Father shook his head. "Things are so difficult right now. The Depression has ruined many people. They get desperate."

Russell held his notepad up. "Do you plan to file a complaint, Michael?"

Father sighed a heavily. "Well, I don't want to. But obviously this is wrong. We can't have people stealing from others, no matter how bad things are. But when you find them, I'd like to know their story. If they're simply in need, I'd like to help."

The sheriff smiled and began writing again. "You're a good man, Michael. Then again, you always were."

Michael patted Russell's shoulder and laughed. "Let's stick with that story, Russell."

"Sure thing." Russell gave him a thumbs up. "I wouldn't want you telling stories on my youth either!"

Rogan lifted the axe above his head, and brought it down with a thud and a grunt. The two-feet long length sawed from a pine log dropped into two neat halves. He wiped the back of his hand across his brow. The light snow meant nothing when chopping wood. The body produced its own uncomfortable heat.

He aimed a few more blows, then set the axe aside and carried up the split pieces to the woodshed behind the Dodds' house. As he exited the woodshed, he spotted Sheriff Kernshaw ambling toward him. At once his chest went tight. What did the sheriff want? Feigning nonchalance, Rogan sauntered to the pile of firewood and picked up another short log.

The sheriff trotted over. "Can I help with that?"

"Sure." Rogan regarded the man with suspicion. He went on splitting wood, wishing the man would go away.

The sheriff carried the split pieces to the woodshed, making small talk while Rogan used the axe. Finally he stopped and stretched his back. "So, listen, Rogan. I need to ask you a couple of questions."

Rogan brought the axe down on the chopping block and reached for the pieces of firewood lying next to his boots. "I told you I was with Cecil all morning last week. I didn't rob the Five and Dime."

Russell held up a hand. "Yes you did tell me that. And I don't doubt your word on it, or Cecil's. But another robbery happened last night. Over at Whitmore's Grocery."

"You want to know if I did it." Rogan stared at the man for a long moment, tamping down the anger rising in his chest. He headed for the woodshed. "No. I didn't."

The sheriff followed him. "Look, I'm not singling you out. I've got a couple other folks I'm going to talk to as well."

Rogan brushed past the man to retrieve the other pieces of split wood.

Sheriff Krenshaw caught his arm. "Would you take a break moving those logs? Stand still long enough to talk to me."

"Fine." Rogan propped his fists on his waist. "I was in the house with Cecil and Elizabeth last night, listening to the radio. We listened to 'The Weston Family Gospel Hour.' After that, I went to my room. I read my Bible for about an hour. The book of Esther. And then I fell asleep." He snapped his fingers in the air. "I did get up for a glass of water around three, but I promise, I went right back to bed."

Krenshaw scrawled notes in a little notebook. He put the notebook in his shirt pocket and gave Rogan a steady look. "I know you have a past with the law. I know what you've been through. But I also know that Cecil says you've given your life to Christ and are a new man now. And if Cecil says it, I believe it. But I have to ask you, because others will ask. And I want to be able to give them answers when they do."

Regret pinched Rogan's lungs. Would he ever get his anger under control? He prayed constantly, but his temper kept showing up. He shoved his hand through his hair. "I'm sorry. I get defensive. Nervous."

The sheriff smiled and reached out his hand. Rogan accepted, and Krenshaw ambled off.

Rogan returned to work, his thoughts rolling. Who was robbing these places? Was the thief dangerous? Rogan prayed the person was caught before anyone got hurt. He knew all too well how badly this whole thing could go.

He split about half a cord of wood before the snow began to fall too heavily to continue working. He put the axe away and went inside where the sound of Elizabeth humming lifted his spirits. The fragrant scents of vegetable soup and fresh baked bread helped melt away the chill of outdoors.

Rogan made his way to the kitchen, licking his lips as he reached for the lid on the bubbling soup. A kitchen towel slapped his hand away.

"And just what do you think you're going to do when you get the lid off?" Elizabeth's green eyes danced. "Lap it up with your tongue?" She tsk'd and set the towel aside. "You'd burn your taste buds off."

"And that would be surely be a disappointment with your cooking." Rogan grinned at her.

Elizabeth giggled. The lines around her eyes deepened with her smile. Even the woman's silver hair seemed to glow. "Go on and get yourself washed up. Cecil should be home for dinner any minute now."

True to her word, within ten minutes the three of them sat at the dinner table, listening to Cecil say grace.

"Elizabeth, honey, this looks delicious." Cecil ladled soup into his bowl.

"You always say that, but thank you. Rogan? Would you like some bread?"

"Yes, please." Rogan accepted the bread from Elizabeth, then the soup from Cecil.

Elizabeth's brow wrinkled as she spread her napkin on her lap. "How is Mrs. Monroe doing, Cecil?"

Swallowing a spoonful of soup, Cecil shook his head. "She's still very weak. But I think she and the children will be all right now that Michael Whitmore has offered his assistance."

The mention of Catherine's father drew Rogan's attention. "What kind of assistance?"

Cecil drank a swig of milk. "He sent some much needed groceries over to the house while I was there visiting. And he also gave young Nathan a job."

"That's wonderful!" Elizabeth exclaimed. "What a blessing that man has been in Sawyer's Gap. And to do such a thing even after being robbed. I do wish the sheriff could find out who has been causing all this awful business. I'd feel much safer."

"We're safe enough with the Lord's protection, sweetheart." Cecil placed his hand on top of Elizabeth's. "But you're right. We do need to pray for wisdom for Russell."

Rogan remained silent on the subject, choosing to direct his attention to his dinner. He also hoped the person would be caught soon, in great part so that suspicion would be diverted away from him.

After dinner, Elizabeth said, "I baked an applesauce cake today. I'll go cut it now. How large a piece would you like, Rogan?"

He grimaced. "It sounds delicious, but do you mind terribly if I have mine in my room?"

"Aren't you feeling well?" She held the back of her hand to Rogan's forehead.

"I'm fine, really. Just tired is all."

"Stop fussing over the boy, Elizabeth." Cecil smiled. "He probably just wants some quiet time to himself before another day of chopping wood."

She worried her brow at Rogan for a moment and then nodded. "Go on to your room. I'll bring you some cake and coffee."

Rogan stood and kissed the woman on her cheek. How different would his life have been if he'd had parents or grandparents in his life like these two?

After eating his cake and drinking most of the coffee Elizabeth had brought to him, Rogan lay back against a pillow. He'd intended to do some reading in his Bible, but tiredness overtook him. He turned off his lamp and rolled over, ready for sleep.

But rifle shot brought him out of bed and scrambling across the floor.

Chapter 4

"Catherine, honestly, I don't understand you." Catherine's mother dropped the green silk swatch on the table and crossed her arms in front of her. "Most young ladies would be utterly beside themselves to have the opportunity to plan such a fine wedding."

Catherine paced the dining room, her feet silent on the thick carpet. "I...I can't focus."

Mother pursed her lips. "It's ridiculous to worry over last night's shooting. Didn't your father say it was likely someone aiming at a night creature and hitting Mr. Walker by mistake?"

Catherine stopped and lowered her gaze to the ring on her finger. With Benjamin staying in the hotel in Sawyer's Gap and her mother going on and on about fabrics, menus, and invitations, it seemed as if she lost a little more control over her own life each day. "It isn't the shooting. It's..."

Mother took hold of Catherine's arms. "If it's the colors, or the food, or—"

Something inside Catherine burst like a balloon that couldn't take any more air. "I don't want to do this!"

Deborah's eyes widened. Her red painted lips parted, but she didn't utter a sound.

Catherine's hand flew to her mouth. Had she really said it? Out loud? Tears blurred her vision. She moved on wobbly legs to the settee by the window and collapsed onto the tufted cushion. A wave of relief brought fresh air to her lungs. At last! At last she had spoken up for herself.

She lifted her head and continued. "Mother, I don't love Benjamin. I never have. He's a nice man and has always treated me well, but he's the one *you* want me to marry."

Her mother's eyes narrowed, and her lips formed a straight line.

Catherine focused her attention on a crystal vase sitting on the fireplace mantel. "I suppose I convinced myself that this is what I wanted as well, but the closer his visit got, the more doubts I had. And now that he's here, and

I've actually spent time with him, even though he has done nothing he could be blamed for, I cannot go through with it." She turned her gaze back to her mother, hoping against hope that she would understand. "This is not what I want."

She held her breath. Surely Mother would respect her only daughter's wishes and call off the wedding.

Mother patted her perfectly coiffed finger wave, smoothed her gray wool skirt, then took slow, deliberate steps to join Catherine on the settee. "Darling. This is just a—a fleeting moment of doubt. Or perhaps, fear of the unknown. But, trust me, marrying Benjamin *is* the right thing for you."

Catherine's breath whooshed out. "But I just said I don't—"

Mother held up her hand. "I heard what you said." Sighing, she rubbed her left temple with her manicured forefinger. "Darling, it's time you stop living in the romantic fantasies of girlhood and accept the realities of womanhood. This marriage will secure your future. It's very important, especially in times such as these. You see how difficult life is for those less fortunate. You see how their children don't even have decent clothes to wear, or enough food to eat." She took Catherine's hand in hers. "Don't you want better for yourself and your children?"

Nausea rolled through Catherine's middle. She pulled her hand free of Mother's grasp. "You married for love though. Why should it be any different for me?"

Her mother lowered her eyes and picked at a stray thread on her sweater.

Chills chased one another down Catherine's spine. An awful thought presented itself. She swallowed hard. "Mother?"

Mother's gaze finally met hers. "I respect your father. I admire him." Her chin tilted proudly upward. "I always have."

Dizziness struck, and Catherine clung to the settee cushion. "But you never *loved* him? Oh, Mother!" She stood, holding her hand to her stomach. "How could you?"

"I just told you." Mother stood and took hold of Catherine's shoulder. "I did it for my future. I did it for you."

Jerking from her mother's touch, Catherine backed away, slowly shaking her head. How could she not have seen the truth?

"Catherine, you are being childish!" Mother waved her hand in the air. "Times were very difficult then, too. Several people I knew and loved died of typhoid fever. The war was beginning. I had no security whatsoever. I could have clung to the same fairy tales you do. I could have married for love. I had that chance. But, do you know where we would be right now? Begging for food and wearing clothes that belonged to five other people before us."

Unable to listen anymore, Catherine ran to the stairway and up to her bedroom, her mother's piercing voice calling after her.

Rogan hid behind a snow covered white spruce, lifted his gun to his shoulder, and peered through the sight. He easily lined up the target, but his finger hesitated on the trigger. Killing an animal didn't use to bother him like it did now. He murmured, "Sorry, fella. But I need to eat."

The single shot echoed through the hills and tall evergreens. His target slumped to the ground. Thankful he only had to shoot once, Rogan trudged through ankle deep snow to where his prey lay on the ground. He picked it up by the scruff of the neck and headed back to the cabin.

Rogan looked up at the sky. "Thank You for your provision, Lord." Charcoal clouds hung low and heavy. The snow hadn't stopped falling all day, and now that the sun had set, the temperature dropped fast. Would a blizzard roll in? Mingled fear and hope gripped him. A blizzard would provide him with some more time to let things settle down in town.

He blew out a breath, the warmth creating a cloud of condensation. What must Cecil and Elizabeth be thinking? He'd taken Cecil's horse and run away without a word to anyone. Cecil had probably called the Dodds, told them he'd run off. Bile rose in his throat at the thought of letting the two families down. Maybe he should have stayed and waited on the Lord sort it out. But people were quick to blame the most convenient target. Just like his dinner he carried right now. The critter was there, alone and vulnerable, so it became his target.

But this was far more serious than killing an animal for food. A good man lay in the hospital with a gunshot wound to his shoulder. Sheriff Kernshaw and the rest of Sawyer's Gap were looking to blame someone. Rogan just couldn't stay and take any chances.

At the cabin, Rogan paused to peer down the long road that led from Sawyer's Gap to his hideaway. He searched the shadows and listened. All was quiet. Nothing stirred. Secure, he walked up the steps to the porch. From behind the door's window, light glowed. He frowned. Did he leave a lamp on when he left? He must have. The day had been so overcast and dark. But he shouldn't be so careless. The cabin wasn't his. He'd not make the same mistake again.

Rogan turned the doorknob and eased open the door. An ear splitting screech filled the night and sent him stumbling backward, heart racing. Thumps and fumbling noises carried from inside. Had an animal gotten in the place? Something was definitely in there, probably feeling cornered. There was nothing more dangerous than a frightened, cornered animal. He set his kill on the porch and took up his rifle. Steadying the gun, prepared to take the shot if necessary, he pushed the door wide with the tip of the weapon.

The hinges moaned a warning. All noise ceased from inside. Rogan scanned the small room, and then he lowered the gun to his side and stared, slack jawed. "What in blazes are you doing here?"

Catherine Whitmore stood in the far corner. She held a frying pan like a weapon. The thing shook so badly in her hand, Rogan knew he could disarm her with little struggle.

Her wide, green gaze darted around the room and landed on him again. Delicate brows scrunched over her nose. She looked from him to the gun and back to him again. She motioned to his gun with the cast iron skillet. "Wh— what are you going to do with that?"

Rolling his eyes, Rogan propped the rifle against the wall. He moved outside, picked up his soon-to-be dinner, and stepped back into the room. He held up the animal by its ringed tail. "Don't worry. I only use my bullets for necessities."

She shrieked.

He held up his hand. "Stop that! You're going to make me deaf, woman! And for cryin' out loud, quit waving that pan around. You're more likely to maim yourself than anyone else."

She stared wild-eyed at the prey in his hand. "What is that...that thing?"

Rogan looked at the animal, head and limbs hanging limp. "Are you really so sheltered you've never seen a raccoon before?"

Catherine angled her head away, her sideways gaze aimed at the raccoon. "What do you plan to do with the wretched thing?"

"I'm gonna eat it. Unless you'd like a new coat. I guess I could make one after I eat. Might take a while. Gotta let the hide dry out and—"

"You can't eat that!" She shuddered as if he'd suggested eating a child.

Rogan scratched his head. "And just why not?"

"Because!" Catherine clanked the skillet onto the stove. The *clang!* bounced off the walls and made Rogan's ears ring. "People do not eat raccoons. It's—it's—appalling." Her nose screwed upward as she lifted her chin and crossed her arms over her chest.

It was true raccoons were about the poorest eating of any forest creature. But she seemed to be taking some kind of stance. Rogan wasn't about to be bullied by a little slip of a woman. No matter how pretty her green eyes were. "Trust me, you'd change your mind if you ever got hungry enough." He scanned her expensive clothes from head to toe. "I wouldn't expect you to understand." He walked toward the dry sink.

"Where are you going? What are you doing?"

At the panic in her voice, he paused and turned around. "I'm going to clean it so I can eat it."

"Oh no." She stared at the dead animal as if it might suddenly come back to life. "Please...please don't do that. Not in here."

The pleading in her voice actually tugged at Rogan. She really was terrified. And maybe sick. Her face had gone white as the snow. He really should be more considerate of— He stomped his foot. Wait a minute! This was *his* hideaway. She still hadn't explained her presence.

"Fine." He advanced on her slowly, raccoon dangling from his hand. She backed away with each step he took, her gaze never leaving the dead animal. "I'll clean it outside. On one condition."

She hugged herself. "W-what condition?"

"That you, Miss Grocery Store Heir, tell me why you are here."

Chapter 5

Catherine stayed on the far side of the room while Rogan tossed the dead animal onto the porch and then crouched to build a fire in the stove. Thankful for a moment to gather her thoughts, Catherine fidgeted with a loose curl. When he finished, he'd clean that awful raccoon, and he'd expect answers. And she didn't know what to say.

She wasn't entirely sure why she was there. She just...escaped. Then the snow had come down fast and thick, hindering her vision, and she needed shelter. She spotted the cabin, she went inside.

When she'd first heard his boots coming up the steps and onto the porch, her heart lurched into her throat. And when he opened the door, sheer terror paralyzed her. But seeing it was Rogan somehow had a calming effect. His presence was both comforting and disconcerting. Why was he here? Did he have something to do with the thefts and the shooting? His rifle, leaning in the corner, threatened her. She shivered. What if he was the one who shot Mr. Walker right in his own home? Was he dangerous?

"How did you get here?" Rogan stood and turned to sit in one of the little chairs near a wood table that had seen better days.

In spite of the warm fire, icy cold fingers traced down Catherine's arms. She absently began to rub them so as to get her blood flowing again. "I—I, um—drove."

"You drove?" Alarm tinted his voice. "Drove what? I didn't see a car out there."

"I parked it behind the cabin."

He leaned back and crossed one ankle over his knee. "Well, at least you thought through that much."

His sarcasm ignited her ire. She planted her hands on her hips. "I am not stupid. I don't want to be traced to this place any more than you do! And why am I the one who has to explain themselves, anyway? What about you? Why are *you* here?"

Rogan's blue eyes darkened. He stared at the fire. "I was here first."

"You were here first?" Laughter erupted from her chest. "I'm sorry, but we are not five years old, and this is not the playground, so I'm going to need a real answer."

He stood abruptly.

She took a step back.

He crossed directly in front of her. "The point is, we can't both be here."

She felt quite small and defenseless with him towering over her. Her tongue stuck to the roof of her mouth.

"I was here first. So you need to scurry back down the mountain. I'm sure your maid, or chef, or someone in that big ol' house has noticed you're gone by now."

Catherine swallowed the hurt at his insinuation that no one outside paid employees would care that she was missing. She lifted her chin and crossed her arms. "I am not going anywhere."

Rogan shoved both hands through his hair and groaned. "It's already dark out. The snow is only going to get heavier. You could get trapped here. Do you really want that?"

"Do you?"

He tilted his head, looking at her as if she'd suddenly grown a beard. Finally he threw his hands in the air. "Fine. Stay. Make yourself comfortable. The bedroom is mine, though." He pointed to a door next to the stone fireplace in the second room of the cabin. "You can take the loft. Now, I'm getting the coon in here and cleaning it for my dinner."

Her stomach rolled. "You are not butchering that animal in here!"

"Oh, yes, I am. I shot it for food. I'm not going to let it go to waste." He cocked his head and glared at her. "And last I checked, you weren't my wife or my mother, so you don't get to tell me what I can and cannot do."

Bile rose in her throat. She was going to throw up. "You said you wouldn't!"

Rogan pointed his finger at her. "I said I wouldn't if you explained yourself. You haven't done so. Besides, it's too blamed cold for me to stay outside long enough to get it gutted and skinned." He brushed past her and swung the door open.

A whoosh of freezing air swept in, chasing away the need to empty her stomach. She muttered, "Thank goodness for small mercies."

Rogan spun back around. "What did you say?"

She offered her most innocent, wide-eyed expression. "Nothing."

His eyes narrowed. He shook his head and stepped outside, slamming the door behind him.

She considered locking him out. But she wasn't hard-hearted enough to let a person freeze to death. Not even a raving lunatic like him. She wouldn't stay in the kitchen and watch him turn that raccoon into stew meat, though.

Catherine hurried into the larger room of the cabin and perused the space to get her mind off the raccoon and its butcher. An embroidered piece hanging over the fireplace drew her attention. She stepped closer, admiring the needlework. A name was stitched onto the fabric—*Tearmann*. She didn't know any Tearmanns. A small black Bible lay on the mantel. She picked it up, gently brushing away dust from the cover. A purple ribbon marked a page, and she opened the Bible.

Isaiah 4:6 had been underlined. She read it in a whisper, " 'And there shall be a tabernacle for a shadow in the day time from the heat, and for a place of refuge, and for a covert from storm and from rain.' "

She traced her fingers over the yellowed pages of the old Bible. The scripture tugged at something deep inside Catherine's being that she didn't quite understand. Grumbles drifted from outside. The poor raccoon was making Rogan work for his food. She smiled. And he hadn't made good on his word to clean the wretched thing inside.

Her tapestry covered suitcase still sat beside the small sofa across from a worn leather chair. She'd better take control now while Rogan was busy outside. She picked up the suitcase and hurried across the floor to the door he had indicated with the bedroom. She stepped inside and clicked the door closed behind her. No moonlight spilled through the window to offer so much as a shadow. Catherine took a step forward and rammed her toe on an immovable object.

Stifling a yelp, she dropped her suitcase and hopped on one foot until the pain dulled. She stretched out her hands and located an iron bed. She inched her way along the soft mattress and encountered a bedside table. More fumbling led her to a lamp of some sort. She fingered it until she located a button. A click brought a dim beam of yellow light. The dry cell battery-operated lantern was far from decorative, but now she could see.

The light fell across the bed—white painted iron with a few rusty splotches—and its blue quilted coverlet. Catherine touched the stitching in the coverlet, smiling. Quaint. Comforting in its own way. And not something Mother would ever own. Catherine gave a nod. She liked it.

As in the living room, dust had built up on the furnishings. She sat on the bed. It creaked and felt less than steady, but it was better than she'd imagined. A stuffed green canvas bag sat on the floor by the bedroom door. Probably Rogan's.

Catherine tried to lift it. For goodness sakes, what was in the thing? She dragged it out of the bedroom and across the floor to the foot of the loft's ladder. Rubbing her back, she scurried to the bedroom and unpacked the few clothes in her suitcase. The wardrobe held her two extra dresses, trousers, and a sweater. A draft drifted across the floor. The foundation must have gaps. Would they be large enough to allow in some creature? She returned to her suitcase while keeping an eye out for any little surprises.

She put her unmentionables in a dresser drawer. Fresh bundles of lavender wrapped in mesh lay in each of the drawers. A pleasant surprise. Whoever had used the old place before them had certainly made themselves at home. She placed her brush and mirror set on the top of the dresser, then lined up her Max Factor make-up, hair comb, and a jar of cold cream. Her copy of *Gone with the Wind* fit perfectly on the bedside table. The book was all the rage with her friends in New York, and she couldn't wait to get started reading it.

When she peeked out of the bedroom, she discovered she was still alone. Logs and kindling waited in the fireplace, so she rolled some old newspaper and lit it from the fire in the stove. Using the newspaper as a torch, she carried it to the fireplace and laid it on the logs. In no time at all a snapping fire warmed the room and brightened her spirits.

Back in the kitchen, Catherine searched the cupboards for a small plate to hold her rose scented soap. She set the soap next to the sink and then stood back and admired it. Giddiness danced through her stomach. She'd never felt so free and independent. But the thought of being found out quickly chased away her momentary sense of independence. Everyone in Sawyer's Gap knew about the old cabin. How long would it take for them to realize she was staying in it?

And Rogan... That was another matter entirely.

By the time Rogan finished skinning the animal, he couldn't move his fingers anymore. He managed to open the door and stumbled inside. The snap of a fire drew him to the main room. Catherine sat on the couch near the fireplace. Questioning green eyes turned toward him. He ignored their magnetic pull and crouched before the fireplace, holding his hands to the flames. He winced against the pain of circulation returning to his fingers. From the corner of his eye, he saw Catherine go into the kitchen.

Rogan made fists with his hands and released them a couple of times. Pretty stupid of him to go out in the cold with no gloves. But in his defense, the temperature seemed to drop much more quickly than he'd anticipated, and skinning the animal took longer. He still needed to cut the carcass into pieces, but the heavy snowfall made him reluctant to go out again.

Catherine approached, holding a wet dishtowel. "Here. Try this." She held the towel open.

He warily held his hands out. She wrapped the warm, yellow towel around his hands with a surprisingly gentle touch. The warmth of the towel began to seep into his hands. He sighed. "Thank you."

She smiled, lifting a delicate brow. "I'm not the wicked person some make me out to be, you know." She returned to the couch. "When I was eight years old, I sneaked outside with the little girl next door. We had been out in the snow for about half an hour before my mother saw me. Sofia—my nanny—wrapped a warm towel around my hands. I still remember the pain." Catherine glanced at his hands. "Are they warm yet? Do you need more warm water?"

"I have feeling in my fingers again." Rogan stared at the towel around his hands. This was a side of her that he had not anticipated. "Your mother must have been pretty thankful to your nanny. You could have gotten frostbite."

Catherine's eyes dimmed. A sad smile lifted the corners of her lips. She stared into the fire. "Mother released her for being inattentive. Funny, huh? My mother couldn't be bothered to watch over me herself, but she fired the one person who was always there for me."

Not knowing what to say, Rogan sat quietly. With Catherine's attention on the fireplace, he could observe her in a way he hadn't been able to before. Her features were much softer, more delicate than he'd interpreted in their past encounters. Her eyes much brighter and...lonely? Her childhood certainly sounded lonely. But it seemed her adulthood had not improved much. Did the man she planned to marry get these glimpses of her, or was she simply a trophy to wear on his arm?

Uncomfortable with where his thoughts were beginning to roam, Rogan stood and laid the damp towel on the hearth to dry. He could feel Catherine's questioning eyes on him. He'd get his gloves, go out and carve up that raccoon for frying. And put some distance between the two of them.

Rogan headed for the bedroom for his duffel. He stopped just inside the door. The bedside lantern flickered, throwing light on a book on the bedside table. His gaze zinged around the room, taking in a hairbrush, mirror, and makeup on the dresser and an empty suitcase yawning open on the bed. He stomped back into the living room. Motioning to the room behind him with his thumb, he frowned. "What is all this stuff?"

"Hmm?" Catherine twisted on the couch to look over her shoulder at him.

"The book and all that—that *female* stuff. Why is it in my bedroom?"

"Oh, that." She stood and faced him. "You see, the loft has no privacy. I simply cannot be expected to sleep up there." She set her hands on her waist and looked up at the loft, then held her hand out to the bag at the bottom of the stairs. "I moved your bag over here. I would have carried it upstairs for you, but it's quite heavy."

Rogan clenched his teeth. This was not going to work. Who did she think she was? In town she may be the queen bee, but here? Here in this cabin she was just another person running from...something. He stretched a finger toward the door. "We are going to get you back down that mountain, and I am coming back *alone*."

"I wouldn't be so sure about that." Catherine offered a satisfied smile. "I peeked out the window while you were out there. The snow is getting quite deep, and it's too dark to travel safely."

Rogan stifled a growl. He'd been out there only minutes ago, in snow nearly two feet deep. She was right. They'd never make it down the mountain without getting stuck. He'd have to wait until morning. In the meantime, though, he'd at least enjoy a hot dinner.

He charged out to the porch for the raccoon. A bloody patch of snow showed where he'd been working, but the animal was gone. "No!" He leaned on the rickety railing and scanned the dark woods, but searching was useless. He made a fist and hit the wall of the cabin. Pain seared through his hand into his arm. "Aaaagh!"

Catherine appeared in the doorway, hugging herself against the cold. "What's wrong?"

Rogan held his hand close to his chest. "The raccoon is gone. Some blasted animal out there just walked right up here and took it. And the snow"—he groaned—"has us trapped. We're stuck here together."

The slight smile on her face before she ducked inside did little to improve his mood.

Chapter 6

Rogan slept fitfully, thinking of Catherine Whitmore and her green eyes, pink lips, and absolutely irritating, invasive, uppity personality. She certainly was no Esther. He woke to the rich scent of coffee and...ham? He squinted at the face on the bedside clock. It couldn't be 11:30. He must have forgotten to wind it last night.

He swung his legs out of the too small cot, stretched his back, and sucked in a breath as his feet touched the cold wood floor. The fire must have died during the night. Otherwise this loft would be the coziest place to be. If the bed were big enough. That alone was reason for Catherine to be stuck up here instead of him.

Clattering sounds from the direction of the kitchen drew his attention. He dressed, including heavy socks, and padded down the stairs. A fire crackled in the fireplace but the logs were hardly scorched. Catherine had built a fire herself? Noises in the kitchen once again piqued his curiosity.

Catherine stood at the old wood stove, her back to him. A faded blue-and-white checkered apron was tied in a lopsided bow behind her back. The bow invited his attention.

Rogan pulled his gaze away from her feminine frame. "Ahem."

She spun to face him. "Oh! Good morning. I hope I didn't wake you." She lifted a coffee pot with a dishtowel wrapped around its handle and smiled at him.

Maybe he was dreaming all this. "Uh, no. I just . . ." He turned around and glanced around the cabin. He scratched his head. No, the cabin and its smiling hostess was real.

"Would you like a cup of coffee?" She didn't wait for him to answer before retrieving a cup and saucer from a cupboard. She set them on the table and poured the steaming black liquid into the cup. "The pipes are frozen, but I melted some snow to make the coffee."

Rogan slowly sat. She was full of surprises.

"Sugar?"

His gaze snapped back to Catherine. To his relief she held a bowl of sugar and a spoon. "No. Thank you."

Catherine put the sugar on the kitchen counter. "I got up in the middle of the night for a glass of water. Of course the pipes were already frozen. But I did some looking around and found some tinned ham in the pantry. I set it by the fire to thaw through the night." She returned to the table with a plate of sliced, cooked ham. Catherine brought him a fork and then sat across from him, sipping from a cup.

Rogan's mouth watered at the warm, salty scent. He picked up the fork and chopped off a bite.

"I was glad to find mason jars of coffee and sugar in the pantry, too. The coffee's good, but it could desperately use some milk." She smiled at him over the rim of her cup. "How's the ham? I thought it turned out fairly edible."

Rogan nodded and spoke around the food in his mouth. "It just might be the best tasting food I've ever had in my life."

"I suppose starvation can do that to a person."

Frowning at her perky disposition, Rogan tried to make sense of what was happening around him. Another thought burst into his mind. "The snow!" His chair scraped against the wood floor as when he stood and rushed to a window. Drifts reached all the way to the sill. He leaned against the wall and sighed. "We're snowed in. Together."

"And here I thought making you some coffee and finding this ham to cook would have endeared you to me at least a tiny bit." Catherine held her arms crossed in front of her. Her brows formed a V, meeting at the top of her nose.

Rogan scrubbed his hands on his face and dropped them to his sides. "I'm sorry. I don't mean to be rude. But this is a bad situation. You must see that."

Shrugging, Catherine began clearing the table.

Rogan intercepted her. "Are you telling me that you aren't the least bit concerned about what people in town must being saying? I've disappeared. You've disappeared . . ."

"I suppose they'll think we've run off together." Another shrug of her slim shoulders. "Let them."

He gawked at her. "Let them? Are you being serious?" Irritation made his ears throb. "How can you be so carefree about it? I don't want people to think I ran off with you!"

Catherine pranced past him, his empty plate in her hands. "I'll have you know there are plenty of men who would want to run off with me! Plenty of men who would want people to think they had run off with me!"

Rogan shook his head, balling his hands into fists. "You're insane. What self-respecting woman would say such a thing?"

Catherine's eyes narrowed. Her cheeks flamed. "The same kind of self-respecting woman who would refuse to marry a man she didn't love. I make my own decisions, and I don't care what others think." She turned on her heel, marched into the living room, and plopped on the couch.

Catherine's hands trembled. She hadn't meant to say anything to Rogan about Benjamin. Ever. But Rogan had such arrogance about him. He made her feel as if she weren't good enough for him. As if she would tarnish his reputation rather than the other way around. She'd tried to be kind, making the coffee and working so hard to cook that hunk of ham. Figuring out how to operate that old stove had been no small feat. And going out in the freezing cold to collect snow to melt had been quite resourceful in her opinion. She swiped furiously at tears slipping from her eyes.

She sensed Rogan's presence behind her. She couldn't speak through the lump in her throat. He moved past her and sat in the wing backed chair. Catherine twisted her body just enough to hide her tears. For a long moment he didn't say anything. Only the crackling of the flames in the fireplace filled the silence between them.

At last he spoke. "Is that why you came here? You didn't want to get married?"

Catherine closed her eyes. Her heart hung like a lead weight in her chest. "I was never in love with Benjamin. I didn't want to marry him. It was all my mother's plan."

The weight that lifted from her shoulders after speaking the words out loud caught her unaware. For so long she had lived with the burden. The dread. She still couldn't bring herself to look at Rogan. As unsophisticated and gruff as he was, there was still something about him that made her feel inferior.

"I'm sorry, Catherine." The way his rugged voice carried the words caressed her heart with a kindness and intimacy that left her emotions exposed. She held her hand to her chest, focusing on the flames in the fireplace.

"Couldn't you just tell your mother you didn't want to marry him?"

A humorless laugh escaped Catherine's lungs. "I tried. But you don't know my mother. To her, marriage is nothing more than a means to an end. And that end being a comfortable—make that *wealthy*—life for herself."

"That's a shame."

"Yes it is. Especially for my father." She bit her lip to stop the sting in her nose threatening more tears. Another few moments passed in silence.

"Cecil thinks a great deal of your father."

Catherine smiled. Everyone thought well of her father. As they should. He was a good man. Who deserved much better than what he got stuck with for a wife. She turned to say as much to Rogan, and she met his gaze. His blue eyes made her breath catch. She'd expected contempt. Instead, she saw compassion.

Gathering her self-respect once again, she sat up straighter. "So, now you know my secret. Why I'm here. It's your turn. What brought you to the cabin in the middle of the woods?"

His strong brow lifted. Flames in the fireplace danced in his eyes. He squirmed in his seat.

"It's only fair." Catherine spread her hands in front of her. "I told you my story. Now you tell me yours."

He blew out a deep sigh. "You know about the shooting?"

"Yes. Mr. Walker." Her pulse quickened. "Did you . . ."

"No." His voice hardened.

Catherine nodded mutely. She dared not argue the conviction in his voice. "Do you know who did?"

"I wish I knew." He stood and walked to the fire to stoke it. He set one foot on the hearth. "Then I could take suspicion off myself."

Distracted by his long legs and strong arms, Catherine cleared her throat and shifted her gaze to the snow forming a glistening carpet beyond the window. "Why are you under suspicion? Have you done something to make them look in your direction?"

He propped his elbow on the mantel and pinched the bridge of his nose. He fingered the pocket Bible on the mantel. "Not since I got to Sawyer's Gap, no. But before . . ."

Catherine tucked her feet up beneath her, spreading her skirt over them for warmth. "Well, we're going to be here for a while. Do you want to tell me about it?"

He didn't look at her. "Not particularly. It's not something I'm proud of."

He moved to the leather chair and sat. "But I guess it's only fair." He brushed something off his knee. The muscles in his jaw flexed. "I didn't have your kind of life growing up." He glanced up at her. "My mother handed me over to my grandparents when I was three years old and I never saw her again. I have no idea who my father was."

Catherine thought of the orphanage in New York she and her mother used to visit. They donated food from the grocery store that would otherwise go bad. She was haunted by the lonely, longing eyes of the children who had no one in the world to care for them.

"My grandparents were too old to keep up with me," Rogan continued, "and I got harder and harder to control the older I got. Eventually they had to ask me to leave." He sighed. "Anyway, last year I...I was arrested for bootlegging in Lander."

He seemed to search Catherine's eyes for something. She didn't know what it was, but she refused to look away no matter how uncomfortable his curious gaze made her. Her heart raced until he looked toward the fire.

"Fortunately, there was a local pastor, Marion Dodds. He visited me while I was in jail waiting to hear my fate. Somehow he and his wife, Frieda, convinced the judge to let me go home with them. They claimed responsibility for me." He shook his head. "I had no idea what a blessing it was that those two came into my life."

Catherine sensed that he'd given her the very short version of his life. Probably leaving out the truly seedy details. She drew in a deep breath. "I suppose they were. Saving you from prison and all."

"Yeah, there's that, too." For the first time that morning, Rogan smiled.

Confused, Catherine tilted her head at him. "What do you mean?"

Still smiling, Rogan eased into the chair, fully relaxed. "Because of them, I met Jesus. I mean, here's this married couple with six kids of their own, and they didn't hesitate to take me in as well." He leaned his head against the chair's high back, grin still tugging at the corners of his lips. "Those kids... There was Raymond, the oldest. You've never seen a harder working kid, although he also had a bit of a chip on his shoulder. He was tough. Protective of his younger siblings. After him was Les, then Norman, then Gerald, and the girls, Bev and Janet."

He started to laugh. "Gerald was a cute little guy. And he had this chicken that loved to chase Janet around the yard. She hated that chicken."

Catherine laughed at the mental image. "It sounds like a lovely home."

"The home itself was modest. Pretty cramped, actually. But there was a lot of love. A lot of laughter. And Frieda's cooking." Rogan rubbed his stomach. "Anyway, one of the rules for me staying there was that I had to go to church with the family. And seeing as how Marion pastored a church, I spent a lot of time in church. But I listened, and I took it in. And because of him, I'm now a follower of Jesus."

Seeing the contentment on his face, Catherine wished she could have grown up in such a home.

"So what's your story, Catherine? How did you come to know Jesus?"

Catherine's stomach tensed. Know Jesus? What did that mean?

CHAPTER 7

Catherine ignored Luke's question and walked to the fire. It seemed to be the only escape when one of them wanted to avoid each other in this place. She picked up the poker and moved logs around for no reason. Sparks and ashes scattered.

"Catherine?"

Rogan's voice her sent her stomach twitching. She faced the kitchen. "I don't know what we'll have for lunch. I used all the ham for breakfast. There are some canned foods in the pantry, but I didn't take the time to read what they were." She chanced a look in his direction.

His furrowed brow and narrowed eyes spoke to his confusion. "Did my question offend you?"

"No. Of course not. It's just that—well, it's private."

He tilted his head to one side. "Private?"

"Yes." She added under her breath, "And it's none of your business anyway."

Rogan leaned forward in the chair. "What was that?"

"Nothing. I'm going to look at those cans."

Escaping to the kitchen, Catherine's mind turned over and over. Why were people so inquisitive about such things? Things she didn't understand. It frustrated her every time she attended services. She sat in her pew next to Mother and Father and listened to the hymns and the preaching. All the people around her seemed so happy, nodding their heads, murmuring "amen." They all had a secret she would never know. It left her empty. And longing. Longing for what? She wished she understood.

She examined the cans one by one—more cans than she'd led Rogan to believe. Canned salmon, beans, various vegetables and soups. Not the fine food she was used to, but they wouldn't starve.

"There's plenty there for us to eat."

Rogan's voice startled her. She jerked to face him.

"I checked it out when I got here. You know, *before* you." The most charming grin tugged at his lips.

Catherine couldn't help but smile back at him. She stepped out of the pantry and watched him pull on his coat and gloves and pick up his gun. Anxiety struck. "You're leaving?"

"I'm going out to see if I can catch us something fresh for dinner."

She released a relieved breath and muttered, "As long as it isn't another raccoon."

Rogan sighed. "Would you please stop doing that?"

"Doing what?"

"Mumbling under your breath like that. You do it all the time."

She huffed. "I do not."

"How many times have I had to ask you to repeat yourself since you got here yesterday?"

Catherine frowned. He did make her repeat herself. An annoying habit.

He pointed at her. "Just think about it. Every time you have to repeat yourself, or you bat those pretty green eyes at me and say, 'oh, nothing,' it's because you're mumbling. And it drives me crazy."

Catherine stuck her tongue out at him.

He laughed and opened the door and went outside.

Catherine shivered against the icy chill that invaded the cozy little cabin. But one thought melted the cold. Rogan thought she had pretty eyes.

Catherine watched Rogan through a cleared spot on the frosty window. He plowed his way through the snow, rifle on his shoulder, so strong and sure. Until Rogan, the men she knew wore fine clothes, were highly educated, poised in society and politics, and thoroughly boring. Rogan was rugged, gruff, opinionated, and thoroughly intriguing. He was masculine and unapologetic. She giggled and covered her mouth with her fingers. What would Mother think if she were to bring Rogan Meuller home? Deborah Whitmore would take to her bed with another of her headaches.

She returned to the warmth of the fireplace. The Bible on the mantel caught her eyes again. The scripture she'd read about a place of shelter appealed to her. That's what this cabin had become for her. Was that what the scripture meant? Catherine worried her lower lip. Rogan seemed to understand such things. Did she dare ask him? Or maybe...

She looked out the window again, scanning the snow-covered scenery for a glimpse of Rogan. He was nowhere in sight. He wouldn't come back until he'd captured their dinner. She tiptoed to the ladder and looked up at the loft. Before she lost her nerve, she scurried up the stairs to where Rogan slept. The bed wasn't made up, showing signs of a restless night. Catherine's brow twitched at the length of the bed. Rogan must have been quite uncomfortable here.

The thought of him lying in this bed sent an odd tremor through her belly. She carefully sat on the edge, feeling as if she were doing something terribly unseemly. She couldn't help but run her fingers over the pillow he laid his head upon. Warmth spread up her fingers into her arm.

A branch outside snapped in the wind with a loud *crack*. Catherine shot to her feet, expecting to see Rogan at the bottom of the stairs, glaring up at her for invading his private space. But no one was there. She held her hand to her chest, closed her eyes and blew out a tense breath. She had to focus on what she came up here for. It must be here somewhere.

Catherine scanned every surface in Rogan's sleeping quarters and peeked in the bag that held his things. She couldn't find it. When she was about to give up, she saw it peeking out from under his pillow. Her heart went fluttery. She reached for the Bible with trembling fingers. Holding what she was sure was Rogan's most prized possession in her hands, she gently opened the worn book. She found an inscription scribbled in the corner of the inside cover.

To Rogan. This book has served me well through the years. Hold it close to your heart, and it will do the same for you. Marion.

So the pastor had given Rogan his own personal Bible. She felt a new respect for what she held in her hands. Thumbing through the ragged edged pages, she noticed a piece of paper tucked into one page. She glanced down at the door of the cabin. No sign or sound of Rogan. Catherine unfolded the paper. Notes from Pastor Cecil's sermon last week on the book of Esther. Catherine looked at the page the notes were tucked into. The book of Esther. Frowning, she wondered why a man would be so interested in a story about an Old Testament woman in the Bible. Then a note caught her eye. Just beneath the name of the book. *My future wife.*

The handwriting matched the sermon notes. Rogan had written this. What did it mean? What could Esther possibly have to do with his future wife? Forgetting the danger of being caught, Catherine began to read the book that seemed to have captured Rogan's attention.

Catherine found the story fascinating and couldn't turn the pages quickly enough to learn what happened next. Fortunately it was one of the shorter books in the Bible, and she finished it quickly. Closing the Bible, Catherine still wondered what it had to do with Rogan's search for a wife.

The door downstairs opened, with a rush of cold air. Catherine froze. Her heart raced. Why, oh why, had she sat here and read for so long!

"Catherine?"

She shoved the Bible under his pillow and closed her eyes. Rogan called her name again. There was no way out. No way to avoid being found out. She slowly rose to her feet and walked to the top of the loft stairs.

"Cath—" Rogan went still. His eyes narrowed, his brow formed a sharp V. "What the—what are you doing in my room?"

Catherine scrambled down the steep steps. "I was just— Curiosity just got the better of— I only wanted to— I'm so sorry, I—"

"Just tell me." His voice was low, even, chilling. "What are you doing up there?"

Catherine stopped at the bottom of the stairs on trembling limbs. Her mouth opened, but she couldn't make any words come out.

"I'd have more privacy in prison than here in this place with you." Rogan shook his head and planted his hands on his waist. "Did you find what you were looking for? A gun maybe? To prove that I'm the one committing all the crimes in Sawyer's Gap?"

"What? No!" Catherine held her hands out and moved closer to him. "It was nothing like that."

"Then what was it?"

She had never seen blue eyes turn so dark. So cold. "I—I wanted to read your Bible." Tears blurred her vision as she braced for his next barrage of anger, knowing she deserved it.

He looked up at the loft and back at her. "Why? Don't you have your own?"

"Of course I do. But it's not something I carry with me."

He gestured to the mantel. "There's one right there. Why couldn't you read that one?"

It was a good question. For some reason, she'd needed to see *his* Bible. But she didn't dare tell him that. He'd want to know why, and she didn't have an answer. "I'm very sorry." She held her hands to her stomach. "I shouldn't have done it without asking you."

Rogan nodded mutely, no longer seething, but the suspicious look in his eyes remained.

Desperate to change the subject, Catherine craned her neck to look behind him, out the open door. "Did you catch anything?"

Sighing, Rogan propped the rifle against the wall. "No. The snow is too deep. Too heavy. The animals are hunkered in, waiting out the storm, just like we are."

His words, *just like we are*, sent a thrill through Catherine's middle. She shook her head. What was happening to her? She was normally so in control, poised, unaffected. But Rogan made her feel things . . .

CHAPTER 8

Rogan sank up to his knees in the snow. Three days stranded in the cabin, and they'd yet to have a real meal. Canned beans only sustained a man for so long. Catherine found one can of peaches in the back of the pantry that morning, so at least they had something different for breakfast this morning.

Catherine... Ever since he'd caught her in the loft the other day, they'd been in a complicated dance. Courteous to each other one moment and jumping down each other's throats the next. She had a kind heart. He knew that. He'd seen it. But she also had a sharp tongue.

So do you.

The quiet voice he'd learned to recognize as God's forced him to stop and be still. He hung his head in regret. It was true. There were many things that had changed in his life since he came to know Jesus, but his temper still needed work.

I'm sorry, Lord. You've been so patient with me. Help me to be as patient with Catherine. And please, help me to rein in my temper.

Rogan peered through the trees and shrubbery around him, using the point of the rifle to push branches aside. He waited. For a noise. Movement. Any sign that an animal had ventured out into the snow. Nothing.

After an hour of fruitless hunting, his legs and feet were numb. If he didn't get back inside to the fire, he risked frostbite. Fortunately the storm had blown over, but it would still take a week or more for the snow to melt enough for them to get back down the mountain. Rogan wondered if the culprit down in Sawyer's Gap had been caught yet.

As he trudged through the snow back to the cabin, yellow lights glowing in the windows in the distance beckoned him. Something about the sight lifted his sprits. He smiled at the image in his mind of Catherine sitting on the couch, reading her book, looking up to smile at him when he walked inside.

It wasn't just the glowing lanterns calling to him.

Rogan pushed the thoughts aside. Catherine didn't know Jesus. She was the furthest thing from his Esther as a woman could get. Again, an unbidden image forced its way into his mind. The look on her face when he'd caught her snooping around the loft. And her confession that she'd wanted to read his Bible.

Would he ever see a day when he didn't have to regret his actions? He shouldn't have been so harsh with her. He should have been happy that she wanted to read the Bible. He should have asked her what she read, and if she had any questions. Instead, the incident had been ignored over the last few days.

He climbed up the steps to the porch. Though defeat accompanied him for failing to catch anything for dinner, relief held him warm in its arms when he opened the door and stepped inside. Just as he'd imagined, Catherine sat on the couch, reading *Gone with the Wind*.

She looked up and smiled. "No luck?"

He smiled back, more to himself than to her. It was nice to have something, or someone, waiting for him. "No. I imagine the animals will start coming back out as the snow starts to melt though. It's getting slushy already."

He pulled off his boots and wet socks, set them by the fire, and then went up to the loft to change into dry socks and trousers. He came back down stairs and pulled the wing back chair closer to the fire. He sat and propped his feet up in front of the flames. His feet and legs tingled sharply as they warmed.

Rogan looked at Catherine, who had gone back to reading her book. He thought again of her sneaking in to read his Bible. The quiet voice deep inside urged him to ask her about it. He fought the urge. But it only got stronger.

"So, uh..." He coughed once. "When you were reading, you know, up there..." He motioned toward the loft.

Catherine glanced up. Her cheeks flushed pink, and she looked away again.

"Did you, uh, read anything...interesting?" He sounded like an idiot. And judging by the look on her face, she shared the sentiment. He held up his hand. "Never mind. It's none of my business."

"Actually, I did."

Rogan's attention snapped back to Catherine. He shifted a bit in the chair to have a better view of her. "Really? What was it?"

She set her book down, seeming to have difficulty making eye contact with him. "I kind of—well, I saw your notes—hidden in the book of Esther." Long lashes lifted just enough for him to see questions in her emerald eyes.

"Oh." Rogan nodded. She'd probably seen his note then, too. Irritation threatened, but he managed to suppress it. "Did you read it? The book of Esther, I mean?"

"Yes, I did."

"What were your thoughts?"

"Oh. My thoughts?"

Her confusion startled him. Had no one asked for her thoughts on a subject before?

"I—well—" Her brow pinched and she sat up straighter. "I thought it was a fascinating story. And I think Esther was a fascinating woman." She paused. "May I ask you a question?"

Rogan's heart began to thump in his chest. "Of course."

"Why were you so taken with the story?"

Smiling, Rogan sat forward in his chair and rested his elbows on his knees. "It's an amazing story of how God made her life complete."

Her frown didn't clear. "How so? I thought it was quite unfair that she was taken from her home and everything she knew, simply because the king wanted her. I understand how God used her to save the Jews, but I don't see how God made her any better for it."

"Don't you remember Pastor Cecil's sermon? The king chose Esther, yes, but she could have made it difficult on him. She could have run, or been a thorn in his side. Instead, she answered the king's call, giving her whole life to him. And when she did that, she found her purpose in life."

Catherine seemed to consider his words carefully.

"You see," Rogan continued, choosing his words carefully, "it's the same with us and God. He is our king. And He chooses us, just like King Xerxes chose Esther. And we have the same choice Esther did. In fact, we have an even greater choice. And when we choose to come to Him, to submit our will to His, to give Him our whole life, we find our purpose."

She nodded slowly. "I hadn't thought of that. I didn't think an Old Testament story would have anything to do with us today."

Chuckling, Rogan sat back in his chair. "You'd be mighty surprised just how much the Old Testament has to do with us today."

How handsome Rogan was when he smiled and talked about things he loved, like the Bible. Catherine thought about his explanation of the story of Esther. No wonder he'd written that note in his Bible. He wanted a wife like Esther. She could never measure up to such an ideal. She could never measure up to *Rogan*. There was probably some sweet, soft-spoken pastor's daughter out there somewhere who would be perfect for him.

And whoever she was, Catherine hoped she'd never have to meet her.

They fell into silence. Rogan in his chair, his eyes closed, soaking up the warmth of the fire. And her, dissatisfied with herself and her future. What was she to do with herself? She had no talents. She had money. That was all. Deep sadness snaked its way through Catherine's heart. What she wouldn't give to live a full life like Esther. To find purpose in her empty life.

The next thing she knew, Catherine awoke to a dying fire. Rogan knelt in front of it, adding logs. The supply on the porch must be nearly gone by now. He looked back at her and smiled. "Don't get up. I'll heat some soup for us."

"No. I'll do it." Catherine stood from her reclined position on the couch.

"I said you didn't have to. I don't mind doing it."

Unexpectedly, anger flared through her. "I guess that would make you feel better wouldn't it? Take care of the spoiled, coddled woman who can't do anything for herself."

"Whoa!" Rogan stood. "What's wrong with you? All I did was offer to make dinner."

"I can do it. I'm perfectly capable. There are a lot of things I can do, you know!"

"Fine!" Rogan threw his hands in the air. "Have at it."

Catherine stormed into the kitchen, snatched two soup cans from the pantry shelf, and slapped them down on the counter. She dropped a pot on the stove with a loud *clank* and began to pry open the lids on the cans. Mid task she stopped. What was wrong with her? Why was she acting so hateful? She hung her head.

That story. Rogan's expectations. Her failure to live up to either of them. Catherine was tired of her life. Nothing but passing time with mind numbing emptiness. Even a criminal like Rogan Meuller had a more fulfilling life than she did. And he spoke of Esther as if anyone could do what she did. It made no sense. Esther was clearly a special woman from the beginning. She was chosen because of her beauty. Although Catherine had been told throughout her life she was beautiful, she hardly had kings demanding that she be theirs.

"It's the same with us and God. He is our king. And He chooses us."

Rogan's words echoed in her mind. She knew God was king. Or Jesus was king. One or the other. Or both. But how did He choose people? He clearly chose Rogan. But how could Rogan know that God chose her? And why would He when there were so many better people in the world?

Questions, accusations and self-doubt clamored in Catherine's mind to the point that she held her hands to her head and squeezed her eyes shut, trying to shut them out. She couldn't. They would not relent. Finally, she stormed into the living room where Rogan sat quietly staring at the fire. "How?"

He looked at her, frowning. "What?"

"How does God choose people? How do you know who He chooses?" She held her arms out at her sides. "It makes no sense!"

Grinning, Rogan held up a finger. "Stay right there."

She opened her mouth to argue, but he set his finger on her lips. "Just for once, will you please listen to me?"

Her lips warmed at the touch of his finger. She stared at him wide-eyed, only able to muster a mute nod.

Rogan bounded up the stairs to the loft, and seconds later rejoined her in the living room. "Sit down."

This time she didn't try to argue. She sat down on the edge of the couch.

Rogan flipped through pages in his Bible. "Yes, here it is." He handed her the Bible and pointed to a spot on the page. "Read it."

Catherine held the Bible in both hands. She recognized the passage and looked up at him. "I already know this passage, I don't need—"

"Read it. Out loud." He folded his arms in front of his chest.

Sighing, Catherine began to read. " 'For God so loved the world, that He gave His only begotten Son, that whosoever believeth in Him should not perish, but have everlasting life.' " She looked up Rogan for further explanation.

He tapped the verse with his finger. "There it is. For God so loved the *world*. That means *everyone*. It's not just a stale passage of scripture, Catherine. It's the truth. He chooses *everyone*." His eyes softened and he sat beside her. "That's how I know He chose you. All you have to do is respond."

Catherine stared at the words on the page of Rogan's Bible. Was it really that simple? If God loved the whole world enough to send His son, then that meant . . . no one was better than anyone else. Could it be true that she was good enough? Tears blurred her vision and spilled onto the page. She swiped them off the page as quickly as she could. "I'm so sorry. I don't want to ruin your Bible."

"Tears don't ruin the Bible. They make it stronger."

She looked in his eyes, seeing all the kindness, and impatience and gentleness and irritable ways that made him so intriguing to her. "How does one—how did you say it?—respond?"

The biggest smile she'd ever seen on his face stretched across his rugged features. He shrugged broad shoulders. "You pray. Ask God to forgive your sins, your shortcomings. Ask Him to take over your heart and your life. After that you learn, day by day, how to please Him. And as you do, He gives you the tools you need to live for Him. It might take some time for certain lessons to set in. I guess you've figured that out by being stuck with me though."

Catherine raised a brow at him and smiled. She thought for a moment about what he had shared with her. "So do I have to do this with the pastor? With you? Can I do it alone?"

His smile faded. "No, you don't have to do it with anyone. You can do it alone if you like."

Nodding, Catherine stared at the verse again. Words she'd heard so many times, but had never truly understood until now. She handed the Bible to him. "Thank you. I'm going to finish heating the soup."

Chapter 9

Finish heating the soup? Rogan stared after Catherine. He'd just shared with her how to give her life to Jesus, and she was thinking about soup?

He sat back in the couch, defeated. He thought for sure she was going to respond to the call of God right then and there.

You didn't.

Again, that quiet voice speaking to him. He thought back to when Marion Dodds first began sharing the Gospel with him. Rogan had resisted just like Catherine. He hadn't believed it was that simple. He didn't think he deserved any part of it. Was that what Catherine felt? How could she feel that? She was so much better a person than he'd been.

As soon as the thought entered his mind, the absurdity of it did as well. He knew better than anyone that no one is good enough. A bootlegger like he was and a high society woman like Catherine were on equal footing when they stood before Jesus. And thank goodness for that.

Catherine needed time to absorb what she'd learned. He got up and joined her in the kitchen, thankful that he'd had the chance to share the gospel with her. Watching her at the stove ladling soup into bowls, Rogan couldn't help the feeling of desire that raced through him. He'd been fighting such feelings since the day he first laid eyes on her. Maybe she was his Esther after all.

She turned and looked at him. "What?"

"Hmm?"

Catherine eyed him for a moment. He smiled. Pink flooded her cheeks and she averted her gaze. "The soup is ready. And we still have canned peaches if we choose, for dessert."

Something about their conversation had opened the floodgates in Rogan. He allowed himself to enjoy being served dinner by her, enjoy her smile, her eyes. She seemed much more self-conscious than usual and squirmed a bit under his gaze. He kinda liked it. But he had to hold back voicing his feelings. She wasn't there yet. He couldn't allow himself to truly love her until she gave her heart to Jesus. Until she responded to her King.

Rogan stared out the window at the slushy snow sparkling in the morning sun. It had taken over a week for the snow to melt enough that they could venture out and try getting down the mountain. The past several days with Catherine had been enjoyable—with bouts of irritation. He smiled to himself. Somehow he suspected it would always be that way with her, and he didn't mind. Maybe an Esther with an attitude was more to his liking than he'd realized.

"It's time, isn't it?"

Rogan turned to face Catherine. She didn't look at him. Her eyes were on the sight beyond the window. Worry lined her forehead.

"I think so. We've been hungry for two days now. What little food was here is gone. And they'll be looking for us soon anyway."

Nodding, Catherine squared her shoulders. "I'll pack my things."

Rogan's heart hurt at the worry he saw written on her face. Would her fiancé be there waiting? Would her mother berate her for running away? Would her reputation be damaged for being here with him? Had they caught the culprit of the robberies and shooting, or was he still the prime suspect? So many unknowns awaited.

There was nothing he could do but pray and hope that things had been worked out while they had been here. Rogan went upstairs and packed his own things. When he came down, he found Catherine in the middle of the floor.

Her gaze roamed the tiny cabin. "I'm going to miss this place."

"Me, too."

"A shelter..." She seemed to drift away for a moment. "I read in that Bible on the mantel, the first day I came here. The scripture where the bookmark is."

Rogan nodded. "So did I. God does use this place as a shelter, doesn't He?"

She answered him with a smile.

They left the cabin together and walked around back to where her car sat. Rogan used a branch to sweep away slush from the windows, hood, and trunk. The '35 Cadillac was a beautiful car for sure. He hoped it had what it took to make it down the mountain.

"Would you mind driving?" Catherine asked.

"Uh..." He made a face. "Are you sure that's a good idea? For us to return together? I was just going to hike back down."

She shrugged. "We've been here for nearly two weeks together. I'm sure they won't be surprised. I'd feel much better if you drove. I don't know how to drive on slippery roads like this."

"All right then." They climbed into the car. He reached for the ignition. "Let's hope it starts."

"Oh it will. I prayed."

His attention jerked back to her. "You—You what?"

Her eyes held a new sparkle when she smiled. "I prayed." She rested her hand on his arm. "I responded to the King, Rogan. Because of you. Thank you for telling me how."

Unable to control his laughter, Rogan clapped his hands. "You are very welcome! I'm so happy!"

Her giggle ignited desire in him that he had no interest in squelching. He cradled her face in both of his hands. "Catherine Whitmore, I have been falling in love with you since that first day I saw you in the Five and Dime."

Wide emerald eyes stared at him. "You have?"

"Yes. I have." Her pink lips beckoned. "May I kiss you?"

"Please do."

She returned his kiss with all the gentleness, love, and kindness he'd imagined. This was his Esther. Better yet, this was his Catherine.

Epilogue

"Mrs. Mueller, Pastor Cecil sent another request for a family outside Sawyer's Gap." Catherine turned and accepted the piece of paper from Betsy Carmichael. Rogan looked over her shoulder to read the note. "All right. Rogan, will you help Betsy fill a box for this family and deliver it before lunch?"

Sixty-year-old Betsy winked at Catherine. "Any reason to spend more time with that handsome husband of yours."

Giggling, Catherine wagged a finger at her. "Just remember, he's taken."

Rogan laughed and draped an arm around Betsy. "I don't know, sweetheart, Betsy's got some pretty irresistible charms." He kissed the elderly woman on the cheek and helped her out the door.

Catherine turned back to the work on her desk. The door opened behind her once again. She didn't turn around. "I knew you'd come back for a kiss."

Her father's voice emerged in laughter. "Well, I wouldn't turn one down, that's for sure."

"Oh!" Catherine turned and stood. "I'm sorry, Daddy. I thought you were Rogan."

"Clearly." He pulled her into a hug and kissed the top of her head. "You know, a year ago, I wasn't so sure this would all work out for the two of you."

"Me either. It took two months to learn it was Daniel Mitchell causing all that trouble in town, and even longer for mother to get over my turning Benjamin down for marriage."

"You did the right thing, honey. I'm very proud of you and Rogan both. Helping me run the store and starting your own charity, giving food to those in need."

Rogan strode breathlessly into the room and took Catherine in his arms. "Excuse me, Mr. Whitmore, but I forgot to kiss my wife."

"No problem, son. No problem. I was just telling her how proud I am of the woman she has begun."

Catherine smiled. "I responded to my King." She looked into Rogan's eyes. "And I found my purpose."

THE END

Promise for Tomorrow

JALANA FRANKLIN

"Cast all your cares on him because he cares for you."
1 PETER 5:7

To my Posse: Thanks for praying for me,
being there for me, and believing in me.
To my kids: Thanks for sharing me with my laptop.
To my husband, Keith: Thanks for your unending belief
that I can to do anything.

CHAPTER 1

Late April 1951
Big Ivey, Wyoming

Margaret sat on her knees on the truck seat and gazed at Daddy through the back window. He stood at the end of the drive while her sister drove her away. He didn't wave. Was he thinking, like her, they'd never see each other again? She tried to memorize every line of his face, every whisker, and every sparkle in the bluest eyes this side of Heaven.

Her sister's voice sniped out. "You need to sit down, Margaret. What if I suddenly had to hit the brakes? You'd go right through the glass."

Margaret plopped down in the seat, and fiddled with the hem of her dress. "I'm not a baby, Camilla. I'm practically a woman, and you need to treat me like one."

Camilla's eyes flashed. "I'll have you know I can turn this vehicle around and drive you right back. I don't have to involve myself in this, you know. I'm only trying to help, and you don't sound very appreciative."

Margaret folded her arms across her chest, rolled her eyes toward the window, and blew out an exasperated sigh. "I do appreciate you. I just don't want you bossing me. If you didn't come get me, I don't know what would have happened. Mama got really crazy this time." She nibbled on her thumbnail, contemplating whether or not to tell her sister about her plans.

Camilla stretched her neck and looked at the rear-view mirror. "You can stay a week, but you'll do all the dishes and the laundry to pay for your keep."

Margaret curled her fingers into fists. "No."

Camilla jerked her head around and stomped the brake pedal, tossing both of them forward. Margaret grabbed the dash to stop herself. An approaching vehicle honked as it narrowly missed them on the driver's side.

"What did you say?" Camilla's icy stare could have frozen a lake.

Margaret breathed a long sigh. "I meant, I'm not going to your house this time. I want to go live with Mrs. Edith."

Her sister threw her hands up, and turned towards the driver's window. "Really?" She placed her hands back on the steering wheel, and began tapping one long polished nail on the top.

Margaret searched for words, but none came. None she wanted to blurt out anyway. Camilla had a sharp tongue, and Margaret didn't want to be on the receiving end of it.

Finally Camilla broke the silence. "And just where did you get the idea to go and live with her? You, of all people, know better than anyone, it won't work. Mama will have you picked up before you even get there. How do you intend to get there, anyway?"

Best time to spring the ride part on her, too. "I was hoping you'd take me." Camilla shook her head. "No. It'll never work."

"Why not? Oh, come on, Sis. Mama'll be expecting me to stay with you, like I always do when she takes a mind to boot me out. You can just take me halfway and come back tonight. She'll never know. You'll go to work tomorrow, like always, the kids will stay with Miss Virgie, and I'll be gone. It's the perfect plan. Please, Camilla? Please?" She laced her fingers together in front of her chest, silently begging.

Camilla laid the back of her wrist across her forehead and left it there, head resting on the back of the seat. "Do you have this worked out with Mrs. Edith, or are you just making this up right now? Because if you're telling me a story, I'm done. I know how you like to dream, Margaret, and I'm sure Mrs. Edith has better things to occupy her time."

"No, no! I've been writing to her since the last time she brought us dresses." She rummaged through her bag and pulled out a stack of letters, tied with a faded pink ribbon. "She gave me her address. Told Mama it would be good practice for school, for me to write to her. So Mama didn't say anything. I know she's opened some of the letters, but I don't think she suspects anything. We've been writing in code."

"Code?" Camilla took one of the letters from Margaret and studied it.

Margaret pointed to capital letters scattered throughout the letter. "See? When you put these big letters together, they spell out a message."

Camilla continued to frown at the letter. "Why would she send for you?"

"Mrs. Edith knows about Mama. She saw one of her fits the last time she came. I was so embarrassed. Mrs. Edith pulled me over to the side and told me she'd help me get away from it, so I've been planning this for a long time.

'Bout six months." Margaret bit at a little piece of skin on the side of her finger. She pulled too much, and it bled.

Camilla folded the letter, and placed it back in the envelope. "So how are you expecting to pay for all of this?"

"Daddy gave me a five dollar bill. Won't it pay for the gas?"

Her sister blew out an exasperated breath. "I'm not talking about that. I'm talking about the rest of the way. If I take you half-way, how will you pay for the rest?"

Margaret raised her brows and smiled. "Mrs. Edith is going to send a check to a post office box at this little town called Sawyer's Gap. Ever heard of it? It's about ninety miles from here. I can stay in a little cabin there. It's up in the woods, I think. Anyway, I can stay there until the check arrives, and then I'll take a bus down to Denver. Now, I know you're thinking it's terrible of me to take money from her, but I don't see it as any different from us taking clothes and shoes from her all these years. I'm in need, and I've already promised to pay her back once I get a good paying job. Unless you want to give me the money."

Camilla snorted. "I don't have that kind of money just lying around."

"Well, Mrs. Edith does, and you know it." Margaret licked her lips and took a deep breath. "So, will you take me?"

James MacKenzie awakened late. He'd intended to check on things at the construction site before his morning ride up the mountain, but the sun peeking through his window over the top of a grove of aspen trees encouraged him to skip the site and make his rounds across the property instead. He dressed quickly, pounded down the railed staircase two risers at a time, and entered the kitchen. Breakfast was over, but a pot of coffee, still hot and half full, waited on the stove. He poured the fragrant brew into his Thermos. The Thermos fit snugly in his jacket's right patch pocket. He wrapped two biscuits and some sliced ham from the icebox in a checked cloth napkin and filled his left pocket. Then, ready for the day, he stepped out into the small fenced-in yard surrounding his parent's home.

He stretched his arms above his head and inhaled the fresh scent of morning as he surveyed the sun's glorious beams highlighting dew covered branches in beautiful shades of green and blue. "Lord, You truly are an artist."

Still basking in the morning's beauty, he ambled to the barn. His favorite horse, Jade, stood ready in her stall. James greeted her with a gentle rub on her velvety nose. "You ready for our ride, girl?" She whinnied a reply. "That's my sweet." He set to work with his bridle and saddle. Within minutes, James led her out of the barn and into the yard. He swung his leg up over the horse's back, talking to her in soothing tones.

The moment he settled himself in the saddle, Jade took off with a gentle canter. Sometimes he thought Jade enjoyed the rides up the mountain even more than he did. Maybe he'd ride all the way to Grandmother's cabin. Jade could rest up in the barn, and he could go inside, read his Bible for a little while, and drink his coffee. Someone needed to check on the place. On his last visit he'd found a raccoon in the kitchen, helping itself to a jar of peanuts. It took a few hours to get him out. The time before that he'd found a hobo, loading his bag with anything loose.

Eager to make sure all was well, he urged Jade to the clearing where his family's cabin had stood for almost seventy-five years. Flowering dogwoods and redbuds created a canopy over the wood shingled roof. He drew Jade to a stop and admired the scene for a few minutes. A photo of this spot would definitely win a prize in any magazine. Good thing not many people knew the old cabin was there, or they'd be flocking to it.

James dismounted and led Jade to the small barn sitting behind the cabin. Tall grass grew along the barn's foundation, and Jade lowered her head and bit off a mouthful. He tethered her and headed for the cabin. He stepped onto the porch, the aged wood creaking as he crossed the wide planks. He reached for the door and then stopped, frowning. A pair of ladies loafers sat right next to the door. They were caked with mud. Creases across the toes and the thin soles spoke of much use. James sent a glance left and right. Was the person they belonged to still around?

Holding his breath, he turned the knob to open the door. He took one step inside. A shrill scream met his ears, and then a shock of pain passed through his head, landing him face down on the planked floor.

Chapter 2

James wanted to get up. His Thermos under his hip bone felt like a boulder. But something heavy between his shoulder blades pinned him down.

"Do not move! Not even a wiggle!" A sharp voice spoke from above him. "I can smash your head in!"

His pounding head made him groggy, but he sorted out that his attacker was a female, she held him down with her foot, and he wasn't supposed to wiggle. He spoke into the floorboard. "So, if I tap my finger, you're going to smash my head in?"

"Of course not."

"But isn't that what you just said?"

"Never mind what I just said!" Her foot crunched down harder. "I promise you, there's nothing here you want, so once I let you up, you will march right back out that door, and head back to wherever it is that you came from. Do you hear me?"

Was she wearing boots? The corners of a heel dug into his spine. Her voice was gruff, too gruff, like she was trying to sound tougher than she really was. James swallowed a chuckle. "If you could just listen to me for a minute, I'm sure we can clear this up. My grandmother owns this cabin."

She let up on her foot enough that James was able to turn his head sideways and get a bit of a look at her. She was just a waif of a girl. Not even a hundred pounds. Blond-haired. And scowling..

She jammed her foot hard again. "Don't look at me!"

"Yes, ma'am!" James turned his gaze to the legs of the dining table and thought about the breakfast he'd passed up for this treatment. A trickle of sweat ran across his upper lip. "But I, um, I think you're wearing my boots."

"What? What did you say?"

"I said those are my boots."

"Not about the boots. What did you say about your grandmother?"

"My grandmother owns this cabin. I'm James MacKenzie." He risked another sideways glance at her. "Did you hit me with the poker?" No wonder his head throbbed unmercifully. Queasiness attacked his belly.

She stepped aside and dropped the weapon. It clattered to the floor, almost bopping him again. "Oh, yes, I did! I'm so sorry, Mr. MacKenzie." She grabbed his arm and pulled. "I have permission to be here. From Mrs. Edith." She'd lost her gruff voice. Now she just sounded pitiful, as if he'd bested her. "Can I get you a glass of water?"

James wriggled free of her hold and eased himself to a sitting position. He leaned against the doorframe and closed his eyes. He touched the tender knot forming on the top of his head. She must have hit him hard.

He squinted at her. "A glass of water sounds really good right now." Maybe he'd pour it over his head. "Even though you're too pretty for the name, I might have to call you Superman."

She gawked at him.

He'd better explain so she didn't think she'd knocked the sense out of him. "You hit me really hard, knocked me down, and took me prisoner." It hurt, but he waggled his eyebrows up and down a few times to show he was teasing.

"And I did apologize!" She wrung her hands. "I am truly sorry for attacking you, but you opened the door without knocking, and I wasn't expecting anyone. Mrs. Edith said the place would be deserted." She gave him a sheepish half-smile, holding her hands palm up.

"Well, for what it's worth, I wasn't expecting to visit anyone. I just came up to check on things."

She crouched before him, her blue eyes wide and uncertain. "Mrs. Edith didn't write to you? Or call?"

"Mrs. Edith..." James frowned. "Who is she? My grandmother has a sister named Edith." He tilted his head, thinking. "But she lives in Denver."

A smile broke over her face. "Yes! Yes, that's her!"

He eyed her. She'd probably found Edith's name in the journal they kept for people to write in. "How do you know Edith?"

She stood and hurried to a bucket on the table. She returned with a dripping tin dipper and held it out to him. "I've known her since I was a child."

He took the dipper and sipped. She must have gone to the spring behind the cabin shortly before he arrived, because the water was fresh and cold. He took another, longer draw, while she talked.

"Mrs. Edith's always bought clothes for me and my sisters. I write letters to her, and she writes me back. We're kind of like pen pals. I'm actually headed to her house, once I leave here." She nibbled on her thumbnail, gazing at him with pleading eyes.

Now that his head was clearing, he fully noticed how pretty she was. Blond hair, not the bleached kind actresses wore but the natural, sun-kissed kind, hung in two thick braids along the bodice of her dress. Eyes as gray-blue as a sky on a cloudy day while rain slowly falls gazed at him. No make-up marred her smooth skin. She would make a fine catch for some young man if she weren't so young and in some kind of trouble. She must be in trouble, or she wouldn't be hiding here.

"Are you a runaway?"

The girl's shoulders tightened, and she seemed to hold her breath for a moment. "Do you want the truth, the absolute truth? If you do, I'll tell you the whole story. If not, then I'll simply tell you that I'm not a runaway." She fumbled with the skirt of her apron, one his grandmother had left in the cabin.

He wanted the whole story, but first he needed to fill the empty ache in his middle. "I'd like to hear it, but you'll have to tell me over some breakfast." He removed the items from his jacket pockets. The Thermos cup was dented, and the biscuits were smashed flat. "I've got biscuits and ham. Would you like one?"

She took one look at the crumbly mess in the napkin and shook her head.

James couldn't blame her. They looked awful, but he'd eat them anyway. "Okay. How about I sit here on the floor, and you can sit there at the table. You talk, and I'll listen." He didn't even know her name. But it didn't matter right then. She needed someone to listen, and he was there, so he'd listen.

While he ate the ham and biscuit crumbs, she told him a bizarre tale of her mother treating her like a servant, expecting her to cook and clean and toil with never a word of thanks. The story reminded him of a fairy tale from a book, except it was usually a stepmother mistreating the hapless child.

"Mrs. Edith saw how Mama was to me, and she promised she'd help me escape as soon as I was old enough. She told me I could stay in this cabin until she sent me money for a bus ticket to Denver. She said she'd send it to a box at the Sawyer's Gap post office. She wrote in her last letter, 'Margaret, I will help you find a job and get a place of your own.'"

So her name was Margaret. It suited her somehow.

She leaned forward in the chair, pressing her palms to her knees. "But you can't tell anybody I'm here. Nobody—not my parents or any of my sisters—

know where I am. Well, except for Camilla. She brought me here. But if my mother finds me, she'll make me go back home, even though she told me to leave."

James frowned. Something didn't make sense. "She told you to leave?"

Margaret nodded.

"Why would she send you away if she wanted you to do all the work?"

She sat straight up. Fire flashed in her eyes. "I'll be eighteen in four months. She said I was old enough to make my own way since I was lazy and didn't earn my keep." Her eyes brimmed with unshed tears. She held her hands up, palms out, as if fending off blows. "Honest, Mr. MacKenzie, I didn't know anyone would be coming up here. Mrs. Edith told me the cabin's only for holidays and such, and that I could stay as long as I needed to."

He stared at her hands. Calluses dotted both palms. Someone was a liar, because those hands didn't belong to a lazy person. James wadded up the napkin and jammed it into his pocket. He used the doorjamb to pull himself to his feet. "Well, miss, I—"

She balled her hands into fists and shoved them in to the folds of the apron skirt. "Don't make me leave. I'm afraid of what Mama'll do to me if I go back. Can't I stay here, Mr. MacKenzie?"

Her story might be far-fetched, but her fear was real. James smiled. "My dad's Mr. MacKenzie. Just plain old James will do for me."

Her eyes flew wide. "You're James B. MacKenzie?"

He drew back. "I am. How did you know?"

She pointed to the mantel. "The journal. I hope you don't mind. I've been reading it."

Ah, yes, the journal. "I mostly write my thoughts and prayers to God, but if you enjoy it, then by all means, read on."

She glanced aside, and he sent his gaze across the small kitchen. Empty cans filled a bucket by the stove, and a few dishes and pans rested on the dry sink. She'd apparently been eating the food he store-housed in the pantry for hunting trips. He'd better replace it.

He turned to Margaret. "What's your full name?"

She nibbled her lip. "Sullivan. Margaret Sullivan."

"All right, Margaret Sullivan. I think we should give your father a call and let him know you're safe."

Margaret bowed her head and pinched the bridge of her nose. "Didn't you hear anything I said?"

"Of course I heard you." He folded his arms over his chest. "I just can't imagine why your mother would come up here to find you if she threw you out. Why would she want to bring back an unwanted child?"

"You don't understand... She doesn't want *me*, she wants to be in control. She... She..." Margaret's eyes brimmed over. She hunched her shoulders and turned away.

An ugly picture formed in James's mind. "Why are you so afraid of her, Margaret? Did she hurt you?"

She jerked to face him. Red streaked her teary cheeks. "I'm never going back. I won't go back."

What should he do? Surely Great-aunt Edith wouldn't help the girl escape unless she thought Margaret was in some kind of danger. He'd have Dad or Grandma give Edith a call. In the meantime, he didn't want Margaret running off.

He spoke gently. "Well, you're safe now. Your mother's not here. You're heading to Denver, and then you'll be too far away for her to find you. Right?"

Margaret's jaw dropped a fraction of an inch, eyes wide. "You...you aren't gonna tell on me?"

He glanced at the discarded poker on the kitchen floor. "Are you going to clonk me over the head again?"

She shook her head so hard her braids flopped.

"Then I won't tell. Deal?" He held out his hand.

Slowly she inched close and placed her hand in his. Her grateful gaze met his, and something warm ignited in his chest. He pulled his hand free and rubbed his sweaty palm along his thigh. Time to leave.

"I've got to go to work now, but I'll bring up some supplies tomorrow morning. I'll also check at the post office. See if you've got anything there."

"Thank you, Mr.—I mean, James."

When she smiled, she was far too appealing. He opened the door. "You're welcome. 'Bye now." He bent over and snatched up the poker before stepping onto the porch. He'd put the weapon in the barn. Better safe than sorry.

CHAPTER 3

The next morning just after sunrise, Margaret stood on the edge of the porch with a cup of tea cradled in her palms and watched for James. She'd never been so eager to see anyone. And it was silly, too, considering how he'd thrown a kink into her plans of buying her bus ticket and quietly sneaking out of town without anyone knowing she was there.

She sipped the tea, trying to swallow the funny feelings that rose when she thought about James. He could probably turn a few heads. The girls at school would swoon over him for sure. All the boys at home combed their hair straight back, but James's shiny black hair hung down over his forehead with a little curl in the middle. Chestnut eyes framed by the longest, darkest lashes she'd ever seen on a man had gazed at her with such tenderness. No one had ever aimed a look of such kindness at her. Not even her parents. And, best of all, he'd said she was pretty. Handsome, kind James MacKenzie said she was pretty.

Heat flooded her face. No one had ever called her pretty before. Mama always said was homely, that she looked too much like Daddy, unlike her sisters who all resembled Mama. But James had called her pretty. Her chest went all fluttery again, remembering it. Wouldn't it be nice to have someone to call her own who said kind things about her? Someone like James...

But why would someone like him even give her a second glance? Mama always told her she'd never marry, because a man with any sense wouldn't pick a girl like her. She'd only be good for work, cleaning some rich person's house, or washing their clothes. Manual labor. That's what Mama'd called it.

A chill crept over her. She hurried inside the cabin and stood beside the stove for a moment. She needed to stop looking back and think about the future. Denver held a lifetime of promise for her. Even a homely girl could find work and purpose. So what if it was only cleaning? At least she'd be taking care of herself. And maybe, just maybe, she would fall in love. With a man who had no sense at all. She giggled, then automatically looked over her shoulder to make sure Mama wasn't listening, ready to pounce.

"Your mother's not here." That's what James had said. The fear fled.

She set her cup of tea down and crossed the floor to the mantel, where the journal she'd spent so much time reading waited. She paged through it, looking at the signatures. Mostly people in the MacKenzie family had written entries, but there were others, too. Margaret's favorites were ones placed in the journal pages by James. B. MacKenzie.

She touched her finger to his neatly penned name. On her first evening at the cabin, after reading one of his entries, she'd scoured the journal for more of his writing. While reading, she'd imagined James much older, maybe even deceased. Reality dawned bright and clear yesterday morning when he'd spoken his name. Margaret could have sworn her heart stopped on the spot. To discover the person whose words had enamored her was young and so handsome was like receiving a heartfelt wish.

When would he get here? Impatience stirred through her. Margaret looked forward to his arrival for more than the food he'd promised to bring. She wanted to get to know James B. MacKenzie better. Reading his prayers to God was water to her thirsty soul. She wanted to know God the way James did, like a close and personal Friend.

She glanced down and noticed little bits of dried mud on the floor. They'd probably fallen from her shoes after her morning trek to the spring. She could stay out of mud if she used the pump in the kitchen, but the spring water tasted so much better. She better sweep the floor before James arrived so he wouldn't think poorly of her staying in his family's cabin. She scurried to the pantry for the broom, and as she went she heard footsteps on the porch, then a knock at the door. Her heart ignited. James was here!

Margaret reached for the door handle instead of the broom.

"Miss Sullivan?"

She froze in place. That wasn't James's voice. She turned the lock on the door and shrank back.

Another knock. "I know you're in there. I've come to take you home."

Margaret dove into the pantry and closed the door. In the small, dark space, she panted with fear.

"Miss Sullivan!" The man banged on the door again and rattled the doorknob. "I'm the sheriff. I can break the door down if I need to, but I don't want to cause the MacKenzie family any trouble, so just open up. Your mother asked me to come find you, send you home."

Sweat dribbled down her forehead and stung her eyes. Margaret blinked in the shadows and hugged herself. She had to make the lawman understand. From the safety of the pantry, she hollered, "My mother told me to get out and never come back, so I'm not going." More sweat trickled down the side of her face, but she trembled too much to wipe it away.

The sheriff's voice came again. "I'm sure it was all a misunderstanding. Your mother misses you terribly. She's been crying for two days solid, she said. You think that's any way to treat your mother? Come on out, and we'll talk about it." The doorknob rattled again, harder this time.

"No!" She didn't mean to shriek, but fear turned her voice shrill. It sounded foreign to her ears. "I'm not coming out! I'm not going back. I'm seventeen. I'm old enough to quit school, and I'm old enough to be on my own."

"Now see here, Miss Sullivan—"

Margaret clenched her teeth and closed her eyes tight. No matter what he said, she wouldn't go with him.

Then Margaret heard another voice. "Hey, Sheriff. What seems to be the trouble?"

James climbed down from Jade's back.

Sheriff Kernshaw clomped over, his hands on his hips. "We have a little problem, but I hope we'll be able to wrap it up fairly quick."

James untied the pack of supplies from the back of his saddle. "What is it?"

"Seems we have a runaway."

He feigned surprise. "A runaway? Here?" He headed for the porch.

"Yes, sir." The sheriff trailed behind James. "Got a call last evening about a girl stayin' in a deserted cabin around these parts. Her mama wants her home. One of my deputies saw a blond-haired girl go in your cabin early this morning. She matches the description the mother gave me."

James set the parcel on the bench outside the door. How would Margaret's mother know she was near Sawyer's Gap? He hadn't told a soul.

Sheriff Kernshaw hooked his thumbs in his belt loops. "I'm sure you'll want to press charges for her breakin' in here like this. Her mama says she's destructive that way. Stays in trouble all the time back home. Stealin', lyin' and the like. You'll be glad to get her off your property." He clenched his teeth together and sucked in air. "Yep, mighty glad."

"Stealing?" James forced a dry chuckle. "Sheriff, you must have the wrong girl. The girl staying here has permission. Why, I was just bringing her up some supplies. See?" He pointed to the parcel.

The sheriff scowled at the bundle and then at James. "Are you saying a girl named Margaret Sullivan isn't staying in your cabin?"

James couldn't lie. "Yes, Margaret Sullivan is staying here, but she hasn't taken anything from us. She isn't hiding out. I'm sure there's a misunderstanding somewhere."

The sheriff scratched his head. "But her mama said—"

"Miss Sullivan's seventeen, Sheriff. That's old enough to be on her own."

Margaret's muffled voice came from the other side of the wall. "I'll be eighteen in four months!"

James choked back an amused snort. She drew her age like she'd drawn that poker.

Sheriff Kernshaw leaned toward the door. "Miss Sullivan? I'm, uh, gonna leave you alone for now and go make some calls. If you are seventeen, like Mr. MacKenzie here says, I don't see how your mama can make you come back home. You'd be old enough to make your own mind up." He turned to James. "I'll let you know what I find out."

Chapter 4

Margaret gritted her teeth together. She wanted a drink of water. Her mouth was dry as a sack of cotton. But she was too scared to come out of the pantry. Eyes closed, she slowly slid down the door, stamina running thin. How had Mama found her? Had James told on her? Wrapping her arms around herself, she pulled her knees up and laid her head on them.

"Superman?" James's voice came from right outside the pantry. "Where are you?"

She found her voice. "You go away. You're a rat!"

"Whoa now. What's all this about? I bring you food, and you call me a rat?"

She glared across the dark pantry. "You know what you did. Now go away. I mean it!"

A soft sigh carried through the wooden door. "If you're talking about the sheriff showing up here, I promise I didn't tell. I thought about it, but I didn't. I've only been to get food. That's all. You can trust me, Margaret. Please come out."

Margaret leaned her head back against the wall and closed her eyes. If he was the same James who wrote all of that stuff in the journal, then she knew he told the truth. He probably wouldn't go away until she went out anyway.

She rose, opened the door a few inches, and peeked out.

James leaned sideways and peeked at her. "That you, Superman?"

Margaret blinked several times, the anxiety of the whole episode coming to a head. Fresh tears welled up. She kept blinking, trying to hold them back, but a couple spilled over onto her cheeks.

James's gaze softened. "Lost your cape today?"

"I got somethin' in my eye." She rolled her eyes from side to side, wiping her lower lids with one finger. She bit her lip to keep it from trembling.

"Must be pretty big to cover both eyes like that."

Margaret ducked her head. "Yeah." She looked at him and then away. "I guess I could use a hanky. Or something."

"How about a hanky and a shoulder?" He took her hand and pulled her away from the pantry. "I'm sorry you had to deal with that. I know the sheriff. He's a good guy, and he won't bother you anymore. I'm sure of it. Here." He pushed a new white handkerchief into her hand.

Margaret dabbed her eyes and then wiped her nose.

"Got something big in your nose too?" He snickered.

"No." She pushed hard on his shoulder, but he hardly even staggered. "You big lug. You're being mean."

"Oh, really? Well, I beg to differ, madam. It appears that my hanky has strategically dislodged a large 'something' from both your eyes, as they are perfectly fine now. I should be your hero."

Margaret tried to smile, but her lips didn't want to cooperate, so she turned away again. "I suppose you are." She sniffed.

"Well, your hero has brought food." He pointed to a parcel on the table. "There's some fresh-baked cinnamon muffins in there. They're probably cold by now, but Grandma said they're just as good that way. And that woman is always right." He winked.

Margaret's tummy went fluttery, so she started unpacking the supplies. "I'd like to meet her. Your grandmother, I mean."

James helped put the items away. "Oh, I think that's a fine idea. She would love to meet you, too. She's very social and loves to entertain guests."

He set two napkins, the muffins, and a small jug of honey on the table. "Shall we?"

Margaret giggled at his playful formality. "Yes, we shall."

They sat down and James handed her a muffin. Before she took a bite, Margaret said, "Do you pray out loud the same way you pray in the journal?"

He stopped with a muffin only inches from his mouth. "Oh, I'm so sorry, Margaret. I didn't pray over the meal." His cheeks glowed pink.

He looked so shaken, she felt guilty. "No, it's fine, really."

"No, it's not. I shouldn't neglect something so important. I guess I got distracted by the commotion." He offered her his hand.

Margaret looked at him, and then to his hand. Confused, she placed her hand in his.

He bowed his head. "Our most gracious heavenly Father, we come to You with thanks in our hearts for the food we are about to receive. I also thank You, Father, for my new friend, Margaret, and I thank You for allowing her to reach us safely. Guide her steps, Lord, and give her assurance as to what You want for her life. In the name of Jesus we pray, Amen."

She stared at him, so humbled by his prayer. He'd prayed for her. And thanked God for her. Margaret wanted so badly to thank God, too, but she didn't know how. She blurted, "I really wanted you to tell me about how to pray. Your prayers in the journal are so beautiful, so poetic. I can tell you spend time with God. How do you pray such prayers?"

James set the muffin aside. "It's like you just said. I spend time with God."

"But how do you get to know Him like a friend?"

He smiled. "That's easy. I read the Bible. When we spend time in His word, He speaks to us. Do you have a Bible, Margaret?"

She squirmed in her seat and twirled her finger around a loose strand of her hair. "No. I never had one."

James took a bite of muffin. "Tomorrow—"

Her pulse leaped. He was coming back again tomorrow?

"—I will bring you a Bible. Everyone needs their own copy of the Bible. God's Word is a roadmap that tells you how to live and how to get to heaven. I don't know what I'd do without my Bible."

She waved her hands. He was going to too much trouble for her. "No, you don't have to do that. I can just read the one on the mantel."

"That little one?" He made a face. "It's old. From the Civil War, I think. Besides, that one belongs here. You need one you can keep. A bigger one that you can mark verses in and write notes in the margins, like I do. It helps to make notes, especially when you find something that really speaks to you." He smiled his heart-melting smile. "Having your own Bible will give you the opportunity to go back and study something you like."

"You're sure it's no trouble?" She held her breath.

"No trouble at all."

He was too good to be true.

The horse found her way to the house without any assistance from James. He wouldn't have been any help anyway. His mind was back at the cabin, with a very beautiful, very seventeen Margaret Sullivan.

She'd surprised him when she'd asked about his prayer life. So many things he took for granted every day, Margaret had probably never experienced.

He'd get her a whole bag of candy before going back tomorrow. Now to deal with Grandmother.

He put the horse in the barn and skirted around the flower gardens, careful to stay out of anything Grandmother could scold him about. Her face was framed in the kitchen window, looking out at him. What would he say? What would she ask? As always, he tried to mask his face with indifference by giving her his best schoolboy grin.

She was washing dishes as he came through the door. "So, how much do you like her?"

James shook his head. "I just met her today."

"Don't matter. I met your Grandpappy on a Sunday, and we married two weeks later. I fell hard, and he did, too. Slapped us right in the face."

The ticking of the old Seth Thomas on the mantel was as loud as a a woodpecker. "Did I say anything about marriage? Anything about falling? No. I didn't."

"You didn't have to. It's written all over your face." Grandmother set the plate aside and wiped her hands dry on her apron. "Shoulda' seen you out there, comin' down the drive. Lookin' all goofy. Good thing you was on Jade or you'd still be roamin' around up there in the woods."

James sighed. "How did you know about her?"

"Your great-aunt Edith called me. Told me that a girl would be stayin' up in the cabin for a spell."

"And just when were you planning to tell me about it? She hit me in the head with the poker. It would have been helpful to know she was there." He shook his head and rubbed the spot.

Grandmother made a sound through her teeth. "If I were you, I'd be finding out everything I could about her. Son, there ain't no picking's of girls left in this town. And I know you've been praying to God for a mate. Ever think He might have put this together?"

James sank into a kitchen chair. "I'm doing God's work, Grandmother. She asked me to help her with her prayer life."

"Call it whatever you want, sweetie. I say you're sweet on that girl." Grandmother sat across from James and patted his wrist. "And that's all fine and dandy. Never seen you lookin' so dreamy, James. Always been so serious."

He stifled a groan. "Grandmother, I am not dreamy. I'm tired. There's a difference."

"Tired, dreamy. Still have it bad for that Sullivan girl. Must be a real looker."

James remembered her soft skin under his knuckles and the clear blue of her eyes. "She is practically a child." He stressed every word. For Grandmother's sake. And his.

She smirked. "I happen to know from Edith that she's nearly eighteen. You being twenty and all, that would make a right smart match. Your Grandpappy was two years older than me."

James jumped up. "Grandmother, you're jumping to conclusions, and you're not the matchmaker you think you are."

"Sit down, James."

He sat.

Her eyes twinkled. "Is she pretty?"

"Yes."

"Do you like her?"

"I...I don't know."

"You like her."

"I do not."

"It's okay, Son. You can like her. You're a big boy now, old enough to find somebody."

James rolled his eyes and flipped his hands in the air. "All right. You win. I like her. You happy?"

"Yes." She moved to the counter and began stacking the dry dishes. "Nothing like a little romance, I always say."

James followed her. "Grandmother, I'm trying to help her get to Denver. Not really a good idea to think about romance."

"Denver, Shmenver. Just keep her here."

He swallowed a laugh. It wasn't that easy. "She won't stay. She's scared her mother will find her."

"And if she's married to you, what can her mother do about it?"

The wheels in his head started to turn. It could definitely keep her mother away from her, but he wanted to marry for love, not convenience. Even so, the idea kept swirling around in his mind.

"See?" She pointed at him, her grin knowing. "You're thinking about it. Makes sense, don't it?"

"Grandmother, right now I have a promise to keep. I told her I'd bring her a Bible. Do you have one I can give her?"

Her face lit. "I've got just the one. Belonged to someone who stayed here once, and she's passed on now." She crossed to the secretary in the corner and pulled out a large, thick Bible from the drawer. She thumped the Book on the table.

James recoiled. "I can see why your friend left it here. It looks like it's covered in mud."

"It is. Needs washing. I believe it got some dirt-daubers nests on it up in the attic one time. I brought it down here for...well, I don't remember why, but it must have been for you. Underneath all that, it's real purty leather." She swirled her hand around above the Bible like a feather duster. "It'll look nice when you get that mud off."

He scratched a fingernail across the cover. Dust formed a little cloud above the table. "Um...would you clean it for me?" He gave her his best little boy face, puckering his lip with all the conniving of a two-year-old.

She snorted. "Fine. Knew you'd wiggle out of it, somehow." She carried it to the sink. Her nimble hands made quick work of the mud. Soon, the beautiful luster of a burnished cinnamon color began to show.

James grinned. "It really is pretty! How about the inside? Any writing?"

"I believe it's got her name in it. She was doin' some travelin' with her husband. They took room and board here for a few days, and she left that Bible here with me. Marked some verses for me to read." Grandmother fingered the pages of the book. "Said she'd come back and get it one day, but she never did. Fine lady if there ever was one. I thought the world of her. She helped me through a rough time when my baby didn't live through the Great Pandemic back in nineteen eighteen."

His heart caught. "You had a baby that died? How come I never knew?"

"Ah, sometimes it's easier to leave things in the past. Doesn't hurt so much that way. Can't cry no tears over somethin' if you don't think about it." Her faraway gaze traveled out the window and up the mountain. A tear glistened on her cheek.

Guilt stabbed him in the gut because he'd made her remember the awful past. "I'm sorry, Grandmother." James wrapped her in a gentle hug and kissed her on the cheek. "I'd better get to the site before Dad thinks I abandoned the company. Love you."

She wiped her eyes and turned back to working on the Bible cover.

James headed out to the work truck. When he got to the end of the drive, he looked back, hoping to see Grandmother in the window like always, but she wasn't there.

Chapter 5

Margaret awakened late the morning after the sheriff's unexpected visit. She slipped on one of her dresses then topped it with a flannel shirt from the loft and a thick pair of wool socks that came clear over her knees. Considerably warmer, she opened the shutters on the windows and let the sunlight stream in.

She scoured the rise for a glimpse of James. Nothing. Yet. She fixed a pot of coffee, poured herself a cup, then stood at the window and watched some more. He'd promised to bring her a Bible, and she wanted to believe him, but as the minutes slipped by and he didn't ride over the rise, doubt crept in.

Tamping down her disappointment, she busied herself dusting and cleaning the cabin. When the sun was a dot directly overhead, even though she wasn't hungry, she got out some of the supplies James brought and began mixing a batch of baking soda biscuits. As she filled the stove's belly with kindling, a noise—a horse's whicker?—met her ear. She leaped up, scattering little chips of wood across the floor, and darted to the window.

James was climbing down from his horse's back at the edge of the yard. Her heart caught. He was even more handsome than yesterday in a blue plaid shirt, jeans, and boots, his hair tousled by the wind. As he tethered the horse to the limbs of a spruce, his muscles filled his shirt sleeves. She'd never seen such arms. Not overly big like super heroes in a comic book but solid like a sculpted statue. He turned from his task and looked toward the cabin. He froze in place, his gaze latched on hers. Margaret's breath hitched in her chest, and the back of her neck tingled all the way up into her hair.

In those few seconds a fanciful picture filled her head of waiting for James to come home from work, greeting him with a hug and kiss, letting him know he was back where he belonged. A foolish notion. He wasn't hers and never would be. She tore her eyes away, heart pounding so hard a wave of weakness washed over her entire body. She slumped against the edge of the table where a pan of biscuits waited to be tucked in the oven. She should get the stove going, but she couldn't move.

She didn't deserve the likes of a godly man. She knew she didn't. But why? Why didn't she deserve happiness? Had she been so terrible? She jabbed her thumbnail between her teeth, afraid she'd ask the questions out loud.

"Margaret?"

Margaret whirled around. James stood in the doorway. "J-James... You came back."

His brows slanted inward, a quizzical smirk forming on his lips. "Didn't I say I'd be back?"

"Um...yes. Yes, you did." Grabbing a towel from the dish rack, she swiped her moist forehead. The flannel must be making her hot. "I've been watching for you..." So much heat filled her face she could bake the biscuits. "I want that Bible you promised." She attempted a smile, sure it looked as fake as a wooden leg, and tossed the towel back to the rack.

His smile was genuine, though. "I'm glad you're so eager for the Bible. I brought one, and also a notebook and pencils from my grandmother. And don't even try to refuse them. She insisted you'd need them." He laid the items on the corner of the table. "I can stay for a while and study with you. Where would you like to start?"

Margaret's stomach plunged into an abyss of desperation. Didn't she tell him yesterday she couldn't quote Bible verses? What should she say without sounding like a dolt? "I'll just let you decide, you being the expert and all."

"Well then, I think we'll start by getting these biscuits baked." His eyes twinkled with teasing.

Her stomach fluttered as he crouched to get a fire going in the fuel chamber. She slid the pan of biscuits into the oven then followed him to the table. To her surprise, he pushed the table beneath the window.

He winked at her. "Let's work here where the sunlight is better. Don't want to strain those pretty blue eyes of yours." He pushed the chairs close to the table and sat.

Margaret stood rooted in the middle of the floor. Twice now he'd said her eyes were pretty. Did James MacKenzie talk like that to everyone, or did he really mean what he said? She blurted, "Do you really think I'm pretty?" She waved her hands at him. "Don't answer. It...it was forward of me to ask."

James gave her a look so intense the breath in her chest ceased to move. He rose and bridged the gap between them in one long stride. His broad hand cupped her chin. "Margaret..."

Sympathy shone in his eyes. She didn't want to hear his answer. She tried to turn away, but his firm yet gentle grip held her captive.

"No. Look at me."

Hesitantly, she lifted her gaze to meet his.

"I can honestly say you are the most beautiful girl I've ever seen."

For as long as she lived, Margaret would never forget those words and that moment. She wanted to thank him, but her tongue lost its ability to speak. Hot tears pricked behind her eyes then spilled over onto her cheeks and his fingers. Abashed, she jerked away and turned her back on him.

"Margaret?" He hand touched her shoulder. "Did I say something wrong?"

She hugged herself. "No."

"You're crying. I did say something wrong." He turned her around.

She kept her head low. "I'm not sad. I'm happy. I'm so happy I..." She sniffed and brushed the back of one finger under her eye. Could she trust him with her deepest hurts? "N-No one has ever told me anything like that before. I...I don't know what to say." She dared look into his eyes. Compassion looked back. More tears flowed.

James guided her to the table and eased her into a chair. He sat across from her and took her hand. "I know we haven't known each other long, but I care about you. God cares about you. He thinks you're beautiful too."

Something warm and wonderful bloomed in her chest. "God thinks I'm beautiful?"

"Yes. He loves each and every person on the face of the earth. He loves us so much, he gave His one and only Son to be the redemption for our sins. Let me show you." He opened the Bible, turned several pages, then angled the Book toward her. "Here, you can read His promise in your very own Bible."

Margaret drew back. "James, this Bible..." She gulped. So large, with a soft red-brown cover made of real leather. "It's so nice." Too nice for the likes of her. "I can't take this."

"Of course you can. Grandmother said someone left it at her house several years ago and never came back for it." His brows pinched. "I hope I haven't offended you by bringing you a used Bible."

She shook her head. "Used doesn't bother me." Hadn't she worn hand-me-downs and clothes from the charity boxes from Mrs. Edith her whole life? The Bible looked newer than anything she'd ever owned. "Are you sure it's okay for me to have this?" She held her breath.

James smiled. "If Grandmother says it's okay, it's okay. Now let's read."

Chapter 6

Over the next two weeks, James rode out to the cabin each day to study God's Word with Margaret. He couldn't stifle his fervency in helping her grasp her worthiness in God's sight, and he delighted in her eagerness to believe it. She reminded him of a sponge soaking it all in.

One evening in early May they sat side by side on the sofa with her Bible draped over his hand, open to the book of John. "Even though the Bible is full of stories, the most important one to me is how Jesus gave His life on a cross so we don't have to die in our sin."

She nodded, her face sweetly attentive.

He cleared his throat and focused on the topic. "Men are all born into sin, and all must be saved through Him. Jesus took our sin upon Himself, and His salvation is a free gift."

"And what does that mean?"

"What does what mean?"

"Salvation is a free gift."

His heart expanded, and he couldn't hold back a smile. "It means, dear Margaret, that you only have to accept it."

Confusion pinched her face.

He caught her hand and led her to the fireplace. He laid the open Bible on the mantel and pointed to the framed embroidery piece. "Read that to me."

Margaret sucked in a low breath. " 'And there shall be a tabernacle for a shadow in the day time from the heat, and for a place of refuge, and for a covert from storm and from rain.' "

He squeezed her hand, inwardly praying for God's Spirit to whisper to her heart. "Think about this cabin. Lots of different people have come through that door, and not one of them have had to pay a penny to stay. Many of them have found refuge from the elements, and many found refuge from the cares of life. In some ways, the cabin is like God. There in times of need, sheltering us from the storm, and giving us a place of rest. One day, though, this little building could let you down. The roof may cave in or the floor might rot. But

God..." He touched the wispy pages of the Bible. "He's *forever*."

"So, what you're saying is...if I tell God I want His salvation, He will just give it to me the same way Mrs. Edith has always given me clothes and shoes and now a place to stay?" He nodded. "That's right."

She chewed her lip for a moment. "Can God help me to find a new life?"

"God can help you with anything."

Margaret placed her hand over the Bible, her brow wrinkling. "I...I want the free gift of salvation, James. What do I do?"

He quickly turned pages to the sixteenth chapter of Acts. "Look here, Margaret. 'Believe on the Lord Jesus Christ, and thou shalt be saved...' "

Margaret whispered, "Believe..." She closed her eyes and folded her hands beneath her chin. "I believe You love me, God. I believe Your Son came to save me from my sins. I believe. Amen." She opened her eyes and a tear slipped down her cheek, but her lips curved into a smile.

James swept Margaret into a hug. "I'm so glad you've accepted the Lord as your Savior. It's a life-changing decision you'll never regret." He let out a shout of hallelujah. "I can't wait to tell Grandmother the good news!"

She wriggled loose, giggling. "Should we celebrate with some of the peach cobbler I baked this afternoon?"

Peach cobbler made for a fine celebration. He grabbed her Bible from the mantel and followed her to the kitchen. As he settled in one of the chairs, something in his pocket crinkled. He swallowed a groan. In his eagerness to study, he'd forgotten about the letter he found in the post office box in town. He pulled it out and held it toward Margaret. "I should have given this to you earlier. It came for you today."

"It's from Mrs. Edith." Happiness colored her face and tone. She opened the envelope and pulled out a folded sheet of paper. When she unfolded it, her eyes flew wide. "Money, James! A check for fifty dollars. I can buy my ticket now—tomorrow even. Aren't you happy for me, James?"

Margaret stared into James's unsmiling face. "What's the matter? I thought you wanted to help me get to Denver. I can go now. Why aren't you happy?"

"I am." A funny smile pulled on his lips. "I'm happy for you...but I'm sad for me." He toyed with the empty envelope.

Her chest fluttered. She sank into the second chair and tried to catch his gaze. "Why sad for you?"

"Margaret, I..." He rubbed his palms across his thighs. "I don't know exactly what to say, but I know I'll miss you." He laid his still sweaty fingers across hers. "There will be an empty spot in my life when you leave."

Her heart melted. She placed her other hand atop his and squeezed gently. "I know. I was thinking of the same thing this morning. But we can write letters to each other the way Mrs. Edith and I always have. And maybe, once in a while, we can talk on the telephone. Wouldn't you like that?"

"No, Margaret. I won't like it. It's not the same as seeing you." He huffed out a breath, then narrowed his eyes and smiled wickedly. "But you can't leave tomorrow."

"Why not?"

"It's Sunday. Buses don't run on Sunday." He leaned back in the chair, clasping his hands behind his head like a sunbather on the beach.

She grabbed a hand towel and slung it across the table at him. "You knew the whole time I couldn't leave until Monday. You're being smug."

James sat upright and waggled his eyebrows at her. "That's right. I am. And you want to know why? Because, Margaret Sullivan, I like you."

Heat exploded in Margaret's cheeks. To cool her face, she grabbed the Bible lying on the table and flapped the cover. Her gaze landed on the presentation page, and she froze, unable to believe what she saw. "James, where did your grandmother get this Bible?"

"She said it came from a lady who stayed a few days with her a long while back. Why?"

Margaret's pulse beat so hard she could hardly sit still. "Is the lady still living, or did she die?"

"What does it matter? You aren't superstitious are you?" His eyes twinkled.

She wasn't in a teasing mood. She jabbed her finger on the name in the Book. "This says Millie Harrison."

He frowned. "Yes. Does that mean something to you?"

Impatience fired her from the chair. She crushed the Bible to her chest. "I need to talk to your grandmother."

James stood, staring at her as if he was afraid she'd start frothing at the mouth. "Why?"

She quivered with contained excitement. "Millie Harrison was my grandmother's name. I never knew her, because she died when my mother was a child. But if your grandmother knew her, I'd love to talk with her."

A lump filled her throat. She swallowed it then whispered, "If this Millie Harrison is the same one as my grandmother, and this was her Bible, she was probably a good person."

James nodded. "I'm sure she was. Grandmother said she thought a lot of her."

Margaret rushed to the door. "Come on. I've got to talk to her right now!"

He caught her arm. "Margaret, it's late, and I'm on Jade. Let's wait until tomorrow. I'll come get you in my truck. You can go to church with my family then have dinner with us. You can talk to Grandmother the whole afternoon if you want to."

Margaret looked out at the evening shadows. James was right. She sent up her first real prayer. "God, please let this night pass fast!"

Chapter 7

Margaret enjoyed the church service. The singing and the preaching was grand. She enjoyed sitting down to dinner with James's parents and grandmother. Such kind people, all so welcoming to her even though she wore her secondhand dress and worn out loafers. No wonder James was such a kind man. He'd had good teaching all around. With every minute in their presence, her admiration for the whole family grew, and leaving for Denver in the morning became less appealing.

When they finished eating, Margaret rose to help clear the table, but his grandmother grabbed her elbow and steered her toward the parlor.

"No, no, my dear. James can lend his mother a hand. You an' me are gonna get good an' acquainted." She chuckled, the sound impish.

They settled on chairs tucked into a bay window, and even though Margaret had lain awake most of the night planning what to ask this woman, she found herself tongue-tied. She'd never known a grandmother. How did one treat a grandmother?

Mrs. MacKenzie didn't have any trouble talking, though, and her eyes twinkled when she talked, lighting up her whole countenance. "Honey, it's so good to finally meet you. I've known about you for years already from my sister. You call her Mrs. Edith, but she's just Edie to me. In all her church-group mission excursions across the United States, she met lots of children, but she never took to one the way she did you. She just couldn't ever get you off her heart. You must be a special one for sure."

Margaret's cheeks heated, but instead of embarrassment she only felt gratitude. God had put people in her life all along to help her see she was worth something. She just hadn't realized it. She ducked her head, basking in the wonderful feelings flowing through her.

"Now, honey," Mrs. MacKenzie said through throaty chuckles, "there's no need to act shy around me. You just be yourself, and talk all you want to. I won't bite. At least, not hard enough to leave marks."

Margaret laughed outright. She wished she could be as bubbly as this woman. Everyone must like Mrs. MacKenzie. She found her voice. "I would like to ask you a couple of questions, if you don't mind."

"Well, ask away." She laced her fingers over her stomach and turned a pert gaze on Margaret.

"The Bible you told James to give me had a name on the presentation page."

"I'm sure it did. Probably had some writing in the margins, too. It belonged to an old friend of mine. But she won't mind you having her Bible, if that's what's worrying you. She went on to her reward a long time ago, but I know she'd be thrilled to think it's being used."

Margaret shook her head. "Oh, no. It's not that. The name is familiar to me."

She fanned her fingers in the air in a nonchalant gesture. "Oh, honey, you couldn't have known her. She died before you were ever born. Why, she didn't even live here. She lived in Nebraska. Just passed through here the once."

"But my mother's people were from Nebraska, and my grandmother's name was Millie Harrison." She swallowed hard, hoping to unearth some long lost memory buried in the mind of the older lady.

"You don't say." Mrs. MacKenzie blinked a couple of times. "Well, I can tell you Millie was married to a good man. Name of Dan."

Margaret gasped. Her grandfather's name!

Mrs. MacKenzie went on. "They helped me through a rough time of it when I lost my little one. Good people. Good, good people..." She seemed to drift away somewhere.

Margaret hated to disturb the older woman's reflections, but there were things she wanted to know. "Did she know the Lord?"

The woman gave a start. "Know the Lord? Why, she an' her Maker was like that." She crossed her fingers up in the air and squinted her eyes. "I don't mind telling you, Millie Harrison was the closest thing to a saint I ever met."

How had a saintly woman raised a bitter girl like Mama? Maybe Mama's bitterness had come from losing her mama so soon. She'd reason that out later. Just knowing her grandmother had been such a godly woman brought a rush of joy. She sighed. "All my life I've wanted somebody to look up to, and now I have somebody."

"Seems to me, young woman, you've had lots of somebodies. My sister, for one. My grandson, for two."

Margaret smiled. "And you, for three."

The older woman waved her hand. "Oh, bosh..." Then her brow puckered. "You know, I got a letter from Millie shortly after she an' her Dan headed on. Letters bein' precious, I'm sure I didn't throw it away. I'll do some huntin' in the attic, see if I can't round it up for you. That is, if you'd like having it."

"I would!" She beamed at Mrs. MacKenzie. James came into the room, and Margaret turned her smile on him. "James, guess what?"

James stopped in front of the chairs. His brows formed a line of worry.

Mrs. MacKenzie sat forward. "What is it, Son?"

"The sheriff is in the kitchen with Mom and Dad. He said a man arrived in town yesterday. He's looking for his daughter." James looked at Margaret. "His blond-haired daughter named Margaret. He's out in the sheriff's car right now."

Margaret's blood ran cold then hot. Dizziness hit with such force the room seemed to spin. Her vision went black, and she collapsed.

Chapter 8

Margaret awakened to a circle of faces, all of James's family members, peering at her from above the sofa. She tried to sit up, but a sharp pain stabbed the back of her skull. She grimaced and lay back down.

James's grandmother laid a wet rag over Margaret's forehead. "Now, you just lie real still, sweetie. You took a lick on your noggin when you fell off that chair over there."

James sat on the edge of the sofa, his thigh so close to her arm she feared she might swoon again. "Are you better now?"

"My head is throbbing terribly."

James's mother said, "I'll get some headache powders." She and her husband left the room.

Margaret scowled at James. "What happened? One minute I was sitting in chair, and the next, I woke up here."

He scowled, too. "You don't remember? We were talking about your father."

It all rushed back. Margaret groaned. How could this happen right when everything was falling into place? She shook her head. "No. No..."

James held her hand. "Didn't you say your daddy was kind to you?"

"Yes, he is. I love him with all my heart." If only she could run into Daddy's arms, kiss his whiskery cheek, bury her face in his shirt and smell the familiar scent of Old Spice. "But if he sees me and talks to me, he'll tell Mama about it, and she'll get all stirred up. She's so hateful when she's upset... I can't let him see me." Worse, what if Mama was with him? She closed her eyes tight, wishing she could faint again.

"Don't worry, Margaret." James's voice soothed her. "Like the sheriff already said, you're old enough to decide where you want to live. With your folks, or in...Denver."

Mrs. MacKenzie's sharp voice intruded. "Go tell the sheriff to bring him in here."

"No!" Margaret struggled to sit up. The rag fell across her face, and she swatted at it.

"Oh, yes. We're gonna get this thing settled once an' for all." She flopped the wet rag back on Margaret's head and then pointed at James. "Get him, James. Now."

When Grandmother spoke in that tone, James did as he was told. He shot an apologetic look at Margaret as he left the room and prayed they were doing the right thing. The sheriff's car waited next to the barn. A gray-haired man sat in the backseat with his shoulders slumped and his head low. He appeared old and haggard, too old to have a daughter Margaret's age. Maybe he wasn't her father after all. James drew close, and the man rolled down the window and looked out. James got a glimpse of Margaret's beautiful blue eyes.

He leaned down and propped his arms on the window sill. "Mr. Sullivan?"

"That's right. Are you the boy the sheriff said might know of my daughter's whereabouts?"

James bit his lip. He wouldn't lie. Grandmother would have his hide. But how it grated his throat to speak the truth. "Yes, sir."

"My wife sent me all the way over here to bring her back. I came. To satisfy her. But..." The man pulled in a breath and his body tensed. His blue eyes bored into James's. "I'm sure my Margaret's not even up at that cabin right now, is she?"

James blinked several times. Was the man playing a game with him? "N-no, sir. She's not at the cabin...right now."

Margaret's father released his breath. His stiff frame relaxed. A smile toyed on his mouth. He stared ahead and slowly bobbed his head. "That's good. That's real good. If she's gone, she'll make something of herself, away from... And I can tell her mama I didn't see hide nor hair of her." He jerked his face toward James, his expression pleading. "Ain't that right young man?"

James swallowed. "I...I suppose so, sir."

"Well then, if you'd tell that sheriff thanks for bringin' me, I'll go back to the hotel. Catch a bus back home in the morning." He sighed. "Maggie ain't gonna like it none, me comin' back without Margaret, but it can't be helped if she's not here." He offered his hand to James. "If you happen to see my Margaret, tell her that her daddy loves her, and...since she really is gone...she won't have to worry 'bout us coming back here. Nobody'll bother her again."

James clasped Margaret's father's hand between both of his. "Yes, sir. Thank you, sir. And..." He swallowed, imagining the agony this man was experiencing to make such a sacrifice. "I'll keep you in my prayers."

He nodded, his eyes watering. "Get the sheriff now, huh?" He pulled loose and rolled up the window.

James trotted to the house, both sorrow and joy propelling him across the yard. He delivered the message to the sheriff, and then he burst into the parlor. "Grandmother, Margaret, you'll never believe what happened."

Mid-August

Margaret rested her temple against James's shoulder. The rickety bench on the cabin's porch was the perfect place to watch the evening sun cast long shadows across the yard. Soon the sun would slip behind the mountains and she'd have to bid the day farewell. Margaret sighed and curled her hands around James's firm forearm, unwilling to see this special day end. It had been the best birthday of her life following the best few months of her life.

She breathed deeply of the mountain air, savoring its flavor and scent. In only a few more weeks, she would become James's wife. He'd proposed in the midst of her birthday celebration, and of course she said yes, but Grandmother insisted on a fall wedding, when the aspen leaves were blazing gold. And they knew better than to argue with Grandmother.

God had blessed her so abundantly! The man beside her loved her and treated her with tenderness she'd never known before coming to Sawyer's Gap. His family had become her family. God had given her a new life in Christ and healed the pain of her past. This cabin had given her a place of refuge in more ways than she could count. She'd hate to say goodbye to the wonderful little cabin. Unless...

She turned her eager gaze to James. "Can we live in the cabin after we get married? Not forever, but for a little while? It's where we met, and I'd love to spend more time with you here."

He laced his fingers together across the small of her back and pulled her closer, planting a swift kiss on top of her head. "You know, I think it would be fitting to spend our honeymoon right here."

"Oh, really? James, could we?"

"I don't see why not. I think it would be absolutely perfect…as long as you leave that poker in the barn, Superman."

THE END

My Best Shot

Eileen Key

And we know that in all things God works for the good of those who love him, who have been called according to his purpose.
Romans 8:28 NIV

To Kim Sawyer, my personal emoticon

Chapter 1

Early 1990s

Fat raindrops pelted the window and woke Bailey Summers. She shoved back the quilt and scooted on her slippers, shivering against the May chill. Almost summer, the mountain mornings brought brisk weather.

"Cold, cold." She drew a bathrobe about her shoulders and opened the front door. Despite the temperature, the outdoors beckoned. Snug in the tiny cabin her friend loaned her, she was quite content. She breathed in the crisp, fresh air. "Away from it all. There's no feeling like it."

Bailey shoved the door closed with one elbow and slippered to the tiny fridge in the corner. She drew out a soda and slurped down her morning caffeine. "Yes, Mr. Reston," she muttered, "coffee would warm me up, but I don't like the taste." Her boss had a daily harangue about her soda intake. Bailey grinned. And she had two weeks away from any of his demands. "Not even a phone to interrupt my day."

After pulling on a T-shirt, jeans and tennis shoes, she found her rain poncho and tugged it over her head. Bailey wadded her oh-so-curly hair into a long ponytail and slipped it through the hole in the back of a San Antonio Spurs cap. Her dad sent her the cap right after they won their championship.

A black case held her Canon camera, lenses and the three rolls of film she'd already shot. She dug the canisters from the bag and tucked them into her suitcase away from the dampness. They represented two days of work and she surely couldn't mess them up.

Bailey chewed her lower lip. "Can't wait to see what's on those." She'd gotten lucky at twilight and taken stills of a doe and her fawn. "Hope those were focused. Boss will have a conniption fit if I don't get at least one good deer shot."

She glanced at her reflection in the mirror over the chair. "Talking to yourself is getting to be a pretty bad habit, old girl." She leaned in closer "Dry, cracked lips, and puffy eyes. Aren't you charming?" She tugged the bill of her cap lower and strode out the door.

The rain had slowed. Bailey steadied her arm and focused on a cottonwood tree as the rain cascaded down the leaves creating tiny waterfalls. *If only I had video.* She took the shot and stared at the scene before her, mesmerized. "God, you have created such beauty, it's beyond my comprehension how people dispute your existence." She shook her head, flinging water across her face with her ponytail.

Bailey spun in a circle. "I don't care, I don't care, I don't care. I'm in the mountains. I never thought I'd get here, but here I am." She jumped a small stream and continued on her wet quest for more unusual shots. The naturalist magazine seemed to eat up her work. When Mr. Reston gave her congratulations, she deferred the glory. "A God-given talent, sir." At twenty-eight, the accolades and few awards she'd won could've caused her to brag, but she knew where gloating led.

Just look at her sister.

Heaving a sigh, Bailey trooped around the back side of the cabin. A large rain barrel stood under the eaves and bright green ivy grew up its side. She snapped a shot from several angles.

"Oh, I want to see what I've gotten. Don't think I can wait another day." She captured glistening drops of water caught in a spider web. "Yeah, I've gotta get this film developed now." Which meant a trip to Sawyer's Gap. Not a hassle, but a return to civilization which she'd chosen to avoid.

Stamping her feet on the porch, Bailey placed the camera bag on a chair and slid the poncho from her shoulders, shaking off water. She scraped mud from the bottom of her shoes, slipped them off and left them by the door. She swooped up the camera and tromped through the door.

Inside, she jerked off her cap and tousled her hair. "Oh, this mess." She glanced in the mirror. "Yep, a red mop. Like a Sesame Street character." She chuckled. If only she could take a picture of herself, she'd send it to her four-year-old nephew. Trevor would certainly want to frame a shot of Auntie B.

Bailey worked to tame the curls and make herself a bit more presentable. The photo lab in town would be open, and she itched to get there. Mr. Reston created an account so all she had to do was give them the canisters and wait a day.

"Yeah, wait. The thing I do best."

The thrumming of rain picked up beating a tattoo on the roof. Walking downhill to her car would be difficult and crossing the small stream might not be a good idea. She stared out the door, disappointment weighing heavily.

"Rain, no pictures, no driving, no TV. Glad I have a couple of books to tide me over." She shut the door and rummaged through her suitcase for a novel. "Let the relaxing begin."

Adjusting the covers, she plopped on top of the quilt, drew it around her damp legs and plumped the pillows behind her head. Once comfy, she started to read.

A thumping rattled the front porch and the floor under the bed. Bailey popped up. "What in the world?" She slung the quilt aside and stood. Surely Wyoming didn't have earthquakes.

The thumping sounded again along with a deep rumbling voice. Bailey held her breath. Someone was outside. She sidled to the kitchen and swiveled about looking for a weapon.

The broom.

She grasped the wooden handle and readied it like a baseball bat. Any intruder in her space would become a home run.

Adam Quincy wanted to run. Just run home. Be done with it all. Instead he found himself hiding out in a lousy mountain cabin with no nearby amenities. He shuffled the grocery sack from one arm to the other and tossed the newspaper on the chair by the door. Drenched, it had kept his small supply of food dry. "Buster, you'd better show up again in the morning. Fresh coffee and doughnuts sound good." He growled as he considered what he'd agreed to. His administrative assistant knew of this cabin and had promised it to be an excellent hide out. Well, that would prove true. "Because it's in the middle of nowhere!"

Adam juggled the sack and reached for the doorknob. His foot caught and he stumbled. A pair of tennis shoes blocked his path. "Reeboks." He shoved them aside with his boot. Someone stupid had left behind valuable shoes. Too bad they wouldn't fit him.

He jiggled the doorknob and swung the door open. He leaned down for the sack of groceries and heard a loud scream and a swish. He jerked upright. His movement had kept him from being beaned with a broom by a mad woman.

"What—"

"Who—"

Adam rooted to the porch. He didn't want to give Crazy Girl any room for an attack. Her wild red Albert Einstein hair and baseball stance let him know trouble could be brewing.

"Lady, wait a second." He held out his hand, as though stilling a horse.

"What are you doing entering my domain?"

Her domain? Who talked like that? "Um, I'm Adam. . ." he struggled for a last name. He certainly didn't want to reveal his true identity to a nutcase. He glanced around, spotting the suitcase. "Adam Case. My friend loaned me the use of his cabin for a few days." He sidled closer, stepping across the threshold, his eyes roving between hers and the skillet. "I certainly didn't mean to startle you." He waved a hand. "Would you mind lowering your weapon?" His lips tipped up. Maybe smiling would calm her down.

Sure enough she lowered the broom a bit, and just as quickly drew up to her full five foot height and spouted out, "You can't stay here."

Adam chuckled. "I sure can. Buster left me here with no car and it's raining. Or haven't you noticed?" He really was wet and ready to change clothes, get out of his damp boots. And have a cup of coffee.

Miss Priss puckered her lips for a moment. "Forget it, buddy. I'm using this cabin for the next two weeks. So you need to leave." She hefted the broom once again. "So get out."

"Lady, I'm sorry about this mix-up, but I'm not going anywhere any time soon." He turned sideways to keep an eye on the crazy one and reached for the grocery sack.

"I said get out." She stomped her foot, her batter-up stance set.

Adam bit his lip and sighed. "And I said no." He set the sack on the counter. "I'm wet and hungry and about to change clothes." He slid his backpack to the floor. "Guess you'd best show me the bathroom or turn around." He shrugged from his windbreaker, tugged his damp shirt up and began to unbutton it.

The girl gasped, cheeks flooding red. "Stop. You can't."

Adam ignored her.

"Over there." She pointed to a door. "Not in here."

Adam suppressed a chuckle. "Yes, ma'am." He waltzed into the bathroom and jerked off his boots, dropping them with a clunk. Mud splattered across his legs. After a change of clothes and a wash up, he grinned into the mirror. "Well, now. Let's get this show on the road." It certainly wouldn't be the first time he'd shared space with a woman he just met.

Chapter 2

Bailey trembled. Who was this guy? She clung to the broom and searched for her shoes and purse, ready for a quick getaway, her heart hammering in her chest.

Rats.

Her shoes—on the porch.

She tightened her grip on the handle and sidled toward the door.

Her camera.

She glanced around. On the bed. The case on the table.

The rolls of film. In her suitcase. Under the bed.

Panic welled and her stomach roiled. She had to flee but couldn't just leave her valuables, her work. She began a sideways slow step inside the room, her eyes on the bathroom door.

She fumed. This guy had taken over the bathroom like he owned the place. She stood still. Maybe he did. Mr. Reston hadn't given her the name of the owners. Holy cow! What if he owned this place and threw her out. How would she get her assignment for the magazine? And if she didn't, how would she pay—

The bathroom door opened and the man stepped out. "Feel better now that I'm dried out." He grinned.

She froze. Her eyes widened. He was an amazing. . . specimen of a man. Broad shoulders which tapered down into a narrow waist. Jeans that hugged his hips in just the right places. Dark hair slicked back from a fine forehead, a perfectly proportioned nose—

Wait.

She wasn't about to photograph this jerk. She wet her lips and slowed her breathing. He wasn't lurching for her in a threatening manner. Bailey closed her eyes for just a second and rubbed her temple. Certainly there was a reasonable explanation.

Her knuckles ached from the death grip on the slim length of wood. She shifted it to her left hand and cleared her throat.

"Sir, we have a dilemma." She leaned against the doorframe, then realized she relaxed her stance and jerked upright. "I must have the use of this cabin for a while. It's necessary to my livelihood."

He glanced at her, an eyebrow lifted. "Your livelihood? What's that supposed to mean?" He rummaged through his grocery sack and retrieved a can of coffee. "You mind if I use that percolator over there? Or is it necessary for your livelihood?" His green eyes twinkled, small creases forming a web around their edges.

Bailey's throat closed up and she shook her head.

"Thanks." He rummaged through a drawer for a can opener, proceeded to fill the coffee pot with water and measure out coffee.

The pungent aroma stung Bailey's nose. She stood in the doorway between the kitchen and gathering room and held the broom like a pitchfork. Best to be safe. Despite the downpour she should leave.

"Who are you?" He fiddled with the stove and set the pot on a burner. "What's your name?"

"Bailey," she croaked. She cleared her throat and tipped her head a bit, striving for an air of authority in this handsome man's presence. "Bailey Summers. And you?"

"As I said before, Adam." He stopped and stared at her. "What are you doing up here by yourself, Bailey Summers?"

By herself. Yep. She was by herself. With a stranger. Yeah, he was the best looking stranger she'd ever seen, but this was stranger-danger if she ever heard of it. Her heart was about to explode in her chest. She turned from his gaze and tightened her grip on the broom handle.

"I might ask you the same thing, Adam. Why are you in this rustic setting?" She tugged her T-shirt down.

"Just getting away from it all." He opened two cabinet doors and finally located what he needed. He reached for a mug. "About to enjoy me some nature." Adam laughed.

A lovely laugh. Bailey looked at his bare feet peeking out from his jeans. Nice toes. *Oh, good grief, Bailey, get a grip. This isn't some romance story.*

"When the rain lets up, I plan to go into town," she said. "We can make phone calls and figure out our problem."

"Your problem, ladybug. I ain't going to town." The coffee was ready and he poured some into a cracked white mug. He took two swallows and sighed. "Best way to wake up and warm up." He settled into a chair by the table and peered up at her. "So if you go to town, you can figure out where you are going to stay. Because this guy's parked here until Buster comes back. And that ain't for a while." He crossed his arms and leaned back pushing the chair onto two legs.

He was pushing it. This gal looked skittish. Wild eyed and wild haired. She stood before him with such a frown, her freckles almost knit together. Cute. If she was in one of his movies, she'd be cast as the little sister.

"Look, Adam." Bailey cleared her throat. "I am a photographer and—"

She droned on but Adam hung on the last word. Photographer. He groaned. Stuck in a cabin with her? His gaze settled on a camera case. Great. Just what he needed. Someone to stick another camera in his face. He was here because he'd smashed a camera and a camera man on the sidewalk in front of a restaurant. He propped his elbow on the table and placed his forehead on his hand. How was it everywhere he went he had his privacy invaded? Buster said he'd made sure no one knew of his location. Only Buster hadn't checked out every photographer on the planet because there was one in front of him, yammering on.

". . .plants and nature. That's the main focus of my career. I work for a naturalist magazine and have to get my pictures finished for an upcoming issue." She heaved a sigh. "My bread and butter." She chewed on a thumbnail, swaying from side to side, a plaintive look on her face. "So you can understand my need for this cabin."

Yes, he understood the need for this cabin. Privacy.

"Look, Miss Summers, I'm sure your magazine can put you up somewhere more comfortable." His gaze roamed the small room. "I'd be glad to chip in to help you relocate—because of the inconvenience. I could even haul your belongings to whatever mode of transportation would take you to town. Is there a mule named Moses somewhere as a beast of burden, or do you have a car I haven't seen?"

Her cheeks flamed red again and her eyes grew wide. "Mr. Case. I'm not moving to another location. This is where the flora and fauna— It's just not—" She drew a hand through her unruly mop of hair. "I'm not sure what to do."

"I am." He sipped a draught of liquid and gave her a steely look. "You go. I stay."

Chapter 3

Bailey trudged through the mud and muck to her Chevy, the film in her pocket and her camera and purse under a rain poncho. With the downpour slowed to a trickle, she had decided to get to town. A call to Mr. Reston would have the intruder removed from her cabin. She hadn't left anything of importance behind with the creep.

Although someone so cute wasn't necessarily creepy.

"Ugh. Stop it, Bailey." She dropped her camera into the front seat, shook water from the poncho and tossed it in the back seat. She cranked the key in the ignition. "This guy is ruining your golden chance." She fishtailed backwards to turn around then pulled the lever into Drive. "You've got to get him *gone*."

Carefully maneuvering down the gravel road, Bailey thought of the pictures she'd taken. She scanned the sides of the road. A fallen log tilted at a forty-five degree angle might make a nice— The car swerved and her heart caught in her throat. All she needed was to wreck her only paid-for possession so she'd best concentrate on driving.

After a white-knuckled few minutes down the switch back road which reduced her speed to a crawl, Bailey entered Sawyer's Gap. Thankfully the rain had stopped so she swung in to the service station and filled up, then grabbed a soda to calm her nerves and paid the attendant.

She'd be so glad when the cabin situation was….situated. How could that jerk just assume he had possession?

"Because he's inside and you're outside, dummy." Bailey groaned and started her car.

She parked in front of the photo lab and clambered from the car. Inside she posted her film in the correct envelopes and was assured the pictures would be ready the following afternoon. She loved this instant service.

Once she finished, Bailey walked to the corner telephone booth which smelled like cigarette smoke and bubble gum. She dare not put her fingers under the shelf holding the phone book. She pulled coins from her purse and slipped them into the slot at the top of the phone. Mr. Reston's secretary answered on the first ring. He was out for the day, but Anne assured Bailey the cabin belonged to one of his relatives and had been secured for the entire month.

"There's kind of a mix-up, Anne. I need to know for sure because some guy named Adam"—what was his last name?—"appeared on the doorstep and thinks he is supposed to stay there."

"I don't have an answer for you right now, but if you call back tomorrow, I will find out for sure."

Bailey thanked her and replaced the receiver. She searched for more coins to call her roommate. Renee's shift at the café didn't start until four, so she was most likely home. And what a story Bailey had to tell. She smiled as she thought of the handsome stranger, then drew in a breath. Intruder, not handsome stranger. And she had to get him out of that cabin before nightfall or she had no place to stay.

But first Renee had to hear—

"Hello?"

"Hey there. What's new in your life? You won't believe mine." Bailey laughed.

Renee gasped. "Oh, girl. Am I glad to hear from you. It's just awful and I don't know what to do. We only have until Friday. Then we have to go."

"Go? Friday?" Bailey frowned. "What are you talking about?"

"We've been evicted."

Bailey gripped the receiver tighter. "What do you mean?" She punctuated each word slowly. "How can we be evicted?"

A light laugh trickled through the phone. "Well, it just happened. I mean, I didn't mean for it to happen, it just did. And now I don't know what to do. We have to be out by Friday. What should I do?"

Bailey pinched the bridge of her nose. "Renee. What. Happened? I left you money for my half of the rent for two months."

"About that. When Conrad's car broke down, I loaned—"

Nausea spread through Bailey's middle. "You loaned our rent money to your good-for-nothing boyfriend?"

Tears clogged Renee's words. "I did, Bailey. And he left. Said he had a gig in Colorado and it couldn't wait. And now I don't know what to do." She wailed.

Bailey pulled the phone away from her ear and closed her eyes, calculating her bank balance. "Renee, I don't have enough to cover this." She bit her lower lip and pushed a clenched fist into her belly. "Would your parents store stuff in their garage for a month? Just until I get a magazine paycheck?" She breathed a prayer for favor.

"Yes. They said they would." Renee sniffled. "I just didn't know what to do without asking you. I mean, I can go home, but now you have no place to live."

Bailey sighed. Renee was right. Without enough money for a hotel room and a stranger in her cabin, Renee was right. In more ways than one.

Adam shuffled onto the front porch, relieved the downpour had ended. He leaned against a porch post and watched a dragonfly buzz a nearby bush. What would he do in this remote area for the next few days? He thought of the wild-haired Bailey and grinned. If she stuck around, they could while away the time. In more ways than one.

She was a cutie. Adam groaned. "Hmph. A cutie photographer. She will end up with her camera poked in my face." He tossed a pebble from the porch. "She'll get back and start in. I know it. They all do." He stomped inside, slouched onto the small sofa and stared at the fireplace. The silence was unnerving. He'd ask Buster to bring him a radio at least.

The hinges on the front door creaked and he heard his current roomie enter the cabin. "So how was the bustling metropolis?" He leaned around the doorframe and smiled at her.

"Fine."

"Did you bring me a surprise from town?" He raised a brow.

"A surprise?" She slid the camera and her purse on the table. "What kind of surprise?"

"I don't know. That's what makes it a surprise." He stood and stretched. "So. Did you find a place to stay? I can help you pack and carry things to your car."

A flush crept up her cheeks. "Uh. No. I didn't."

Adam suppressed a chuckle. He'd get his wish for company after all. "I noticed there's room for two. I guess I can let you have the loft."

"The loft?" Bailey jerked around and popped her hands on her hips. "I sleep in the bedroom, mister. You can take the loft." She tipped her head.

"After all, it's the gentlemanly thing to do."

"Gentleman?" He took a step in her direction. "You're assuming I am a gentleman?"

Bailey edged toward the stove and placed a hand on the skillet's handle. "Am I wrong?"

Adam barked out a laugh. "No, you aren't wrong. My mama raised a gentleman. And I'm more than willing to sleep up there. Thank you for sharing." He moved closer and spun the skillet handle from her reach, then grabbed the coffee pot. "This is still warm, want some?"

She shook her head, the wild mop of curls ruffling. Opening the refrigerator, Bailey pulled out a package of cheese, butter and a soda. "No, I need sustenance. Grilled cheese for me."

Adam almost drooled. He hadn't had a homemade grilled cheese sandwich in quite a while. He tilted his head, slumped a shoulder and fluttered his eyelashes, trying for that look of longing, bringing to life his last movie part as an undercover cop. He'd been a beggar on the street. "May I have one, too? Please?"

Bailey froze and stared at him.

He straightened, his stomach muscles tightening. He'd just spoken the exact lines from the movie and reminded a photographer that he was a well-known actor. *Stupid move.*

"Never mind. I'm sure I can fix—"

"I don't mind at all. I just wondered why you were acting so goofy." Bailey leaned over and lit the stove, popped cheese between slices of buttered bread and placed them in the skillet. She lifted a spatula from the drawer and watched the pan, her back to him, shoulders stiff.

Goofy? He had just reenacted a critically acclaimed part which she thought was goofy? Who was this woman? And just why hadn't she suggested taking pictures?

The buttered bread sizzled and popped. Bailey grabbed two small plates from the cabinet.

"Were you a cook in a diner?" Adam pointed to the spatula. "Seems like you know the right end of that thing."

"Nope. Just cooked simple things for a long time." She flipped the sandwiches, a golden brown patina covering the bread. "Had to care for my sister as well as myself from an early age." She slid a sandwich on a plate. "After we eat, we can discuss living arrangements. In the morning we go to town so you can call your friend to come get you." She slid the plate toward him. "Lunch is served one time only. For tomorrow you move."

Chapter 4

Bailey ate a piece of toast, grabbed her camera, and tromped through the woods looking for anything remotely interesting that wasn't male. Adam was so handsome and would make a wonderful model with that thick black hair and startling green eyes. But she'd not ask him to pose. And he'd be gone by this time tomorrow.

She sighed, a pang of disappointment rolling through her middle. Why in the world did that make her feel sad? She'd only known the guy a few hours. But she had to admit, she'd enjoyed the short bit of time.

Water pinged from the trees in a erratic rhythm, forming a symphony around her. The air stung her nose, the earth smelled so fresh. She stopped and surveyed the area. A rabbit darted through the underbrush and Bailey squatted, stilled, and waited for any more signs of movement. She had a few bunny pictures, but who knew what this tiny creature might bring?

"What are you doing?"

His husky voice broke the stillness and scared the living daylights out of her. She lurched forward and landed knees first in a mud puddle, camera held high above her head.

Adam reached over and grabbed the camera. "Oops. Guess I shouldn't have used my Indian tracking skills and been so silent." He slung the camera strap over his shoulder and held out a hand. "Let me help you."

Bailey glared at him. She wore her favorite pair of slacks and now they were mud-caked. Of course she hadn't changed before she left the cabin. She'd been in such a hurry to leave his presence, she'd scurried for the door as soon as possible.

She grasped his hand and electricity shot up her arm. Bailey jerked free and tumbled backward, creating quite the splayed display. She stared at him. His cheeks were flushed and he rubbed his hands down his jeans.

"Sorry." He croaked. "Didn't mean to let go, I was trying to help."

She gave a light laugh and scrambled to her feet. "Clumsy of me." She brushed hair from her face and reached for her camera. "Thank you so much

My Best Shot

for saving this baby. I'm truly grateful."

"No problem." Adam scanned the area. "What were you photographing?"

Bailey smiled. "A bunny rabbit." She pointed to the tangle of bushes. "He was peeking out from under there, framed perfectly." She frowned. "Until we caused such a ruckus."

Adam lifted his hands. "Hey, said I was sorry. Just got bored and wanted some company. Didn't mean to ruin your *best shot*."

He'd lifted his hands and put air quotes around the words best shot. Bailey frowned. "Well, it might have been my best shot. Who knows?" She sighed. "I'm trying to make some money with these pictures." Money she surely needed for a new apartment. A small headache started as she recalled her roommate's words. "It's a tough business. Mr. Reston was kind enough to give me this job and I want to do well."

"I'm sure you'll do fine." He grinned. "Where will I see this fascinating display of your work? In a gallery?"

Bailey's lips turned up. "No, in print. To accompany magazine articles on wildlife and ecology. It's a broadening field and I'm excited to be a part of a project to keep this part of Wyoming…well, Wyoming." She spun in a half circle. "Have you ever seen anything as beautiful as this area? The flora and fauna? The animals? Water bubbling through the creek?"

"Whoa." Adam spun around then faced her. "Who is flora and fauna and where did they go?"

"Ha ha. Very funny, sir. You know well what I mean." She pointed at the horizon to the mountains. "Have you ever seen anything so beautiful?"

Adam was tempted to say he was looking at something beautiful, even with the streak of mud across her forehead. The pert, crazy-girl's beauty shone through her expression as she talked about her work. Bailey was the real deal. She wasn't some plastic Hollywood model trying to make it in the world. Her words were genuine.

"It is beautiful out here. Lonely, but beautiful." Adam toed the edge of the mud puddle with his boot. "Glad the rain let up. Glad to be outside." And he was. Truly. He'd grown up moving from one shabby apartment to another with his single mom. Now that he was in the money, she lived in a new house he'd purchased miles from him—not that she got on his nerves much. He picked up a stick and tossed it toward the bushes. "Maybe we can scare up Bugs Bunny again."

Bailey gave a half-hearted laugh. "Maybe or maybe not." She tromped down the hillside a bit and Adam trailed behind her. She glanced over her shoulder at him.

"Do you mind if I tag along? Got nothing better to do."

She shrugged. "Just watch your step."

They walked to the burbling creek. After the rain, it was full and dancing around rocks and through crevices. Adam bent and retrieved a handful of rocks. He tossed them into the water one at a time. "I used to skim these across the lake when I was a kid." When he'd had a dad. A sinking sensation ran through his middle. He hadn't thought of his dad in a long time. Wonder where he was?

This is ridiculous. Too much free time to think. He hurled the remainder of the rocks into the water.

Bailey squinted up at him. "You okay?"

He dusted his hands together. "Sure. Think I'm having a caffeine crash though. I'll head back to the cabin while you search out a magazine spread."

Adam knew his remark was sort of rude but at the moment he only wanted to be away from Bailey. This whole outdoor experience with a good-looking, fresh, kind woman was unnerving. Maybe Buster's idea wasn't such a good one. Maybe he would accept Bailey's challenge and leave tomorrow. He needed a script to study or television to watch. Something to distract him from wisps of memories long tucked away under a flurry of activities.

A rabbit darted across the path and Adam almost called to Bailey but it disappeared before he could get the words out of his mouth. He did hope the kid could find a good photo. She seemed sincere and deserving. Not like the piranhas he faced in the big city. He shuddered as he recalled the anger which coursed through him as the photographer clicked photos that day. In all honesty, he was mad at himself for his poor performance.

He'd been so sure he could land a part in the stage play. His one true desire the stage—not film—with the live audience listening, feeding your inner being. And he hadn't been chosen. The celebration dinner with Buster and two other friends had turned sour. He had stomped out of the restaurant into a large camera lens. With a hard shove, the camera flew and the cameraman went over the curb. He wasn't even sure what all happened after that. He only knew there were no charges pressed, and Buster hustled him to the hinterlands.

The grilled cheese sandwich he'd eaten earlier began to curdle in his stomach. He'd left town without a thought to the man's condition. After seeing Bailey tumble in the mud trying to shoot a picture of a rabbit he could imagine what the guy in Hollywood faced.

"Oh man. I'm a total jerk." Adam brushed hair from his forehead. He needed to at least call. "Okay, that does it. Tomorrow to town with her." He took three more steps before the crevice gobbled his boot. His knee gave way.

The pain was as though a nail had been driven into the bone beneath the kneecap. He froze for a few seconds then tried a step. He made it to a tree and leaned against the trunk, a sheen of perspiration dotting his brow. "Holy cow. Not this!" The earlier nausea started again as he felt the knee tighten and start to swell.

This wasn't good. This wasn't good at all.

Chapter 5

Bailey found a boulder and perched on the edge to rest. She'd not found any more spectacular scenes to shoot. Not good. She needed a hit—something to knock it out of the park. One of those "Wow, she needs a bonus" pictures. She ran a fingernail around the buttons on top of the Canon. "Come on, sweetie, make Mama proud."

Time to plan. She had this cabin for a couple of more weeks, as soon as Mr. Wonderful left, that is. She could stand to share the small space for one night, fully dressed with her camera and purse clutched to her chest. She chuckled at the picture. Maybe this guy wasn't as scary as she first thought.

"But then don't they always say they never suspected their nice neighbor was a killer, Bailey?" She whispered and shook her head. Too many mystery books in her life. She'd close the bedroom door and make it until morning if she had to read all night. Maybe she'd even sleep with the broom.

She pushed off from the rock and realized the call to the ladies' room was imminent. She turned on her heel and headed toward the cabin, following the same trail which brought them to the creek.

Bailey spotted Adam at the neck of the trailhead, leaning against a tree. *Guess Mr. Muscle-man isn't in shape after all.* Although he looked spectacular at the moment. She mentally framed a shot and wondered if she could focus the camera without him spotting her. Then he looked her direction, and she waved, the moment gone.

His face paled and worry lines creased his brow.

Bailey sped up her steps. "Hey, there. Everything all right?"

"Hunky-dory. Peachy-keen." A muscle in his jaw twitched.

Bailey drew up next to him. She eyed his stance which spoke of something other than normal and noted his smile didn't reach his eyes. "Adam, what's wrong?"

He pointed to his knee. "Something gave way. I think it's my old football injury."

Despite herself, Bailey laughed. "Old football injury? There's a worn out excuse if ever I heard one."

"True though. Two years of college ball and I blew my knee. This is the same type of injury, I can tell." Adam massaged his left knee. He glanced up at her. "And, as much as I hate to ask, I'm going to need help back to the cabin." He tipped his head and held out his arm.

"Sure." Something in Bailey's middle fluttered. She slid the camera on her left side and tucked under his arm. Adam bent over and leaned on her shoulders. Bailey inhaled sharply. He smelled of woods and a touch of something musky. Her heartbeat picked up the pace. She gave him a shaky smile. "Let's go, quarterback."

"Wide receiver." He held out his right hand. "Old Catch 'em Walker."

Bailey chuckled. "If you say so, sir. Just don't catch any tree roots as we go." With much grunting, groaning and effort, they crutched him up the trail.

After three short breaks, they reached the cabin porch. Adam sank on the step, propped an elbow on his good knee, and put his forehead in his hand. "This isn't good, Bailey. I'm sorry. Hope that wasn't too hard on you."

"I'm fine." Bailey entered the cabin and took her camera to the bedroom. Hard on her? Surely her chest would explode with her heart racing. She'd never been so close to a man. She'd helped to support strong shoulders and inhaled the musky scent of him. Not an aftershave, just . . . him. With each hitch of a step, she became more and more aware of the man and could feel a flush crawl up her face.

Adam stirred up new emotions. And she wasn't sure she liked them.

Adam leaned against a porch post, exhausted and a bit nauseous. The grinding climb had taken its toll. He wanted to crumble into a ball and not move, but not moving wasn't a solution. He had to haul himself inside and prop up this knee, get it iced.

"Excuse me. Bailey?" He hated to depend on the kid, but had no choice. Her fresh look and breezy attitude stirred up emotions he wasn't sure he knew how to handle. Flirting was as much a part of his persona as breathing, however being real... now that would be a new experience. "Bailey?"

"You called, Catch'em?" She stood in a mock bow in the doorway. "What might I do for you now that my camera is safely stowed." She walked to his side, dropped to the porch step and pointed to his knee. "Bet you need to ice that." She tipped her face toward his.

Tiny freckles peppered her forehead and nose. Adam stared at her. If you drew a line from one to another, you'd create quite a portrait. He closed his eyes. Sheesh, the pain was causing his head to go all wonky with weird thoughts.

"You're right. Ice is called for. I need to prop it on a pillow first." He glanced back at the door. "Think you can help me inside?"

"Hey, we managed a mountain, we can certainly manage the rest." She stood and propped her hands on her hips. "Look, it's too late in the day to make it to town. I don't think we can hobble across the creek to my car—" A frown wrecked her freckles. "Unless you think you need an immediate x-ray."

"No, I recognize this sprain. Believe me, I've been down this road." He pushed against the post and stood with his weight on his good leg. "For now, ice and rest is all I need." He spun toward the door and wobbled, a precarious balance on the edge of the porch.

"Hang on, hang on." Bailey captured him around his waist. "Don't tump over or we'll be in a sad shape for sure."

Adam grinned. "Tump over? Now there's a new one."

Bailey slid her arm tighter against him and cinched him close to her. The bouncy ponytail tickled his arm. "Tump is a great word. Tumble and dump all in one." She leaned forward a bit. "Now on three…"

Together they made it to the sofa where he plopped down. Bailey scurried to the bedroom and returned with a pillow. He turned sideways on the small sofa and reached for the pillow.

"No, this won't do." Bailey dropped the pillow. "You don't fit there. You're too long."

"I can scrunch sideways and it will be fine." The nausea had begun again. He needed to get settled so it would abate.

Bailey marched into the bedroom, and soon loud thuds battered the floor. "What are you—"

"C'mon. We're moving again." She bent forward and inserted her shoulder under his arm. "To the bedroom where you can be comfortable."

Adam sighed. Despite the relief he knew would come from stretching out on the bed, he felt a touch of unease. "That's your room." He hefted his weight from the sofa and onto her shoulder then gave her a cocky grin. "And I appreciate you sharing it."

Bailey pulled away a bit and punched him lightly in the stomach. "Don't even think it, Catch'em. I'm moving to the loft. You ain't catching this girl, that's for sure."

CHAPTER 6

Bailey awoke, stretched, and yawned as morning dawned. She'd spent much of her night in the loft tossing and turning in an attempt to get comfortable. She was able to peer over the railing and check on his closed bedroom door before she tucked under the quilts.

True, she hadn't had the need to clutch a broom to her chest because she was pretty sure Adam was unable to climb the narrow staircase, but knowing he slept nearby made her—aware. She'd listened closely to his light snore and drifted to sleep, only to awaken with the need to go downstairs to the bathroom. She had lain in the dark willing herself to go back to sleep, but it was useless.

With trepidation, she'd climbed downstairs, tiptoed to the bathroom and made it back up the stairs with little noise. Adam's snoring had stopped completely at one point and she'd frozen in her tracks.

In the morning light she laughed at herself. What had she expected? An attack? A tinge of disappointment slithered in. Truth be told, maybe some interest. She rolled to her back and ran her hands through her hair. The man—very handsome man—hadn't even noticed her. He'd been intent on settling onto the bed, calling her to fetch him towels filled with ice, even another grilled cheese sandwich, yet he'd not appeared attracted to her at all. Their chitchat had been totally superficial. Most of it about his earlier football injury and rabbit pictures.

"Crazy woman. One minute you're hauling around a broom to bash his head in and the next you're bellyaching because he's not flirting with you. What do you want?" She flipped the quilt back and reached for her jeans. She knew the answer to that question, but wasn't about to dwell on it. Having a home and family didn't seem to be in God's plan.

Hauling her camera, purse and a change of clothes upstairs had been about all she could manage last night, so her toiletries and hairbrush remained on the sofa. Maybe Adam was still asleep and she could sneak into the bathroom—

"And what? Fancy up for a hunky guy who doesn't even know you're alive?" Bailey reached for the first step with one foot, her camera slung over her shoulder. "Not in this lifetime." She'd grab an apple and head out to shoot pictures. "Flora, fauna, and maybe bunnies, Bailey. That's it."

When her foot hit the floor, she turned to reach for her overnight case and jolted backward.

"Good morning." Adam stretched out on the sofa, a hairy leg flung over the arm rest. "Sleep well? I did. This mountain air and that comfortable bed is a winning combination." His lips twitched.

Bailey clutched the camera against her stomach. "You scared the liver out of me."

Adam chuckled. "Liver transplant required?" He pointed to his knee sticking out from the shorts he wore. "Reckon you can grab me a towel with ice in it before you head to the hospital?"

She glared at him, and then walked to the kitchen. "I supposed I can help out the wounded." Bailey picked up a towel from the sideboard and flapped it in the air. She pulled out the aluminum ice tray and plopped it on the counter with a whack, then released the center lever and poured the cubes into the towel. Once it was firmly knotted, she carried the icepack to Adam.

"Glad to know you slept well, Catch'em." She handed him the icepack. "You snore."

Adam shifted the pack onto his knee and groaned. He squinted in Bailey's direction. "I do not snore."

Bailey smirked. "Do too. Or there was an animal inside the cabin." She reached for her night case and carried it into the bathroom. "And it snored." With those words she clapped the door shut.

Good grief, did he get better looking during the night? She leaned against the sink and peered into the wavy mirror. Corkscrew curls stuck up all over and a crease ran down her cheek from the pillowcase. "Or am I worse?"

Adam watched the bathroom door waiting for the Kewpie doll to reappear. He'd almost laughed at her Raggedy Ann morning look, but stopped himself. He found himself drawn to this girl he'd known a mere twenty-four hours because of her sincerity. She'd been a real Florence Nightingale last night, making sure he ate, his icepack wasn't leaking, the pillow was plumped. He'd watched her like he would've watched a ballgame. For any misstep, any false move, any insincerity. And found none. Like he'd thought.

"Yeah, she is the real deal. Too far from your world, Quincy," he whispered.

He sighed and shifted on the sofa. A world he had to avoid for a bit. Adam hadn't realized until he lay in the dead quiet last night how jumbled his life had become. Like a kaleidoscope the thoughts tumbled about. People—painted faces and ruby-smeared lips; lines to memorize with words he'd been taught not to utter; parties where you overlooked antics of celebrities because they were important to your career.

"Career. A train wreck." What did he want in this life? Here he was thirty-one and churning out activities daily to kill time. Nothing worthwhile. Where was his drive? The desire he'd had in college to make a mark? "Made a mark, all right, Adam. A huge black one that can't be erased." He shifted the ice pack to a more comfortable angle. Though his leg felt better, he was loving the attention. Maybe he'd lay low a tad longer.

He stared at the embroidered piece on the mantel. Place of refuge. Yeah, that's what he needed, all right. Refuge from the outside world. To be encapsulated, free from making wrong choices.

The bathroom door popped open and Bailey stepped into view, fresh-faced, with the minty smell of toothpaste following her.

"How about breakfast?" She looked at the end table. "Didn't spot your morning cup of Joe at your side. Need some? I can sure burn it." She dropped her suitcase at the foot of the steps and waltzed into the kitchen. "Scrambled okay? Toast?" He heard the refrigerator door open. "No bacon, but I can make a cheese omelet if you'd like." The stove hissed on and the skillet banged against the grill. She poked her head around the corner. "Diner's open. Cook is ready." Her lips tilted in a smile. "What's it to be?"

Adam's breath caught in his throat. What's it to be? All he wanted at that moment was the cook in his arms. And that could never be. Ever.

"Cook's choice." His throat clogged. "Coffee would be great." He cleared his throat, the thought of refuge dwindling. "Then I will give you a phone number to call when you go to town and I will get out of your hair."

Forever.

Chapter 7

Out of her hair? Forever?

Bailey served up coffee and a cheese omelet with a false smile tipping her lips. A sinking feeling had assaulted her insides when Adam gave her his friend's phone number. He'd leave and she'd never see him again.

Why did that make her so sad?

"Are you sure you don't need anything else before I go?" She filled his coffee cup and dumped the second tray of ice in a towel. She peeked around the corner at him.

His mouth downturned and a frown creased his brow. "Nah. I'll be fine." He sat up and jerked a hand over his T-shirt. "Just call Buster, give him the update and he can come after me." A perfect white smile crossed his face. "Then you'll have your solitude once again."

Solitude. Highly overrated.

Turning back to the kitchen she lifted the dirty skillet from the sink and scrubbed it clean with a paper towel, greased it and set it on the back burner. Her hand lingered on the handle, smiling at her recent weapon.

Man, life turned on a dime.

Bailey wiped the countertop and replaced the dishes in the cupboard. Kitchen clean, she was ready for the trip to Sawyer's Gap. And didn't want to go. Once she made that phone call, Adam would disappear from her life—and boring routine would return. She heaved a sigh, leaned against the counter and closed her eyes.

"Lord," she whispered, "I don't know this guy from..."—she snorted a laugh—"from Adam. And I've not prayed for him at all. Don't know anything about his walk with You. If that's a conversation we are to have, would You open the door?" She paused and gazed about the small, cozy kitchen and out the front door. "And if You want rain to pour down so I can't go outside, that would be fine with me."

She stepped to the door and opened it. Inhaling a deep breath of fresh mountain air, she eyed the rays of sunlight streaming through the trees. "Guess I'm bound for town." She shut the door and twisted a curl back behind her ear.

Adam sat on the sofa, the icepack in a lump on the floor. Bailey swooped it up and reached around the doorframe to toss it into the sink. "I stuck the ice tray back in the freezer for the next go round." She swiped her hands down her jeans leg. "If you're sure there's nothing else you need, guess I will head out."

He shook his head. "All is well." He gave a half-hearted laugh. "Guess you can go."

"Lot of guessing going on, Catch'em." Bailey tugged her ball cap on. "So guess I'm gone. I will try to remember your surprise."

Adam raised a brow. "Surprise?"

Bailey clapped her hand on the table. "Yesterday you were disappointed I had no surprise for you. So today, I shall do better." She spun around, grabbed the camera bag and headed toward the door. "See you later."

"Later." The reply sounded feeble.

He must be feeble-minded. A golden opportunity to spend time with a beautiful woman in a remote location and he gave her Buster's number so he could be rescued? What kind of lame-brain move was that?

"The right move for once, Quincy." Adam pushed from the sofa and hobbled toward the kitchen door. Bailey was out of sight. He sighed. "Yeah, the right move. This kid doesn't need to be involved with someone like me."

He reached for a kitchen chair and rested his hand on the ladder-back. Pinching the bridge of his nose he stood still as a depth of sorrow pierced his heart. He glanced at the tablet and pen which lay toppled into the fruit stand. He drew out the chair and sat, pulling the paper close. With a moan, he began to write an "I'm sorry" list. His mom had drilled the exercise into him when he was a wild teenager. He'd not used the 'fess-it-up method in a long time. Maybe in this quiet place he could rid himself of some of the soiled memories.

The chair quickly grew uncomfortable and he withdrew to the sofa. He doodled on the page, jotted another name and then stared at the mantel once again, noting the Bible verse stitched on the embroidered piece. A small black

Bible was pushed to one side under the frame. He hitched over and grabbed the book, and sat back down. He opened to the table of contents and eyed the frame again.

"Isaiah 4:6." He thumbed the pages to the table of contents then found the scripture. "*And there shall be a tabernacle for a shadow in the daytime from the heat, and for a place of refuge, and for a covert from the storm and from rain.*" A tabernacle. In one film he'd used a tabernacle as a hideout. He looked at the words again. A refuge. A hiding place. He gave a small smile. "Check, check, check. I sure need all of those at the moment, God." The smile quickly drew to a frown, and he heaved a sigh. "Okay, while we are talking, let me just say I like the kid. She's— different. So protect her, God. Give her what she wants. I bet she'd be grateful. Seems like that kind of person."

"I'd be very grateful." Bailey's voice pierced the silence. "And I want only what God wants for me, thank you very much."

Adam swiveled about and felt his face flush. "Where did you come from?"

Bailey giggled. "Got to the car without my keys." She plunked the camera on the end table. "Can't go far without those." She edged closer and eyed the Bible. "Interesting reading?"

Adam tilted his head in the direction of the fireplace. "Read that and was wondering what it said." He rubbed the black book cover. "This is one old book."

"Been around for a couple of thousand years." Bailey slid into the chair and crossed her legs. "I find it stimulating reading."

He cleared his throat. "I bet it is." His thumb drew circles over the cover, almost in an effort to draw solace from the book. "I've just read parts." Parts. Scripts, acting, pretending. Parts. Not real in a very long time. The ache under his breastbone intensified. "What's your favorite part?"

Bailey's face relaxed and a serene smile crossed her face. "Now that you've asked"—she held out her hand—"may I?"

He placed the small Bible in her hand and watched as she flipped pages. Obviously she knew where she was going. Her freckles drew close as the tiny frown crossed her forehead, and a lock of curls edged from the cap. His fingers burned and he longed to tuck the strands in their rightful place. Whoa, he had no business thinking like that. And while she was Bible reading. For crying out loud. Guilt panged inside his ribs. "Not like the others, Quincy."

"Hmmm?" Bailey peeked at him. "Did you say something?"

He shook his head, not trusting his voice.

"Then here it is." She held out the book, a finger pointing at a specific place.

"Just read it to me, please."

Bailey eyed him for a moment, the silence ringing in his ears. "Sure. It's John 3:16—"

Adam snorted. "The sign they hold up at the football games? That John verse?"

"That John verse. Central to the book, Catch'em. Once you read and digest this, your life will never be the same."

Never be the same. What more could Adam want?

Chapter 8

Bailey knew her life would never be the same. She'd learned at church camp about sharing her testimony, telling others about Jesus, but she'd never ever had such an opportunity as the one before her. Adam was like a sponge. His eyes glistened with tears as she told of how her relationship with Jesus had gotten her through her mother's illness, her father's death, and her sister's choices which so affected Bailey.

"The modeling jobs Ginger had led to bad behavior, and she got hooked on drugs. It seemed like her life was over. The real Ginger disappeared. I bailed her out of jail a few times, then it got where I couldn't afford that." Bailey thumbed a tear from the corner of her eye. "Made me feel like I'd left a pet at the pound the last time she called and I wasn't able to help." Bailey scooted further back in the chair and dangled a foot in a lazy circle. "When she did get out, I lost contact with her."

Silence loomed for a few minutes as Bailey's throat constricted. Swallowing hard, she continued, "Then a friend of mine shot photos of a slum in downtown Denver and there right before me, was Ginger." She sniffed and closed her eyes. "I couldn't believe it. Just down the street from our office. And out of reach—even though I searched for her." Bailey toyed with the tissue she'd pulled from her overnight case. "My prayer partners and I doubled up the efforts, and I wish I could report all is well, but that isn't the case. Yet." A smile twitched her lips. "I won't give up. Ginger gloated about her glamorous life then took a plunge I wouldn't wish on anyone. So sad."

Adam nodded. "Yeah, I know people like that." He placed the fragile Bible on the end table. "That lifestyle grabs you by the throat and you're quickly a goner." Adam leaned forward. "I'm really sorry to hear about your sister."

Bailey brightened. "You can always pray for her. Ginger Summers."

He tilted his head. "Not sure my prayers would help much."

"Adam, may I ask you a personal question?"

He nodded.

"Do you know for sure that Jesus is your personal Savior?"

"I—" A red flush crept up his face and he averted his gaze. "Bailey, I'm not sure how to respond. Do I believe in God? Yes." He pointed to the Bible. "And what you read me? Yes. I believe that. But I'm not a good person. There's a lot of stuff—"

"Ha!" Bailey shot to her feet. "Catch'em. That's the point." She waved a finger in his face. "None of us are good. And we all have a lot of *stuff*. That's why Jesus went to the cross. All we gotta do is have faith and ask for our sins to be forgiven. It's so simple, and we want to complicate it. But the Gospel is not complicated. It's all about a relationship with Jesus Christ."

She plopped on the edge of the sofa, her knee bumping his. He grunted. "Oops. Sorry."

Adam shifted his leg and placed his foot on the floor. "Bailey Summers, you have given me much to ponder." He stood. "And ponder it I will."

Bailey frowned. "Promise?"

"Promise." He hobbled toward the bathroom. With his hand on the doorknob he glanced back over his shoulder. "Seriously. I promise I will think on this conversation while you go to town and call Buster."

Relief tinged with disappointment sagged through Bailey's chest. Surely he would keep his word. And if he didn't, God would. Scripture never returned void.

Inside the bathroom Adam sagged against the doorframe and listened to Bailey's retreating footsteps. He used to keep promises, but lately that seemed too difficult. It was better to keep the plates spinning, fool everyone. Not let on how frightened he felt. He slid down the door and crouched on the floor, the ache in his knee a faraway pain. Not like the one knifing him in the middle.

Adam Quincy Walker. Movie star. "What a joke." He massaged his temples. "God forgives sins. That clean cut kid might believe it's that easy, but it just can't be. Not for me. Nothing's easy for me." He chuckled. "Oh, a pity party in a bathroom. What a kicker, Quincy. Or wait. The real me. Walker." He shoved to his feet, propped his hands on the sink and stared into the mirror. He needed a shave. "Adam Quincy Walker, when did you become such a…a pushover?" He snorted in disgust and limped back to the sofa.

The Bible on the end table beckoned. Adam placed his hand upon the worn cover and shoved it away. "Not today."

Bailey drove slowly to Sawyer's Gap. Once she made the phone call to Adam's friend, he would leave. A sinking feeling grabbed her stomach. Had she shared too much, or not enough? What if his promise was empty. "Cut it out, you are not the Holy Spirit." Bailey cringed. Those were the very words her sister had hurled at her. "Okay, okay. Not my problem. I did my bit, now it's out of my control."

She chewed on her lower lip and guided the car into a parking spot in front of the photo lab. The phone booth at the corner sat empty. Bailey tugged the slip of paper with the phone number from her pocket. In a while, she could have her solitude restored. Why did that leave her sad?

"Because you've spent a day and a half with a handsome man. One who paid attention to you, stupid." Bailey shoved out of the car and started toward the phone. As she approached, a man walked around the corner and pushed into the booth. A smile crept across her face. "Reprieve." She turned toward the photo lab where her money-making photographs waited.

Once the pictures were tucked under her arm, Bailey had no more excuses. She waited until the phone was free, stepped inside the booth, ignoring the cigarette smoke/bubble gum aroma and dropped change into the slots. She dialed the number. It rang three times.

"The number you have dialed is no longer in service."

Bailey glanced at the slip of paper, retrieved her quarters, and dialed once again.

And listened to the drone of the operator.

Chapter 9

"What do you mean no longer in service?" Adam's red face and wrinkled brow appeared in the kitchen doorway.

"Just what I said. I called three times and got the same response." Bailey used two forks to toss the lettuce and other ingredients in the bowl. She set those aside and peered in the refrigerator. "Do you want salad dressing? I picked up two kinds at the store."

"I want to know what's going on with Buster." Adam stomped to the table.

Bailey watched him "Seems your knee is better."

He massaged his kneecap. "Yeah, it's getting there. I told you. Rest and ice. That's all I need." He plopped into a chair and propped his elbows on the table, dropping his head into his hands. "Can't figure this out." He spun the small piece of paper his direction. "This is the correct number, I've dialed it myself many times. How could it be wrong?"

Bailey placed salt and pepper shakers on the table along with the salad bowl. She grabbed two plates and a couple of forks from the dish drainer and set them down. "Um, maybe it is out. Of. Service. As in, not working?" She pushed a plate toward him. "These things happen." She pulled out a chair and sat. "Of course, maybe your friend couldn't pay his bill."

Adam glared at her. "That's not true. He makes a killing off of—"

Bailey lifted a brow. "Off of what?"

"Never mind." He dipped his fork into the salad bowl and scooped half on his plate. "This looks good."

"Yeah. Lettuce never looked so good." Bailey reached out and stilled his hand. "Why do I get the feeling you aren't telling me everything?"

Adam jerked his hand aside. "Don't know what you're talking about. Once we eat, you can help me to the car and I will locate Buster. Then I can get out of this God-forsaken—" He broke off.

"God-forsaken?" Her lips twitched in a half smile. "Seems like God's been speaking to you right here, Catch'em, so it's not forsaken." Bailey filled her plate and let the subject of secrets drop. Maybe she'd get Adam to open up more with silence instead of questions.

He leaned back in his chair. "Bad turn of a phrase. Let's just say I'm ready to return to civilization."

She chewed thoughtfully. "Me, not so much. Still have wittle wabbits to photograph, if de big bad boy is through stomping through de woods." She wriggled her eyebrows.

Adam stared at her and then a deep rumble of laughter erupted. "You're one crazy girl, you know that?" He toyed with his fork. "Does this mean I get to stay another night?"

Bailey nodded. "I'm not in the habit of throwing people into the woods." She paused and sighed, then added softly, "Only into jail."

"Hey, now. Forgiveness and all that jazz."

"Yeah, all that jazz."

The muscles in Adam's jaw worked furiously. He wanted to tuck this kid under his arm and protect her. The brokenness from this morning's conversation about her sister played across her features. He knew too many gorgeous wanna-be models and actors who had gone the same direction. He wondered if any of those had praying family members.

The promise. Now that he'd made her a promise to think about God, he was sure he had someone praying for him. Not that he'd done much else in the last couple of hours. It was hard not to do in the silence. He needed music or television to drown out the thoughts bombarding him. Yeah, the stuff.

"You finished?" Bailey pointed to his half-eaten salad.

He nodded and stood. "If you'd put all that in the sink, I'd like to stretch my leg and stand, so I will wash." He jerked his chin in the direction of her purse. "Didn't you say you had work to do with your pictures?"

With Bailey busy and in another room, he could corral his mind. A smile crossed his face. He had enough noise in his brain to drown out real thinking.

He ran hot water and stirred in dish soap, a mound of suds growing over his fingers. He couldn't remember the last time he'd washed dishes. All the time as a kid, but lately— too many willing to do for him: the movie star. He snorted.

"What?" Bailey called from the other room. "Did you say something?"

"Nope." Adam swiped at the last fork and placed it on the dish rack. He wiped his hands on a towel and hung it neatly over the stove's handle, then took a look around the small kitchen. A broom sat in the corner so he grabbed it and swept clumps of dirt out the door. The activity made him feel useful. Normal. "So not a movie star, Quincy." He leaned against the doorframe and stared at the glorious view.

The sun bore directly down and bounced beams from small puddles. Fingers of light wiggled through the gently swaying trees. He could see how amazing this cabin in the woods—this refuge—was.

And God had led him here.

Adam stiffened at the stray thought. All this God-thinking. He gave the broom a hearty push and shoved bits of leaves from the front porch. If only he had a broom to swipe through him.

"I cannot believe this." Bailey's cry echoed through the stillness.

Adam spun about, dropped the broom and jerked into the living room. "What's wrong?" He limped to her side.

She was seated on the floor, the pictures she'd taken spread across the sofa. She looked up at him, unshed tears causing her eyes to darken.

"Hey, kid." Adam bent forward and peered at the shots. "What's wrong?"

Bailey sniffled and ran a hand through her curly mop. A mop he wished he could tangle his fingers in.

"None of these are right." She stared at him. "None of these are"— she formed air quotes—"my best shot." A sob caught in her throat. "I'm desperately in need of a good sale, because…" She hiccupped. "I'm homeless right now… just like Ginger." Her sobs increased, she placed her elbow on the sofa and tucked her face in it.

Adam patted her shoulder. "Hey, kid. It's going to be all right."

Homeless. What in the world did she mean?

Chapter 10

Bailey tossed the pile of pictures on the floor and dropped to the bed. She was exhausted. Her head pounded in tempo with the rain. The storm had blown in by late afternoon and erased any idea of Adam returning to town to check on the phone number. She'd escaped any further explanations by scurrying upstairs for a nap. She could hear Adam humming downstairs.

"Hey."

Bailey punched the pillow and rolled over. No use in conversation. He didn't want to talk about God, she didn't want to talk about homelessness, helplessness, poverty... "Good grief, you're a mess." She muffled her words into the feather pillow.

"Hey, Bailey." Adam's voice sounded nearer.

"What?"

His hand knocked against a step. "I'd come up there, but you might have to help me down." He laughed. "Come downstairs. I'm lonesome. And you're not asleep, I heard you talking."

"Maybe I talk in my sleep."

"Maybe. But I bet you're just restless with this storm." He rapped the wood again. "Come play." He feigned a whine. "I'm bored."

Despite herself, Bailey laughed. "Okay. Okay. You win." She shoved to her feet and descended the stairs. "What's that?" She pointed to the box in his hand.

"Monopoly. I found this and a couple of other board games in the closet." He nodded toward the stack of boxes on the end table. "We could have a rousing round of Chutes and Ladders if you prefer."

Bailey tugged the box from his hand. "I love Monopoly. I'll play if I get to be the banker." She slid to the floor. "Only time I ever have any cash in hand." She cringed. She didn't need to bring up the state of her affairs lest he hone in on the homeless remark again.

After arranging the board on the end table, settling Adam on the couch with a glass of water, a bag of Fritos, and a pillow, they were ready to play. The rain and wind pounded the windows, but Bailey soon found herself relaxing and enjoying the evening.

Adam crunched a chip and tossed the dice. He moved his figurine and landed on Boardwalk. Her property.

"Pay up, buddy." She wiggled her fingers in his direction.

He fumbled with the play money. "I'm almost broke. Geez. We need to head to Vegas with your luck."

Bailey giggled. "Not a chance. This is my only form of gambling."

Adam sighed. "Well, my old man lost enough for a chalet on a hill in Switzerland when we lived there."

"You lived in Vegas?" Bailey raised a brow. "Glamorous. See or meet famous people?"

"Elvis left the building before I was born." Adam handed her some bills. "And it ain't so glamorous when you're a kid and your old man ditches the family."

"Wow. Sorry."

He sighed. "It happens. Life can kick you in the gut." His brows rose. "As well you know."

"True." Bailey lined up the cash in her growing stack. If only it were real. She blinked back stinging tears and swiped the dice up in her hand. Best move on from personal subjects she didn't want to address.

A roll later she'd landed in jail. No get out of jail free card, either.

Adam's mouth twisted in a crooked smile. "Ha, right where you belong." He crumpled the bag of chips in a wad and stood up. "Break time." He pointed to his loot. "No cheating, either."

"Hey, I don't cheat, Catch'em." Bailey stretched. "What time is it?"

He limped toward the bathroom and glanced over his shoulder. "Why? You got an appointment or important phone call coming in?" He shoved the door open and disappeared.

Bailey leaned against the couch, a shy smile creeping up her cheek. "Nope." She whispered, "I'm right where I'm supposed to be."

Monopoly had helped them kill time, until Bailey couldn't quit yawning and crowed about winning. He'd conceded defeat and reassembled the game in the box. She'd disappeared upstairs, and now he flopped back and forth in bed.

He ground a hand over his face and groaned. Vegas. What a memory to stir up. He had danced around the subject and he noticed she had too. What was it with this kid? She definitely had family problems. Why did he feel such empathy for someone he barely knew?

"Because she is the real deal. You seldom meet those anymore." He stared into the blackness. "And she obviously doesn't have a clue who I am." A sharp pain stabbed his middle. "Quincy, you're ticked she doesn't know who you are." He propped up on one elbow. "For the love, man. You're here to avoid the press, and you've got a photographer upstairs who doesn't even know you and you're ticked." He flopped back and chuckled. "Crazy. You're just plain crazy."

He pinched the bridge of his nose. "She needs money. Your face makes money." He jerked upright, the quilt tumbling to the floor. "There you go. Be the hero." He slid from the bed and padded to the bathroom to stare in the mirror. "Shave, black T-shirt. A shot in the woods against some flora or fauna." He grinned. "And the kid makes money from a picture I *want* taken." He ran water over his hands and splashed his face. "Win-win, I think. She'll take more than Monopoly money to the bank."

His smile died. "Then she'll know who I am and learn I'm a jerk." He wiped his face on a towel and turned off the bathroom light. Once back under the covers, he punched his pillow and tried to settle his knee. "What difference does it make? After we leave here, the magic will evaporate. Life returns to the circus."

Unless you choose differently.

"What? How?" Adam jolted upright. "I don't understand."

But he knew. He knew the choice he needed to make from the talk he'd had with Bailey; he knew from the words which had jumped from the pages of the Bible. He knew deep down inside.

Adam's heart rat-a-tatted against his chest keeping time with the rain. A lump formed in his throat as a tear slid down his cheek.

Yeah. He knew. And the discussion of the most important relationship ever began in his dark bedroom.

Chapter 11

"Quit fidgeting, will you?" Bailey glared at Adam, trying for indignation, and failing completely. She could feel heat rise in her cheeks and angled the camera at his face once again. "I don't want to miss the lighting." She peered through the lens and groaned. "Stop it, Adam. You're ruining the picture."

Adam struck a pose as The Thinker. "What about this one?" He laughed and waggled his fingers in her direction. "Come on, Bailey. Lighten up. We've got time."

Bailey stomped her foot. "No, we don't. Not for the shadows I want. So please cooperate." She titrated the camera's filters. "Now lean one foot back against the cabin step." She pointed at him. "Be careful, don't stumble."

"Why here?" He followed her directions. "Why not out in the woods?"

"I like this rustic setting." She stared at his black hair, glistening in the bright sun. The tips of her ears burned. How could she say so she'd take home a memory of a lifetime? Her throat constricted and her eyes stung. This man had completely captured her heart in a mere two days. *What an idiot.* "Now stand still while I walk." She took a few steps to the left. "I know it's weird, but photographers can capture different angles and create a completely different shot."

"Don't I know it." Adam jerked his T-shirt down.

Bailey lowered the camera. "Adam, what part of be still do you not understand?" She frowned. "Is your knee getting tired?" They had been outside for almost an hour.

"Yeah." Without another word, he stomped up the steps and inside. The thumps didn't make him sound too crippled.

"Okay, then." Bailey capped the lens cover on and looked at the blue sky. All traces of the storm from the night before were on the ground, and the bright sunshine warmed her face. "I'm sure I have some good ones. To town it is."

She'd promised Adam they'd trek back to Sawyer's Gap this morning, but he insisted on a series of photographs before they left. And with such a handsome subject, she certainly didn't mind. He wasn't the cute bunny rabbit or doe and fawn promised to Mr. Reston, not her money shot, but it was the least she could do for a friend.

"A friend." Her pulse sped up. "All that amazing man can ever be, Bailey-girl. A friend." She sighed, kicked mud from her tennis shoes and stepped on the porch. "Someone like him must have a dozen girls lined up. And you're certainly not in the running." That sadness tugged at her once again. The deep-seated lonely. . . "That only prayer can ease. Stop whining, thank God for this amazing experience, and shut up." Bailey lifted her face up and smiled. "Thanks, Lord. It's been real."

Adam growled in the receiver. Buster's phone number still rang as disconnected. Great. His agent bailed? Now what? He thumbed his right eyelid and ran a mental Rolodex for a number. His mom? What would she know?

She answered on the third ring. "Adam, honey. Where are you?"

"I'm on a shoot, Mom." He lied to her so often it came natural. "What's new there?"

"Adam. The police were here looking for you." She sighed. "Honey, it's Ron Carnes."

"Buster?" Adam straightened and pulled the phone booth door closed. "What's wrong?"

"He had a heart attack, Adam. He is in critical condition at the hospital. The policeman said he asked for you before they loaded him into the ambulance."

"Mom, I'm in Sawyer's Gap, a small town up in the mountains." He spoke swiftly, spouting directions he needed for transportation. He glanced up the street. "Call his office, and let the secretary know. I will meet the driver in town at the diner." He replaced the receiver and shifted his weight on to his stronger leg. The hike to Bailey's car had caused his knee pain to flare up, but it didn't match the pain in his heart.

"God, please watch over Buster and keep him alive." His murmured prayer shot out and surprised him. Buster had been like a dad to him for the last few years. He didn't want to lose someone else he cared about.

Bailey stepped out of the photo lab. Her bouncy, curly pony tail flapped under her ball cap and made him smile. That cute kid. Another pang shot through him, tightening his throat. He was about to lose her. "God, another request. This for one I know You care about." He prayed for Bailey and her sister.

She grinned in his direction and pointed to her car. He limped out of the phone booth and met her. "You get the film turned in to—"

"Oh!" A screech filled the air. "Wow!"

"It's him. It's really him." Another screech.

Adam closed his eyes and let the proverbial sound assault him. Something quickened inside. Wasn't fear or anger. Unfamiliar. He swung around and waved a hand at three teenage girls standing on the sidewalk. "Hey, ladies." His throat grew dry.

"Adam Quincy!" One teen bounced nearer. She placed a hand on the hood of the car. "Can I have your autograph?" She reached out her hand with a paper bag and a pen.

"Sure." He swirled his famous AQ across the bag and raised a brow toward the other two. One girl hung back as he signed another paper bag. Adam smiled at the shy teen. "You sure?" He tilted his head in his famous puppy dog look. "I'm willing."

The girl shook her head. "No, thank you, sir. I don't want to bother you."

"No bother, sugar. It's how I make a living." Adam gave a tight laugh and watched as the girl snatched the pen away from her friend. He signed the third time, gave a salute and slid into the front seat with a sigh. The girls formed a tight group and watched as Bailey backed from the parking spot. Adam didn't look her way.

The magical reprieve had just been broken.

Chapter 12

Bailey couldn't form words as she drove back to the cabin. Her brain whirred like a movie reel: scene to scene to scene. Adam Quincy? The man in the car was Adam *Quincy*? Granted, she wasn't much of a movie-goer, but she didn't live under a rock. Or maybe she did.

She glanced at Adam's profile. How could she have been so blind? So stupid? She'd shot photographs of one of Hollywood's most glamorous men. And played Monopoly with him. Had shared a cabin for two nights—

A groan escaped her lips.

"You okay?" Adam swiveled in the seat to face her.

She gave a tight smile. "Sure." Her heart raced and her cheeks burned. "Fine."

Adam sighed. "Look, Bailey. I'm sorry about what just happened. I hope you weren't embarrassed."

"Of course not." The words squeaked from her lips. She bit the inside of her cheek. Now she was embarrassed.

He slid his hand down his thigh and massaged his knee. "I'll be out of your hair soon. My agent had a heart attack, and Mom's making arrangements for someone to come pick me up. I need to grab my gear and come back to the diner and wait for a ride. Would you bring me back?"

"Of course I will. A heart attack?" Bailey took her eyes from the road momentarily. "I'm so sorry. What's his name? I'll add him to my prayer list."

"Buster." Adam sighed. "Ron Carnes, actually, but Buster to me. He's been like a big brother-dad." He stared out the side window. "I just can't lose him."

"We can pray. God is always ready to hear his people when they cry out to Him. He wants to hear from us." Bailey navigated the last turn and parked her car. She reached for the door handle, anxious to be away from Adam. Here she was with a ball cap clapped on her unruly mop, no makeup, and dirty blue jeans. He must think her a real mess after being surrounded by beauties every day. Her cheeks still stung and the tips of her ears burned. She clenched a fist against her stomach, pressing down the rising emotions.

"Wait." Adam reached for her elbow. "Before you get out." He squeezed and then released her arm. "I have to say something."

Bailey settled against the seat and watched as muscles in his jaw worked.

"First off, thank you for spending time with me. I seldom have that luxury. I know I crashed your solitude and"—he grinned—"the search for the best shot, but you cannot understand how wonderful and relaxing the last two days have been."

Bailey stirred in the seat. "You're welcome? I guess that's the appropriate words to use." She tilted her head and smiled. "I've enjoyed the time, too." She swiveled toward the door.

Adam chuckled. "There's more. I want you to know how important you've become to me."

She froze, her back to him, her throat tight, tears threatening.

"Bailey, please look at me."

She did, her heart pounding so loudly she was sure Adam could hear it. He met her gaze, then looked at her lips. Her breath hitched. A kiss? Was that possible? No, she mentally nudged that thought away. "What?" she croaked.

Adam toyed with the gear shift in the center console. "You know that whole Bible discussion we had?" He swallowed and paused, then spoke softly, "It took. I believe, and it's because you were brave enough to talk to me about God. No one has ever done that before." He looked toward the cabin, barely visible through the trees. "This place of refuge, away from prying eyes and the clamor of work—well, it's been a healing time. I can never thank you enough."

A tear seeped through her lower lashes and trickled down her cheek. His words of life—eternal life—were much better than a kiss. "Oh, Adam," she breathed. "What a blessing."

"Yes, you are." He leaned forward, placed his fingertips under her chin and lightly brushed her lips with his. "Thank you." He grasped the door handle and climbed from the car.

Bailey watched him limp up the incline. With one finger on her lips, she heaved a sigh.

Adam Quincy had just kissed her.

Yes, he'd kissed her. Given away his heart to an imp.

Adam reached for the front door knob then glanced back at the car where Bailey sat. How he was going to miss this girl. This cabin. He looked toward the mountains, the majesty of the scenery seeping into his soul. Wouldn't it be amazing to experience such peace at home?

"Could never work, Quincy, so staunch these feelings now." He shoved the door open. "She would never want to be a part of your world." He clomped to the bedroom and shoved his clothes into the duffle bag. Zipping it up, he looked at the tiny Bible he'd brought into the bedroom to read. He reached for it and rubbed a finger over the barely visible filigree on the cover. "This stays. It's the heart of the cabin." He touched his lips to the book, limped to the living room and placed it gently on the mantel. He stared at the embroidered piece of fabric. *Place of refuge.* "I don't know who left this, but thank you."

With that, Adam felt he was ready to leave. Bailey had remained in the car to shuttle him down the mountain, so he tugged the bag onto his shoulder and headed out.

In the kitchen, he tapped the broom's handle and grinned. "Batter up," he whispered through dry lips. Man, leaving someone like Bailey Summers was hard. He inhaled and exhaled slowly. Time to paste on his act. He could never let her see his heart.

He flashed her a bright smile once he was in the front seat. "Time to get back to the real world, huh?" He plopped the bag on the floor between his feet. "Nice little vacation, but gotta pay the bills. I know Buster lined up one audition in three weeks. Hope he had all of that squared away before he conked out."

Even to his ears he sounded callous. Well, so be it. This was who he was now.

Adam Quincy, actor. And this part required his ultimate attention lest he slip into his real skin and hurt the wonderful woman behind the wheel.

CHAPTER 13

Three months later

Bailey pulled the magazine from the mailbox, leaned against the porch post and sighed. The doe and fawn graced the front cover. Her heart galloped as she ran her fingers across the picture. Where had Adam been when she'd shot this one?

"Oh, stop it, dummy." Bailey trudged up the steps into her apartment building. She'd been so blessed to find this efficiency. Mr. Reston was so pleased with most of her pictures, he'd given her enough of an advance for a deposit and first month's rent. To top it off, he'd reverted the rights of the remainder of the photos back to her, and she sold eleven more pictures to nature magazines. She'd not received copies of many of them, but it certainly boosted her spirits.

Bailey reached across the kitchen table for a frame she'd purchased. Sliding the magazine inside, she held it at arm's length. Was this bragging, to hang your accomplishments on the living room wall?

"Hope not, Lord. But I am so proud of this…" Tears clogged her throat and she swallowed hard. "My best shot."

Bailey tapped a nail into the wall and hung the magazine. She stepped back to admire the small fawn curled up so tightly near the doe. The lighting had been perfect that morning.

The last morning.

Once she took Adam down the mountain, the cabin and scenery dulled. She had called Renee, stayed with her for a week before Mr. Reston helped her out.

Bailey slid onto the sofa and reached for an unopened envelope of pictures. She fingered the tab, then tossed it back onto the end table. Pictures of Adam. Her best shot was probably in that envelope. Opening it wasn't something she was ready to do. She knew she could garner big money for a superb picture of Adam Quincy. After all, he graced the front of many magazines sitting by the checkout stand in the grocery store. But she would never sell his picture. He meant too much to her.

A tense feeling gathered under her breastbone. Bailey crossed her arms and drew them tightly to her chest. The pangs of loneliness for a man she'd known all of two days hadn't abated. No matter what she did, thoughts of the soft kiss kept her awake. She replayed every moment of their time together.

Bailey groaned. "Every moment you acted like a goofball." She ran a hand over her fluffy ponytail. "Mr. Best-dressed surely did see you looking good, girl." She shoved from the sofa and grabbed her purse and camera bag. The gig to shoot a friend's kid's birthday party didn't pay much, but money was money. She would take what she could get.

Adam couldn't take it anymore. He dropped the script on the floor and paced the hotel room. Three days in Denver and all he could think about was Bailey Summers. A two day... what? Fling? No, that indicated more than Monopoly and sandwiches. A two day friendship.

"A two day refuge." He gazed at the mountains in the distance and thought of the mountains outside the cabin door. Had he been too crass to notice their beauty? The majesty of God's handiwork? He sighed and dropped into a chair. "If so, Lord, I'm sorry."

This new attitude of thinking about God and instant prayers made him chuckle. When he'd stood by Buster's bed and offered to pray, his agent had looked at him as though he were foreign. A good sign. Because he wanted to be foreign in actor-land. He wanted to be different inside and out. The opportunity to tell about his new, changed life had afforded itself several times, but unlike Bailey, Adam hadn't spoken about it.

"Chicken." He sighed and pinched the bridge of his nose. "Big chicken. Bailey would've spoken up to Trina." His co-star had made herself readily available, and Adam had worked hard to escape her clutches. Trina grabbed him outside a restaurant and planted a hard kiss. Just in time to get a picture for the front page of some rag. He could've taken her inside, bought her dinner and talked to her about the miracle in his life. Instead, he pushed her aside and scrambled to the waiting cab.

He'd never make it as a witness for God. "Just not my part, I guess." He bent over and reached for the script. "Better study the one I'm suited for."

The phone rang interrupting his study time. A call to the set.

Adam shrugged on his jacket, gathered the script and headed into bedlam. He knew photographers waited outside the hotel, like crows on a wire, so he hoped the limo had the door open.

The revolving door swung him onto the street and into the melee and the face of a man he knew. The photographer he'd punched a few months ago. Adam jerked back and stopped. Flashes of light pierced his eyes.

"Hey, buddy." Adam pressed his hand against the man's shoulder. "Got a second?" He nodded toward the car. "I'd like to speak to you, if that's okay." The puzzled look across the man's face made Adam chuckle. His heart rate sped up. Here was an opportunity he didn't want to miss. "No fists, I promise. Just words."

Wonderful words of life.

Chapter 14

The strident ring of the phone jolted Bailey from sleep. She squinted at the clock. Four-fifteen. She swallowed, her throat dry, and croaked a hello.

"Miss Summers?"

"Yes."

"Please hold."

Bailey stared into the darkness. Please hold? For whom? She struggled to sit up and pulled the blanket against her chin, her hand trembling. At this time of night, a phone call couldn't be good. She willed her heart to slow down and waited.

"Bailey?"

The deep voice resonated in her ear, through her brain and straight into her heart. She was sure it would burst.

"Adam? What— How did you get my number"

"An assistant with directory assistance. Look, I know I woke you, and I apologize, but I'm in London and this was the only time I could find to call. I need to see you."

"Why?" Bailey bit her lip. Had that word escaped? She should've jumped for joy with a hearty yes.

"Please. I'll be back tomorrow. Would you have dinner with me?" She heard him draw in a breath. "It's important. I can have a driver pick you up at seven if you'll give me an address."

Bailey nodded then said, "Sure. Sounds like a plan." She repeated her address.

"See you soon."

With that the call disconnected. Bailey held the receiver until the operator croaked would she like to make a call. She hung up and slid under the covers.

She had a date with Adam Quincy. Holy cow! She had a date with Adam Quincy.

Bailey jumped from the bed, flipped on the light and jerked the closet door open. What did one wear on a date with a movie star? She ran a hand through her curls. Would Lorena Mery have time to work magic on her hair? She poked a foot into the pile of shoes on the floor. Did anything there look presentable?

Bailey's hands shook and she gathered them against her chest. "Okay. Stop the foolishness. It's probably not a date." She closed the closet door. "He wants those pictures. Or he wants to talk about God." She turned the light off and climbed back into bed.

Yes, that was it. He wanted to talk to her about God, the Bible, and Scriptures. Something, which at the moment, eluded her. Brain power. The call had caused her to envision Adam Quincy, the movie star, not Adam the Monopoly-playing cripple.

She sighed. Didn't matter, he was coming and she was going. "Amazing, Lord. Please use this evening to Your glory."

After a rough hour tossing and turning, Bailey headed to the shower. She would search out Lorena, find a decent outfit and be ready for her meeting—not date—with Adam tomorrow at seven.

The following day, time stretched out, but by six forty-five she was parked in front of the window, watching for a car. When it arrived, she gulped. "A stretch limo?" She grabbed her purse and, out of habit, reached for the camera bag. Her hand fell to her side. "No, my *friend* doesn't need me to take any pictures, I'm sure."

She locked the door behind her and stepped out the door and into a new world.

Adam licked his lips and nodded a thank you to the maître d. The private dining room he'd reserved was perfect. Not too romantic, but secluded from prying eyes. He folded his hands on the table, ran his right thumb across his left thumb, reached for the napkin, flapped it open, then dropped it on the plate. He swallowed, his throat tight. He glanced at his watch and sighed. He wasn't this nervous in front of a camera.

"Something wrong, Catch'em?" Bailey slid into the chair across from him.

"Not now." He stared at her; the freckles on her nose had been powdered and her unruly mop tamed. The cute girl was now a beautiful woman. He met her gaze. "How are you?"

"Doing well, thanks." She tipped her head. "I see you've begun another picture. Congratulations."

The thought of the real world and the fantasy world colliding nearly sent Adam reeling from the table. He didn't want to talk movies with Bailey. He wanted to talk about—

"Thanks. But we're not here to discuss me." He tipped a hand toward her. "I saw the deer pictures. So congratulations to you, too."

Bailey grinned and reached for her water glass. She took a sip leaving a trace of lipstick on the glass. Another change. He'd not seen her in makeup at the cabin.

"Thanks." She cleared her throat. "It's really good to see you." She gave a light laugh. "In person, not just on a magazine stand."

"Yeah, well, that's part of my life. Can't change that." He toyed with the knife and fork by the plate. "Look, Bailey, I've asked you here for a very important reason." He straightened and narrowed his eyes. "I found Ginger."

Bailey's forehead wrinkled. "Ginger?" She whispered.

"Yeah, your sister. I found her." He leaned forward and propped his elbows on the table. "There was a casting call when we were here last." He looked down and then met her gaze once again. "I'm sorry I didn't call." He had so much to tell her. "Anyway, Ginger appeared. Gave her real name. I saw the list and had the casting director locate her. She auditioned and made the cut." He reached across the table and grasped her fingers. "Bailey, I know where your sister lives. She's in a small apartment with another girl and has work. Until this set wraps, at least."

Bailey's fingers twitched.

He tightened his grip. "I can take you there."

She nodded, a tear tracking down her cheek. "Thank You, Jesus."

Adam smiled. "Pretty much sums it up, I think."

A waiter approached but Adam waved him away. This wasn't the time for a meal, it was a time for a reunion.

He stood and held out a hand. "Ready to go?"

Bailey swiveled in her seat and clutched the table. Her eyes, full of unshed tears and uncertainty scanned his face for a moment. Then she rose. "As ready as I'll ever be."

Adam held out his elbow and tucked her hand through the crook. It felt so right.

Then he turned toward the kitchen. To avoid being on the front page, they'd have to sneak out the back door. He hoped she was ready for that.

Chapter 15

Bailey's throat constricted and she struggled to swallow. Her chest was so tight she considered asking the driver to head to the ER. Was it really possible Adam had found her runaway sister? She swiped at her cheeks, makeup smearing across her palm. What did she care about dripping mascara? She was with her friend, Adam Quincy. And he'd found Ginger.

They had changed from the limo to a smaller car and the driver swept them down the freeway and exited after a few minutes. She'd been unable to speak, unable to think of anything except meeting with her sister. Adam hadn't tried to make conversation. Instead, he'd held her hand.

Her friend: Adam Quincy.

They arrived at a small housing project, older apartments in a seedier part of the city, but the area appeared under renovation. Oh, how she hoped Ginger was renovated as well.

"Bailey?" Adam gripped her hand tighter. "We changed cars but I can't change my appearance. If you think having me go in would be distracting—"

She gasped. "I can't do this without you. Please." She tilted her head and looked at the apartment building again. "What if she's not there? What if she doesn't want to see me?" She swung her head side to side, a frantic panic rising up.

"Hey. Look at me." Adam pressed a finger under her chin and tilted her head toward his face. "Stop. Let's pray."

She slumped against the seat and closed her eyes. "Pray, of course. The first thing that should've crossed my mind."

Adam placed an arm around her shoulders, drew her against him and whispered words of peace. Bailey's rat-a-tat heart surely resounded through the car. She squinted at this guy who held her, who had helped her. He did seem changed. She drew in a deep breath and felt a river of calm flow through her. When he said amen, she squeezed his knee. He flinched.

"Sorry, Catch'em. Didn't mean to hurt you." She pecked him on the cheek with a tiny kiss. "Thank you so much. I don't have enough words to say thank you."

Adam pressed his forehead to hers, "Bailey, I could never thank you enough for braving the elements and storming the refuge to help me understand about God's grace. I have so much to tell you." He reached for the door handle. "But for right now, we have someone to meet."

Bailey stared into his eyes and then nodded, a glimmer of recognition causing a shiver of excitement to course through her. If he had so much to tell her, that meant they would communicate with each other again. She wasn't sure she could stand any more excitement.

Ginger and Bailey held on to each other and swayed inside the sparsely furnished apartment. Adam cleared his throat in an attempt to gain control of his emotions. The reunion was all he could've hoped for. The two sisters cried and laughed uncontrollably. He found himself caught up in their excitement, longing for a strong connection of his own.

Ginger shoved her dyed-brown hair from her eyes and stared at him. "Adam Quincy?"

The familiar squeak tinged her tone and he looked at his shoes.

She reached for his hand and squeezed it. "Thank you, sir." Ginger faced her sister. "I didn't know how to come back, how to be me again." She pulled Bailey to two folding chairs and they sat. "I've been clean and dry for almost a year. I have a job…" She shot a look at him. "Your doing?"

Adam held out his hands. "Nope. Must've passed muster with someone else, because I didn't pull any strings."

A tender smile crossed Ginger's face. "Wow. Thank You, Jesus."

Bailey swooped over and hugged Ginger. "Words I've been hoping and praying I'd hear," she sobbed. "Oh, sister-of-mine, you're really here."

Adam stepped into the foyer of the small apartment to avoid intruding on this personal moment. He leaned his back against the wall and closed his eyes. The little place here should have an embroidered hanging. Seems it had become Ginger's place of refuge.

He jerked upright when Bailey threw her arms around him. "Adam Quincy, friend-not-movie-star, I love you."

"What?" Adam pulled her back enough to stare into her eyes.

"I love you, silly." Bailey grinned up at him.

"You're welcome, I was glad to be a part of this miracle." The words caught in his throat and he clutched her shoulders tighter. "Bailey, you don't know what you're saying."

"Oh, yes I do." Bailey stood on tiptoes and kissed him square on the lips. He leaned in to the kiss and deepened it. Her arms tightened around his neck.

She sighed and pressed her face to his chest. "Adam Quincy, friend-not-movie-star, I love you."

Adam laughed, a flood of love welling up. "Bailey Summers, not-a-photographer, I love you too. I'm not sure how this will work, you being part of this crazy world I live in but—"

Bailey threw her head back and met his gaze. "Let's give it our best shot."

THE END

My Dwelling Place

K. Marie Libel

How lovely is your dwelling place, O LORD Almighty! My soul yearns, even faints, for the courts of the LORD; my heart and my flesh cry out for the living God. Even the sparrow has found a home, and the swallow a nest for herself, where she may have her young—a place near your altar, O LORD Almighty, my King and my God. Blessed are those who dwell in your house; they are ever praising you. Blessed are those whose strength is in you, who have set their hearts on pilgrimage.
PSALM 84:1-5

To my posse, in whom I have found dear friends for life.

CHAPTER 1

Wichita, Kansas

Fear gripped Autumn Brady's stomach as she secured her seat on the bus and tucked her small suitcase under her feet. At least she hoped it was fear causing her stomach to clench painfully and not something wrong with the baby. She waited impatiently as other passengers boarded and found their seats. A nervous glance at her watch told her the bus would depart within a few moments. It couldn't leave fast enough. Autumn was half convinced she'd be yanked from her seat and dragged back home before she even had a chance to escape. But she'd been more careful this time, timed it just right, given no clues as to her plan. Surely it would work. It had to.

As the bus lurched forward, carrying her away from her home, her fear was gradually replaced with fragile hope and she placed a protective hand over her still-flat stomach.

My baby.

She still couldn't believe a new little life grew inside of her, just under her heart. Funny how two pink lines on a stick had given her the strength to do what she'd not been able to do for herself.

"Don't worry, little one," Autumn whispered. "I'll keep you safe. I promise."

She leaned her head back in her seat and closed her eyes against the nausea welling up with the not-so-gentle sway of the Greyhound bus. She'd used cash for her ticket, just in case. She couldn't take any chances that her husband would be able to track her down. She was pretty sure Rick wouldn't think to look for her at her cousin's house in Wyoming. She and Whitney hadn't spoken in years, aside from the obligatory Christmas card and accompanying letter each December. But that's why Autumn had chosen to go there; not just because Wyoming was a far cry from Kansas, but because if Rick were to look for her—and she was certain he would—a cousin in a distant state with whom she barely spoke wouldn't even cross his mind. That was her hope, anyway.

Lord, please keep me and my baby safe. Don't let him find us.

A single tear slipped from beneath her lashes. How had she gone from a giddy bride to a frightened runaway? Rick had been everything she thought she wanted—handsome, charming, and romantic. He'd swept her off her feet, and within three months of their first meeting they were planning a wedding. It was like a fairy tale come to life. Unfortunately, within three months of the wedding, the beatings had begun.

Autumn involuntarily winced as she remembered the blows. Sometimes he would only deliver one—a warning she was getting on his nerves. Other times there would be so many she would black out—her punishment for dinner being cold, or wearing too much makeup, or daring to stand up to him.

The first time she'd tried to leave, she hadn't gotten any further than the front door. He'd made sure she understood her mistake in trying to leave him. She never tried to leave again. Instead she learned to walk on egg shells and try not to upset him. Nothing she did was ever good enough though. Nothing ever would be. Eventually his fists broke her spirit, and she accepted that this would be her life. . .if she could even call it a life. For her it was mere existence.

Until she learned she was pregnant. That discovery fueled a new fire in her, and for the first time in a long time she felt the urge to fight. This broken, defeated existence that had become her own would not be her baby's fate.

The bus hit a bump and Autumn shifted, trying to find a comfortable position. Her back ached, her stomach rolled with nausea, and she longed to stretch her legs. But she wouldn't complain. Each moment on the bus, uncomfortable as it may be, afforded her one more mile of freedom.

A small smile tilted her lips, despite her discomfort. Freedom. What a wonderful word. She still didn't know what she would do once she reached her destination, but for now just the journey was reason enough to celebrate. Soon she would be in Sawyer's Gap, Wyoming, and she would start a new life where no one would ever hurt her again.

Sawyer's Gap, Wyoming

Micah Hodge fell to the ground, clutching his chest, and released a loud groan. "Please," he begged for mercy, "no more. I surrender!"

He was answered with a shriek before the little girl threw herself onto his stomach, forcing all the air from his lungs. "Oomph. You're gonna kill me, kid." He tickled her belly until she squealed and ran away from him.

Flat on the floor, he looked up at his best friend's husband. "Can't you control that rascal?"

Dean Lawson laughed and offered a hand to help Micah off the floor. "Trying to control a three-year-old is like trying to lasso a tornado. Besides, you started it. Lacey was perfectly calm before you showed up."

"What?" Micah affected a look of innocence. "All I did was give her some candy."

Whitney, Micah's best friend from childhood, glared at him. "After I told you it was too close to bedtime for her to have sugar. You got her all hyped up."

"Aw, come on. It's my right as an honorary uncle to give my darling niece candy. I can't resist that face. Besides, you can't stay mad at me anyway." Micah grinned at Lacey, who giggled and latched onto his leg. He tousled her mop of blonde curls and scooped her up into his arms. "Mom and Dad aren't going to let me spoil you anymore if you don't calm down, Miss Lace."

She buried her face in his neck, and he breathed in the scent of her shampoo. How did they manage to make kids shampoo smell like pure innocence?

"You do spoil her." Whitney reached for her daughter and Micah reluctantly released her.

"I can't help it. I'm crazy about this little imp." He made a face at Lacey and she rewarded him with another adorable giggle.

"Sounds like you need to have one of your own to spoil," Dean offered with a smirk as he picked up stuffed animals and pieces of Lacey's princess tea set off the floor.

"Would love to, but I kind of need a wife for that first. And if you haven't noticed, I don't exactly have any prospects." Micah plopped onto the couch and waved goodnight to Lacey as Whitney carried her to bed.

"What about joining the singles group the church just started?"

"I don't know, not really my style." Then again, his "style" hadn't gotten him anywhere other than a few casual dates with no sparks whatsoever.

Maybe it was time for a reevaluation.

Dean rolled his eyes. "Gotta start somewhere. How long has it been since you've been on a date?"

A knock on the door saved him from having to answer. Micah jumped up off the couch. "You're busy, I'll get it."

He just might hug whoever was on the other side of the door for sparing him the humiliation of admitting how long it had been since he'd last been out with a woman. *Fourteen months.* He inwardly cringed. Totally embarrassing. Meeting someone in a small town was just so hard. You already knew everyone and had either tried dating each other or had no interest in dating each other. Not exactly the best recipe for romance.

Lord, it would sure be nice if you could bring me someone.

Micah swung the front door open and nearly staggered backward a step. The woman standing on the threshold was stunning. Dark hair framed her heart shaped face and accentuated her blue-green eyes, which sparkled brilliantly under the porch light. She was a vision, despite looking weary and confused.

Wow, Lord, You work fast. Micah cleared his throat and did his best to stop staring. "Hi. What can I do for ya?"

The woman's eyes darted to the silver numbers above the door, then down to a piece of paper in her hand. "I'm sorry, I must have the wrong address. I was trying to find Whitney and Dean Lawson."

"You've found them. Come on in." He stepped back and motioned her inside.

She tentatively stepped around him into the living room. "Thank you."

He held out his hand. "I'm Micah. I'm a friend of Whitney and Dean."

She glanced at his extended hand for several seconds before reaching out and accepting his handshake. Her fingers had barely touched his before she quickly withdrew. "Autumn Brady. I'm Whitney's cousin."

"Nice to meet you." Something about this woman seemed very vulnerable. Micah got the feeling she didn't want him too close and he wondered what had her so skittish. Had he stared too hard at her when he opened the door and made her uncomfortable? That would be just like him, making a fool of himself in front of a beautiful woman he'd just met.

"Who is it, Micah?" Dean called from the kitchen.

"Um, it's Whitney's cousin, Autumn Brady."

Dean poked his head around the corner, his eyebrows knitted into a V.

"Autumn?"

Whitney appeared from the hallway and stopped in her tracks when she saw her cousin. "Autumn? What are you doing here?"

Autumn twisted her hands. "I'm so sorry to just drop in on you like this. I should have called first. I was just afraid—"

Whitney rushed forward and drew Autumn into a hug. "Well, I'm happy to see you, but this is a surprise." She led Autumn further into the living room. "Are you okay? Where's Rick?"

Micah watched as Autumn's eyes began to water. He didn't know what was causing her to cry, but his heart immediately went out to her. He eyed the small suitcase by the front door and reached to bring it inside. Obviously Autumn planned to stay for a few days. He toyed with the doorknob, unsure of whether he should stay or go. He didn't want to intrude on a family reunion, but he didn't want to leave the presence of this beauty quite yet either.

Dean caught his eye and motioned him into the kitchen. Relieved at having the decision made for him, Micah joined him and helped to get drinks for everyone. The two men carried glasses of iced tea out to the living room and set them on coasters. Whitney had Autumn wrapped in a tight embrace and was rocking her back and forth like she did when comforting Lacey. Autumn's eyes were red and puffy from crying, and tear tracks stained her cheeks. Micah's mind reeled with questions, but it was not his place to ask so he settled into a recliner and tried to look inconspicuous.

"Autumn needs to stay with us for a while, Dean." Whitney rubbed Autumn's back in a motherly fashion. "She's left Rick."

Micah's heart sank. So the lovely Autumn was married. Separated, apparently, but still married. *Guess it's over before it even began.*

Dean leaned forward in his seat. "I'm sorry to hear that, Autumn. You're more than welcome to stay for a few days." He gave her an apologetic look. "But the only place we have for you to sleep is on the couch. I don't want to sound rude, but how long were you planning to stay?"

Autumn sniffled and Whitney glared at her husband. "She needs our help, Dean. Let her get through a few days at least and then we can figure something out."

"I still don't understand why you came here, Autumn." Dean reached out a hand and placed it on Autumn's knee. The girl jerked and winced—an odd reaction. Dean leaned back. "Honestly, I'm not upset you're here, just confused. What's going on?"

"Dean. . ." Whitney's tone warned.

"No, it's okay." Autumn pulled away from Whitney's embrace and wiped her hand across her cheek. "You both have a right to know the whole truth."

She reached for her glass of tea, drained half the contents, and then drew a deep breath as if trying to summon strength. "I came here because it was the farthest place from home, and the least likely place Rick was to look for me. I can't risk him finding me. I just can't."

Her voice wavered, and Micah thought he detected a hint of fear mingled with desperation. From what was this woman running?

"Are you saying Rick doesn't know you've left him?" Dean questioned, concern evident in his tone.

"I'm sure he's realized it by now. But I left no note and there was no discussion about it if that's what you mean." Autumn sat up straighter. "But you don't understand. I had to do it that way or—or—"

"Or what?" Whitney asked gently.

"I fear he would've killed me," Autumn whispered brokenly. "You see, that's why I left." She pulled up her sleeves and revealed arms marked with large bruises, some obviously fresh, others on the mend. "There's more, but I will spare you those."

"Oh, Autumn," Whitney breathed, a catch in her throat. "I had no idea. I'm so sorry."

Dean heaved a sigh. "So you ran as far as you could. I suppose I can understand that, given your circumstances." He shook his head and his eyes filled with sympathy. "I'm sorry this has happened to you, Autumn. It's not right for a man to treat a woman like that, especially his wife. I can't even imagine—"

Dean swiped his face with his hand. "I want to help you, Autumn, truly I do, but I have to be honest with you. I'm concerned. What if Rick *does* think to look for you here? He's obviously a violent man and I have a wife and young daughter to think about."

Whitney gasped. "We can't just throw her out into the street, Dean! She needs our help, and we *will* give it to her."

"Whitney. . ."

"We are *not* throwing her out, Dean."

Whitney and Dean stared hard at each other, neither one willing to back down. The tension in the room was palpable, and Micah shifted uncomfortably. He'd seen the two of them have little spats before, but never had he heard

Whitney speak so vehemently to her husband.

Autumn stood up and took to twisting her hands again. "Please, don't argue. The last thing in the world I want to do is cause problems between you two or put your family in danger. I'm so sorry I didn't think of that. I will find somewhere else to go."

Whitney stood too and put a protective arm around Autumn. "You have nowhere else to go. You'll stay right here."

"No, really, I don't want to cause problems here. Please, I'll be okay. Don't worry."

Autumn's attempt at bravery touched Micah's heart. If only he could open up his home to her. But what would people think? What would *she* think?

"Wait!" he exclaimed as an idea struck. Why hadn't he thought of this sooner? "My family's cabin. No one is staying there. It probably needs a good cleaning, but it's vacant." He turned toward Autumn. "It's up in the mountains, very private. You can stay there as long as you need."

"Oh no, I couldn't do that." She shook her head.

"Why not?"

Autumn blinked. "Well, because. . .I don't even know you. Or your family. I can't just impose on a stranger's home like that."

Micah smiled gently. "Actually, you can. That's sort of what the cabin is for. It's a place where anyone in need of refuge can go for as long as they need it. And if anyone is in need of refuge, it's you."

"Oh, Micah, that's perfect!" Whitney gave his hand an excited squeeze. "I can't believe I didn't think of that either. She can't go tonight though. It's dark outside and she's been traveling too long already today."

"I'll drive her up there tomorrow afternoon. I'll need a chance to clean the place up and stock the fridge first." Micah grabbed his jacket. "I'd better get going. I'll do some grocery shopping tonight and make sure the cabin is ready for you tomorrow, Autumn."

"Wait, I don't need you to buy me groceries or clean for me. I don't have much money but I have enough for some food. And I can certainly manage the cleaning by myself." Autumn met his eyes, and he felt his knees go a bit weak. "I appreciate your kindness, but I don't want to trouble anyone. Please, let me do the cleaning and shopping. Simply offering me a place to stay is help enough."

He started to argue that it was no trouble, but then he saw her eyes glimmer with stubborn pride, and he nodded. After everything she'd been through, she probably needed to feel self-sufficient. He could understand that. "All right. Enjoy your visit with your family, and I'll come pick you up early tomorrow afternoon to take you shopping and then up to the cabin." He paused, not wanting her to feel as if he was bossing her around. "That is, if that's all right with you."

Autumn turned a hesitant look to Whitney.

"It's okay," Whitney assured her. "I've known him practically my whole life. You can trust him."

Micah stepped forward. "Yeah, I might be a pain in her neck, but I'm pretty harmless." He grinned, hoping to put Autumn at ease.

A soft chuckle escaped her lips and she smiled for the first time since walking through the door. "Okay. That sounds fine. Thank you, sir."

"Micah, please." He made a face. "*Sir* makes me sound old."

Autumn laughed again. A beautiful sound. "Micah, then."

The sound of his name on her lips caused butterflies to flit around in his stomach. *Get ahold of yourself, man. She's married.*

He tipped an imaginary hat. "See you all tomorrow then."

Micah let himself out, and as he closed the door behind him he had the eerie sensation that this beautiful, vulnerable woman—married or not—would not easily be erased from his mind. As much as Micah might be attracted to Whitney's cousin, she was not someone he could pursue. A disappointment to be sure, but a fact he would have to accept. Still, her situation saddened him and made him want to help her in any way he could. So, he would head up to the cabin tomorrow morning and at least make sure there would be clean linens and the electricity and plumbing were in working order before he took her up there. The rest he would let her do for herself as she requested.

"Lord, I truly want to help her," he prayed as he climbed into his car. "She needs protection and people around her who care about her. Help me to be a friend to this woman and to not wish for things that can't be."

Chapter 2

Autumn stepped across the cabin's porch, through the door, and found herself in a small but functional kitchen. Micah set the grocery bags down on the counter top and motioned for her to take a look at the rest of the place. She peeked through the kitchen door and let her eyes roam the cabin which was to be her new, albeit temporary, home. It was small, but she didn't need much room. Besides, the layout and decor possessed a warm, cozy touch that made her feel...safe.

Been a long time since I've felt that.

"This is really nice, Micah. I can't thank you enough for letting me stay here." Autumn leaned against the door frame and watched him start to pull groceries out of the bags.

"It's my pleasure. This cabin has been sitting empty for quite a while. It needed someone to come in and give it life again." Micah began putting groceries in the fridge. "Unfortunately, since it's been empty, it really does need a thorough cleaning. Are you sure I can't help you with that?"

Autumn joined him in finding places for the items in her grocery bags. "No, but thank you. I can manage on my own."

Autumn could tell by his expression he didn't like leaving her alone with the chore, but he respected her wishes. "Okay. I brought some cleaning supplies up this morning. There are also clean sheets on the bed in the bedroom, but not in the loft. I just assumed you'd want to sleep on the main floor. I also put some fresh towels in the bathroom. If I missed anything, just make a list. I'm happy to supply anything you need while you're here."

She gave him a sidelong glance as he pulled paper towels and cleaning spray from what appeared to be a pantry. She'd just met this man, and already he was being so kind to her. She didn't understand his motives, but in her experience a man wasn't nice to her unless he wanted something or was trying to pull the wool over her eyes. Would this Micah turn out to be the same?

True, he'd been a complete gentleman while they'd done the grocery shopping and during their time in his car. He'd not made one romantic overture or inappropriate comment toward her. Still, she wasn't ready to let her guard down yet, even if Whitney said Micah could be trusted.

"That's everything." Micah brushed his hands along his pant legs. "You should be set for at least a week with these groceries. But like I said, if you need anything else just let me or Whitney know. Hopefully that trac phone we got you will give you a good enough signal up here. Here's my number. . ." He grabbed a notebook and pen off the table and scrawled his phone number on it. "This is my cell, so call any time. As long as I'm not with a patient I'll answer right away. Otherwise I'll call back."

Autumn took the paper from him. "With a patient?"

He smiled. "I'm a nurse at the hospital on the edge of town. I work kind of strange hours sometimes, but I'm only part time so I can usually be available if you need anything."

"You're a nurse?"

"I know, I know. A male nurse is not a commonality, but we do exist."

"Oh, I didn't mean any offense." Autumn shrugged. "It's just that. . .well, that explains things."

Micah raised his eyebrows.

"Why you're being so nice to me, even though you just met me." Autumn smiled. "Nurses are genuine nurturers. You can't help it, can you?"

Micah laughed. "I guess not."

"Well, thank you for your kindness. It means a lot to me." Autumn looked around at her new dwelling. "I really hadn't thought farther ahead than getting to Wyoming. I should have realized I couldn't just stay with Whitney and Dean indefinitely, and I certainly should have considered their safety, even if I don't think Rick would look for me there."

Micah reached out to touch her arm and she did her best not to flinch. He wasn't Rick. He wouldn't touch her with the intention of hurting her. Still, those inner instincts were hard to squelch. As if he sensed her discomfort, he quickly dropped his hand but his eyes remained filled with compassion.

"You were scared. I'm sure all you could think about was getting away. I'm just glad you made it here safely. Even if your husband did show up at your cousin's house, all she would have to say is she hadn't seen you. He'd never find this cabin. You're safe here," Micah reassured her. "And this can be your home for as long as you need it."

Autumn felt her eyes well with tears. She laughed at herself as she brushed them away. "Sorry, it must be the pregnancy hormones getting to me."

"You're pregnant?"

Oops.

"Um, yeah." She instinctively covered her stomach with her hands. "I hadn't planned to say anything to Whitney until I made it through my first trimester. Just in case. . .you know."

Micah stepped forward. "Sure, I understand. I won't say anything. But are you receiving medical care?"

"No, I'm only eleven weeks along, by my best estimate. My main focus was not letting Rick's fists anywhere near my stomach and planning my escape."

She watched Micah's eyes narrow. "Did he ever hurt you in a way that could have affected the baby?"

"No." She closed her eyes and tried not to let her emotions take over again. "I did everything I could to protect my baby, even if I couldn't protect myself."

"You should have a medical exam anyway, possibly even a sonogram." Micah's voice took on an edge. "If he hit you frequently, you should be checked for internal damage, just to be safe."

She shook her head regretfully. "I agree I should probably see a doctor soon, but I don't have much money, and if I file insurance it will get back to Rick where I am. I can't risk that."

Micah pursed his lips. "My shift starts in a couple of hours. I'll speak with a couple of the physicians in OB and explain your situation. Maybe they can work something out with you so you can get the care you need during your pregnancy."

"You don't have to do that."

"I know. But you can't go through your pregnancy without some kind of medical attention. Soon you'll need to start regular checkups, get on a prenatal vitamin, and someone is going to have to deliver the baby." He took on a teasing tone. "Unless you planned on doing that yourself, too?"

Autumn laughed. "Like I said, I guess I didn't plan very far ahead. You're right, I need to think about these things now that I'm safely away from Rick."

"Well, you'll have plenty of time to think up here." Micah headed for the door and stepped out onto the porch. "I need to get going so I can get ready for work, but like I said, call me or Whitney if you need anything." He grimaced, a regretful look shadowing his face. "I hate leaving you up here without a vehicle, but I'll get together with Dean and Whitney and see if we can figure something out on that, too. In the meantime, one of us will come up every day to check on you, okay?"

She leaned against the door frame and wrapped her arms around herself against the early April chill. "You all are doing so much for me already. I feel funny about imposing on everyone so much."

Micah locked his eyes with hers. "You're not an imposition, Autumn." He motioned inside with his chin. "There's a Bible on the mantel. Look up Matthew 25:40."

With that, he offered a warm smile and climbed into his car. Tapping his horn twice as a goodbye, he drove off and left her alone in her new home. She closed the door and immediately moved to the living room. She took down the pocket-sized Bible. Though she hadn't attended church in a couple of years—Rick wouldn't allow it—she was still familiar enough with the Bible to be able to quickly find the verse Micah referenced.

And the King shall answer and say unto them, "Verily, I say to you, inasmuch as ye have done it unto one of the least of these my brethren, ye have done it unto me."

She smiled and carefully closed the worn cover. The language was as old as time, but the meaning was timeless. Micah was letting her know he would happily help her, not because he wanted something in return or because he felt obligated, but because his faith taught him to selflessly reach out to those in need as Jesus had done. Even though she'd just met him and really didn't know him well, she sensed Micah was the type of person who actually took pleasure in helping others.

Autumn took comfort in knowing Micah was a God-fearing man. Between that knowledge, Whitney's assurance that Micah could be trusted, and her own observation of his genuine willingness to help, she felt her guard let down a notch. Perhaps Micah would prove trustworthy after all.

She sure hoped so, because she could really use a friend right now.

Micah pulled up to the Lawson's house and, since Whitney knew he was coming, let himself in. Lacey immediately came running for him and he scooped her up in his arms. "Hey there, Miss Lace. How's my favorite girl?"

"Good!" She wrapped her arms around his neck and gave him a slobbery kiss on the cheek. "Mommy, my Micah's here!"

Whitney came out of the kitchen and smiled. "I see that. Are you going to hog all his attention or can I talk to him for a minute?"

Lacey wiggled to get down. "You talk. I gotta play."

Micah chuckled and put her down. She took off like a shot down the hallway to her room, and Micah made himself comfortable on the couch.

Whitney sat on the other side and angled her body toward him. "Did you get Autumn settled in at the cabin?"

"Yeah, she's got everything she needs for at least a week. But I told her to call one of us if she needs anything else. I don't like that she doesn't have a car though. What if she needs to come into town for something?"

"I didn't think of that. I guess having a vehicle is something we just take for granted." Whitney crossed her arms. "You're right, she needs some transportation of her own instead of being completely dependent on us for rides. I'll talk to Dean when he gets home from work and see if we can figure something out."

"Maybe talk to Pastor Doug too. He might have some ideas," Micah suggested.

"Good idea. I'll give him a call." Whitney squeezed his hand. "Thank you for taking care of Autumn today. I'll do what I can for her, but taking care of Lacey is a full time job in itself. I really appreciate you stepping up to help."

Micah waved the compliment away. "You're my best friend and she's your family. You know I'd do anything for you and Dean. Besides, she's obviously been through a lot and could probably use all the friends and help she can get right now."

Whitney scowled. "I still can't believe Rick did that to her. He seemed like such a nice guy at their wedding. I guess he had everyone fooled."

"Abusers usually do."

"You should have seen her at her wedding." Whitney's eyes grew misty. "She looked beautiful and so happy. She said meeting Rick was like a dream come true. It breaks my heart that her dream was shattered so brutally."

Micah pictured Autumn in a wedding gown, her hair pulled up in an elegant style, her eyes radiating with joy. He had no doubt she'd been a beautiful bride. The lovely depiction his mind created disappeared and was replaced with an image of Autumn cowering in a corner, suffering blow after blow from the man she loved. His gut clenched painfully. "I'm glad she got away. She's lucky. So many women never escape that life."

Whitney shook her head. "Do you think Rick will come looking for her here?"

"I don't know. I think he'll for sure look for her, but I couldn't tell you where or how far he'll go. I guess all I can say is keep your eyes open and be careful."

"I still wish she could have stayed here with us. I don't like the thought of her in that cabin all alone."

"Me either, but I don't think she minded. If we can find a vehicle for her, she won't be so isolated and can come into town if she needs something or wants to visit you guys." Micah stood. "I've got to get to work. Let me know if Pastor Doug has any ideas."

Whitney walked him to the door and gave him a quick hug before he left. "Will do. I'll give her a call later to check on her too."

Micah nodded and jogged out to his car. As he drove to the hospital for his shift, he made a mental To Do list. From what little he knew of her, Autumn was a sweet gal with a soft heart in spite of everything she'd been through. She also had the makings of a great mother. Already she'd risked her own safety to give her unborn child a chance at a normal life.

Whitney may not know it yet, but Autumn would need a lot more than a car in the coming months with a baby on the way. And Micah intended to make sure she had everything she needed.

Chapter 3

Autumn unpacked the last shirt from her suitcase and placed it in the dresser drawer with the others. In her haste to get out of the house as soon as Rick left for work, she hadn't taken much with her, only what would fit in the small suitcase. As she looked at her meager wardrobe, she cringed. How she wished she'd had more time to prepare. But ever since the first time she'd tried to leave, Rick always called the house phone an hour after he arrived at work, and every hour after that until he returned home. If she didn't answer the phone, he would leave work to find out why. Her window of opportunity had been short. She'd had to pack fast and travel light.

Unfortunately, that left her with very little to live off of. She'd managed to secretly tuck away some of the grocery money over the last few weeks, but it was a puny amount. She would not rely on her cousin and Micah to keep her kitchen stocked, so she would have to buy groceries as needed. Even with the small amount of food she would consume alone, her money wouldn't stretch very far.

As if the mere thought of food was too much, her stomach growled loudly, reminding her she hadn't had any dinner yet. She padded to the kitchen to assemble a simple meal. As she settled at the table with her sandwich and a glass of milk, it occurred to her that soon her belly would start to grow and she would need to purchase some maternity clothes. The baby would also need things; clothes, blankets, diapers, a place to sleep. . .the list would be endless.

And she had no money for any of it.

The milk turned sour in her stomach and she shoved her plate and glass away. Dropping her head into her hands, she groaned. "What am I going to do?"

As she leaned forward, her necklace swung and bumped her wrist. Slowly she sat up, then removed the chain from around her neck and cradled the pendant in her palm. Rick had gifted her with the necklace on their wedding day, and she'd never taken it off. Even after the abuse started, she'd worn the necklace and clung to hope that someday the dreams she had when he'd gently hung it from her neck would one day be fulfilled.

Now it was just a reminder of dreams broken. The hope of any kind of "happily ever after" with Rick was gone. It was time for a new dream—a dream that was no longer about herself or her own happiness, but that of her child's.

"I can pawn it."

She smiled at the idea. Fourteen carat white gold with genuine diamonds and sapphires, it was a stunning piece. She knew she wouldn't get what it was worth, but it should bring a nice amount. It was a start, at least. When Whitney called to check on her an hour later, Autumn shared her idea with her cousin.

"Sure, Autumn, if you're sure that's what you want to do." Whitney told her there was a pawn shop in the next town over. "There's also a mall if you want to do some shopping."

"Thanks, but I think for now I should save the money." Autumn longed to tell her cousin about the miracle growing inside of her. Besides, she'd already let it slip to Micah that she was pregnant. She didn't want him to have to keep secrets for her. "Whitney, I have to tell you something. I—I'm going to have a baby."

Autumn heard Whitney's gasp and then a short squeal assaulted her ear. Autumn pulled the phone away from her ear and laughed. "I take it you're happy?"

"Autumn, that's wonderful news! I'm so happy for you." Whitney's gushing lifted Autumn's joy. "Oh. . .that's why you left Rick now, isn't it?"

"Yeah."

"Oh, Cuz. . ." A sigh wheezed through the phone. "This isn't going to be easy for you, is it?"

Tears immediately filled Autumn's eyes. "No. But this little one will be worth the struggle."

"Well, Dean and I will do anything we can to help. I still have my maternity clothes so you're welcome to borrow those."

Autumn breathed a sigh of gratitude. Whitney had just eliminated one huge expense. Now if she could just figure out the rest.

"I still have some of Lacey's baby clothes, too. You can also use those if you'd like." Whitney giggled. "Well, as long as it's a girl, that is."

Autumn laughed. "Hey, at this point I'm desperate enough to dress a boy in pink if I have to."

"Don't worry, we're going to figure all this out. One way or another, you won't be left in need."

Autumn gripped the phone. "Thank you. I don't know what I'd do without your help."

"God led you here for a reason. I can't promise much, but we'll do everything we can for you and your baby."

Before her emotions had a chance to take control again, Autumn ended the call with a promise to be ready by ten o'clock the next morning for Whitney to pick her up. She wandered to the window and gazed out at the dusk engulfed view—nothing but trees and sky. It was lovely up here. Lovely and quiet. Autumn was no stranger to being alone—she'd been forced to give up her friends and she'd lost her parents to a car accident not long after she married Rick—but something about being alone in this cabin away from civilization was much different than being alone in her house. The quiet here was almost deafening.

"God led you here for a reason." Whitney's words rang in Autumn's mind. Her decision to come to Wyoming had seemed the most logical choice. But was it God who had put the idea in her head, ultimately leading her to this place?

She went back to the mantel in search of the Bible she'd found there earlier. A tapestry she hadn't noticed before caught her eye, and she withdrew it from its place on the mantel. *Place of Refuge*, it read. That's what Micah had called this cabin last night—a place of refuge, something of which she was in desperate need. Lord knew she'd prayed enough times to be free from her husband, to find somewhere safe. Was this how He'd chosen to answer her prayers?

Her heart thrilled at the thought that God might care enough for her to bring her to this place where she could be free from the clutches of her husband and safely bring her baby forth into the world. Her eyes traveled to the stitching beneath the header. *Isaiah 4:6.*

She latched onto the Bible and found the page, then read the passage out loud. " 'And there shall be a tabernacle for a shadow in the daytime from the heat, and for a place of refuge, and for a covert from the storm and from rain.' "

Autumn sank into the couch cushions and lowered the Bible to her lap. "Hmm. Well, this doesn't look much like a tabernacle, but I do feel safe here." She absently fanned the pages, enjoying the crinkling sound they made as they flipped through her fingers. She wondered how many others had sought refuge in this cabin and looked for comfort in the worn pages of this little Bible. "I hope you all found what you needed," she whispered into the air, feeling a sudden kinship with the memories hidden within the walls of this cabin.

"Did you bring me here for a reason, Lord?" Autumn closed her eyes and held her breath, hoping for the miracle of an answer to break the quiet surrounding her. A moment later, after hearing nothing but her own heartbeat, she sighed and opened her eyes. It was probably too much to hope for, hearing God's voice out loud. Why would He choose to talk to her anyway? She was nobody. Hadn't Rick told her that enough times?

Her eyes travelled down to the Bible in her lap. The pages lay open, exposing the book of Psalms. Autumn knew the chapters to be the beautiful, heartfelt writings of King David. Now there was a guy who had some problems. Yet, in spite of how far David had removed himself from God, God still loved him and showed him forgiveness and mercy. If God could do that for David, why wouldn't He look upon her with the same love and mercy?

As her eyes skimmed the pages, a single phrase—*dwelling place*—caught her attention. She held the Bible closer to read the small print. *How lovely is your dwelling place, O LORD Almighty! My soul yearns, even faints, for the courts of the LORD; my heart and my flesh cry out for the living God. Even the sparrow has found a home, and the swallow a nest for herself, where she may have her young— a place near your altar, O LORD Almighty, my King and my God. Blessed are those who dwell in your house; they are ever praising you. Blessed are those whose strength is in you, who have set their hearts on pilgrimage.*

Autumn's hands tensed on the Bible as she gripped it tighter and read the words again and again. The words seemed to speak to the deepest part of her soul—the part of her that cried out to God and yearned for a place to belong, to be safe and protected. In many ways she had done just as the verse said, set her heart on pilgrimage. She'd left her home, fled from oppression, and ventured into the unknown for a chance at a new start. How weak and terrified she'd felt from the moment she stepped foot outside her front door, yet a strength that wasn't her own had propelled her forward, bringing her here, to this place—this place of refuge, her dwelling place.

Moments ago she'd wished for an audible voice to answer her question, but this verse—words from another time and another place—provided her answer more powerfully than if the Almighty had let her ears hear a simple yes. He'd used this Bible, His holy word, to relate to her situation and speak to her in a way she would truly understand.

"Thank You, Father," Autumn prayed as her eyes pooled with tears of gratitude. "Thank You for bringing me here. I trust You to protect me and my baby."

She placed her hand over her abdomen. "Give me strength, Lord. I really need You now."

CHAPTER 4

Four Months Later

"You're robbing me blind," Micah grumbled as he handed Autumn a wad of money.

Autumn laughed as she counted the Monopoly bills and added them to her pile. "Lucky for you it's not real money."

Their Saturday game nights at her cousin's house had become one of Autumn's favorite things, something to which she looked forward all week.

Whitney rolled the dice to take her turn and groaned when she landed on Park Place—Autumn's property. "I've never seen anyone as lucky as you in this game. You're bankrupting all of us."

"Next time we should play with real money," Autumn joked as she collected her payment from Whitney.

Dean got up from the table. "I'm going to go check on Lacey before Autumn takes all my money, too." He gave her shoulder an affectionate pat before leaving the dining room, and Autumn smiled up at him.

"How about we take a refreshment break?" Micah suggested.

"I'll go get some sodas. Water for you, Autumn." Whitney winked and headed toward the kitchen. "Be right back."

Autumn affected a mock pout. "What if I wanted soda?"

"You know it's not good for you," Micah chided good-naturedly.

"Yeah, yeah." Autumn shifted in the dining room chair, trying to make more room for her bulging belly. "Oh! The baby's on the move again. Want to feel?"

Micah immediately reached his hand out, and Autumn guided him to the spot where the baby was tumbling around. "Amazing. I think you've got a little gymnast in there."

"I never get tired of feeling her move." Autumn smiled. The warmth of Micah's hand penetrated through her shirt, and she marveled at how comfortable she had grown with him to be able to share such an intimate moment. Over the last few months he'd managed to convince one of the OB's at the hospital to treat her for free during her pregnancy, helped to find her a vehicle through a good Samaritan at the church, and kept her company on his days off. In truth, he'd become one of the closest friends she'd ever had, and she could easily see why Whitney had claimed him as her best friend. He was a good man. Between Whitney, Dean, and Micah, she finally felt a part of a family.

A sense of gratitude filled her chest, and she spontaneously placed her hand over his. "Thank you for being such a good friend to me."

He looked up in surprise. His eyes reflected something she couldn't quite define, but he blinked it away before she could ponder it further. "I've grown to care about you very much."

"Am I interrupting something?"

Whitney's entrance into the dining room caused Micah to jump back and withdraw his hand from her belly as if he'd been burned.

"I was just feeling the baby move. It's an active little one." Micah laughed, but it sounded forced to Autumn's ears. He sprang up from his chair. "Think I'll go see what's taking Dean so long."

As Micah raced off, Whitney raised one eyebrow. "What was that all about?"

Autumn shrugged. "You've known him longer than I have. I haven't figured out his weird moods yet."

Whitney set cans of soda on the table and handed Autumn the bottle of water. "If I didn't know any better I'd say he had feel—"

"What?"

"Uh. . .nothing. Forget about it." Whitney avoided Autumn's eyes as she sat back down at the table to wait for the men to return.

"What were you going to say?" Autumn pushed.

"Nothing. Really. Forget I said anything."

"Whitney—"

The home phone rang and Whitney leaped up to answer it, effectively avoiding any further comments. Seconds after Whitney's cheerful "hello," her face visibly paled and she looked at Autumn with wide, panicked eyes.

"What's wrong?" Autumn struggled out of her chair and moved toward her cousin.

Whitney covered the mouthpiece. "Autumn, it. . .it's Rick."

Autumn's knees buckled and she slipped to the floor. She heard rapid footsteps, and then two strong arms came up under her and half-carried her back to her chair. Micah knelt in front of her and turned her face to meet his eyes. "Hey, look at me. You almost passed out over there. Are you okay?"

Autumn shook her head. "It's Rick." Terror nearly closed off her vocal cords. "On the phone. Right now."

Micah jumped up from the floor. "Hang up, Whitney. Just hang up."

Rick's faint voice came through the phone line, impatiently repeating Whitney's name.

Autumn shook her head. "No, I want to know if he knows I'm here. I need to know." She nodded at Whitney. "Put it on speaker?"

Whitney hesitated then pushed the speaker button. "I'm here, Rick. Sorry about that, I was...distracted. Haven't talked to you in ages. What's up?"

Would Rick hear the tension in Whitney's voice? If Rick didn't know for sure that Autumn was here, she sure didn't want to give him any reason to come looking.

"Well, Whitney, I got an interesting phone call this morning. Would you like to hear about it?" Rick's voice—cool, controlled, yet condescending—sent goose bumps up and down Autumn's arms. She knew that voice, and it never meant anything good.

Dean entered the room and Whitney quickly held a finger to her lips and pointed to the phone. *It's Rick*, she mouthed. Dean's posture immediately stiffened, and he joined the three of them around the phone.

"Whitney?" Rick questioned.

"I'm here. I'm not sure why you'd call me to talk about a phone call you received, but go ahead."

"Well, I think you'll find it very interesting. See, my wife—your cousin—went missing about four months ago. But I suspect you already know that. I wasn't having any luck finding her. And then it hit me. She couldn't have had much money with her. She would have needed cash. But where would she have gotten it?" He paused, enjoying this game he was playing.

"I'm sure I don't know." Whitney's voice trembled slightly.

"Well, my dear wife took off with a rather expensive necklace, an anniversary ring and her wedding ring. They would have brought in a decent price if she decided to pawn them. Since I paid for those items, I figured they belong to me so I reported them stolen. This morning I got the call. Guess what turned up in a little pawn shop in Wyoming? Can you guess, Whitney?"

Autumn's lungs felt frozen and she struggled for a breath. Micah caught her hand and rubbed small circles across her palm with his thumb. "Breathe," he whispered.

Whitney looked helplessly to Dean.

"That's enough of this," Dean muttered. Louder, he said, "What do you want, Rick?"

"Oh, the husband is on the line, too. Well, it's like a little family reunion, isn't it?" His mocking voice made Autumn cringe.

Dean said, "I don't know what you're after, but you're barking up the wrong tree by calling here, so why don't you leave us alone now."

"Oh, I'm pretty sure I've called the right place," Rick countered, his tone icy. "It took me a little while to figure out why she'd go to Wyoming, but then I remembered Autumn had a cousin there. I dug out the address book and sure enough, there were your names with an address in Sawyer's Gap, Wyoming, which just happens to be a mere twenty miles from where my wife pawned her jewelry." He laughed, a hard, brittle sound. "Crazy coincidence, don't you think?"

"I'm not playing games with you, Rick. What's your point?"

"My point is I'm coming to get my wife, and you'd better not stand in my way. Whatever she's told you, it's her word against mine and she's got no proof of anything. If you try and keep her from me, I will call the authorities and report you for kidnapping. We can do this the easy way or the hard way, but she *will* be coming home with me."

Rick's words brought back vivid memories of a time not so long ago, but a time that had—until this moment—started to feel like another lifetime ago. He used to say that to her all the time. *We can do this the easy way or the hard way, but you* will *obey me.* Autumn began to shake uncontrollably.

Micah put a comforting arm around her, and she tried to will her body to be still.

Dean disconnected the call without bothering to acknowledge Rick's threat. "Whitney, go get Lacey. Pack a couple changes of clothes for her."

When Whitney didn't move, he barked, "Quickly! I don't know how long we've got."

Whitney seemed to come out of her trance and scrambled down the hallway to Lacey's room. Dean turned to Micah. "Take the girls to the cabin. Stay there with them. I'll stay here and deal with Rick when he shows up."

"Maybe you should call the cops." Micah helped Autumn out of her chair. "We all saw the bruises when she showed up here that night. Surely if we told the cops that, they wouldn't let Rick leave with her."

"Can't take any chances. Just get them to the cabin where they'll be safe and we'll go from there." Dean opened the linen closet door and reached to the top shelf where he withdrew a small, hard black case.

Autumn stared at the case. "Is that...?

"It's a pistol. I've never had to use it before and I hope I don't have to tonight, but I'm not facing him unprotected."

She nodded mutely.

"Does Rick have a gun?"

"No, I don't think so. I never saw one, at least. I don't think he even knows how to shoot."

"Good. Still doesn't hurt to be prepared." Dean turned toward the hallway. "Whitney, hurry! I want you out of here now!"

Whitney came around the corner, Lacey in one arm and a backpack in the other arm. "We're ready."

Micah took Lacey, who was still half asleep and transitioned to his arms limply. "Autumn, if you'll give me your keys I'll drive."

Autumn found her purse and handed him the keys, grateful he was taking over the chore. The way her hands were shaking she'd probably run them all off the road.

"Do you have your cell on you?" Dean asked Whitney as he wrapped her in a tight hug.

"Yes, but. . .aren't you coming with us?"

"No, I'm staying here."

Whitney drew back. "Dean, you can't! We don't know what this guy is willing to do to get Autumn back."

"He has to be dealt with, babe, or he'll just keep coming back. We'll work it out, man to man. Don't worry." He delivered a soft kiss to her lips. "Now get to the cabin. I'll call you in a little bit."

Whitney's eyes shone with uncertainty, but she kissed her husband and whispered, "Be careful. I love you."

Autumn's eyes teared up. "I'm sorry I brought you all into this. I'm so sorry."

"It's not your fault." Whitney spoke firmly even thought her face pinched in anxiety. "Let's get you back to safety."

Autumn took one last glance backward as they exited the house and climbed in the car. Dean stood by the window, back rigid and fists clenched,

pistol at the ready by his side.
Please, God, protect him. Protect all of us.

Micah caught Autumn sneaking another glance out the cabin window. "You're going to drive yourself crazy, Autumn. Come away from the window. Sit down and rest your feet."

She moved to the couch and sat, but her hands twisted in her lap. "Part of me is convinced at any moment I'll see Rick's face peering through the window."

"There's no way he could know about this cabin," Micah reminded her. "You're safe here."

Whitney paced restlessly back and forth in front of the fireplace. "I can't stand this waiting. Why hasn't Dean called yet?"

Micah stepped into her pathway. "I'm sure everything is fine. We don't know how far away Rick was or when he'll show up. Try to relax."

Whitney rolled her eyes. "Easy for you to say."

Easy? If she only knew. Micah was exhausted from trying to keep the two women calm when his own nerves were so on edge. He wouldn't let them know how bothered he was by Rick's phone call. He trusted Dean to take care of himself, but the thought of anything happening to Autumn had his stomach in knots. He stole a glance at her, and his chest tightened painfully. She looked so vulnerable, so frightened. He wanted to wrap his arms around her, smooth her hair and hold her close. But of course he couldn't do that. She would find that far too intimate, and she'd be right.

If only. . .

He shook his head. No, it didn't do any good to go down that road. As hard as he'd tried not to, he'd fallen in love with Autumn. But those feelings would have to remain his secret alone. Despite her circumstances, she was still a married woman. He would not dishonor her or God by revealing the love he couldn't help feeling for this beautiful, sweet woman. As difficult as it was, he would keep it tucked deep inside and simply be content to have her in his life as his friend.

Whitney's cell phone trilled, breaking the tense silence in the room. She fumbled the buttons before finally pressing the right one. "Dean? Are you okay? What's happening?"

Micah and Autumn both leaned forward, straining to hear what Dean was saying. Whitney's eyebrows crinkled. "Uh-huh. . .yeah, we're all fine. Lacey's asleep in the loft and we've just been waiting to hear from you. . . Really, are you sure?. . .Well, if you think that's best, I understand. . . Okay, be safe. . . I will. . . Love you, bye."

Whitney ended the call and shrugged as she met Autumn's eager gaze. "Rick still hasn't shown up. Dean suggested we all try to get a good night's sleep. He's set the security alarm at home and will sleep on the couch just in case Rick shows up during the night. He'll call in the morning. Or before if something happens."

Autumn released a huge sigh. "I don't know if I'll be able to sleep with this hanging over our heads."

"Me either, but he's right. We should at least try. Who knows what tomorrow will bring?" Whitney tucked her cell phone in her pocket. "I'll sleep up in the loft with Lacey. Looks like you're stuck with the couch, Micah."

"That's okay." He offered Autumn his hand, and she allowed him to help her off the couch. "Do you mind if I go in the bedroom to get an extra pillow and blanket?"

"Of course not." She said good night to Whitney and followed him into the bedroom. "I'm sorry there's not another bed for you. I feel bad about relegating you to the couch. It's not even long enough for you to stretch out." She bit her bottom lip. "Maybe you should take the bed and I should sleep on the couch. I'm shorter."

"Absolutely not." Was she out of her mind? What kind of man would he be if he let her—at almost seven months pregnant, no less—sleep on the couch while he enjoyed the luxury of a bed? Not to mention lying in the same place where Autumn rested every night would drive him crazy. "You will stay in your room. I will take the couch."

He pulled a pillow and thick blanket from a storage chest at the foot of the bed and turned to tell her good night. The bedside lamp she'd flipped on illuminated her hair, and with her gauzy white sundress floating loosely around her frame, she looked angelic. He swallowed hard.

"Good night, Autumn. Do try and get some rest, okay?"

She nodded and offered him a small smile. "Sweet dreams."

If she only knew.

He made himself as comfortable as was possible on the too-short couch and prayed while he waited for sleep to come. It seemed he'd no sooner drifted into sleep than a hand shook him awake. He dragged his eyelids open to find Whitney kneeling in front of him. "What's wrong? Did you hear from Dean?"

"Yes." She whispered raspily. "I don't want to wake Autumn yet though. Micah, Rick is dead."

Micah sat straight up. "What? Dean *shot* him?"

"No, he never showed up. Dean said the home phone rang about half an hour ago and it was a police officer. Apparently Rick was driving too fast and he crashed. He was pronounced dead at the scene. The police found our address in his GPS and our number was the last one he'd called on his cell, so the police called us looking for next of kin."

Micah rubbed his hand over his face. "Wow. . ."

"I know."

"How do we tell Autumn that her husband is dead?"

"Rick is dead?" Autumn's shocked gasp from the bedroom doorway startled them both.

Micah rushed to her side and guided her to the couch. "Come sit down. I know this must be a shock to you. I'm so sorry, we didn't know you were up."

"What happened?"

Whitney filled her in, all the while holding Autumn's hand. "Are you okay?"

Autumn's eyes had a glazed over look. "I—I don't know what I feel right now."

Micah gently rubbed her back. "It's okay if you're sad. I know he hurt you, but he was still your husband, and I know you must have loved him."

"My love for him died a long, slow death with every strike of his hand. But. . .I didn't want him dead. I just wanted away from him." Autumn's head slowly shook back and forth. "I can't believe he's really dead. Really gone."

They sat in silence for several moments, simply letting the reality of the last several hours sink in. Whitney put her arm around Autumn. "Why don't you try to get some more rest? It's the middle of the night, it's been a really long day, and this is a lot to take in."

Autumn nodded tiredly.

Whitney chafed Autumn's shoulder. "Do you want me to stay with you?"

"No, I'll be okay. Thanks." Autumn moved trance-like into the bedroom and shut the door.

Micah embraced Whitney in a hug. "I have to admit, I'm glad Rick didn't show up at your house. Who knows what would have happened."

"God protected all of us, that's for sure." Whitney yawned.

Micah watched her climb back up to the loft and then he resettled himself on the couch. "Thank You for Your protection tonight, Lord," he whispered into the dark. "I didn't know Rick, but he obviously had some problems. I have to be honest, Lord, I'm glad he can't hurt Autumn ever again. I hope he found peace with You in his final moments."

Micah looked toward the closed bedroom door. Was Autumn lying awake, trying to process the fact that she was now a widow? "I don't know what Autumn is feeling right now, Father, but I pray You will bring her healing and peace. I—I love her, Lord. I want her to be happy."

He was sure he'd be awake for the rest of the night, but sleep eventually overtook him and he rested dreamlessly until the sun peeked its rays through the window and cast its warm glow over his face.

Hearing soft breathing, he stretched and sat up to find Autumn at the window. Sunlight glinted off tears that traced silently down her cheeks. "Autumn? Are you okay?"

She turned toward him, making no move to wipe her tears away. "When Rick and I got married, I loved him so much."

He nodded, his throat tight.

"The man he became—that wasn't the man with whom I fell in love." She turned back to the window. "I accepted long ago that the Rick I loved was gone from me. I've mourned that loss already. The Rick that I left behind was heartless, violent. He didn't love me, he only wanted me back because he thought I was his property."

She paused, and he let her gather her thoughts. A long sigh expelled from her lips, and her shoulders slumped. "I'm sorry he's dead. But all I keep thinking is. . ." She turned toward him again and relief flooded her eyes. "I'm free." More tears spilled down her cheeks.

Micah closed the distance between them and wrapped her in a comforting embrace.

She sobbed with the broken relief of a woman whose spirit had been battered and bruised but was now being restored. "I'm free. I'm free."

Chapter 5

The cold wind nipped at Autumn's ponytail, pulling strands out to whip around her face. It stung her skin, but she wouldn't go back inside yet. After sitting in front of the fire inside, she found the cool invigorating. The leaves were in their final stages of falling from the trees, leaving the land with a forlorn, barren appearance. The scent of snow was in the air, and Autumn wondered if the ground would be covered in white before nightfall.

The baby rolled and kicked hard, and Autumn rubbed her protruding belly, trying to calm the restless infant in her womb. Her back ached horribly today, and the baby's frantic movements weren't helping. "I know you're anxious to get out of there, little one. I'm anxious, too. But you've still got a little ways to go, so try to calm down, hmm?"

The baby's due date was the day after Thanksgiving, but Autumn secretly hoped she'd give birth a few days early and would have her baby in her arms on Thanksgiving day. She couldn't think of any greater reason to celebrate a day of thankfulness. Not that every day wasn't filled with prayers of gratitude. Autumn thanked God every day for giving her a new start.

The gray sky begged for sunshine. Cold, dreary days such as this usually made her feel melancholy, but Autumn's heart still sang songs of praise. During her marriage, she'd separated herself from God. It hadn't been a deliberate choice, just a gradual shutting down of her heart. But since coming to this cabin, the dwelling place God had provided, the door to her heart had been reopened and her spirit had been renewed. She felt a kinship with her Savior here that she'd never felt before. Perhaps it was because she spent the majority of her time alone, but she found herself talking to Him more than she'd ever done, even before Rick when she was an active church-goer. Her faith had come alive for her here.

She inhaled a deep breath, letting the cold air seep into her lungs. When the burn became unbearable she turned to go back inside to the warmth of the cabin. Behind her she heard tires crunching over the rough ground and she smiled, not even needing to look to know who she'd find pulling up to the cabin. Micah was such a frequent visitor she knew the sound his car made as it approached. In fact, she'd grown to know a great many things about him—she couldn't remember ever being so *aware* of another person. She knew how he smelled, the sound of his laughter. Even the air around her seemed to become charged when he was near.

Autumn wasn't sure what to do with the feelings she'd developed for Micah. It was probably too much to hope that he could care for her the way she'd come to care for him. After all, she was nine months pregnant. Why would he want her like this? But her heart still hoped just the same.

She heard his car door shut and she left the cabin door open, knowing he would follow her inside.

He entered the kitchen and quickly shut the door behind him, blocking out the cold. "Why in the world are you standing out in the cold without a coat?"

"Hello, it's nice to see you, too," Autumn teased.

Micah gave her a sheepish grin. "You know I'm always happy to see you. But seriously, are you trying to make yourself sick?"

"I was only out there for a few minutes. I didn't know you were coming up today. Don't you have to work?" She reached behind her and rubbed at the ache in her back.

"Not today. I couldn't reach you on the phone so I just drove up."

"I'm sorry, it's on the charger. I guess I didn't hear it."

"No big deal. It gave me an excuse to see you." Micah blushed as the words left his mouth. "I mean, to check on you."

Autumn felt her own cheeks warm. The thought that Micah might look forward to seeing her as much as she'd grown to look forward to seeing him made her heartbeat speed up.

Micah cleared his throat. "I heard on the radio that a storm is moving in. I thought it might be wise for you to ride it out at Dean and Whitney's place."

"No, I'd have to sleep on the couch, and I'm pretty sure half of me would be hanging over the edge." She chuckled as she looked down at her belly. "I'll be fine here. I have everything I need."

"I don't know. These storms can get pretty bad up here. If it snows enough, you might be stuck for a few days." Micah's eyebrows creased together. "I don't like it."

"You worry about me too much. I'll be fine."

"I worry because I care." His eyes grew soft.

Her heart thrilled at the words, even if they didn't carry the weight she wanted them to. "I know. And I appreciate that."

A deep pain tightened across her abdomen and wrapped around her back, and she bent over slightly, her hands immediately gripping where the pain hit.

In a flash, Micah was at her side. "How long has that been happening?"

"It hasn't, not really." The pain eased and she straightened. "My back has hurt something awful today, but other than that nothing more than some strong Braxton-hicks."

His eyes narrowed in concern. "Are you sure they're just Braxton-hicks?"

"Pretty sure." She watched his lips purse. "Stop it, you're making me nervous. The baby's not due for another two weeks. I'm not in labor."

"Well, I'm going to stay with you for a few hours just to make sure." He took off his coat and hung it over a chair. "So, what's for dinner?"

After enjoying a meal together—which Micah insisted on preparing—they sat in front of the fireplace with a deck of cards and played round after round of Solitaire. As they listened to the wind pick up outside, Autumn tried to conceal each pain that came, but she couldn't help wincing at some of the stronger ones.

Micah checked his watch. "You're still having them, aren't you?"

"Only a few. Honestly, it's no big deal. Nothing like the doctor said it would be when my labor started." Autumn rolled her eyes at his worried expression, even though his concern touched her. "I'm *fine*, Micah."

He grunted and gathered up the cards. "Have they gotten any closer together?"

"No, I don't think so."

She struggled to get up from the couch, and he reached out to help her up. "What do you need? I'll get it for you."

"Thanks, but you can't help with this particular need." Her face warmed as she looked pointedly toward the bathroom.

"Oh." Micah let out a short laugh. "Well, by all means then. . ."

As she waddled past him, he called after her, "I'm going to make sure you've got enough firewood to get you through the next few days before I leave."

"Thanks." She finished up in the bathroom and came back out to find snow all over the kitchen floor. "What in the world?"

Micah was removing his coat and shaking snow from his hair. "Apparently while we've been playing cards, Mother Nature has been spitting out quite a bit of snow. I won't be able to make it back into town until it calms down."

Autumn's heart skipped a beat. "So...you're staying the night?"

"Yeah, possibly more than one, depending on how bad it gets." He looked up and caught her eye. "Don't worry, I'll sleep in the loft. I'll be a perfect gentleman—cross my heart." He grinned and crossed his finger over his chest.

Autumn laughed. "I believe you."

But the thought of him being in such close proximity for such a long period of time made her palms sweaty. He'd said it might be more than one night. How would she possibly be able to hide her feelings for that long when she wouldn't be able to get away from him?

Oh, please don't let me make a fool of myself.

He grabbed a dish towel and scrubbed at his damp hair. "Hot cocoa?"

"Yeah, I'll make it." She hobbled to the pantry, trying not to let on how intense the pain in her back had become. Knowing him, he'd probably insist on watching her sleep just to make sure nothing happened without him noticing.

They downed mugs of hot chocolate and Micah re-stoked the fire to make sure it would burn through the night, all the while listening to the wind pick up speed. Finally the call of her bed became too much for Autumn, and she bid Micah a bashful good night.

Once she was snuggled under the covers, she prayed for the pains to ease enough for her to be able to get some sleep—and to not be consumed with thoughts of Micah sleeping under the same roof as she. She trusted him completely and knew he would never do anything to compromise her integrity. But with the way she felt about him, she feared she'd unwittingly let her secret slip and that would make being confined together in the cabin rather awkward.

"One thing at a time," she whispered to herself. "Just focus for now on getting some sleep."

She pulled her knees up as far as she could and cradled her stomach, willing herself into a restless sleep.

Micah tossed and turned on the stiff mattress, unable to relax enough to get to sleep. Aside from the fact that sleeping under the same roof as Autumn made him restless, he was truly worried she might be in the beginning stages of labor. A thousand what-ifs ran through his mind like a broken record.

Stop it, you're driving yourself crazy.

Hopefully Autumn was right and was just experiencing Braxton-hicks contractions, which wouldn't be uncommon at all. He needed to just chill out and trust that everything would be fine. It was just hard not to worry about her when he loved her so much.

He chuckled dryly to himself. Wouldn't she be shocked to know he was secretly in love with her? He'd wondered a hundred times what her reaction would be if he ever told her how he felt. Surprise? Revulsion? Embarrassment? Or maybe, just maybe, she'd smile and say the words back to him.

Well, he could always dream, anyway.

He stretched out on his back and consciously took deep breaths in and out to calm his mind enough to rest. His thoughts were just beginning to slip into nothingness when he heard a tiny cry from down below. He strained his ears, trying to determine if it was the wind or Autumn he'd heard. A second cry, louder this time, floated upward.

"Micah!"

He flung the covers back and raced down the steps from the loft. He stopped at her closed bedroom door. "Autumn?"

He heard her groan, and then in a strained voice she told him to come in. He turned the knob and found her sitting on the edge of her bed, bent over and crying. He rushed to kneel in front of her. "What's happening? What's wrong?"

"I—I don't know." She spoke through sobs. "The pains kept coming, and then all of the sudden this *stuff* just came out of me."

Micah suddenly realized her nightgown was soaking wet. He flipped on the lamp and a quick check confirmed the bed was wet as well. *Oh, no.*

He took her hands in his. "Autumn, look at me. Listen, your water broke. You are definitely in labor."

"But—but the baby's not due yet! I can't be in labor!" She shook her head frantically.

"It's okay, it's only a couple weeks early. Sometimes they come a little earlier than planned." He spoke soothingly to calm her and to calm himself. "But Autumn, I can't get you to the hospital in this storm and I don't think an ambulance would make it up here either."

She looked at him wearily. "Then what do we do?"

"Well. . ." He took a deep breath, certain she would not like his answer. But he had no other choice. "I'm going to have to deliver the baby."

Her eyes grew wide. "You're. . .*what?*"

"Come on, let's find you a dry nightgown or a robe."

"Micah—"

"If you can get yourself changed, I'll change the bedding and get everything comfortable for you." He began to pull the soaked sheets off the bed.

"Micah."

"Do you need help getting changed?"

"*Micah!*"

He turned toward her. "Are you having another contraction? Do you need to sit?"

She gaped at him, hands cradling her belly. "You cannot deliver this baby! Are you out of your mind?" She doubled over and moaned.

He grasped her and supported her weight while she waited for the pain to pass. When it seemed the contraction had ceased, he calmly rubbed her back. "Of course I can. I'm a nurse, I've done this before. I know what I'm doing."

"That's not the problem. I'm sure you know what you're doing, it's just that. . .that. . ." Even in the dim lamp light he could see her cheeks flaming red, and he suddenly understood her reticence.

He led her to a chair in the corner and knelt in front of her so they were eye to eye. "I understand, Autumn. I know this is going to be incredibly personal and is probably embarrassing for you. If we had any other options right now, I would not be putting you through this. But the baby is coming, whether you're ready or not."

He gently wiped a tear from her cheek. "I realize this will be. . .uncomfortable. . .but I'm glad I'm here. Imagine if I hadn't come up here tonight. You'd be going through this all alone." Another tear slipped from her lids and he wiped it away. "Try not to think of me as Micah, your friend. Think of me as Micah, your nurse. I promise I will take good care of you and make sure your baby is brought into the world safely. Can you trust me to do that?"

Her eyes still held a trace of panic, but she drew a deep breath and let it out slowly. "I trust you."

"Good." He stood. "Now, can you get changed by yourself while I take care of the bedding?"

She nodded, and he helped her from the chair.

"Put on something loose that can be pushed up, okay?" Micah turned his back to her to offer her some privacy and began remaking the bed, laying thick towels over the mattress before putting on new sheets. When he felt her step behind him, he asked "Are you dressed?"

"Yes." She whispered, her voice taut.

"Do you think you can walk around the cabin for a bit? It will help speed up the labor."

"I'll try."

He held out his arm and she latched onto it, letting him bear the majority of her weight. For three hours they walked in circles around the cabin, with Micah checking her progress—much to Autumn's obvious humiliation—each hour. Finally, as the darkness outside began to fade, she told him breathlessly, "I can't walk anymore. Please, can I lie down?"

Her contractions were coming steadily every two minutes, and Micah knew she was getting closer. "Yes, let's get you comfortable and I'll check you again."

"Oh, goody," Autumn deadpanned.

He hid his smile and helped her into the bed. "I'd say you're dilated to about a nine. Shouldn't be long now."

She let out a long, loud moan as another contraction hit. He took her hands and allowed her to squeeze his fingers until they lost feeling. "Breathe, Autumn, come on now, breathe..."

Finally she flopped back against the pillows. Sweat dotted her forehead, and he went to retrieve a cool washcloth from the kitchen. As he wiped it across her clammy skin, he smiled down at her. "You're doing so well. I know this is hard without any pain medication, but you are so strong. I'm amazed at how strong and brave you are."

"I never. . .thought of myself. . .as either. . .of those things." She panted as she braced for another contraction.

"You are though." He smoothed her hair away from her face. "You're amazing, sweetheart. Soon this will be over and your baby will be in your arms."

This brought a smile to her face. Micah's heart was so full of emotion watching the woman he loved go through such pain, he feared it would burst from his chest. Even in the throes of agony, she was still so beautiful, so strong. He was in awe of her. In spite of the physical awkwardness of the situation, he felt so privileged to be the one to help her bring her baby into the world. Never in his life had he been so glad he had the skills to assist in the miracle of childbirth.

Autumn groaned. "Micah, I feel strange. I feel. . .pressure. . .a lot of pressure."

He moved to the foot of the bed. "The baby's crowning. I can see its head." He settled himself in front of her on the bed. "You're going to have to push now. With the contractions, okay? Are you ready?"

She nodded tensely and bore down. For half an hour she tirelessly pushed while he offered soft words of praise, coaxing her to keep going. Finally, a cry pierced the room and Micah quickly placed the baby on Autumn's chest and covered them with a clean blanket.

"Oh, Autumn, she's beautiful."

Autumn gazed down at her baby's face. "She? I have a daughter?"

"Yes. And she's just as beautiful as her momma."

Autumn's face glowed with unabashed joy and she lovingly stroked the dark strands of hair on the baby's head. "My baby girl," she breathed.

"Do you want to cut the cord?"

She looked up at him. "No. You—you should do it."

He felt the strangest urge to cry, but he swallowed hard and reached for the scissors he'd sterilized earlier. As he severed the physical tie between mother and child, the baby began to fuss. "She probably wants to nurse. I hate to take her from you, but I need to check her airway and look her over real quick before you can nurse her."

Autumn reluctantly handed her over, keeping her eyes glued to her newborn daughter until Micah finally placed the baby back in Autumn's arms. Seeming to have lost—or forgotten—her embarrassment, Autumn pulled her robe to the side and positioned the baby so she could nurse her. Micah turned away and busied himself with the post-birth procedures. When he was finished he quietly exited the room to give Autumn time alone with her daughter.

He treated himself to a hot shower, the warm water soothing the tense muscles in his shoulders. He knew it was no coincidence Autumn hadn't heard her phone ring yesterday when he'd called. If he hadn't come up to the cabin, she would have had to go through her labor and childbirth alone. God knew their needs before they did, and He was faithful to meet them every time. "Thank you, Father, for keeping Autumn and the baby safe, and for making sure I was here and giving me the skills needed to deliver the baby."

After quickly drying off and, regretfully, putting the same clothes back on, he knocked on the bedroom door. "May I come in?"

"Please do."

At some point she'd gotten up and put on sweat pants and a loose T-shirt. She sat propped up in the bed with the baby nestled in a blanket in her arms. "Do you want to hold her?"

"I'd love to." He moved to the side of the bed and perched on the edge. Autumn carefully transferred the sleeping baby to his arms. She fit perfectly in the crook of his elbow, and as he gazed down at her tiny face, he was immediately smitten. "She's perfect. You did an amazing job."

"Thank you." Autumn smiled tiredly. "So did you." She placed her hand on his arm. "Thank you, Micah. I can't say that enough."

"Thank you for trusting me." He couldn't take her eyes off the baby in his arms. "What's her name?"

"Madison Grace. After my mother."

"What a pretty name you have, little Maddie," Micah cooed as he softly stroked her cheek with one finger.

A few moments of silence stretched between them, and then Autumn shifted her position against the pillows. "Micah?"

"Yes?"

"You called me sweetheart."

Her voice was so soft, so hesitant, he barely heard her. When her words registered, he slowly met her gaze. "Yes. I did."

"Why?" There was no condemnation in her tone, just honest curiosity.

Micah struggled for a response. "I—I guess I. . ."

She waited for more, and when he didn't continue she offered a weak smile and broke their eye contact. "It's okay. It was just one of those things. . .a term of endearment that doesn't mean anything. I understand."

He thought her eyes held disappointment, though he couldn't be sure. Was it possible she'd *liked* it when he used the endearment?

Lord, could she possibly have feelings for me, or am I reading this wrong?

He felt a subtle nudge to tell Autumn the truth, and he immediately balked. What if he was wrong and she shot him down? What if he further embarrassed them both? Was it worth the risk?

His father's voice intruded in his mind. *"Anything in this life worth having is worth taking the risk to get it, son."* How many times had his dad told him that as he was growing up? One look at Autumn and little Maddie, and he knew they were both worth the risk.

He drew a long breath and gathered his courage. "I called you sweetheart because. . .because I've wanted to call you that for months. I didn't mean for it to slip out when it did, but I'm not sorry I said it."

Autumn's head snapped up, and she searched his eyes for truth. "What do you mean, you've wanted to call me that for months?"

He snuggled the baby closer, feeling an odd sense of security from having her in his arms. "I mean, I've wanted to call you sweetheart ever since I realized that. . .that I'm in love with you."

He couldn't look at her as he said the words out loud for the first time. His heart raced with the fear of her rejection, and he focused his gaze on the baby. What would he do if she told him she didn't feel the same?

"Please look at me."

He barely heard her whispered plea over the beating of his heart, and he grudgingly met her eyes. They shone with hopeful expectation.

"Do you mean it?"

He could not lie. "Yes. I love you, Autumn. I hope that doesn't scare you or upset you. I understand if you don't feel the same way. I won't ever say it again if you don't want me to. I just want to have you and little Maddie in my life, and if it's only as your friend I'm okay with that."

She reached for the baby. "Well, I'm not."

His heart sank as he let her take her daughter back. Her words stung. She didn't even want to be his friend anymore? He'd taken the risk and lost everything. His throat felt tight as he forced out a reply. "I understand. I'll leave you alone." He stood up and started to walk away, his heart feeling as if it would break in two.

"Don't leave."

He paused, but didn't turn around to look at her. Why wouldn't she just let him go before he broke down in front of her? Couldn't she afford him a little dignity after rejecting him?

"Please come back."

He shook his head, remaining rooted to where he stood. He couldn't face her right now. It hurt too much.

"Micah. . .I love you, too."

His heart stopped and he spun around. "Wh—what did you say?"

She smiled. "I said I love you too."

"But. . .but you just said. . ."

"I said I wasn't okay with just being friends because I want more than that. I want a life with you." She ducked her head bashfully. "I love you, Micah."

His feet made quick work back to the bed. Only seconds ago he'd feared his heart would break from losing her, and now he feared it would burst with the relief and love that swelled almost painfully.

"Call me sweetheart again." She smiled, her eyes glistening with unshed tears.

"Sweetheart. . ." he breathed as he tenderly cupped her cheek with his hand. Slowly, gently, he leaned forward and pressed a soft kiss to her lips. "I've been waiting forever to do that."

He felt her smile curve against his lips. "Do it again."

She didn't have to ask twice. He kissed her with all the emotion in his heart, and when he withdrew he delivered a kiss to the baby's forehead. "I love you, Autumn. I love you so much. And I already love little Maddie. We could be a happy little family, don't you think?"

She nodded, her tears spilling over her cheeks. "We could."

"Marry me." He lovingly wiped her tears away. "Please say you'll marry me."

A joyful laugh bubbled up from within her. "Well, since you asked so nicely."

He grinned. "That's a yes?"

"Yes, Micah." She laced her fingers through his and kissed his hand. "Nothing would make me happier."

Epilogue

Christmas Day

The air smelled of pine and cinnamon from the garland draped over the fireplace and the candles that flickered from all around the room. A full, brightly decorated Christmas tree graced the corner by the fireplace, its lights twinkling as brightly as the candles' flames. A fire crackled in the fireplace, giving the room a cozy warmth on this cold eve.

Pastor Doug stood in front of the fireplace with Autumn and Micah facing him, holding hands and smiling unabashedly at each other like the newlyweds they were about to be. Whitney, Dean, Lacey, and Micah's parents stood around them in a half circle, serving witness to the small, intimate wedding ceremony.

Micah's mother cradled the baby, already having staked her claim as Grandma. Autumn wished her own parents could have been here, but she imagined somehow they knew how happy she was now. She looked into Micah's eyes and saw everything she'd ever wanted—a man who cherished her, a family to call her own.

As they recited their vows to each other, Autumn silently thanked God for bringing her to this place, for using it to give her a new start. She'd found refuge in this cabin, her safe place. Surrounded by these cabin walls, she'd fallen in love with Micah, fallen in love with God, fallen in love with her daughter...it was only fitting that in this place of refuge she and Micah and little Maddie would become a family.

They would stay here for a few more days for their honeymoon, then would move into Micah's house in town. The cabin would once again be empty, waiting for the next person who needed it. Somehow, in the serene glow of the fire reflecting off the wooden walls, she felt the presence of all those who came before her, and knew that God would faithfully continue to use this cabin as a place of refuge and healing. Autumn prayed the cabin would be as much a blessing to the next person as it was to her.

"By the power vested in me, I now pronounce you man and wife." Pastor Doug smiled widely and winked at Micah. "You may kiss your bride."

"Finally!" Micah pulled her to him and just before he placed his lips on hers, whispered, "I love you, sweetheart."

Her smile was uncontainable. "And I love you. Now kiss me already."

He needed no further encouragement. He playfully dipped her and sealed their future with a kiss.

THE END

If you enjoyed this compilation of stories, please look for

THREADS OF TIME

another novella set from
Wings of Hope Publishing.

Wings of Hope Publishing is committed to providing quality Christian reading material in both the fiction and non-fiction markets.

Made in the USA
Lexington, KY
23 July 2015